P9-DFO-937

# LIBERTY
★ ★ ★ ★ ★ ★ ★ ★ ★ ★ ★ ★ ★ ★ ★ ★
# 1784

## BAEN BOOKS by ROBERT CONROY

*Himmler's War*

*Rising Sun*

*1920: America's Great War*

*Liberty: 1784*

**To purchase these and all Baen Book titles in e-book format, please go to www.baen.com.**

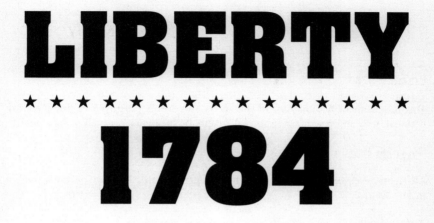

# LIBERTY

★ ★ ★ ★ ★ ★ ★ ★ ★ ★ ★ ★ ★ ★ ★

# 1784

# ROBERT CONROY

A Baen Book

Baen Publishing Enterprises
P.O. Box 1403
Riverdale, NY 10471
www.baen.com

ISBN: 978-1-4767-3627-3

Cover art by Kurt Miller

First Baen printing, March 2014

Distributed by Simon & Schuster
1230 Avenue of the Americas
New York, NY 10020

Library of Congress Cataloging-in-Publication Data

Conroy, Robert (Joseph Robert), 1938–
  Liberty 1784 : the second war for independence / Robert Conroy.
      pages cm
  ISBN 978-1-4767-3627-3 (hardback)
1. United States—History—Revolution, 1775–1783—Fiction. 2. Alternative histories (Fiction) 3. War stories.  I. Title.
  PS3553.O51986L53 2014
  813'.54—dc23

                                          2013051061

10   9   8   7   6   5   4   3   2   1

Pages by Joy Freeman (www.pagesbyjoy.com)
Printed in the United States of America

## Acknowledgments

On a number of occasions I've been asked how I get a book published. I respond by saying I've never gotten a book published. All I've ever done is write it, which is a very satisfying experience and never a chore. Getting a book on the shelf, or online, is due to the hard work of my agent, Eleanor Wood, and the superb people at Baen who are always ready to assist or inform. They do all the heavy lifting. I just watch and learn.

And finally, to Quinn and Brennan: I think you're old enough, but I don't have a vote.

# Introduction

G EORGE WASHINGTON NEVER SUFFERED A TRULY CATASTROPHIC defeat during the revolution, although he certainly had numerous opportunities to fail in a manner that would have ended the war.

His inexperience as a field general nearly saw his army destroyed at Long Island, and it was only good fortune that saw a British relief fleet defeated off Yorktown since a second British fleet arrived shortly after Cornwallis' surrender. And the other times he took the field to confront the main British Army, he was generally less than successful, as with Brandywine and Germantown, while some consider the battle at Monmouth to have been a draw. To be fair, he did have his share of victories such as Trenton and Princeton, but they were relatively minor actions against smaller segments of the British army.

Washington had to keep his army intact in order to keep the revolution alive. A serious defeat could have devastated the revolution that began in 1775. But would it have meant an end to the revolutionary spirit, or simply a temporary lull in the fighting?

In "Liberty," the first British relief fleet does arrive in a timely manner off Yorktown in the Fall of 1781, does defeat the French fleet (which should have happened if only the British had been smarter). Cornwallis then goes on to rout the Americans and Washington, who had gambled all in an attempt to trap and defeat Cornwallis; thus ending a war that had gone on for years.

However, I do not believe it would have meant the end of the revolutionary spirit. Instead, I believe that numbers of hardcore revolutionaries would have migrated westward, much in the manner that the South Africans did to flee the British only twenty years later. They would have done so to keep their freedoms and to save their skins from a vengeful British government.

Yet, how far could Americans run and how far would the British, fearing a resurgence of the revolution, chase them?

I believe that the British would have recognized the presence of a "free" nation as a great threat and would have chased them hard and far to bring the rebels to heel or to destroy them.

Thus, the story of "Liberty."

—Robert Conroy

For more information about books and
events, please check out my new website,
robertconroybooks.com. It includes my email
address and I promise to try and respond.

# Prologue ★ ★ ★ ★ ★ ★ ★ ★ ★ ★ ★ ★ ★ ★ ★ ★ ★ ★ ★

MAJOR JAMES FITZROY WRAPPED HIS CLOAK ABOUT HIS SHORT, spare, lean body in a vain attempt to keep out the cold spring rain that was soaking London and anyone foolish enough to be outside. At least he wasn't suffering alone, he thought as he sniffled and wiped his running nose on his already wet sleeve. If misery loved company, then he was in good company indeed.

To his right and slightly to his front was Lieutenant General John Burgoyne, his commander, distant cousin, and mentor. The weather didn't seem to bother the general. He loved the theater and considered himself an actor and an actor was always on stage. He wouldn't let a simple thing like a freezing deluge upset his composure, while Fitzroy tried and failed to emulate him.

Burgoyne chatted amiably with the brothers Howe—Admiral Richard Howe and General William Howe. General Howe had been excoriated by Parliament for not attacking the rebels more aggressively during the revolution's early months, and it was assumed that his presence at today's ceremony was a punishment for his failure to act decisively. The admiral was there to represent the Royal Navy. He hadn't actually been disgraced, although some said that Admiral Howe could have ended the war years earlier had he only been more aggressive in stopping Washington's retreat from Long Island to Manhattan. It was accepted that the Howe brothers had sinned in the eyes of the king by being less than enthusiastic supporters of the war against the colonies.

1

Prime Minister Lord Richard North and his companions were smiling and gloating. To Fitzroy, it was unseemly. A man was about to die. Even a criminal or a traitor was entitled to die with a modicum of dignity. North had not been a strong supporter of the war, but he had supported his king and now the moment of triumph was at hand. After today, North had made it known that the chaotic and violent situation in France would become his primary focus.

Even Lord George Germain, the Viscount Sackville, had risen from his sickbed to see this day of harsh justice. It was widely understood that Germain wouldn't have too many more days on this earth. His replacement in control of North America, Lord Stormont, stood by impassively.

The Tower of London had always been one of Fitzroy's favorite places, but not this day. It was both a medieval fortress and a complex group of buildings covering a fairly large area of ground. The actual "Tower," a surprisingly elegant white stone keep, had originally been built by William the Conqueror to control the Saxons. It was alleged by historians that the overall site also held Roman fortifications. Numerous other buildings, walls, and battlements had been added to the original Tower. The entire complex was both a symbol of strength and a strategic point on the Thames. All of these made it a marvelous prison for those guilty of crimes against the crown, although it was rarely used as such in these times.

"When will this damned circus start?" snarled Edmund Burke, a man who had spoken out against the War in the Americas. Was he being punished too? Fitzroy thought it likely.

"I believe he's saying his prayers," North commented with a cold smile. "And a damned good thing if you ask me. The bastard's going to burn in hell."

Fitzroy shuddered. Men should die in bed surrounded by loved ones or in battle proving their courage. They should not be executed by their fellow men in a brutal and coldblooded ritual. At least this death would occur in relative privacy. There would be no screaming and drunken mobs numbering in the thousands as was normally the case for a major execution, and was beginning to occur with horrifying frequency in France, a nation that was falling apart. There was too much risk that the masses would riot if it was held at Tyburn Hill. Tyburn was normally used for the hanging of thieves, while this would be the decapitation of a traitor.

Only the few dozen gathered in the rain had been invited and would witness it. Nor would any member of the royal family dignify the proceedings by their presence, although Fitzroy suspected that some younger members of the House of Hanover had sneaked on to the grounds and were looking on from windows above. He hoped they learned something from watching this murderous ritual, although he doubted it. The Hanovers, now led by the often ill George III, were as stubborn a bunch of Germans as had ever been produced. At least the current George actually spoke English, a skill never quite mastered by his predecessors, in part because they never considered themselves English.

The door to the chapel opened and red-coated guards emerged. "About time," muttered Burgoyne. Fitzroy stifled a smile. Perhaps the great actor truly was feeling the weather. Burgoyne was no longer a young man, which made it even more likely.

In the guards' midst stood a very tall man with a shock of short white hair that showed hints that it might once have been red. He wore nothing more than a long nightshirt that hung below his knees and a pair of badly scuffed shoes. His legs were white and knobby. He looked like a lunatic from the insane asylum at Bedlam. His once powerful body was now but skin and bones. His flesh was pale and why not? He hadn't been outdoors in a number of months. For security's sake, even his trial had taken place in the Tower. Nor had he been shaved in several days, which made him look even scruffier, even more the lunatic, although they all knew that was not the case. The prisoner blinked and looked around at those assembled. He started to smile and quickly closed his mouth. He had no teeth and looked ghastly as a result. Still, he managed to look like a predator, a caged tiger. Fitzroy stifled a shudder. This was the enemy.

The prisoner was led to the chopping block. A powerfully muscled, masked man leaned on a longhandled ax and stood patiently by. Death would be swift, not like the drawing and quartering that some felt the traitor deserved. Thus, he would not be hanged, and then let down while still alive, and would not suffer the agonies of castration and having his genitals stuffed into his mouth, followed by disembowelment before his limbs were ripped from his still living body. No, thought Fitzroy, England was too civilized for that. This cold morning would only bring a decapitation.

"Hurry it up," muttered North futilely. There would be a deliberate pace to this sad event.

The guards guided the man to the block. He did not struggle or protest. They pushed him to a kneeling position.

"Not yet," bellowed Burke.

"He had a fair trial," North said angrily. "Not that he deserved one. He was found guilty of treason and an armed rebellion that took years to quell. It nearly broke the treasury, and almost brought England to her knees. He deserves the justice we are about to meet out."

"Has he any last words?" Burke asked. "Prisoner, speak now if it is your wish."

"Or forever hold your peace," laughed North and turned to his companions. "Damned difficult to converse with a headless man, I dare say."

The prisoner looked up. His eyes were alert. There was surprising force and strength behind them. He smiled so his bare gums didn't show, proving that the man still had his pride.

"I will only say that you can never win," he said through tight lips. "This sad day merely delays the inevitable. You can never stop men from being free." With that, he turned away disdainfully. "Do your duty and be damned to you," he said to the executioner.

"Not very eloquent for a man's last words," said one of North's toadies.

The prisoner laid his head on the block and signaled to the executioner who raised his ax and lowered it in one brutally swift and efficient movement. The small crowd gasped involuntarily as the separated head rolled onto the ground as blood gushed from the torso.

"Dear God," that same toady said and began to puke. Fitzroy hoped he ruined his lovely yellow leather shoes as he felt his own gorge rise. He controlled himself with great effort. He wondered what the young royals hiding above were thinking. Or were they also puking? He thought he heard the muffled sounds of screaming and crying. Good, he thought, learn what death is about.

The executioner reached for the head. He found a handful of hair and held it up, dripping blood onto the ground. For a horrible instant, Fitzroy thought the man's eyes were yet alive and glaring at him, blaming him. Then they glazed over and the jaw went slack.

"Death to traitors," said Lord North and others took up the chant. Even the shivering Germain managed a wan smile. Fitzroy noticed that Burgoyne was silent, as were Stormont and Burke. It didn't matter.

It was 1783 and George Washington was dead.

# Chapter 1 ★ ★ ★ ★ ★ ★ ★ ★ ★ ★ ★ ★ ★ ★ ★ ★ ★ ★ ★ ★

DEEP INSIDE THE BOWELS OF THE *SUFFOLK*, A ONCE PROUD merchant frigate, Will Drake thought he felt the rotting hulk of the prison vessel move. He paused in fear. The ship was a derelict. She had no masts, merely grotesque stubs that looked like broken teeth showing where they once had been. She was anchored at the end of a dock, parallel to the shore, and was thought to be thoroughly wedged in the mud and thus immune to wind and storm. She couldn't move. She barely shifted and quivered with the tide, although the ship sometimes creaked and moaned as if it was alive and ashamed of its current life. The *Suffolk* and two others rotted silently off the city of New York in the Hudson River.

Will gathered his strength and moved to a higher deck in the hull of the large ship. He'd thought that the *Suffolk* had likely sailed to China and India, which explained the double rows of gun ports to protect her from pirates. Now it was going to be his coffin. He looked at his gaunt and terrified fellow prisoners and some of them shared his concern as to the ship's unexpected and frightening movement. Most of the other men consisted of little more than a layer of skin over a skeleton, and were too far sunk in despair and sickness to notice or care. Whatever happened, they would be dead in a very short while.

The *Suffolk* had been Will's prison for almost a year and a half, although she and her sister ships had been convict ships for many years before.

Will had been taken prisoner by the British when Clinton's army had burst out of New York following the catastrophic American defeat at Yorktown and the subsequent collapse of the Revolution. It was just plain bad luck that a Redcoat patrol had found him and even worse luck that he had been identified by a man who knew him and told his captors that he was an officer.

It was then that he realized the rules of war had changed. Hitherto, officers had been kept in reasonably pleasant circumstances until either paroled or exchanged, while the enlisted men lived lives of privation and squalor. This was because the British feared retaliation against their own officers. Now, with the rebellion crushed, there was no need for niceties and Will quickly understood that the victors wanted the rebellion's leaders permanently out of the picture. Most of the newly captured enlisted men had been flogged, branded, and released, while the men currently entombed in the hulks were officers and quietly forgotten. Cornwallis now commanded in New York and he was considered to be a hard man, but Will wondered if he was this cruel? After the agonies of branding and flogging, the British kept lower-ranking officers like Drake in floating hells like the *Suffolk*. Senior ones had been shipped away, either to England for trial or prisons in the tropics.

Will had managed to survive, but it hadn't been pleasant or easy. By the time he'd been caught, many of the hundreds jammed into the filthy hold of the *Suffolk* had been weakened or would soon be dead. He'd quickly realized that being Christian or noble simply meant dying sooner rather than later. He'd swallowed his pride and his scruples and done what was necessary to continue living as long as he had. He'd taken food and the rags that passed for clothing from the obviously unconscious and dying and the recently dead, doing so before anybody else could get to them; thus keeping a semblance of his strength. He'd fought for positions in the ship that were relatively dry, or weren't suffocatingly hot in summer, or freezing in winter. There was no comfort to be had in the stinking bowels of the prison ship at any time.

All the time he'd done this, Will had begged God for forgiveness and cursed the British for putting him in this horrible position.

Fortunately, the British guards on the *Suffolk* were lazy and incompetent swine who spent most of their time drinking the cheap gin or rum they'd bought by selling provisions meant for the prisoners. The guards had no idea how many men were down

below since the prisoners, with Will's connivance, had stopped
sending corpses up to be taken away as that would only mean
a reduction in their already inadequate food ration. Instead, the
prisoners kept the rotting corpses in the lower holds until the
bones could be slipped out through the barred gun ports at
night. Thus, as the numbers of prisoners declined, the amount
of food each of the survivors received actually increased, despite
the pilfering from the guards. The additional stench from the
rotting bodies was scarcely noticed.

They rarely lacked for drinking water, even though it was
frequently foul. They were north of the city of New York and
high enough up the Hudson River so that only the strongest of
incoming tides or storms would make the water undrinkable. It
was often brackish, but rarely so salty that it couldn't be drunk.
Other hulks lay off Brooklyn, in the East River, where the water
was tidal, brackish and generally undrinkable. Will and the others on the *Suffolk* were actually the lucky ones.

Will had lost many pounds from his once sturdy frame, and
the fact that his teeth were loosening meant that scurvy was on its
way. If nothing happened to save him soon, he would die a painful
and lingering death and join so many of his comrades in either
the river or a shallow grave. It did not appear that the victorious
king and his Parliament had any intention of freeing the prisoners
they'd swept up during and after the war. Will wondered if anyone
even remembered that the prisoners existed. Will had heard that as
many as ten thousand American soldiers had died in the hulks. He
feared that someday someone would strip his own cadaver naked
and drop it into the filthy bilge. The thought of his bones sliding
into the river sickened him even further. He wanted to weep in
despair, but decided not to waste the energy. Stay alive. Survive.
There was always a chance of life until the moment of death.

Along with physical imprisonment, there was the maddening
lack of knowledge of events in the outside world. He could look
longingly out the gun ports at rural life in New Jersey. Farms
like the one he once owned were being worked and life was going
on very pleasantly for people who were either Tories or who had
made peace with their conquerors. Will wondered if they even
gave a thought to the wretches in the *Suffolk*.

Every now and then a new prisoner would arrive, and be
pumped for information. The British were strong everywhere, they

said, but there were rumors of rebel colonies out in the west. In particular, there was one that was apparently called "Liberty." It made sense, Will thought. The vastness of the continent would attract many people who would trade space to get away from the claws of Mother England.

Once upon a time, he'd had a family and a profession, but his parents were dead of smallpox, and a brother had been killed at Brandywine. He had cousins, but they were Tories. He was thankful that he didn't have a wife and children outside somewhere waiting and wondering if he was dead or alive. Widows and children faced a life almost as miserable as his. They could starve, or, including children, be forced into prostitution. Or they could die of the pox or a hundred other diseases that afflicted the weak. No, he was thankful he was alone. Of course, he thought ruefully, that meant he would die unlamented and unmissed if he didn't get off this damned ship.

At least he could move about in the innards of the *Suffolk*. At first, he and all the others had been chained to the hull, but the chains had pulled away from the rotting wood, and splinters had been used to pick the locks and free the men. The guards made no effort to rechain them. Whatever happened in the dangerous world below decks was none of their business. Live and let live was the guard's motto, or was it live and let the rebel bastards die?

He felt it again. The ship was moving, trembling, groaning. What the hell was happening? The others were talking nervously. The ship shuddered, this time strongly, and a couple of the men who were standing fell down.

Will dropped to his knees as the ship slowly began to tilt towards the river. A loud sound like a screaming animal was heard as rotten wood gave way. On deck he heard the guards yelling and running around in confusion. It dawned on him—the *Suffolk* was falling apart and capsizing.

The list grew worse and the ship shook violently as the sounds grew louder. Prisoners began to scream as they recognized their peril. Suddenly, the ship fractured herself and Will glimpsed the blessed glare of sunlight before torrents of green water rushed in through the hole. As others ran from the gaping hole in her hull, Will moved toward it. He had an idea. It was desperate, but what did he have to lose besides his life?

When the inward rush of water slowed, Will took a deep breath and dived underwater and through the hole. He brushed against the wooden side of the hole and felt pain as his skin was scraped, but nothing stopped him. His lungs ached from the exertion and his own weakness, but he forced himself to stay underwater and not to surface where he could be seen. In agony and with his vision turning red, he pushed himself away from the slimy hull of the dying ship.

He could hold his breath no more. He rose to the surface, gasped and gulped welcome fresh air. He quickly looked around. There was pandemonium on board the sinking *Suffolk* and on the shore beside her. The hulk had broken in half, spewing prisoners and dropping guards into the river. Gunfire crackled as guards shot at prisoners floating in the water. The two halves of the *Suffolk* were on their sides and breaking up into smaller chunks.

A good-sized piece of her deck floated by and Will grabbed at it. He held onto it and sank below it. There was a pocket of air and he sucked it. He could feel the current taking him downstream and away from the shore. He was free of the prison ship, but for how long? He willed himself to make no movement, no splashes, nothing that would attract attention. He wanted to be a part of the slowly moving planking.

He drifted. The sounds seemed to fade away. He realized that he was naked. The rags he'd once called clothing had fallen apart in the river. He was cold and it dawned on him that he would freeze to death before he drowned. He was already having difficulty feeling his legs and his grip on the planking was weakening.

His makeshift raft bumped against something and he looked out from under. He'd collided with a small and decrepit wooden dock and was well within the city of New York. There was no one on the dock. Will decided he had to take his chances and get out of the water. With the last of his strength, he ripped off a piece of sodden and rotting wood to use as a knife. He would use it on himself before going back to another prison ship.

Will's chances of escaping were negligible. He was a naked, weak, and cold rebel in a Tory city. He was gaunt and his long hair and beard made him look frightening. His wooden knife was a puny weapon that probably wouldn't break a man's skin, much less kill him. He laughed bitterly as he thought about using it to commit suicide. He climbed on to the dock and rested on his hands and knees. He vomited water on the dock. He was doomed. A kitten could take him prisoner.

"What you gonna do with that little bitty thing, rebel?"

Will turned towards the sound. He was so disoriented that a man with a wagon full of hay had gotten within a few feet of him. Almost idly, his mind in a daze, he noted that the driver was a Negro.

"You from that ship that sunk up there, ain't you?" The Negro laughed. "Them English is going crazy tryin' to catch everybody." He gestured to the pile of hay. "You want them to catch you?"

"No," Will managed to say through shaking and blue lips. He was too tired to even try to cover his nakedness.

"Didn't think so. My name is Homer and I ain't Greek. Now get your skinny ass up there in the wagon and cover up under the hay. And don't make no noise, either."

Will did as he was told.

A few hours later, Will was in paradise, busy scrubbing himself with soap made from ash and dirt after being drenched with buckets of sun-warmed river water. Not even his prolonged swim in the Hudson River had removed more than a year's worth of filth. Nor had it done anything to his long and matted beard and hair, which Homer first cut off and then shaved. When they were done, Will was raw all over, but he was clean.

Homer pointed to a welt on Will's left buttock. "What the devil's that?"

Will laughed wryly. "The bastard British branded me. That's supposed to be an 'R' for rebel, but I screamed and squealed and twisted so much that ugly blob is what resulted."

Homer nodded. "I thought that's what it was. Somehow I thought that only black people got branded and then only slaves, although I guess you were a slave of the British. Either way it's a vile way to treat a man."

Will sat down on a rickety chair and wrapped himself in a blanket. He was freezing and, as his condition improved, he didn't want to be naked in front of his new companion. He was also completely spent.

"Now what?" he asked.

Homer stood and stretched. He was a big man and Will guessed his age at forty or so. "You rest up for a bit, and then we'll figure that out after we get some food in you. If I tried to feed you now, it'd be a waste of food. You'd probably puke it up again thanks to the seawater you drank."

Once again Will did as he was told.

Sarah Benton and her cousin Faith hugged each other and waited for the dawn. They were in the small western Massachusetts town of Pendleton's one prison cell as guests of Charles Braxton, the sheriff. They were to be punished by spending a day in the stocks for speaking ill of the king. The population of Pendleton was only a couple of hundred, but many of them were Tories and most would be there to watch the two women's discomfort and humiliation.

Sarah Benton was twenty-six and ten years older than Faith. She felt guilty for her cousin. It was Sarah's sharp tongue that had said that the king was responsible for the war and the death of Tom, the fine man who she considered to be her husband. Faith just happened to be standing by when she made the comment, but that meant nothing to Sheriff Charles Braxton. His authority included the ability to punish minor offences, and a day in the stocks for Sarah's impertinence was what she and Faith would suffer.

Sarah was certain she could handle it, but she less was less so regarding her cousin. Plump little Faith looked terrified. Why, Sarah wondered? It couldn't be all that bad, could it?

She'd known little about Pendleton. She and Tom had lived somewhat closer to Boston, but after his death in the war, and with Boston being a virtual British garrison, she'd decided to move west to her cousins. A woman alone, especially the widow of a rebel, was not safe with so many angry and vengeful British soldiers roaming around. The British and Tories were in a vengeful mood.

Of course, it now seemed that sleepy little Pendleton, with a population of about two hundred living in clean, well-appointed homes, wasn't all that safe either. Sheriff Braxton was a virtual dictator appointed by the British in Boston to control this area and he did so with a hard and often cruel hand.

"Come on out for your day in the sun," exclaimed Sheriff Braxton with a sarcastic laugh. Deputies came in and separated the two women. A sobbing and unprotesting Faith was led down a hallway to another room. Sarah was led by the arm to Braxton's office where she was pushed against a wall. She heard voices through it, but nothing to cause her concern.

Braxton glared at her. "A day in the stocks is not pleasant, Sarah Benton."

"I think I will survive. Would it help if I apologized for my wicked tongue?" She did not offer to pay a fine. She had no money, and the sheriff knew it.

"No. What's said cannot be unsaid, any more than water can be put back in a bucket after its spilled. You must be punished."

"I see."

"But your punishment can be changed. You're an attractive woman, Mistress Benton." He reached out and touched her light brown hair. Sarah gasped in surprise. "And a pleasant figure, too. Nice and firm and trim, not soft and plumpish like your cousin." His hand slipped into her dress to her breast and squeezed, while his other hand groped between her legs.

"Stop that," she said weakly. His hands hurt her. Braxton was a very large and strong man and she could not break his grip as he continued to paw at her. He could overpower her with ease if he wished to. His pelvis was against her and she could feel his erection straining against her.

The sheriff laughed. "Don't protest your virtue, Mistress Benton. You claim you're a widow, but you're a whore since your so-called husband was a rebel. It also means you are no silly little virgin. But don't worry; it'll be nothing like what you're worrying about. I won't rape you. Last thing I need is some bitch like you going to the parson saying I'd forced her to spread her legs for me, or worse, winding up with a little bastard running around town and looking like me." He laughed again. "Christ, my wife would kill me slowly if that happened."

"What then do you want?" she asked.

He took her hand and put it on his erection. "You take this in your mouth and do what comes naturally."

She pulled her hand away. "I won't."

"Your cousin is doing it right now."

"I don't believe you."

He spun her around and clamped his hand over her mouth. He opened a sliding window separating the two rooms and pushed Sarah to it. Faith Benton was naked to the waist and kneeling between the knees of one of the deputies. His pants were at his ankles. He was grinning hugely and groping Faith's full young breasts as her head pumped up and down over his groin. Faith's eyes were closed as if she was hoping this was all a nightmare.

"Your cousin will milk all three of my deputies and then be sent on her way. All you have to do is service just one person, me, and then you can go home as well."

Sarah wanted to cry and throw up. Pendleton wasn't a refuge. Instead, it was a newer form of hell. "Never," she said in a voice that was almost a whimper.

Braxton laughed, "Your choice."

Within moments, Sarah was locked in the stocks. Her legs and arms were spread out in front of her and her bottom was on a rail. Discomfort quickly turned to pain. Worse, the sun was rising and she was already sweaty and thirsty. But at least she had her pride, but she was beginning to wonder the price of her pride. Out of the corner of her eye, she'd seen Faith running down the road to her uncle's home. Faith hadn't turned to look at her.

Minutes became hours and her position became agonizing. Braxton came by and smiled down at her. "Too bad it's too late to change your mind."

"I would never change my mind," she said with difficulty. Her tongue was dry.

Braxton laughed and walked away. He turned back to her. "Next time you might not think that way, and, trust me, there will be a next time. Even if you don't say something slanderous, I can always find a half dozen people in this happy little town who'll say you did. You'll either do what I wish or you'll spend many days in my stocks."

Sarah felt a wave of growing despair. When she got out of the stocks—if she got out of them—she would have to find another place to live and do so quickly. Some place far, far away from a monster like Braxton. She looked up as two young boys laughed and ran up to her. They pulled her skirt up above her thighs and roared with glee as her bare legs were exposed. One of them knelt between her legs and looked while the second pinched her breast until someone hollered and chased them away. She thought the voice sounded like her aunt. Other citizens of Pendleton amused themselves by pelting her with rotten vegetables.

A woman stopped beside her and leaned over. "Here, take this."

It was a pitcher of water and the woman held it to her mouth. Sarah thanked her and gulped eagerly. The woman stepped away and began to laugh. It was Sheriff Braxton's wife and she began to cackle loudly.

A moment later, Sarah's stomach churned and cramped. She would have doubled in agony, but the stocks held her firm and she couldn't move. Another cramp and her bowels released, sending a torrent of brown filth gushing through her dress and onto the ground. The half dozen people still gathered around the stocks howled in laughter.

The sheriff's wife grabbed Sarah's hair, pulled her head back, and glared at her. "You refused my husband, didn't you?" she hoarsely whispered. "That means he's gonna be angry and take it out on me. I've got to suffer because of *you*, you arrogant bitch. So now you get to suffer."

The agony grew even more intense. Sarah passed in and out of consciousness. She thought she heard her uncle's voice and then Sheriff Braxton's.

"You have to set her free."

"It's not sunset yet."

Braxton eyed her uncle carefully. Even though Braxton was strong and an experienced fighter, Sarah's uncle Wilford was a blacksmith and had a reputation of his own for settling issues.

"That's blood on the ground below her. She's bleeding from her insides. She may be seriously hurt by that concoction your witch of a wife gave her. If she dies, I will accuse the two of you of murder and I will have more than enough witnesses to satisfy a court, even a British one. For God's sake, Sheriff, you've proved your point."

There was silence and she felt hands fumbling at her wrists and ankles. Sarah fell free of the stocks. Hands eased her to a lying position on the ground. She cried out as her muscles protested and her stomach spasmed again. She was lifted up and placed on something firm, wooden. She felt motion as her uncle's wagon took her away.

Will held the bowl of broth in his hand and savored the warmth and the exquisite odor. It was chicken. He loved it. It was the most delicious thing he'd ever tasted. He held it to his lips and drew in a swallow. It was his third bowl of the day and he felt his strength returning with each sip.

It had been a week since his escape. Homer, the middle-aged colored man who had rescued him had fed him a steady diet of broth and vegetables with an occasional piece of fruit. Not only was Will's strength returning, but his teeth were no longer loose and aching. He felt he could walk for miles although he knew that was a fantasy. It would be a long time before he could hike anywhere. He relished his freedom even though he was a fugitive in hiding and had even less space in Homer's basement than when he'd been in the hold of the *Suffolk*. He concluded that freedom was a state of mind, of the spirit, and had nothing to do with wealth or the size of a dwelling. Homer lived in little more than a hovel and seemed to be quite content. For the moment, so too was Will.

They were in the basement of a building that had burned during the great fire that had ravaged much of New York when the British took it over in the early years of the war. If he looked out through a crack in the building's foundation, he could see the charred remains of old Trinity Church, which helped him place himself. He'd been to New York on a number of occasions both before and during the war. Before the war, it had been on business or pleasure, but during the war it was to gather intelligence from the occupying British.

Even though he was an officer in the Continental Army, his real skill was as a spy.

Homer usually disappeared during the day and occasionally at night. Once he returned with a collection of clothing that more or less fit Will. It included several pairs of boots that Will tried on before finding a pair that were comfortable.

"What do you do for a living?" Will asked.

"I fix things. I'm very handy. I don't take work from carpenters and such so they leave me alone, except sometimes when I help them with carrying and lifting. But if some old lady needs a leaking roof fixed, or somebody needs a stable cleaned, or something like that, I fix it."

Will fingered his shirt. It was a little large, but maybe he'd gain weight and grow into it. "Do they pay you in clothing?"

Homer shrugged. "Sometimes they don't pay me at all. Sometimes they think they can just fuck the nigger because the British aren't going to make them pay up."

Will grinned. "So you take what's owed you?"

"Yes."

"So that makes you a thief, doesn't it?"

Homer grinned back. "Not in my book. Besides, you want me to return them clothes and maybe turn you in just as naked as they day I found you?"

Will returned to his broth. "So why didn't you? Turn me in, that is. After all, didn't the British abolish slavery? I would've thought you would be a supporter of theirs."

"I was never a slave, so they didn't do nothing to free me. They couldn't give me something I already had. All they can do is take it away—and that concerns me. See, I was born of free blacks, who were also born free. Nobody in my family was ever a slave, at least not that I know of. I even served in the British Army along with a lot of other colored men because we thought the British would be better for us then you rebel people. Of course, the British lied. Now they're trying to forget every promise they made to colored folk, and they're even letting slave catchers from the south look for so-called escaped slaves. The British are gonna keep peace with the southern planters by ignoring the existence of slavery. The slave catchers ain't too particular who they catch. I ain't gonna be caught." He smiled grimly as he patted the hilts of the large knives he had in his belt and his boot. "I've defended myself before and will do it again. In my world, killing to keep your freedom ain't a crime."

Will was not surprised by Homer's statement that he had served the king. The British had raised several detachments of militia consisting of black soldiers, but with white officers, of course.

"So why did I save you? Because what they was doing to you prisoners was as wrong as slavery is to black people. I saw how they jammed you all into them big boats and I saw how they carried dead people out. That was wrong, evil. They call themselves Christians, but they aren't if they do that to other people."

"So you're a Christian?"

Homer shook his head. "Didn't say that. I am what I want to be and I ain't seen nothing in Christianity that makes me want to be one."

Will put down the now empty bowl. His hunger was satisfied for a while. Perhaps soon he could try some meat. His body had begun craving it. "All right. What do we do now?"

"They've stopped looking for escaped prisoners. Good news

is they've taken them all off the other boats and put them in warehouses. I've heard that General Cornwallis is furious that so much of the money intended for the prisoners has been stolen. At least warehouses don't sink. Still the prisoners are starving, just not as badly. But they don't know who's missing because they don't know who was on the *Suffolk* in the first place."

Will exulted. They weren't looking for him. Hell, they didn't even know what he looked like, much less what is name was. "I want to get out of New York."

Homer laughed. "Can't say as I blame you. I do have an idea. When you're stronger and things are really quiet, we will rent a horse and wagon like I'd done when I picked you up, and take it north across the Harlem River. You need a pass to get out of this town, but that's no problem. After that there's no British patrols, at least none that will pay any attention to a white man and his slave. You will pretend to be my master and I will be the lowly slave riding in the back of the wagon. No one will suspect a thing."

Will thought the plan had the virtue of simplicity. But he had been caught by a random patrol. The letter "R," for rebel, had been branded on his buttocks, and if caught and stripped, he'd be hanged. And so would Homer who was willing to risk his life to help him.

And who was to say that the same wouldn't occur even across the Harlem River after the two of them had parted and he was alone.

"Homer, just suppose I do get caught. They would realize that someone helped me. They would force me to tell them everything and lead them to you."

"Do you know where you are right now?"

"Enough to lead someone back here if I was forced to."

"Then don't worry about it because I won't be here. There's no reason for me to stay here. I'll move."

"But I know your name."

Homer laughed hugely. "Do you?"

Owen Wells liked climbing the rigging of a great sailing ship, and the HMS *Victory* was the greatest of them all. Only a few years old, the massive ship of the line still seemed shiny and new. She'd entered the fleet in 1778 and taken part in the two battles of the Ushant where Owen's skills as a sniper had gained him recognition. The *Victory* carried upwards of a hundred great guns and was the pride of the Royal Navy. She displaced about 3,500 tons and had a crew of almost nine hundred men. She had patrolled off Boston during the revolution and had acquitted herself well fighting the French, although some thought it a shame that she had missed the climactic battle off Virginia that had ended the revolution. Owen didn't care. People had a nasty habit of dying during battles. He'd already lost a number of mates.

Owen didn't have to be climbing the rigging at this time of the evening. He was off duty and could have been playing cards, reading, or cleaning his kit. He was a Royal Marine, not a seaman, but he was good at climbing and it gave him a chance to be away from the other marines and sailors who frequently ridiculed him. They called him ape, or monkey, because of his physique. He was short, squat, and dark haired. His arms were disproportionately long and heavily muscled, which enabled him to swing through the rigging with consummate ease.

This strength meant he'd won most of the fights with people who'd initially tormented him. If he got them in his massive arms, it was all over. He would wrap his arms around their chests and squeeze until they either gave up or passed out. He hadn't yet killed a man with his strength, but he'd come close and that would be bad. It was one thing to kill an enemy, which he'd done, but entirely another to kill a fellow British crewman.

Along with being very strong, Owen was also a deadly shot with his musket. His place in combat was in the rigging, firing down on an enemy deck after clearing the enemy's rigging of their own riflemen. Lately, that had meant the French, and he'd killed several of them.

Owen was only twenty years old, but had been a Royal Marine for seven years. He'd enlisted after lying about his age and after finding that the local sheriff and squire were after him. His crime was poaching on the squire's grounds and eating the squire's damned rabbits, which was how he'd learned to shoot and track. He'd only shot the squire's rabbits because he was suddenly an orphan and was hungry. For killing rabbits they'd had him flogged before turning him over to the pressmen from the navy.

From his high perch, he could see the *Victory*'s captain far below on the quarterdeck. He'd never been on the quarterdeck.

That was officer's territory, and that struck him as strange. After all, it was just wood planking. The captain was accompanied by Admiral Sir William Cornwallis and General Sir John Burgoyne. Sir William, he'd heard, was the younger brother of Charles Cornwallis, the governor general of the colonies. As if it mattered to him. He toyed with the idea of spitting down and seeing if he could hit either of his mighty lordships on the head. He decided that was not a wise idea as he'd be flogged until his bones showed through, although the thought of hitting someone so important with a gob of spittle made him smile.

The *Victory* was the flagship of an enormous British fleet heading towards the American colonies. Even though it was a dark night, he could see the shapes of a score or more merchant vessels and a half dozen escorting warships, including other massive ships of the line like the *Victory* and a number of smaller, swifter frigates. He'd heard that the French navy wasn't much of a threat anymore, but it didn't pay to take chances.

Owen had made a decision. On reaching the New World, he would desert. The country was vast and, even though the British ruled the land, he was confident he could disappear in it. He had some money saved up from winning shooting matches, and, as a marine, he would likely be sent ashore to guard the sailors while picking up stores as he'd done before. His job would be to see the sailors didn't desert, and no one would be watching for him to run. He'd acquired a reputation for being trustworthy and it was time to use that to his advantage.

Somehow, he'd get civilian clothes and maybe a musket for protection from the red savages, or even the outlaws who, he'd heard, roamed the land outside the cities. He couldn't keep his smaller, naval version of the Tower musket as that would be too obviously property of the king. He thought seriously about joining the outlaw rebels to the west of the colonies, but discarded it. The army in the convoy was being sent to destroy them, which meant they would be destroyed. He'd never seen rebel soldiers, but he had seen the British and a rebel mob would never stand against them.

At least that was the plan. He shuddered at what could happen to him if it all went wrong. He'd be lucky if they shot him or hanged him. More likely he'd be flogged to death. He shuddered again. He'd been flogged once while in the navy, fifty lashes. He'd screamed after twenty and his back still bore the scars on top of the ones given back in England. He'd been hit with a short knotted rope called a starter a thousand times, but that didn't count. Everybody got hit like that. He'd worked hard at being a good marine and there was talk he might be promoted. Sure, he laughed, in a hundred years. Thanks to his squat physique, he didn't wear a dress uniform because none would fit him, which meant he could never command in the ranks. What he did wear was a large man's uniform that draped all over him.

Burgoyne and William Cornwallis appeared to be arguing. He wondered about what. He could hear the sounds of their voices but couldn't make out the words or meaning. He thought of the damage he could do to the British cause with his musket if he had it and shot down at them. He was Welsh, not British, and he'd been taught to respect and fear the British, but never to love them.

He wondered what he'd be when he was free.

"Get your lazy ass up," Homer said jovially. "We be leaving now."

It was the middle of the night, and Will had been dozing on a pile of rags. "What's happened?"

"There's a whole goddam fleet coming in and it's gonna be bringing more Redcoats than can be counted. They'll be crawling all over the place and all of a sudden I don't think this is a good place for us to be."

Will dressed quickly. He had nothing else to carry with him. At least it wouldn't look all that much like they were running away, he thought ruefully. He realized there was another problem involving British security.

"We don't have passes."

"Yes, you do." Homer rummaged in his pocket and pulled out a piece of paper. It identified the bearer as Thomas Wolfington, a merchant from Providence, Rhode Island. His date of birth said he was in his late thirties and the document carried all the appropriate stamps and seals. "Like I said, you white people need the pass. Nigger slaves don't need one. Lucky us."

Will examined the paper. "Where'd you get this?"

"Off of Thomas Wolfington of Providence, Rhode Island, where else? He was drunk as a lord and fell down in the gutter."

"Won't he miss this when he wakes up?"

"He won't wake up, leastwise not on this earth. I dumped

his sorry ass in the river. He's probably halfway out to join that British fleet right now."

Will grimaced. Homer had killed a man on his behalf. So what if the man was probably a Tory, it was murder, not battle. But then, did he want to run the risk of being picked up in a city that was full of Tories and soon to be inundated with British soldiers? As with all he had done to survive on the prison hulk, he would beg forgiveness later. Now it was long past time to go, and if Mr. Thomas Wolfington truly was dead, then he was a casualty of a brutal and ongoing war.

Very early in the morning, they rented a wagon and a horse. They promised the stable owner they'd have them back in a day or two and headed north to the Harlem River. As planned, Will drove while Homer sat behind him, the picture of docility.

There was excitement in the air. The overwhelmingly Tory city of New York was expectantly awaiting the arrival of the fleet. There were those who said they could see a forest of sails from the church steeples, which made the need for their departure even more imperative.

Will and Homer rode north against a tide of people heading for the waterfront to take in the scene. The stolen pass got them through the city's defenses without a second glance by the guards who were far more interested in the fleet's arrival. Once outside of the city, Manhattan Island was scarcely occupied. An occasional farmhouse broke the monotony as they rode north, but there were few of those and a number of them had been destroyed. Charred ruins near the road showed that hard times and years of warfare had fallen upon the people who had attempted to live there. The fertile land was strangely barren. The trees had been cut down for firewood, and only high weeds grew where once there had been forests.

A number of miles farther on along the trail called the Post Road, Will gazed wistfully at the Harlem Heights where the rebel army had handed the Redcoats a bloody nose following the over-whelming British victory at Long Island. The British had thought the Americans were finished, but they'd been wrong. Will prayed they were wrong again and that there really was a place called Liberty. But the feeling of depression returned when they passed by the site of Fort Washington, where more than two thousand Americans had been captured by the British.

When they finally reached the Harlem River, more than a dozen miles north of the city, it was getting dark and only a couple of very bored British soldiers examined Will's pass. A dozen others and an ensign commanding them lounged around a dilapidated farmhouse a hundred or so yards away. One scrawny white man and a colored servant were not a threat to their safety. The soldiers were even friendly, and Will allowed himself a moment's fleeting sympathy for them. This wasn't their war either. The soldiers said that they were annoyed at the arrival of the fleet and the thousands of reinforcements General Burgoyne had brought with him. The soldiers and sailors would be additional competition for the city's whores.

Will grinned in mock sympathy. "Don't worry. I understand most of the women in New York are whores already, so there'll be plenty to go around." It was almost the truth. Someone had calculated that one in five women in New York were prostitutes, while others had jokingly said it was the other way around.

The soldiers laughed appreciatively and let the two men pass onto Dykeman's Bridge that took them across the river. When they were several miles farther away, Will and Homer paused. It was night and the moon gave only a little light.

"This is where we part," Homer said.

Will nodded. He was on his way to Connecticut to see if a piece of property owned by his family still existed. He wasn't certain what he'd do when he got there. It was just a small dairy farm, but it was a link to his past and had been in his family for generations. If asked by anyone along the way, he would continue to be the late and unlamented Thomas Wolfington.

"Not going back to New York?" Will teased. "What about returning the horse and wagon?"

Homer grunted. "Fuck the guy who rented them to me and fuck New York. Nothin' there but Redcoats wanting me to shine their boots or kiss their asses. And like you said, all the women are whores even though all the money in the world won't get them to fuck a black man. No, I'm on my way to Boston."

"Homer, there are even more Redcoats there. It's almost a prison."

"I ain't that stupid, Will. I'm just going near Boston. The British are only in the city, not the surrounding area. I understand that the people up there are a lot nicer to colored people than elsewhere in the colonies. Who knows, I might even get laid. And you? Where will you go after you've satisfied your curiosity about that farm?"

Will had given that a lot of thought. He wondered if he'd be able to escape his past and live peacefully as a civilian farmer. Then he wondered if he even wanted to be a farmer. He'd studied for the law, but soldiering was almost all he knew. And he was damned certain he didn't want to be a farmer under an English yoke.

"You're going to wind up at Liberty, aren't you?" Homer chuckled.

"If there is such a place. Maybe it's mystical, like Camelot, and doesn't even exist?"

"I have no idea what this Camelot is, Will, but if it doesn't exist, then why are the British going to send an army against it? Naw, Will, there's something out in the west and I don't know if it's called Liberty, or Fort Washington, or Jerusalem, or what in hell. But odds are, that's where you'll wind up."

# Chapter 2 ★ ★ ★ ★ ★ ★ ★ ★ ★ ★ ★ ★ ★ ★ ★ ★ ★ ★

GOVERNOR GENERAL SIR CHARLES CORNWALLIS RECEIVED HIS younger brother William in his private quarters in Fort George on lower Manhattan. They embraced fondly.

"Thank God, a friendly face," the recently appointed governor general of the thirteen colonies said.

Sir Charles Cornwallis' responsibilities were awesome, since they included both civil and military matters, and he looked tired and haggard despite being refreshed at meeting his brother. Privately, he sometimes wondered if he'd been rewarded or punished with this high office.

He'd recently been particularly distressed when one of the prison hulks had fallen apart and disgorged more than a hundred emaciated prisoners into the river where most of them drowned. Until then, he'd naively assumed that the civilian contractors who were running the prison ships were at least doing what they were being paid to do—feed, clothe and shelter the prisoners at a minimal level until London could figure out what to do with them. Embarrassed and ashamed at what he'd seen and belatedly recognized, Cornwallis had ordered the surviving prisoners out of all the hulks and into warehouses where British soldiers now guarded them and assured that they received sufficient food and at least a decent level of comforts. A recent inspection showed most of them improving and he'd sent a message to Lord Stormont describing what he'd found and how he hoped it wasn't being repeated in other prisons where rebels were being held. He'd heard rumors that conditions for senior rebels in Jamaica were even more vile. The rebels deserved to be punished severely, but not starved and abused until they died.

"Good to see you as well," William said. "And how's the luckiest man in the world this day?"

It was a joke they shared every one of the infrequent times they got together. The elder Cornwallis' victory at Yorktown had been as unexpected as it was total. On the verge of surrender, his men starving and out of ammunition, the relieving British fleet had arrived with both supplies and reinforcements. That they'd also destroyed a poorly handled French fleet under Admiral DeGrasse in the great victory at the Battle of the Capes had been an added bonus.

Refreshed in mind and body, the British had surged out of their fortifications and defeated the now dispirited combined French and American forces. The defeat had turned into a rout and the rout into a slaughter in which the rebel army had been destroyed and George Washington taken prisoner.

William, known as "Billy Blue" behind his back, took a brandy from his older brother. "My voyage with General Burgoyne was fine and thank you for asking. Now, what are you going to do with the great man and the little army he's brought over?"

Charles Cornwallis chuckled. "I suppose I'll obey my orders, presuming they make any sense. Of course, I'm not sure it makes any sense at all to ship an army, however small, over here when the real war is taking place in France."

Shortly after the French and American collapse, an attempt by the French monarchy to raise taxes to pay for the debacles had resulted in France being torn apart by a sudden and violently anti-monarchist revolution. The new taxes had started a civil war that was rending France into bloody pieces. Horrified by the violence of the revolution in France, and tormented by the possibility of a similar republican uprising in England, King George III had sent over an army led by Lord Jeffrey Amherst to France to help the monarchists crush the revolution. France was where most professional soldiers wished to be and was where Charles Cornwallis thought he should be. Still, he had doubts. Yorktown had taught him the fickleness of fate on the battlefield.

France was also a war that was not going particularly well for

England. The small British army had not had a major impact in trying to restore its version of order on the French, and the efforts of the French monarchists had been just as dismal. As a class, both Cornwallis brothers considered the French aristocracy to be a pack of fools.

"And just how popular is Burgoyne's adventure in England?" Charles asked.

"Emotions are mixed," his younger brother answered. "Many wish Burgoyne a swift victory, while others want the rebels left alone, feeling that enough blood and treasure has been spent in subduing the colonies. Others feel that the rebellion in France might spread to the English peasants and that terrifies them. In sum, the war against the American rebels is unpopular with a sizeable portion of the English people and that includes a growing number in Parliament. Burgoyne will have but one chance to win. If he fails, there will, at best, be an independent American nation out in the west. It is entirely possible that all of the colonies would rebel again and win."

"I will meet with Burgoyne shortly," Sir Charles said with a hint of distaste. "The man is too flamboyant for my taste, and he did lose an army at Saratoga."

His brother laughed, "Whereas you only almost lost one at Yorktown."

Sir Charles grinned happily. "All right, you have me there. And of course I have advance knowledge that he is here to do something about that damned rebel enclave out west and I'm going to be ordered to render whatever assistance possible while, at the same time, governing thirteen fractious and largely unrepentant colonies in the King's name."

Billy Blue Cornwallis made a mock bow. "And of course you will obey your orders like a good soldier and to the best of your ability."

Governor General Sir Charles Cornwallis matched his younger brother's bow, "Up your arse, Billy."

Major James Fitzroy followed General Burgoyne into Lord Cornwallis' large but surprisingly spartan office in Fort George at the foot of Manhattan Island. Cornwallis took one look at Fitzroy and made a gesture that he should leave. Fitzroy did as told, but positioned himself outside the door so that he could hear the conversation, just as Burgoyne had earlier told him to.

Cornwallis was stood behind a large desk and table which was littered with papers. "What on earth were our lords in London thinking, General Burgoyne?" he said after formally acknowledging the other's presence.

"I believe it's quite simple, General," Burgoyne said with a hint of smugness. "We all want the rebels finally crushed and that is my assignment. When the rebels are destroyed, peace will be assured and then the second phase of pacification will begin."

"I have no problem with your taking on the rebels in their forest lair, but it is Lord North's concept of pacification that disturbs me."

"Oh?"

Cornwallis looked through a window at the harbor. Scores of warships and transports were anchored near the fort, and unloading large numbers of men and vast quantities of supplies. Even so, the harbor of New York was so enormous it somehow seemed largely empty. The large expanse of protected water hinted at what the North American colonies could become with the proper British control. New York had the potential to become one of the world's major ports.

Cornwallis turned and faced his guest. "Several things bother me. First is the amount of taxes the colonists are going to have to bear. Yes, I know the war has to be paid for somehow, but we are now going to heavily tax those people who supported us in the rebellion and remained loyal, and that bothers me immensely. Please don't forget that the colonists were divided into three unequal parts. There were the rebels, the loyalists, and those who stayed uninvolved. The rebels should be punished, but not the others.

"Second is the idea of restrictions on jobs, pay, and travel. London seems to be hell bent on turning the remaining colonists into medieval serfs. Benjamin Franklin said that he foresaw England turning these colonies into something equivalent to Ireland—a land full of impoverished and sullen people, governed harshly. If that is the case, it would be a very foolish policy indeed. The Irish are unarmed and have no place to flee to, but it is totally different here. Many, perhaps most, Colonists have their own weapons, and they are perfectly capable of both using them and going westward. This is what so many have done, and which is why you are here."

Burgoyne made to interrupt but Cornwallis stopped him. "Then there is the king's idea of establishing a North American nobility to oversee and overawe the poor benighted peasants. What will they do, make Benedict Arnold the Duke of Pennsylvania? Or would Earl of West Point be more appropriate? Lord, that would be ironic justice, wouldn't it? Will every hamlet and village have its overweight and over-dull squire with his fat and unmarriageable daughters?"

Even though he didn't like what Cornwallis was saying, Burgoyne had to smile. "Please don't forget the poor sod's shrew of a wife."

Cornwallis laughed at the mental picture. "Oh, that'll inspire loyalty to the crown. Is the king aware that a previous monarch, James II, tried pretty much the same thing a century or so ago? It failed miserably, and it was one of the factors in James Stuart losing his crown. The colonists have no history of nobility and are singularly unimpressed by titles. Even the loyalists will resist such efforts. Many of the most loyal will insist on the colonial custom of shaking hands as if with equals instead of bowing to one's betters."

Burgoyne had turned almost beet red. "And why do you imply that our efforts will fail?" Burgoyne said. "We must have peace and economic stability to support our war in France. There cannot be an enemy in our rear."

"Of course we must have peace," Cornwallis replied sarcastically. "Let me see. Since the collapse of the rebellion, the French monarchy has been assailed by two groups. First are the Constitutionalists under the boy general, Lafayette, and the second are the Republicans, who are little more than an armed mob intent on killing everyone who disagrees with them. The Constitutionalists wish to control the king, while the Republicans wish to depose him. Either group frightens our king and his lordships in London since, if successful, the disease of rebellion could spread to England's own sullen peasants.

"The two groups have chased King Louis out of Paris and off to Calais, where he is protected by the Royal Navy and the British Army. They are trying mightily to put him back on his throne with the help of the third group, the supporters of the status quo. This includes just about everybody the average Frenchie hates, and that includes an incredibly corrupt Papist clergy."

"France cannot be allowed to slide into anarchy," Burgoyne said. "We need taxes to restore Louis."

"And why not? Since when did our ancient enemy become our new friend?" Cornwallis shuffled through some papers on his desk. "Still, I must support you. I have my orders, insane though they are."

Burgoyne's complexion had paled slightly. He was visibly shaken by the unexpected response from someone he'd thought was a supporter. "According to the orders, Lord Cornwallis, you are to give me ten thousand British soldiers. Along with the four thousand I have brought, I will have a truly formidable force that will crush the rebels."

Cornwallis glared at Burgoyne. "Did their lordships remember that I only have fifteen thousand regulars in all of the colonies? That will leave me only a relative handful to protect them should you fail and I do not consider the few Loyalist militia regiments we have as either trained or reliable."

"I don't believe I will fail, General."

"Do you know what you're up against?"

Burgoyne smiled. "Approximately two or three thousand rebels, including women and children at a place called Fort Washington, or, if you prefer, Liberty. Either name will suffice as long as it's the same place. It is located on the southern end of Lake Michigan and can be approached either overland from Fort Pitt or Detroit, or by water around Michigan from Detroit."

"Correct," said Cornwallis, "Except that Liberty, the name of the village outside Fort Washington, is but one of a number of similar places out in the west. It is, however, by far the largest. London seems to have forgotten that literally thousands of rebels fled to the west, either individually or in groups, and have built a score of villages and forts."

"Sir, I assumed that there would be other rebels. Otherwise, fourteen thousand to crush a few thousand rebels would be a ridiculous waste of resources that could be utilized against France."

Cornwallis sighed. There were times when he was heartily sick and tired of the colonies. Some days he only wanted to spend some time back in England where he could better cherish the memory of his late and beloved wife, Jemima. He wanted a different posting. He'd been promised the governorship of India after his victory at Yorktown, but that had been cancelled. He would stay in the American Colonies until—if?—events calmed down.

Cornwallis smiled inwardly. If Burgoyne succeeded, then perhaps he could be replaced as governor general and promoted. Perhaps his replacement would be Burgoyne and wouldn't that be marvelous justice to see the elegant Burgoyne stuck in the squalor of New York instead of reveling in the delights of London. Perhaps, Cornwallis thought, he'd get an army to fight the French? If Burgoyne failed, why it would be London's fault, wouldn't it? Cornwallis decided that he would make sure that no mud from any possible failure by Burgoyne splashed on him. He would do everything his orders required. He would support Burgoyne. Of course he would.

"Shall I assume that you will take possession of Mr. Washington's skull and bones from me?" Burgoyne asked.

The look on Cornwallis' face showed what he thought of bringing the barbaric trophies across the Atlantic. Again, friends in London had forewarned him that Washington's skull and a number of other bones would be sealed in a trunk along with some of Washington's personal possessions. So far the existence of what Cornwallis considered to be vile relics was a secret. If the word got out, the Tories would want them destroyed with great ceremony, while the rebels would want them enshrined in a North American version of the Vatican. If anything, the damned bones should have been kept in London.

"The box containing them will be left with me and locked away for what I hope will be forever," Cornwallis said grimly. "If Lord North or Stormont want Washington's bones displayed prominently, let them come and do it."

Burgoyne nodded. "Which is precisely what I would do. I protested, but was overruled."

Cornwallis smiled in a belated attempt at conviviality. "You will have my total cooperation, General Burgoyne. In anticipation of your orders, I have already notified the various units and garrisons under my command that you will be using many of their men. Some will reduce their forces, while others will have to close up, temporarily, one hopes. The situation will be precarious, but you're right. The return on investment will be well worth it if the rebels are finally crushed. If all goes well, you will have the beginnings of an army in a few months and you'll be able to begin campaigning in full strength by next spring."

Outside the door, Fitzroy's jaw almost dropped. Next spring before they could even begin? He'd known it would be a long campaign, but he'd expected to be back in England well before next spring. What in God's name had he gotten himself into?

It took Sarah Benton several days to recover her strength. In the meantime, the outcry against Sheriff Braxton had grown large enough to attract the attention of the British government in Boston. As a result, he had been chastised for his excesses and warned never to do it again. Braxton had laughed off the punishment. He would do as he damned well pleased. However, he would wait a very short while before beginning his ways anew.

As a result, Sarah was often hesitant about going outside. Either the sheriff or one of his deputies was always hanging around the white picket fence outside her uncle's home. On the rare occasions she did venture outdoors, they would tease her lewdly. Braxton also said it was only a matter of time before she would again have the choice of a day in the stocks or giving him sexual gratification. Of course, he'd added, it would be two days in the stocks for a second crime.

Sarah was despondent. Was this going to be the way of the rest of her life? If so, how long would the rest of her life be? She'd spoken with Faith and found that it hadn't been the first time Faith and other village women had been forced to perform for the sheriff and his deputies. She suspected that her own aunt had been one of those abused by him, but dared not voice her concern.

"You live with it," Faith had said, her voice bleak with bitterness and shame. "You do what you have to and get on with your life."

In many ways, Faith was still a child, and it pained Sarah to see her so abused and depressed. She knew that Faith felt guilty. In an obscene way, Sarah had suffered the most, while Faith endured only the humiliation. But perhaps humiliation was worse than anything.

Deep down, Sarah knew that she would ultimately lose to the sheriff and the thought repelled her. Not the act, but the sheriff. She had done such a deed for her husband, Tom, but that had been an act of love, not vengeance or power. Worse, the deputies let it be known that she would be servicing them as well and as often as they wished. They were going to break her, and she knew that anyone could be broken.

Then one evening, Uncle Wilford made a simple pronouncement. "We're leaving."

Faith and Sarah were surprised, while Aunt Rebecca simply beamed. "I've sold the property and we're heading west," Wilford said.

"There are Indians and outlaws out there," Faith wailed. "We'll be robbed and scalped."

"Could they be worse than the sheriff and his men?" Aunt Rebecca replied with a cold fury that confirmed Sarah's concerns that her dear old aunt had been forced to perform for the sheriff as well. Was it because of something Rebecca had done herself, or had she done it to protect Faith? Or her husband? Probably the latter as Wilford was fairly outspoken. Sarah wondered if her uncle even knew or suspected.

"I have no plans to go all that far west, Faith," Uncle Wilford added gently, evading the fact that Indians would always be a menace no matter where they went. There were Indians near Pendleton but they were mainly a pathetic bunch of drunken beggars, something to be scorned, not feared.

He continued. "I do not plan on totally leaving civilization. I think we will find a place in Pennsylvania that will be far enough from the sheriff and the damned English who are so corrupt and cruel as to put a man like Braxton in charge of us."

"Don't say it so loud," Faith said, looking around in fear.

"Unless the sheriff's under the table I don't think he can hear us," Sarah answered with a tight smile. Under the iron rule of Sheriff Braxton, Pendleton was an evil place and she would be glad to be rid of it.

Uncle Wilford continued. "I sold the place as is to someone from Boston. A Tory, so he and Braxton will be happy with each other. I have the money and we'll just pack up and leave quickly. We can be miles away before the sheriff even realizes we're gone. We can lose ourselves in a vast country such as this."

To himself he hoped it was true. He'd heard rumors of terrible British oppressions to the west under the command of Banastre Tarleton at Pittsburgh.

Now even Faith looked excited. "When do we pack?"

"We'll start tonight," Wilford said. "I want to leave at sunset tomorrow."

A thought chilled Sarah. "Uncle, did you say the buyer is a Tory?"

"Yes."

"And did he pay in gold?"

Wilford laughed, "Of course. Did you want him to pay in Continentals?"

"Then I think we should leave tonight, and I think we should only take what we can carry. Leave everything else."

Her uncle looked shocked, while Faith looked puzzled. "But why, Sarah?" she said.

"Because no Tory would miss a chance to get back the money he's paid to a rebel. They'll raid us and rob us. Or worse, since Braxton will doubtless help them recover their money. And we'll be considered criminals for planning to leave without permission."

Uncle Wilford stood, anger contorted his face. "She's right. I'm a fool for not recognizing the peril I was creating. We pack now and we run."

They waited until dark and moved into the woods near the house. The women were dressed in men's clothes so they could ride the horses they were leading, along with a couple of other pack animals. What few personal possessions they brought were carried in pathetically small sacks. They had only two weapons, a musket carried by Wilford, and a fowling piece carried by Sarah. Wilford had to leave his blacksmithing tools since they were too heavy to carry. He only retained a large hammer that he said he'd like to use on either Braxton's or the Tory land buyer's skulls. Sarah seethed with anger at the injustice of it all, while Faith sobbed softly.

They were less than a mile away from their house when they heard horses in the distance, coming closer. They stopped and waited silently, holding their own horses' heads down so they wouldn't respond. A line of riders moved past them less than a hundred yards away. Sarah counted seven men and thought she recognized the bulk of Sheriff Braxton on the lead horse. When they were past, she asked her uncle if he recognized the buyer of the house as well. He did and snarled that he'd like to kill the son of a bitch.

"We should ride away now," said her aunt.

"No," Uncle Wilford said. "We'll wait until they're distracted." A grim smile played on his face.

The riders circled the comfortable and quiet-looking frame house and dismounted. What looked like a candle shone through an open window. Funny, Sarah thought, I don't remember seeing that candle before, but it does make it look like the house is occupied. She wondered if that was the distraction he mentioned? If so, it wasn't much of one. As she watched, the men smashed down the front door and rushed inside.

Uncle Wilford swore and then smiled with a cold fury. "The bastards. But now watch."

A moment later, the soft glow in the window became much brighter and, suddenly, flames erupted from the house. Wilford chuckled harshly.

"I rigged the oil lamps to spill if someone tried to come in through the doors. If I can't have the house, then no would-be Tory thief's going to get it either."

An explosion lit the night and men tumbled from her uncle's home. At least two of them were on fire and writhing on the ground, screaming at the top of their lungs. Others grabbed buckets from the well and doused the burning men while the house was quickly consumed. Sarah and the others hoped that one of the men burning was Sheriff Braxton or the thief of a Tory who had come to rob them. Wilford thought it likely that one was indeed Braxton. For all his faults, Braxton wasn't a coward and he would have led his men inside. One of the burning men was being ignored and obviously dead, while the other was frantically being treated by his companions.

Sarah smiled grimly as they mounted their horses. She was confident that no one would chase them this night. Even Faith looked pleased. The war against the English was not over.

Will Drake found his Connecticut property easily enough, but he didn't particularly like what he saw. Instead of a neat, clean, well-painted, and tidy house and barn, the main building was almost a ruin and the barn looked like it would fall over in a mild breeze. He had lived there until the end of his boyhood and had fond memories of the house and his family. Now, it looked like a shell, a mausoleum, and a tawdry one at that.

Worse was the presence of Francis and Winnie Holden, his cousins. They had never been close and Will had always suspected them of Tory leanings. Their presence on the property reinforced it—otherwise how would they have gotten the property that was rightfully Will's?

They were thoroughly surprised to see him, but greeted him cordially enough. Will looked in their eyes and could see it was all superficial. Their eyes were cold and wary, even fearful. They wondered why he had come, and what he wanted.

"I know you're surprised to see us living here," Winnie said nervously. She and her husband were obviously not thrilled at Will's unexpected arrival. "But we bought the place at a government sale. It'd been seized for nonpayment of taxes after it was abandoned. I can't imagine you'd be displeased. After all, it's staying in the family."

"Of course not," Will said evenly and with great effort. They were in the small kitchen eating some kind of stew prepared by Winnie who, in Will's opinion, should have let someone else cook. Still, it was food, and he wasn't that far from his days in the *Suffolk* to pass up a meal.

"We had no idea what'd happened to you," Francis said. "It was as if you'd dropped off the face of the earth. Heard rumors, though, that you were in a British prison."

"I was for a bit, but they let me go," Will lied.

"But I heard they were still keeping officers." Winnie said.

Will forced a laugh. "I wasn't an officer when the war ended. I got broken to the ranks for hitting a man senior to me. The man was a coward and I damn near killed him."

It was yet another lie, but he didn't trust his cousins, and was beginning to regret coming. He didn't doubt that they'd gobbled up the property for far less than what it was worth, and he didn't doubt they feared his presence as a potential claimant on what was now their land. He knew they'd turn him in if they suspected him of being an escapee.

"What are your plans?" Winnie asked, so transparent and cautious that Will almost laughed.

"I just want a good meal with you folks and then I'm heading west to start over. I'm satisfied that everything is in good hands here, and I want to start my life up again. If you'd be kind enough to give me breakfast, I'll leave first thing in the morning."

They both nodded and smiled happily at the thought of him leaving so quickly. "We'd be honored," Winnie said, her normally sour face breaking into a smile.

"And tonight I'll sleep in the barn. I'm used to that sort of thing and I wouldn't want to put you nice people out."

He got no argument from Francis and Winnie. In the barn, Will spread a blanket they'd given him on some straw and pretended to go to sleep. After a while, he heard a rustling outside and then heavy breathing by the wall. Cousin Francis, he decided, was about as quiet as a herd of horses. When Francis went back to the house, Will followed him far more silently.

"He's sound asleep," Francis told Winnie. "If I leave right now, I can get help and be back in a couple of hours."

"Why not just let him leave like he says he's going to," Winnie hissed.

"Because the bastard's a rebel and, besides, there's a ten-pound reward for turning in escaped prisoners. Or did you believe that bullshit about him being demoted from officer for fighting? The Will Drake I remember was too self-righteous to get his sanctimonious ass in that kind of trouble. We turn him in and we get the reward along with seeing that he doesn't ever trouble us about this land."

At least they think highly of me, Will thought as he listened through the glassless window.

They argued a little more, but Francis prevailed. He left at a trot and Winnie sat on a chair with a musket across her lap and stared fixedly at the door.

Will decided he wanted that musket. It was fairly new and looked as if it had been cared for. He took a rock and threw it at the barn. Winnie, who had been half dozing, awoke with a start and ran to the door, her musket held firmly before her.

As she stepped outside, Will slipped through the window and hid beside the door. When Winnie turned and entered, it was simplicity itself to grab the musket's barrel and yank it from her. He laughed as he saw it wasn't even cocked. Winnie, however, started to scream. Will shoved her back down in the chair and clamped his hand over her mouth.

"Winnie, I am not going to hurt you unless you make me, so be still. But if I do have to hurt you I will do so very terribly. Do you understand?"

She nodded, he eyes still wide with terror. Will released his hand from her mouth and replaced it with a gag made from dirty torn cloth. He tied her arms and legs to the chair while she moaned. Her nightdress had fallen open and her flat, sagging breasts were exposed. Will shook his head. He'd been a long time without a woman, but he wasn't that desperate. He fastened her nightdress, which calmed her, took the musket, and went outside into the darkness. He had human prey to stalk.

Will moved about a half a mile away from the house and down the rude path that his cousin had just used. He settled himself in some brush and waited.

He didn't have long. The sound of footsteps and gasping breath told him that his cousin had returned and had brought some help. As Will had hoped, there was only one other man. He didn't think his cousin would want to involve too many people. They'd have to split the reward even more ways if he had.

Will let them shamble past him and began to follow a few yards behind. He wasn't worried about being detected. They were fixated on the farmhouse and were making a lot of noise. Francis looked unarmed, but the other man had a musket, and a pistol was stuck in the waist of his pants. When they got to within a few hundred yards of the house, Cousin Francis and the other man stopped and gathered themselves, breathing deeply. He heard them murmuring a plan. They would approach the barn as quietly as they could and surprise what they expected would be a sleeping Will.

They were so intent on what was ahead of them that they paid no attention to their rear. Will did not think twice about such a thing as fighting fair. He'd been in too much combat to believe that killing someone else before he could kill you was not fair. You did it in order to survive.

Will approached them and, when he was within a few yards, he fired, shooting the man with the musket in the back. As Francis turned in shock, Will ran up and hit him in the head with the stock of the now empty musket.

It was over in seconds. He checked the man he'd shot. He was dead with a hole in his back that left a gaping exit wound in his chest. Francis was out cold, and a lump was forming on his skull. Will hoped he hadn't killed the greedy, treacherous fool, and then wondered why he cared.

After pushing the dead body well into the field where it couldn't be seen, he dragged Francis into the house. No one was near enough to have heard the shot, or they simply didn't care. Winnie began to moan again when she saw her husband's bloody and unconscious body.

"You're not stupid," Will said to her. "I'm going to loosen your bonds so you can get yourself out of them in a while. If anybody tries to follow me, I'll kill them just like I did that other Tory bastard outside. Remember that I didn't kill Francis, even though I could have and with ease. He stole my farm and was going to sell me back to that stinking prison for ten miserly pounds. Your husband is a cruel cheap shit. Even Judas wanted thirty pieces of silver."

Francis began whimpering and groaning, so Will tied him up as well. He again turned to Winnie and loosened both her bonds and her gag. When he was satisfied she could get help for herself and dear Cousin Francis, Will searched the house for useful things to take with him. He settled on an ax, a knife, a bullet mold, lead, and powder. They had some bread and dried meat, so he took that as well. He also now had two muskets and a pistol. You could never have too many weapons, he thought. He would never be taken alive.

As he stepped out into the night, he checked the stars and headed roughly west. It was in that direction that Fort Washington, and whatever Liberty was, were said to be. He only wondered just how far away they were.

Major James Fitzroy thought the city of New York was depressing and squalid. More than thirty thousand people, many of them enthusiastically if belatedly proclaiming their loyalty to King George III and the government of Lord North and General Cornwallis, were jammed into its narrow and winding streets. There were two exceptions to the rule of narrowness, Broad Street and De Heere Street, which was also called the Broad Way. These seemed to be the center of what life existed in New York.

Much of the town was still in ruins from the fire of 1776, and little had been done to rebuild. That took money, and the country was still in a state of war.

Fitzroy was puzzled. He wondered why, if the people were so solidly behind the king, were so many of them ignoring him or worse, glaring at him when they thought he wasn't looking? In the weeks since his arrival, he'd noticed that he got better service in a tavern or a shop when he didn't wear his uniform. He was beginning to think that the veneer of loyalty in the colonies was very thin indeed.

He had a small room on the second floor of a pleasant inn on Wall Street, once the site of the city's walls and now a place where merchants and investors congregated. At least they'd used to when the city was vibrant and alive. It was an easy walk to Fort George, which meant that he didn't have to live in the cramped officer's quarters inside the fort. No matter how small and overpriced his room might be, it was his and a hundred times better than living with his stinking and dirty brother officers.

Adding to the city's problems was the influx of soldiers and sailors from the fleet and convoy. Admirals like William Cornwallis could and did live in elegance on their ships, but army officers had to go ashore, as did their men. This meant imposition and resentment as soldiers were quartered in civilian homes. It was ironic in that the forcible quartering of soldiers in private homes was one of the issues that had caused the rebellion in the first place, and now those who'd remained loyal were suffering from it.

Fitzroy sighed. It was the small price the Loyalists had to pay if they wanted the damned western rebel force stamped out and British control over the colonies strengthened and completed. The newly arrived army would pack up and leave soon, marching in stages to Albany and then to Fort Pitt. General Burgoyne had seen the irony of his army marching to Albany from New York. Albany had been his goal when he was defeated at Saratoga in his attempt to march south in 1777. He still cursed Generals Howe and Clinton for having abandoned him instead of marching to join him as he'd understood the plans to be.

Less ironic was the choice of Burgoyne's lieutenants. General Banastre Tarleton commanded the British garrison at Pitt, which made him a logical choice even though he had the reputation among the rebels of a barbarian and a butcher. It was thought that knowing that Tarleton was advancing on them would terrify the rebels into surrendering or fleeing. Fitzroy had his doubts, even considering it wishful thinking. Tarleton had a habit of murdering his prisoners, which made surrendering to him an adventure. Thus, others thought that Tarleton's presence would inspire desperate opposition. Burgoyne and Cornwallis were less than thrilled, but had no choice. The orders came from London.

Even more controversial was the choice of one of the other generals, Benedict Arnold. London thought the former rebel general and now turncoat in the service of England would inspire large numbers of Loyalists to his cause. So far, the effect had been exactly the opposite. Even the staunchest Loyalists had been repelled by the idea of the turncoat Benedict Arnold commanding an English army.

Fitzroy went downstairs to the restaurant portion of the inn and took a seat a small table. His friend, Captain Peter Danforth, entered a minute later. The two men drank a tankard of passable ale and ordered a fish dinner, fresh from the Hudson River. Seared in butter, it was, as always, excellent. On complimenting his host, the innkeeper had again reminded him that he had a cousin, a young woman, who ran a similar facility in Albany. Fitzroy would make it a point to pay a visit, although he did think it ironic that everyone in New York seemed to know the army's plans. He was especially intrigued that a young woman could handle such a business out in the wilderness.

"One thing I will hand to the colonists," Danforth said, wiping his chin, "they do have excellent and hearty food. And why not, with all these rivers and forests to hunt and fish from?"

"And no one to tell them where and when they might hunt," Fitzroy added.

"At least not yet," Danforth said. "Once the last of this stupid war is over, then we shall turn this vast land into a proper English province with proper English squires and nobility in charge. Then we shall see order in the Americas, which will then turn into lands of peace and prosperity. Lord, I hope some of it rubs off onto us."

"Peter, it will be interesting. Personally, I see more migrations to the west if we are overly harsh. Just look at the resentment the quartering of a few thousand soldiers for a short period of time has caused in this miserable excuse for a town."

"They'll get over it," Danforth said. "It's not like they have a choice if they want to serve their king."

"One can hope," Fitzroy said.

"I hate this place," Danforth said while picking a stray fish bone out of his teeth. "They have taken everything that is bad in an English city and brought it here to New York, while leaving out all of the good. What we have is all the squalor of London and none of the elegance and refinement. Do you realize there are no proper theaters in this miserable excuse for a town?"

Fitzroy smiled, "How terrible for you."

"Well, take me with you when you go and joust with the rebels. At least I can participate in a theater of the absurd."

Fitzroy almost laughed. Captain Peter Danforth was short, plump, and ruddy-faced. Behind his back, his men called him "Apple," and he looked like he would want to be nowhere near the hardships of the frontier. For that matter, Fitzroy had his own doubts about staying alive in the wilderness. "I thought you liked working for Cornwallis?"

"I do. He's a great man. But nothing's going to happen in New York that would help advance my career. Although I do have some money with which to purchase further advancement, it is not all that huge an amount. Thus, I must augment my funds with glory. Do tell me there's an opening on Burgoyne's staff?"

Fitzroy sympathized with his friend, although only to a point. By any definition, Danforth was far better off monetarily than Fitzroy. The problem was that Danforth didn't always realize it. Or was it that Fitzroy was so bad off in comparison? All the money Fitzroy had earned—well, looted—during his tour of duty in India had gone to buying the commission and rank he now held. Nor would there be any more money from his family. They were fond of him and he of them, but there was simply no money to share. He was on his own to make his fortune. It was too bad there were no jewel-covered temples in the Americas crying out to be plundered.

Still, how transparent of Danforth, Fitzroy thought. Danforth loved the theater as did Johnny Burgoyne. All Fitzroy had to do was mention that a man of Danforth's ability and interests was available and Burgoyne would jump at having him on his staff. Burgoyne had been mildly disappointed by Fitzroy's lack of interest in things theatrical and this would make the old man happy. Of course, nothing was quite as simple as all that.

"I will put in a good word for you, Captain Danforth, but will you be spying on him for General Cornwallis?"

Danforth smiled easily and without guile, "Of course."

The two men laughed. It was near closing time and one of the tavern girls smiled at them. She was plain-looking and skinny, but she was a woman. Danforth grabbed her and pulled her to his lap. She squealed in mock dismay as he slid his hand underneath her skirts and between her legs.

"I think we should celebrate my new position?" Danforth said to her.

The girl smiled and ran her tongue across her lips. "Any particular position you'd like, dearie?"

Owen Wells walked at the rear of the squad of soldiers accompanying the sailors into town. Even though they were in supposedly friendly territory, he held his musket tightly. It was night and who knew what lurked in New York's narrow streets. Loyal to the cause or not, it was quite obvious that some New Yorkers would rob and rape a nun if they had a chance.

Adding to his nervousness was the fact that this would be his one and only chance to desert. Tomorrow the HMS *Victory* would up anchor and sail back to England with the admiral and the other ships of the convoy. There he'd heard the *Victory* would take up patrol duty off the coast of France. Of course, the officers hadn't bothered to notify him of their plans; instead, they talked openly about them as if he was a piece of the furniture or part of the hull.

Owen scanned the area for a chance, any chance. He had purposely fallen behind by a few steps, nothing serious that would concern the idiotic and pimply-faced young midshipman in charge of the men sent to get special supplies for the officers. These included wines, tobacco and other expensive foodstuffs that mere sailors and marines would never smoke or taste. The bulkier normal supplies had already been loaded and getting these luxuries from local merchants was the last of their tasks.

A narrow alley appeared to his left. Owen took a deep breath, turned, and darted down it.

"Owen, what the devil are you doing?"

Christ, he thought. It was Alan, another marine. Owen had lost track of where he was. At least the sod hadn't hollered. The rest of the unit had disappeared around a corner. "Sorry," Owen said and hit him in the stomach with the butt of his musket. Alan crumpled. Owen quickly stripped off Alan's jacket and tied him up with it, stuffing Alan's own filthy kerchief in his mouth. He hated doing it, since Alan was a decent sort, but he was also a loyal Englishman who would have called for help.

He pulled some trash over his former companion and headed down the alley. If it was a dead end he would have a lot of explaining to do. It wasn't. He continued on, even crossing several narrow and garbage-strewn streets without anyone noticing. Better, he heard no hue and cry behind him. They hadn't even noticed he'd gone.

Owen's luck smiled on him again. Despite the hour, laundry hung on a line and it included articles of men's clothing. He grabbed a couple of shirts and pants and headed away. He found a niche and changed quickly. The clothing was big but it would suffice. Except for being very large around the shoulders and arms he was small to begin with and the damned Americans were so much larger than ordinary Englishmen. Now in civilian clothes, he hid his musket and uniform underneath a pile of rubbish and looked for a way off Manhattan. He hated leaving the weapon, but no one in New York walked around armed with a Tower musket. He kept the socket bayonet. He decided he would feel naked without some sort of weapon.

Again luck favored him. He reached the Hudson River and spied a small boat tied up to a small dock. He jumped into the boat, cast off, and headed downstream in the dark waters. He used an oar to steer the boat in the direction of the black blur that was the land to his right front. If he made landfall on what he thought was Staten Island, he would be free. If he missed, he ran the risk of being swept through the narrows and out to the ocean where he would doubtless die.

Fitzroy and Danforth eyed each other as they followed their respective leaders, Burgoyne and Cornwallis, into the small room off Cornwallis' quarters at Fort George. Cornwallis closed the door, which quickly made the room stuffy and uncomfortable. There was a table and chairs, and a large map of the colonies was pinned to the wall. They took their seats.

"First of all, General Burgoyne, I am so thankful that you have accepted Captain Danforth onto your staff."

Burgoyne smiled. "He and I have much in common. And may I assume that he will be your eyes and ears while on the expedition?"

If Cornwallis was surprised by the bluntness of the comment, he didn't show it.

"But of course. Although one wonders just how he can be my eyes and ears when he's five or six hundred miles away."

"A good staff officer can accomplish miracles, gentlemen," Danforth said with an impish grin. The comment caused both generals to laugh, which released any tension that might have been in the air. Danforth was Cornwallis' spy and now everyone knew it. Fitzroy thought he'd have been court-martialed if he'd said anything so cheeky.

Cornwallis continued. "As you were busy seeing to the forces you just landed, I took the liberty of giving orders to those parts

of the garrisons of Charleston and Boston that will report to you.
I hope you don't mind."

If Burgoyne was upset by the gentle reminder that the army
still belonged to Cornwallis, his superior, he didn't show it. "Of
course not," he said.

"Good. The merchant transports that brought your soldiers from
England, along with a couple of frigates, will be sent to Charleston
to gather up the men you will be getting. The fleet will then continue on to Boston and pick up those men from that garrison. The
entire host will then sail up to the St. Lawrence and then down
to Quebec, where the men will disembark and await your orders."

Burgoyne looked puzzled. "That means my army will be divided.
I had intended to march it intact from here."

Cornwallis shook his head as if talking to a child. "I strongly
recommend against it. The problem of maintaining a proper level
of supplies will be simplified if there is more than one force to
supply from several sources.

"Besides," Cornwallis added, "there is no danger from an American attack. Tarleton's scouts from Pitt and Detroit say the Americans
lack the resources and the will to attack this far to the east. I see
no difficulty in your marching from here to Pitt and joining with
Tarleton, while Arnold and the rest march from Quebec to Detroit."

"I see," said Burgoyne, clearly unhappy at the thought of his
army even temporarily fragmented and out of his control. It was
also evident that he was less than thrilled that Arnold would
hold an even temporary independent command.

Cornwallis ignored Burgoyne's displeasure. "I've also given
directions that a number of sailing barges be constructed at
Detroit and elsewhere along Lakes Erie and Ontario. I think you
will find them handy if you wish to transport any or all of your
army by water around the Michigan peninsula."

"And why would I wish to do that?" Burgoyne bristled.

Cornwallis stood and walked to the map. "Because it may be
as much as a thousand miles from here to where Fort Washington and this Liberty place may lie, and I would think you had
enough of the North American wilderness the last time you tried
to march through it."

Burgoyne swallowed and forced a smile. The distances shown
on the map were misleading and the American wilderness was
sometimes impenetrable, a fact he had indeed learned during

his ill-fated Saratoga campaign of 1777. While he had succeeded in dragging hundreds of wagons and numerous cannon down from Canada, it had taken an eternity, exhausted his army, and permitted the Americans the opportunity to gather their damned militia and destroy him.

"You are correct, sir," Burgoyne admitted.

Fitzroy was stunned. A thousand miles? Burgoyne only had to go a couple of hundred at most in his attempt to take Albany in 1777. It had ended in ignominious failure at Saratoga. Worse, on the map it looked like a trifle in comparison with the distance between New York and the rebel stronghold.

"I'm sure you will concur, General Burgoyne, that sending men and heavy supplies by water is faster and more efficient than having your entire force plowing through the woods and devouring all their supplies as they go, which, I believe, was part of your problem the last time."

Burgoyne flushed at the reminder, but concurred. "I will continue construction of more of the appropriate craft as soon as we reach a suitable base. They will be similar to what are sometimes referred to as bateaux, but they will be larger and uniform in construction. Like you, I will refer to them as sailing barges, although I admit that the word 'bateaux' has more Gallic charm."

Fitzroy glanced at Danforth and saw shock and dismay on his face. A thousand miles? Building boats? What happened to the lightning strike to destroy the enemy? Fitzroy fought the urge to laugh at his new friend. Instead, he would do it later over several glasses of wine and not in the presence of two senior generals.

Of course, he too was less than thrilled at the thought of going so far into the untracked wilderness and for what was obviously going to be a protracted period of time. But then, how untracked could it be if he American rebels had sent several thousand people into it and created settlements? Buoyed by that thought, he winked at Danforth who nodded surreptitiously. Tonight they would eat, get drunk and find a couple of reasonably clean New York doxies to pleasure them. It was the least they could do before they set off on behalf of their king and country.

# Chapter 3 ★ ★ ★ ★ ★ ★ ★ ★ ★ ★ ★ ★ ★ ★ ★ ★ ★ ★ ★

O WEN WELLS TWISTED AGAINST THE ROPES THAT BOUND HIM, but to no avail. His captors had tied his hands behind him with the rope wrapped behind a tree. He could kick his legs if he wanted to, but that would likely get him nothing more than another beating, and he'd had enough of those in the several days he'd been a prisoner of the scruffy bandits who'd captured him. His face was a mass of bruises and his ribs ached where he'd been kicked. The beatings only stopped when one of them realized that Owen needed to be alive for them to collect the reward from the British.

Owen's escape from Manhattan Island had gone extremely well at first. He'd managed to land his stolen boat on Staten Island, and had carefully snuck across to New Jersey and then into Pennsylvania. There he'd felt emboldened enough to work his way openly north and west. He'd had no specific plans. All he wanted to do was put time and distance between himself and the authorities in New York.

He'd been no fool and had kept away from the trails and occasional road. He also avoided contact with the few households and bypassed the villages. He assumed that anyone who looked prosperous was a Tory, while anyone who looked impoverished would turn him in for a reward. If he saw a traveler, he hid in the brush. During the days and weeks of his journey, he'd rehoned the skills he'd possessed as a youthful poacher in his native Wales. Although he occasionally regretted throwing away his musket, he didn't need it to catch food. A trap and snare made from local materials were more than enough to catch rabbits and squirrels and he reveled in their taste when cooked over a small fire that was also easy to make.

Thus, getting caught was gallingly stupid. Why had he thought he was far enough away from British-controlled land to ask someone how far he was away from this "Liberty" place? He had naively presumed that people so far from New York and well into Pennsylvania would be rebels and that he could drop his guard. But no, he had run into a small band of bounty hunters looking for rebels and deserters just like him, and now he faced being dragged back to New York and hanged if he was lucky. If he was unlucky, he'd be sentenced to a thousand lashes, which meant that he would be flogged to death, screaming his lungs out for the mercy of death while the white bones of his ribs and spine were exposed to the air. He'd seen men whipped like that and watched as they became something less than tormented animals before they finally died.

Stupid, stupid, stupid he said to himself. The four-man bounty hunter team was now drunk and asleep. The bayonet he'd kept lay beside one of them. It was further proof that he was a deserter.

The small fire they'd burned was dying out and Owen wished they'd thought enough to feed him. They hadn't, and were only giving him water to sustain him. They'd rather reasonably decided that it made no sense to waste food on someone who was going to die anyhow, and a weakened prisoner was easier to control.

Owen froze when he sensed rather than heard motion in the trees behind him. It was not an animal—too large. It had to be a man. Maybe it was an Indian who would slice his throat and then scalp him. As horrible as it sounded, that would be preferable to what the Royal Navy would do to him when they got their hands on him. Whoever it was, he was only tolerably good at prowling through the woods. And whoever it was apparently didn't want the four sleepers to wake up, which meant he wasn't on their side. Owen tried not to hope and didn't make any kind of a sound or move. His captors were drunk, but that didn't mean they might not suddenly wake up and get vicious.

He continued to hold still when he felt a gentle tugging at the rope that curled behind the tree to which he was bound. It sagged and he was free. A firm hand on his shoulder meant that he should stay still. He did as he was told. Then the hand tapped him and gestured for him to move away from the camp. Owen's muscles were cramped and he found it difficult to walk silently, but he managed to do so without alerting the sleeping outlaws. His rescuer followed a few seconds later.

When they were a ways away, Owen whispered. "Why didn't you kill them?"

His liberator turned. He now carried a pair of muskets taken from the bandits and a pistol was stuck in his belt. Owen didn't see his bayonet and didn't care. The hell with it, he thought.

"It would be murder and I've done enough of that lately. Don't worry. They won't follow us without weapons."

Owen gulped at the response. "Then tell me who you are."

"I have the guns so you tell me first."

Owen thought that was reasonable. After all, hadn't the man risked a lot to untie him? He told him and, as they continued to trot through the forest, he quickly explained that he was a deserter from the Royal Navy and how he'd managed to get his stupid self captured. He added that he sincerely hoped his new friend had nothing to do with the English.

The other man laughed. "I'm Captain Will Drake of the Continental Army. If you really want to find that Liberty place I'll help you. If it exists, of course."

"You've been there, Captain?"

"No, but I think I stand a better chance of finding it than you do."

Owen grinned. "And you're less likely to make a fool of yourself by getting caught like I did. I'd be honored to serve under you, Captain."

"I thought you might," said Will. They'd come to the place where Will had been camping. They were a couple of miles away from the bounty hunters' camp and had heard nothing of an alarm behind them. The four men would have a most unpleasant surprise in the morning. Perhaps they'd even be thankful that their throats hadn't been sliced.

Will handed him a spare musket. "Take this."

Owen grasped it and checked it out. "You think those bastards might still come after us?"

"No. I'd been watching them for about a day and I don't think they can track very well at all, not that I'm that much better."

Owen chuckled. "You were good enough to free me without alerting them, Captain. Personally, I don't think those four could find their asses in the dark with both hands."

★   ★   ★

Sarah and her family had also traveled into Pennsylvania, but that only put them close to the English troops headquartered at Fort Pitt and the adjacent city of Pittsburgh. Banastre Tarleton, the English general commanding the sprawling area, had troops and patrols on the lookout for people heading to and from the rebel enclave out west. His cavalry roamed the trails and roads looking for people to stop and question.

Thus, when they heard the thunder of hooves behind them, they quickly ducked into the thick bushes that lined the trail they'd been following. They dismounted and held their horses steady. Sarah and the others held their breath as about twenty green-coated cavalry pounded past. "Tarleton's men," her uncle muttered. "Dragoons, and Tories all, damn them."

They waited. The enemy seemed to be on a mission, looking for someone or something. Finally, Uncle Wilford stood. "Time to get moving, I guess. But we're staying off the trail."

There was no argument. They began to move cautiously through the woods on foot, leading their horses to keep them quiet. After a short while, they heard the sounds of cries and screams. They looked at each other. Whatever was happening up ahead could have easily happened to them. Nobody wished ill on anyone else, but that's how it sometimes happened. They'd gotten lucky and that's all there was to it.

Wilford led by a few yards. He paused and signaled the others to wait, but that Sarah should come forward. He indicated that she should crouch or crawl and she complied. He pushed the branches of a bush aside and she saw what had happened.

A group of maybe a dozen travelers had been intercepted by the dragoons who had just ridden past them. There were men and a handful of women along with a couple of children. The women were on the ground, naked, and were being held down and raped by Tarleton's men, who were whooping and hollering as they took their turns. The men in the group, also naked, were all bound and gagged, except for one man who lay limp and bloody on the ground, probably dead. The children ran around screaming hysterically and were ignored by the British, except for one who was kicked by a dragoon when he tried to get close to one of the women.

"We can't help them," her uncle said sadly, but firmly. "It might not be very Christian to ignore them, but we don't want anyone to see us or the same thing might happen to us. If we stay south of Pittsburgh, we might avoid British patrols. I understand there's a mighty river that flows westward to the Mississippi. We make it to the river perhaps we can get a boat to take us farther west."

Sarah thought her uncle was grasping at straws, but said nothing. In truth, she had nothing to add because there were no other options. She wondered what would happen to the surviving travelers. Would they be allowed to continue their journey, naked and abused, or would they be killed? Or arrested? Sarah shuddered. Could have been us, she kept repeating to herself. Clearly this Tarleton was as bad as Sheriff Braxton.

They had to get past the British patrols before they could be safe. Her knowledge of the area's geography was scant, but, like her uncle, she did recall hearing of several rivers that met at Pitt and at least one of them then flowed west. She thought it was the Ohio. Of course they couldn't get a boat at Pittsburgh, but perhaps he was right. Maybe they could find something.

A keening wail from one of the abused travelers cut like a knife and drew them back to the tragic scene less than a hundred yards away. She parted the bushes to see better. The dragoons had mounted their horses and were riding off slowly, while the travelers, now only half dressed and trying to repair the torn clothes that had been ripped from their bodies, were gathered over the man who'd been lying on the ground.

"We can help them now," she said.

"A penny says that man is dead and we can't help at all," said cousin Faith, who had quietly joined them.

As the travelers moved the pale body Sarah could see that the man's head was bloodied and smashed. Worse, his limbs were totally limp. Even at a distance, they judged the situation as hopeless. What made it worse was the commonly held knowledge that Tarleton's green-coated dragoons were likely all Tories, men who also called the colonies their home. Sarah wondered how they could commit such crimes against people who were their neighbors. Of course, she thought ruefully, there was the little matter of a war that had raged for six years and, in many ways, was a civil war pitting brother against brother, neighbor against neighbor. That she and her family were heading west was proof that vengeance was the rule of the day. She wondered just how she would have behaved towards the Tories if the revolution had succeeded.

Silently, they led their horses away. In a bit, they mounted. The tragic scene reinforced their hatred for the British and the correctness of their decision to head west.

Sarah thought that the only good thing to come from their journey was the irony that they were all healthier and stronger than when they'd lived in Pemberton. Sarah felt that she was stronger mentally and physically. She had lost weight, and little plump Faith looked like she'd gained confidence as she shed pounds. So far, they'd had little trouble finding berries and vegetables to eat, and there was fresh water in abundance. An occasional fish, or a trapped rabbit or squirrel, had rounded out their diet.

Of course, all the health in the world would mean nothing if Tarleton's horsemen caught up to them.

Will and Owen lay on the ground and stared intently at the half dozen armed men who rested on the small hill a couple of hundred yards in front of them. The men just stood there, nonchalantly holding their muskets, while their unfettered horses grazed contentedly. Behind them was yet another stand of thick forest, which puzzled Will. If the men wanted to be unseen, all they had to do was move a few feet into the woods and they'd be invisible. Also, if it wasn't for the weapons, they could have passed for workmen taking their ease while the boss was away. They exchanged food and drank from canteens as the two men watched. The group exuded quiet confidence which further concerned Will. They acted as if they owned the forest.

The riders had been easy to spot. Owen and Will had crept as far as they could through the forest and into the brushes without being seen by the armed men. Perhaps, Will thought, the riders had been *too* easy to spot.

There was no real trail or path as they headed west, but there were places where the presence of previous travelers could be discerned and this was one of them. When paths were obvious, the two men didn't follow them. Instead, they worked their way parallel to them, hoping that they would not run into an ambush. The sight of the armed men in front of them confirmed their choice.

"Who do you think they are?" Owen asked.

Will didn't respond. The answer to the question was crucial. They were far enough west, they hoped, for the band of armed men to possibly be American rebels. Still, there was no guarantee

of anything. They could be Tarleton's men, or outlaws like the
men who had seized Owen. Hell, he thought, they could be that
same group with a couple of more men added to it. They had
a major decision to make. Should they try to evade them or go
up to them? The wrong step could prove fatal.

"I wish I had a telescope," Will muttered.

"I wish I could fly," Owen chuckled.

"We can go around them. It'd mean a big detour, but it may
be the best way."

Owen was about to say he agreed when several more horsemen
joined the group and they all spread out. "Shit," he said. "Now
we'll have to wait forever."

"I wouldn't think so," said a deep voice from their rear. "Now
get up slowly and raise your hands above your heads and don't
even think of trying for your weapons."

Owen and Will did as they were told. When they turned around,
a group of five men had muskets leveled at them. They wore no
uniform, except for a patch of blue cloth sewn to their chests.
One large man with a reddish beard and a ruddy complexion
wore the insignia of a sergeant and was their leader. He also had
been branded on the cheek with the letter "R." Will saw that a
couple of the others bore the same scar.

The sergeant spoke. "Now, just who the hell are you and what
are you doing so far west?"

The scars meant that the men were American soldiers. Or at
least they had been at one time. Who knew what they were this
day? "We're trying to get to Fort Washington," Will said. "Or
Liberty. Either will do."

"So is everybody, or at least that's what they say," the sergeant
responded. "Now answer my question, who are you?"

Will stood tall and allowed his arms to slowly drop to his side.
The soldiers didn't seem to mind, even seemed slightly amused
by his small act of defiance. "I am Captain Will Drake of the
Continental Army, and this is Owen Wells, late of His Majesty's
Navy. We are traveling together."

"I hope you're not together for security's sake, considering how
easily we caught you," the sergeant said.

Will winced as the others guffawed at their expense. They had
fallen for an old trick. They'd been gulled into believing that
the men in plain sight were dangerous when the real threat was

creeping up on them while they were transfixed. The trick may have been as old as the hills, but it had been skillfully done.

"I told you who I was, now, who are you?" Will asked.

The big sergeant straightened slightly. "Sergeant William Barley, Second Regiment, New Continental Army."

Will nearly gasped with relief. Assuming the armed men were telling the truth, they had finally found the rebel forces.

"If you're not lying about yourselves, you'll be welcomed," Barley continued. "Of course, if you're lying, we'll hang your asses. A lot of British have tried to get into Liberty and Fort Washington and maybe some have succeeded, but that doesn't mean I'm going to let in everybody who walks up and knocks. Is there anyone who'll vouch for you at Fort Washington so you can vouch for the squatty little Brit?"

"Up your ass," snarled Owen and the troopers laughed.

Barley laughed too, but kept his musket aimed squarely at Owen's stomach. "You look like a Brit, you sound like a Brit, and you say you were a Brit, so why shouldn't I think you're a Brit spy. Anybody can claim they've deserted now can't they? Helluva thing to prove, though. I guess we could turn you back to the Redcoats, and if they hang you, then it would prove you were telling the truth."

"Watch," Owen said. He carefully removed his jacket and then his shirt. He turned and showed the Americans his back. It was covered with scars and welts. "Now ask me how much I love fucking King George and his goddamned Royal Navy."

"Jesus," said Barley, fingering the branding scar on his own cheek. "You pass, little man, at least for the moment. Put your shirt back on." He turned to Will. "Now you, Captain. I don't doubt that you have a brand scar on your leg, along with other marks, but those will get you only so far. So, who'll vouch for you?"

"Who's at Fort Washington?" Will asked.

"General Greene knows you?"

Will thought quickly. He'd seen Nathanael Greene on a number of occasions, but doubted that the general who'd been Washington's second in command would recall him from Adam. Still, it was a comfort that a general of Greene's stature was at Fort Washington.

"Probably not."

"Then how about Wayne or von Steuben?"

"I doubt it. What about Alexander Hamilton?"

Barley shook his head. "He's rotting away in a prison in Jamaica, and, if you're a spy, you'd have known that."

"We could guess all day, Sergeant Barley, and maybe not find a match. Why don't you take me in and then sort it out?"

Barley nodded. "Makes sense. We'll have to treat you as prisoners until we can turn you over to General Tallmadge."

Will felt like laughing in relief. "Is General Tallmadge's first name Benjamin?"

Barley relaxed slightly. "It is. Will he vouch for you?"

Will couldn't stop grinning. "Yes he will."

Major Fitzroy sat behind a small table in the tent that served as Burgoyne's headquarters near Albany. The air in the tent was stuffy and he was sweating like a pig, but decorum would not let him remove any of his uniform while interviewing colonials. Had to impress them, he thought, and then wondered if they were at all impressed by the idiocy of wearing a heavy wool uniform in the middle of summer. He decided he didn't want to know.

"Next," he called.

A large man entered and stood before him. Fitzroy almost choked. The man was a thing, an apparition, an escapee from hell. His eyebrows were gone and his nose little more than two holes in the raw, red skin of what passed for his face. There was next to nothing in the way of lips, exposing broken and rotting teeth, and the man's ears were equally raw lumps with holes in them.

But the apparition was real and could speak and his eyes showed fury and hatred. "You can stare if you like, Major. Everyone else does. I know what I am and it doesn't bother me anymore. The Indians and many of those who know me call me the Burned Man."

"You surprised me, that's all." Fitzroy was also surprised that the creature spoke English instead of the language of Satan but did not say so.

"Indeed. Regardless, I am here to volunteer."

"In what capacity?" Fitzroy asked as he tried to gain control of the situation. Perhaps the creature wanted to be their resident bogeyman.

"I wish to be a militia officer. I've brought a band of fifty men who feel like I do towards the rebels, and who want me to lead them, and I'm certain I can get more to join me. We want to kill rebels."

"Did the rebels do that to you?"

Something ghastly that might have been a grin flickered across the man's ruined face. "You are quite perceptive."

Fitzroy caught the sarcasm and flushed. "What happened?"

The man shrugged. "The vicious and cowardly bastards set a trap for me while I was trying to enforce the king's law, and I fell for it. There was an explosion and I was covered with burning oil. My friends put out the fire by dousing me with water and covering me with dirt. There are more scars on my arms and chest if you wish to see."

"No thank you," Fitzroy said, controlling a shudder.

Fitzroy noted that one of Burned Man's hands was missing two fingers and the other more resembled a claw then something human. Some of the wounds were so raw that he wondered if the man shouldn't be in bed recuperating.

"You're right, Major, it didn't happen all that long ago and everyone thought I was going to die, including my whore of a wife who ran off with another man while I lay in agony. But I didn't die and I won't die until I've had a good measure of revenge. I caught my slut of a wife and her bastard lover and killed both of them. I let her watch while I cut off his head, and then I chopped off hers and put it on a fence post beside his. But there's still the rebels who did this to me and I want them dead as well. I know I should still be resting and regaining my strength, but that doesn't help me kill rebels, now does it?"

"I suppose not," Fitzroy said.

"And I want to destroy the particular group of damned rebels who did this to me," he snarled. "That is one way I will become stronger. Hate will keep me going. I trust you won't stand in my way when I find them?"

Fitzroy thought quickly. The decision was easy. The Burned Man said he had brought fifty men and, if they were anything like their horribly mutilated leader, they would be useful and highly motivated. He had a disquieting thought that the Burned Man's band would be very difficult to control and discipline, but he reasoned that many terrible things would happen to both sides in the course of the campaign. He put aside his doubts. He had an army to help form and a war to win.

Fitzroy stood up. He did not extend his hand to shake. The thought of touching the Burned Man's mutilated skin was too repugnant. "As long as you and your men obey orders, they are welcome. And those orders might mean deferring your vengeance for the common good. Is that acceptable?"

"It is as long as it's not forever."

"Good. Welcome to General Burgoyne's army, and I'll have the papers made up to confirm your rank of militia captain."

"Excellent."

"Of course, I will need your real name. Burned Man might do to identify you to the red savages, and even better if you were one, but you aren't an Indian, are you?"

Burned Man laughed harshly and Fitzroy nearly recoiled at the stench coming from his mouth. "Isn't my skin red enough for you? But you're right. My name is Charles Braxton."

Tallmadge greeted Will warmly. He rose from behind his desk of raw planks and the two men shook hands. "God, it's good to see your smiling face, Captain."

"Good to see yours, too, Major." Will winced. He'd used Tallmadge's old rank.

"Correction, Will, I am now a brigadier general."

"Congratulations, sir." It did not escape Will that Tallmadge was, at most, only a couple of years older than he, and like so many American leaders, quite young for their rank. And inexperienced as well, he thought. To the best of Will's now incomplete knowledge, Tallmadge had never commanded men in battle. He'd always been a staff officer. Had things changed?

"I wonder about any congratulations," Tallmadge said. "I often think I hold this rank because there's no one else around to give it to. We've got a number of soldiers, but damned few real generals to command them, and even fewer lower-ranking officers to lead them. The British managed to capture so many of us after they promised amnesty and then broke their promise."

"Where are they? I didn't see too many of them in the hulks."

"The senior officers are imprisoned in Jamaica, which is where so many of the middle-ranking officers are also held. Many are being forced to work in the fields under brutal conditions. We are developing plans to get them out, but it will be dangerous work at best. I gather they never figured out that you were on Washington's staff or that you worked for me."

"They did not."

Will had indeed been on Washington's staff. Tallmadge had been his direct superior and the two of them had gathered intelligence and had run some of Washington's spies. Had the British realized that, Will would have either been hanged or would now be rotting in Jamaica, a place from which there was even less chance of escape than from a prison hulk.

"Washington's dead, you know," Tallmadge said grimly. "The bastards chopped off his head. Rumor has it they've sent the skeleton here to America to impress us with their sense of fair play and justice. If it is true, I hope it will inflame true Americans."

"I'd heard about the execution but not about the bones."

Tallmadge shook his head sadly. "Will, the last time I saw General Washington, it was night and Tarleton's cavalry were swarming all over us and he'd been knocked from his horse. When the enemy was too numerous, I admit that I cut and ran. They already had Washington in their grip and there was nothing more I could do. I wanted to live and I'm not ashamed to admit it."

Will could not criticize Tallmadge for his decision. He too had been in the act of fleeing for his life when he'd been caught. Will was saddened by the memory.

Tallmadge's face contorted with anger. "I saw Washington fighting like a tiger until they wrestled him to the ground. They wanted him alive, but it cost them. I know you recall that Washington was immensely strong. He killed at least two of them with his sword and one with his bare hands before they finally captured him. And then I ran away as fast and as far as I could. When I was far enough away, I threw myself into some bushes and stayed there until dawn," Tallmadge said. "Nobody came looking for me. I wasn't important enough."

Will filled in his old commander with his own story, of realizing that the army no longer existed, of his own capture, his almost miraculous escape from the prison hulk, and his subsequent travels to Fort Washington.

"As always," Tallmadge said approvingly, "you've been resourceful and a little ruthless. A good combination for an officer, especially one who's job is to gather intelligence from a vicious enemy."

Will laughed at the rough compliment. "You mentioned a shortage of senior officers. Just who is here? I heard that Nathanael Greene commanded."

"In theory he does, but he is desperately ill from a lung disease he caught while in a British prison. He spent several months in a dungeon that often flooded before we found him and freed him. In a couple of days he too would have been on his way either to the Caribbean or the afterlife. In truth, he may never recover."

That comment dismayed Will. Nathanael Greene had been Washington's trusted and most able second in command. If Greene was not able to lead the American army in the field when the British arrived, then who would?

Tallmadge shrugged and answered the question. "We have Anthony Wayne, von Steuben, Schuyler, and Willie Washington, and that's about it. We understand that others may arrive, but that's the future, not the present. Of course, we're a little better stocked with politicians. John Hancock is president of the rump group we call the Continental Congress, and Benjamin Franklin, recently arrived from France, does his best to annoy Hancock and is succeeding marvelously. Seriously, we are in desperate straits."

"How can I help?"

Tallmadge smiled. "You just did. When you walked in the door, you solved a problem for me. I will talk to Greene or Schuyler about getting you a rank commensurate with your skills and our needs, and then we'll send you back towards where the British are assembling. Assuming you're up to it, of course."

"I don't need rank, Major, I mean General, and, yes, I am up to it."

"You may not feel you need the rank, Will, but I do. You have both experience and intelligence, and that makes you unique." Tallmadge steered him to the door. "Come. Let me show you around my domain. Among my other duties, I command the garrison here at Fort Washington."

Fort Washington was less than impressive. An earthen wall covered with logs and topped with wooden spikes ran about a hundred yards in each direction and formed a very large square. There were numerous blockhouses, but only the ones at each corner contained cannon, and those were small three and four pounders, which would be almost useless in a real fight with a determined and professional British army. The walls would certainly keep red Indians out, but would not present much of a barrier to the forces rumored to be on their way. He did see how it could be improved significantly by digging a moat, adding abattis made of tree limbs, and other barriers, thus strengthening the dirt wall. However, it would never be a serious deterrent to the British Army.

Inside the walls were numerous log and even a few frame buildings that housed the garrison as well as quarters and meeting rooms for the Congress. Outside the ramparts, there were literally hundreds of log cabins, earthen dwellings, and tents. They ran in all directions and there appeared to be little in the way of city planning.

Tallmadge waved at them. "Everything you want is out there, including hardworking people trying to make a living, and other people trying to steal it from them. In sum, a real city has sprung up here in the wilderness. I don't know why, but a number of whores decided to make the trek with us. Perhaps they're here to help out Congress in their efforts to fuck over the entire country."

Will laughed. "Some things never change."

"Seriously, it is not as chaotic as it looks. Everyone works here, and that includes the women, the young, and the old. We grow wheat, corn, and other crops. When we want something more substantial, we gather fish in abundance from the lakes and streams, or hunt for our own food, primarily deer and wild birds including ducks and turkeys. We have some cattle and a growing number of chickens. We make many of our own weapons out of metals brought from the north, and train for the war we know will come. If nothing else, General Schuyler is a good organizer, so no one goes cold or hungry. Schuyler is in charge of the men, while Mistress Abigail Adams is in charge of finding tasks for the women. Her husband, John Adams, is a prisoner in Jamaica."

"So this is what is called Liberty?" Will mused.

"There's really no such precise place," Tallmadge answered with a smile. "It's more of an idea, a concept. Liberty is everywhere and nowhere, if you will. There are dozens of communities like this, although this is by far the largest, and they are all referred to as Liberty along with more specific names. Still, this is the place most people refer to as Liberty."

"I hope you're not offended, General, but the fort is not imposing. The cannon are far too small and too few to be effective. The earthen walls, however, should dampen the effects of small cannon, but would be destroyed by anything large."

"We have eight guns in all," Tallmadge said. "The British sloops that patrol along the shoreline carry as many on each ship, but that's all we were able to bring with us when we frankly ran like the devil from the British."

"Warships?" Will exclaimed. "Just where the hell are we?"

Tallmadge laughed. "About ten miles south of the southern-most point of Lake Michigan. We are just past a swampy area where two rivers run into the lake. The Potawatomi call it the Checagou, or at least they did until we drove them away, which didn't endear us to them or to the other tribes in the area. They seem to be getting used to us, however. Of course they don't have much choice. Some of our people call this settlement by the Indian name, but that's a matter of small import.

"Along with the British, the Potawatomi and other Indian tribes are another set of enemies to watch out for. Right now, they are sitting back waiting to see who wins the coming war. Whenever it is apparent that one side will win, they will pounce on the losing force and then try to curry favor with the victorious army. Under the circumstances, it is precisely what I would do."

"I see," said Will. "Let me sum this up. You have a fort that could be knocked over by a strong wind, damn few weapons, not enough generals to command a poorly organized army, and far too many lawyers. Is that correct?"

"Indeed it is, Will."

They returned in silence to Tallmadge's office. "Will, I want you to take a patrol down to the Ohio River and check out rumors of a significant British presence there, one that could move down the Ohio and then up north to threaten us. I need to know if that force actually exists. Is it a real threat, nonexistent, or nothing but a nuisance? How many men do you need?"

"Do you expect me to fight them?"

"Not at all, except for your own defense. I want information, not a victory."

"Then a small patrol will do." Will thought for a moment. "I want Wells, of course. He may be a foreigner, but he moves through the woods like an Indian. And I'd also like that Sergeant Barley who caught me so cleverly. I would think a dozen men would do nicely. It'd be enough to protect ourselves and not enough to tempt us into fighting a battle."

Tallmadge grinned. "Good thinking. And when you come back you'll be at least a major."

★　　★　　★

Half a dozen large canoes snaked down the wide and dark Ohio River. With the exception of the lead canoe, each contained a family group and their possessions, which, since most of the people were virtually penniless, meant there was more than sufficient room for all the people.

Sarah Benton and her family were in the last canoe and, like everyone, scanned the overgrown banks of the deep and westward flowing river. The vegetation was thick and they could see little of anything that might be in the forest. Even though they were well west of Fort Pitt, they felt they were in the most dangerous portion of their trip. The British had patrols out looking for rebel groups and they'd been told that skirmishes were frequent. Rumor said that Tarleton feared an attack on Pitt and would do anything to be forewarned. Worse, as Sarah had already seen, the British troops were vicious and thought they had a right to abuse and rob Americans.

The caravan tried to keep well out from the riverbank where a sudden attack could overwhelm them. It meant they were visible from a ways off when the weather was clear, but it couldn't be helped. Fortunately, this day an almost providential mist covered the river and helped hide them.

The six canoes were led by a guide named Micah and two of his friends. They were scrawny and their clothes were ragged and filthy. However, their weapons were clean and in good condition, a necessity in the wilderness. Micah and friends had gathered what they referred to as "pilgrims" and, in return for payment, promised them safe passage westward to where they could trek north to American-controlled land.

Neither Faith nor Sarah quite trusted Micah and his companions. He seemed skittish and often declined to look them in the eye. Sarah and Faith still wore men's clothes as did several of the other women traveling with them. The wilderness was not the place for traditional proprieties.

"I don't trust him," said Faith, echoing their concerns. They knew nothing about Micah except for the fact that he was willing to guide them for money.

"I don't either," said Sarah. "But I don't think we had much of a choice. It is either go west with him or someone like him as a guide, or stay back and someday be captured."

"He keeps staring at my breasts," Faith added.

Aunt Rebecca snorted. "Perhaps if you kept your shirt fastened, and if your pants weren't so tight, he wouldn't be looking so intently."

"Why have charms if you can't use them?" Faith sniffed, causing Sarah to conclude that her little cousin had begun to recover from her ordeal with Braxton's deputies, and that she wasn't as innocent or naive as Sarah thought she was. Of course, how innocent could anyone be after suffering at the hands of Braxton and his men? Innocent perhaps, but naïve? Never.

Micah signaled with his paddle and the canoes veered closer to the shore. "Why," Sarah asked. No one knew and Micah didn't respond. They generally only went to ground at night, but that was a long time away.

"Maybe he sees something," Faith said, and wondered just how and what he might see through the mist and the dense foliage.

"I won't be happy until he sees the place where we can get off these things," Sarah groaned. "Kneeling like this is worse than the stocks." Not really, she thought. Nothing would ever be worse than that day.

Faith giggled. "Don't you like paddling a canoe like a Red Indian?"

Sarah declined to respond. At least they were going with the current and not fighting it. Tom signaled another change and they followed the leading canoes still closer to the land. Ahead of them and on the far side of the wide river, the mist parted for an instant and they saw several other canoes heading the opposite direction, and what looked like armed men in them. The mist returned and covered them.

"Ours or theirs?" muttered Uncle Wilford.

"I don't wish to know," Sarah said.

What if the men in the other canoes had been a British patrol? Strange, Sarah thought. If it was a British patrol, might they soon be paddling over to intercept the boat? Perhaps their luck had held and they really hadn't been noticed.

A musket blast shattered the silence. It was followed by another and another and then by screams from the lead canoes. At least one had tipped over, spilling its human contents into the river. In horror, Sarah saw a man's body floating face down and trailing blood from a gaping wound in his head.

She turned to her left, where the riverbank was close. Men were standing on it and shooting at them. Micah had betrayed them. He had led them into this trap.

More musket fire and more screams filled the air. Sarah picked up a fowling piece and shot at a man only a few yards away. He clutched his leg and fell screaming into the water. It occurred to her that there weren't all that many attackers and that they weren't British or Americans. She realized that they were nothing more than bandits. If they were taken by them, it would be worse than being captured by the British. From what they'd heard, the outlaws were little more than animals.

Wilford fired his musket at another man and missed. A bandit jumped into the canoe and clubbed Wilford down to his knees while Faith screamed and jumped on the man's back. Sarah pulled a knife from her waist and slashed at another man who grabbed her and tried to throw her into the water.

Fortunately, Faith had distracted Wilford's attacker long enough for him to pull his own knife and stab his assailant in the stomach. Aunt Rebecca helped out by clubbing another bandit with a paddle and then pushing him into the river.

They had regained control of their own canoe, but the others were either capsized or being fought over. Micah's canoe, of course, was controlled by him and he now turned it towards Sarah's. The three men originally in it had been reinforced by two of the attackers from shore. With five strong paddlers, there was no way they could outrun Micah's canoe.

"Load," Wilford yelled.

One fowling piece and one musket wouldn't be enough, but it was all they had. Silently, they vowed to sell their lives dearly. Sarah was bitter that it was all coming to this. They would be killed, but not until they were robbed, tortured, and the three women raped. That the women were wearing men's clothes as a disguise wouldn't fool their new attackers any more than it had fooled their traitorous leader, Micah. She thought about putting the fowling piece into her mouth and blowing her brains out. No, she thought. She would take at least one more of them with her. Besides, if she fought hard enough, perhaps Faith or one of the others would escape. Logic said it was a fool's thought, but she could not bring herself to die at her own hand.

The outlaws' canoe was only yards away when both she and Wilford fired and, to their horror, missed. Micah and his cronies hollered with glee. Micah stood up unsteadily and grabbed his crotch, screaming what he was going to do to the women.

They had only gotten a little closer when a volley of gunfire swept Micah and the others off the canoe and into the river. Sarah watched incredulously as more gunfire was directed at the few remaining attackers on the shore. Those bandits promptly turned and ran.

They were safe, at least for the moment. But why and how?

Homer's trek alone from Manhattan Island began quietly and stayed that way for several days. There were few roads leading towards Boston, merely paths at best, and he walked them carefully. He was fully aware of his vulnerability as a lone black man in a land not that far removed from being a savage frontier.

He could not carry a musket or a pistol as white farmers or city-dwellers would find him threatening. They might even take it into their heads to shoot first and ask him his business over his lifeless corpse.

No, he would stay in the shadows of the trees that lined the miserable excuses for roads and endure the additional hardship that it entailed. The few people he had seen had behaved in such a way as to reinforce his plan. Once, a woman in a field screamed when she saw his dark skin and ran back to a cabin. A few seconds later, a man with a musket emerged and aimed it at him, telling him bluntly to get the hell away from his property.

Homer had complied, of course, but wondered to himself if a rampaging Iroquois war party would have gotten the same or better treatment. He also wondered if the poor couple had ever seen a Negro before. He could always go back to New York, he thought. Nobody there would have missed him in the first place. But no, it was time to start something new, a series of thoughts that had been triggered when he pulled that poor naked and starving white man from the river.

"Hold up, nigger."

Homer froze and cursed silently. He'd permitted himself to be lulled and now two men stood just a few feet in front of him, their muskets not quite pointed at his chest.

"Damn, Abel, look what we got. Another fucking escaped slave."

"I do think you're right, Joshua."

"So what do you think we should do with him?"

"I am not a slave," Homer answered with a trace of indignation. "I am a free black man, and I'm on my way to Boston to find work."

"Bullshit," said Joshua. "You're a fucking escaped slave and we're going to arrange for you to go back south to your master."

Homer was incredulous. "Don't you know that slavery's been abolished by the British?"

Joshua laughed. He was clearly the pair's leader. "Nigger, you might just be surprised to know that a lot of people down south are simply ignoring that announcement. And you should know that there are a lot of other places like those owned by Spain and France where slavery still exists."

This can't be happening, Homer thought. He had to do something. "I have money. Let me buy my way out of this."

Abel shook his head. "Amazing. Not only we get a slave to sell, but he has money as well to help pay us for our inconvenience. He ain't armed so I think I'll just take it. You keep him covered, Josh."

Abel stepped forward and reached for Homer. For an instant, he was between Homer and Joshua. Homer shifted his left arm and the knife he had strapped above his wrist slipped into his palm. He rammed it into Abel's heart and stepped to his left, pulling out the other knife that was below his right elbow. This one he threw at an astonished Joshua, taking him in the throat. He quickly grabbed the musket from Joshua who was clutching at his throat while blood gushed down his shirt.

Homer laughed. As he'd thought, it had never occurred to the fools that a Negro would fight back.

Homer dragged the two bodies a few yards into the forest. If he was lucky, the animals would turn them into unrecognizable slabs of meat and piles of bones in a very short while.

In the meantime, he had some decisions to make. First, he would no longer travel unarmed. He selected the better of the two muskets and threw the other away. He also took their gunpowder and bullets and, surprise, had found some money on their bodies, which he added to his own purse.

Where to go was the next decision. He decided that Boston was not a good idea, if the presence of Joshua and Abel was any indication of the welcome a black man would receive. No, he thought, he would head north, far north. He would go to Canada. Even though it was British-controlled, it might be safer for him than in the colonies.

If, he thought ruefully, anywhere would be safe for a black man.

# Chapter 4 ★★★★★★★★★★★★★★★★★★

THE TRIP SOUTH FROM FORT WASHINGTON TO THE OHIO RIVER had been fruitless. From prior experience, Will had known that gathering intelligence was often like that. For every valuable piece of information you found, you wasted time chasing a hundred useless ones.

Will was now convinced that there was no significant British presence on the Ohio River. Of course, he and his men couldn't check every canoe and flatboat for the odd spy or scout, but there was no army to threaten Fort Washington or the various villages collectively known as Liberty. Hell, he decided, there probably wasn't even a company of Redcoats between him and Tarleton's headquarters at Fort Pitt.

"See that, Major," said Sergeant Barley, pointing in the direction of the opposite shore.

Will was still not quite comfortable with his new rank. A few months ago he'd been a prisoner. Now, he was a major in the American Army. Tallmadge had bestowed the rank on him just before they departed. Will didn't really care what rank he held. He just wanted to stay free and stop the British.

He followed Barley's gesture and saw a line of canoes in the shadows of the other side. With the mist on the river, they could easily have missed them.

Will thought quickly. A handful of canoes could not contain an army, but they were coming from the direction of Fort Pitt.

67

Thus, they might be spies or scouts for the British. If nothing else, they would be civilians who had knowledge of what was going on closer to Pitt. With their information, perhaps it wouldn't be necessary to get any nearer to Pitt and Tarleton's soldiers.

Barley read his mind. "And it would be a helluva lot easier paddling with the current than against it, sir."

No argument there. Paddling upstream was brutal. Even though they were strong and in shape, and that now included Will, their arms and shoulders ached with the effort of arguing with the strong currents of the Ohio River.

"We'll let them pass and turn into their rear," Will said.

Their unexpected presence in the other canoes rear might frighten them, or even cause them to shoot, in which case his men would shoot back. He decided it was a chance worth taking. Innocence or guilt could be proven later.

They drifted for a bit and then turned and began to paddle with the current and across the river. They'd gone about half way when they heard gunfire. Will didn't hesitate. "Everybody get ready to shoot," he ordered. "Now paddle harder."

They came upon the fighting within minutes. Bodies were in the water and there were individual struggles in those canoes that hadn't capsized. It was too dangerous to fire their weapons. They couldn't tell who was who. Then he saw a canoe with a handful of scrawny men in rags bearing down on another canoe that was in distress and appeared to contain what were clearly women though they were wearing men's clothing. He quickly concluded that they were the victims and that the others were the attackers and fervently hoped he was right. Will pointed out the target canoe and gave the order to fire. Muskets roared, spilling the outlaws into the river in a display of very good shooting since the rocking action of the canoes made aiming difficult.

Will's men roared into the fighting and ended it quickly, killing the surviving outlaws with tomahawks and knives. Will had a pistol, but didn't find a target. None of the men in the canoe they'd fired on had come up from underwater and he presumed they were dead. He saw a small group of the outlaws on the riverbank suddenly dart into the woods.

"Let me go, sir," asked Owen.

"Just take some of the men with you, Corporal, and try not to get hurt."

Wells nodded and grabbed a couple of his new friends and headed into the woods where they quickly disappeared. Will almost felt sorry for the outlaws. Even the frontiersmen who came with Barley were impressed by his tracking skills.

In the short amount of time he'd been with the new American Army, Wells had proven himself to be an outstanding woods-man and an incredibly accurate shot, along with being a solid, experienced soldier thanks to his years in the Royal Navy. Will was thinking of recommending him to a lieutenancy.

Will gathered up the surviving pilgrims on the riverbank. Out of what he was told was more than twenty, only nine survived. Five were women and there was one child, a boy about seven, who clung to his mother. Most were in shock from the sud-denness and savagery of the attack. Well, not all of them. One brown-haired woman glared at him. "I killed one of them," she said, "and would've gotten another but my gun misfired."

"You did well," Will said. He noted that she was really quite attractive, even though she was filthy, exhausted, and dressed in unbecoming men's clothes. Two other women were helping an older man with a leg wound. He would leave them alone. They were in good hands.

"And who are you, sir?" she added.

Will almost bowed. "Captain—I mean Major—Will Drake of the New American Army."

The woman sagged visibly. "Then we've made it to safety?"

"I hope so."

"My name is Sarah Benton," she said and then named the others. She was about to say more when Wells and the other soldiers returned. "We found one dead a little ways up and caught up with the other two of them real easy. They made a path like elephants." Wells had never seen an elephant but he knew they were huge and it made sense that they would leave easy trails to follow.

Will gestured. "And?"

"Oh, sorry sir, we killed them."

Will grinned. "What are you sorry for, Wells? They deserved killing."

"Yes sir," Wells said, not quite certain that a major made jokes with corporals. He understood the rank might be equivalent to that of captain of a ship, and those worthies never made jokes, at least not to ordinary folk like him. He fixed his eyes on Faith Benton. She caught him looking and smiled before returning to ministering to her father.

"New American Army?" Sarah asked. "What happened to the Continental Army?"

Will shrugged. "It lost. It's time to start anew with a new name."

Sarah thought it made sense. "Will you take us to Liberty?"

"With pleasure, Mistress Benton. In a way, you're already there."

Fitzroy was amazed that you could actually take a sailing ship up the Hudson River all the way to Albany. With a landsman's lack of knowledge of rivers and things that float on them, he thought that the south-flowing current would be too strong to fight and that the crew would spend all their time at the oars, or sweeps as they were called. However, he found that a skilled captain could take advantage of the winds, do some sideways sailing he thought was called tacking, and arrive at their destination without too much difficulty.

Since the few roads northward were miserable at best, traveling by water was more than a convenience; it was both safer and swifter. It was no wonder that the larger and more important cities in North America were located on navigable waterways. So too were the major cities of England, he realized with mild chagrin.

It had been just such a sailing ship from New York that had brought a welcome addition to the British forces and some unwelcome news.

The addition was General James Grant. Like Burgoyne, he too was a lieutenant general, but his orders were to serve under Burgoyne. Grant was quite fat, almost obese, and had little interest in underlings. He tolerated Fitzroy because he was Burgoyne's aide and distant cousin. Otherwise he was almost uniformly arrogant, rude, and contemptuous, which did not endear him to others on Burgoyne's staff.

However, Grant could fight. Like many British commanders, he believed that the bayonet was the superior battlefield weapon for British infantry. Cold steel in their guts and the rebels will run, just as they had at Long Island and Brandywine, was his often stated motto.

Burgoyne had professed delight over Grant's arrival. For all his faults, Grant was a vast improvement over Tarleton and Arnold.

It meant Burgoyne now had an experienced and seasoned second in command in the sixty-four-year-old Grant. It further meant that he didn't have to depend on Arnold and Tarleton, whom he considered mediocre talents at best. Now he could create three unequal divisions: Arnold's, Tarleton's, and a third grand division under Grant.

But it was not all good news. The war in France had deteriorated into bloody anarchy. The three factions fighting for control of France were now reduced to two. The French moderates, or those who wanted a constitutional monarchy like that of England's, had been defeated by the radicals who were making every effort to kill all the aristocrats and nobility they could find. Savage and bloody massacres were taking place all over France as long boiling hatreds overflowed, causing cascades of blood. Some of the most ancient names in the French nobility had been wiped out, hacked to bloody pieces by outraged peasantry.

The second group consisted of the monarchists who wanted the king restored to his throne and life resumed as if the revolution hadn't happened. Of course, this would occur after the appropriate revolutionary ringleaders had been executed for treason, and tens of thousands of others sent to prisons and worked to death as slaves.

Neither Burgoyne nor Fitzroy thought that France could ever return to an earlier world. Fitzroy had little sympathy for either group. Almost all of the French nobility he had met felt that the peasants they ruled were barely human at best and that they, the nobility, were godlike in comparison. Fitzroy felt that the nobles deserved some punishment for their actions in oppressing the peasants, but being hacked to death was far too extreme for the taste of Englishmen. The Bourbons might be fools, but killing them all was not a solution.

"Sad," Burgoyne said, "but the voice of reason is often overwhelmed by that of passion. Hatred and vengeance are so much more satisfactory than contemplation and compromise."

Fitzroy nodded. "And Calais has fallen?"

"Yes and our army has almost all fled to England, in effect leaving France to the French. Lord Jeffrey Amherst has been defeated, which must have been a great shock to him. He had a very high impression of his own abilities. You recall, don't you, that he declined to command our forces in the colonies? As I recall, he felt that fighting rebels was beneath his dignity. The bumbling French king and his idiot queen Marie Antoinette are now in London."

"Sir, I've read the reports, but I still find it difficult to believe that we were defeated by a French rabble."

Burgoyne wagged a finger at him, teacher to pupil. "Fitzroy, never forget that it almost happened here a few years back. If the population of the colonies had been larger and more compressed, perhaps they too could have become the brainless hordes like those that simply overwhelmed our army at Calais without any thought of their own casualties. They might have taken New York or Yorktown and chased us out."

"But we still hold Dunkirk, don't we, General?"

"For the time being, yes, and for what reason? Oh, I know the rationale will be for us to use it as a base for future operations, but I rather think we'll soon be walled into the city and port and never be able to break out."

Burgoyne poured himself a brandy. He gestured for Fitzroy to help himself, which he did. "Our orders have changed, Major, and I need you to go to Tarleton, wherever he is."

"Yes, sir." Recent messages had General Tarleton shifting forces between Pitt and Detroit in anticipation of Burgoyne's arrival in the spring.

"This should not surprise you, Fitzroy, but as a result of the defeat at Calais, their lordships in London want most of their army back to defend England. They are terrified that the French might somehow cross the Channel and lay waste to England or worse yet, that the unwashed English multitude will rise up like the French peasants and commence slaughtering country squires. They are particularly fearful it will happen in Ireland, or even Scotland, or dear God, Wales. It appears that nobody likes us all that much. Therefore, I will have one chance and one chance only to win this war. If we falter, then the rebels will be left unmolested at best to form their own country. At worst, they will be inspired to further rebellion, rise again, and attack the cities in the east."

"Dear God," Fitzroy muttered.

"Dear God, indeed. And if we do win, or rather, *when* we do win, the government of the colonies will not be as originally planned with the Loyalists as a privileged group lording it over those who rebelled or simply wavered. Instead, it will be a military government. Thanks to the upheaval in France, London will not tolerate the possibility that there might be another revolution here, so the colonies are to be disarmed and all properties will revert to the king who will decide who will possess them as tenants and not as owners."

Fitzroy was shocked. "But that effectively makes landless peasants out of even the Loyalists who now believe they own their property."

"Correct, which means they won't be able to vote either for local or colony representatives. That also precludes the already remote possibility that someday there might be elections for seats in our Parliament. And your second and unsaid assumption is also correct. The takeover will be perceived as a betrayal by the Loyalists who supported us all these years. The exact details are in a package of documents General Grant brought. It's called 'Plans for the Future of the American Colonies,' and it's to remain a secret. You will read it of course, so you can understand its importance to me and to Tarleton. You will impress on Tarleton the urgency to be ready for anything and to keep the report as secret as we can for the time being, which means until we've destroyed the rebels at this Liberty place. A man like Tarleton usually needs no urging to go out and kill people, but one never knows and I've certainly learned not to assume anything."

Later in the privacy of his quarters, Fitzroy read the fairly lengthy document with both astonishment and dismay. There was good reason for it to remain a secret. It was inflammatory at best. It had the potential to outrage the most loyal of colonists. He finished, and returned it to the chest and locked it.

Fitzroy's quarters were in a private room above a large and fairly decent tavern, the one recommended by his innkeeper in New York. It had proven a pleasant surprise at many levels. When he returned there in the evening, he always wrote of the day's events in his journal. He referenced reading the "Plans," and how they dismayed him, but did not go into detail.

There was a tap on the door and Hannah Doorn, the owner of the tavern, entered. She was a blond widow in her mid-thirties, very attractive although a little plumpish. And better, she liked him, which meant he received far better treatment than an ordinary guest, and the tavern was well appointed in the first place.

Hannah Doorn was a sort of woman he'd never met before. Not only was she quite lovely, but she possessed business acumen and had numerous financial interests in Albany and further west. She was a shapely reminder that the Dutch presence predated the British and, although it had faded in New York, places like Albany still had a number of Dutch families and merchants. Typical Dutchies, he'd concluded on meeting Hannah and others. They made money everywhere, just like the Jews.

At least as surprising, Hannah was an artist. Her drawings and paintings of life in the area were quite exact. She wanted to sketch him, but he'd demurred, at least so far.

Hannah wore a floor-length robe which swirled as she walked across the floor and exposed a length of bare leg. "I think you should go down to dinner before the food is all eaten," she said.

"You're right, of course," he said. Hannah set a good table. Not up to London standards, but damn good and hearty nonetheless. "But must it be right now?" He pulled on the sash that held her robe together and it opened. As expected, she was naked underneath and totally blond. She laughed and they fell jubilantly onto the bed.

She was a wild thing, he thought moments later as she wrapped her legs around him and drew him deep inside her, and she really seemed to like the idea of bedding British nobility. Of course, he'd told her he was the most minor of nobility, but that meant nothing to her. She said he intrigued her.

Their coupling was sweaty and brief, a promise of even more satisfying things to come. "Now you really had get to dinner before your hoggish fellow officers eat everything, especially your friend Danforth. His stomach seems bottomless."

He grinned happily and concurred. When he was dressed he kissed her fondly on the forehead. She really was a fun creature. Too bad he would have to leave her and head west where he was afraid that the only women would be flat-faced and stupid Indians who likely carried every disease known to man.

"Do you want me to wait for you?" she asked as she stretched out like a yellow-haired cat on his bed, utterly shameless.

"No, I've got some errands to attend to." Like playing cards with Danforth and a couple of others and taking their money. He was always short of money. "May I wake you when I come back?"

She smiled coquettishly, enjoying the fact that she was still naked and that he was staring hungrily at her.

"Of course, my dear Major, you go and I'll clean up your room. It seems like we've made quite a mess of it."

When he was gone, she dressed quickly, picked up the scattered bedclothes and made the bed. Then she checked the door and bolted it. Fitzroy's journal was on the table and, as usual, unlocked. She scanned the day's entry. She was puzzled. What on earth was the "Plan for the Future of the American Colonies," and why on earth did Fitzroy think it was so awful that it had to be kept secret?

She put the journal back where she'd found it. Then she unbolted the door and stepped into the hallway. Once in her own room, she would write the question as a message and send it on its way west where others could try and figure out its significance.

She laughed to herself. Fitzroy was sweet but he thought he was so superior. He didn't realize there was more than one way to screw the British.

After their rescue, and escorted by Will and his men, Sarah, her family, and the other survivors of the raid canoed farther west and then walked north from the Ohio towards Fort Washington. During the several weeks it took, she had a number of pleasant conversations with Major Will Drake. They'd solemnly exchanged stories of the horrors they'd endured. For her sake, she could not imagine anything as despicable as keeping naked, freezing, and starving prisoners incarcerated in a hulk like the *Suffolk*. She almost wept at the thought of so many young lives ending in the ships anchored in the Hudson River and elsewhere off Manhattan Island. Damn the British for their cruelty.

To her immense surprise, she found herself opening up to Will about what happened to her after she refused the sexual offer from Sheriff Braxton. She omitted the fact that Faith had accepted the offer and noted the look of gratitude in Faith's eyes when she realized what they were talking about. Faith was more than a little interested in the squat and muscular Welshman, Owen Wells, and didn't need her past brought up at this time, however involuntary her actions might have been. Sarah had made one choice and Faith another.

Still, Sarah concluded that whatever had happened to her was dwarfed by the prolonged agonies inflicted on Will.

On arrival at the sprawling community of Fort Washington,

Sarah and the other women were assigned quarters in barracks made of logs and raw wood and assigned bunks that were even more crudely made than the barracks. The buildings were hot and stifling, and she wondered just what they'd be like in the winter with the wind and the snow blowing through the cracks. If she was still in them, she would see to it that the cracks were filled with mud, which would keep out the worst of the weather.

Of course, they were separated from Uncle Wilford, although Aunt Rebecca was with them. They were assured that there were married quarters, just not enough to go around just yet. Faith allowed that she was old enough to live away from her parents and the American authorities accepted that. Sarah had doubts, but kept her peace. If Rebecca and Wilford were satisfied, she would be too.

Sarah was further surprised when each of them was asked to write a summary of their skills on a page of paper. If nothing else, she thought wryly, it would separate those who were literate from those who weren't.

A couple of days later, she and Faith found themselves seated across a table from a pleasant-looking woman who seemed older than someone not yet forty. And why not, Sarah thought. Abigail Adams' husband John was likely dying in Jamaica.

"I hope you two are willing to work," Mistress Adams said with a faint smile.

"We are," Sarah answered for the two of them.

Abigail turned to Faith. "Your father is a blacksmith, is he not? What do you know of working with metals yourself?"

Faith was astonished. "Surely you do not expect me to be a blacksmith?"

"Of course not," Mistress Adams answered sharply. She was not used to having her questions answered with another question. "I only want to know if you've worked with metal."

"I have," Faith admitted.

Mistress Adams relaxed and smiled. "Wonderful. While the men are out training for war, those women who have some skills will take their place. We have also found that many women have the dexterity necessary to work with weapons. We would like you to help assembling muskets. Do you accept?"

"Certainly," Faith said, just a little overwhelmed by Mistress Adams. After all, she was the wife of one of the leaders of the revolution.

"Excellent." Abigail Adams turned to Sarah. "I have a very cranky old man who needs a clerk and a nursemaid." She held up the paper Sarah had written. "According to this, you obviously read and write well, and you say you took care of your father before he died."

"I did," Sarah answered with some hesitation.

Abigail's eyes twinkled. She really was quite attractive when she was happy, and she seemed to be enjoying the conversation with Sarah for some reason.

"Don't worry, Mistress Benton, I will not have you emptying chamber pots or wiping drool from the mouth of some demented old goat. No, there is an older man who may or may not be a little insane, but is certainly eccentric, and who is quite capable of caring for himself. He needs a clerk as much as a housekeeper, and he works well with women. Sometimes too well, if you understand my meaning."

Sarah laughed. "I believe I can stop an old codger from pawing me."

"I don't doubt it at all. Do you accept?"

Do I have a choice, Sarah thought. She did not want to work assembling muskets with Faith, whatever and however one assembled muskets in the first place.

"Of course," Sarah smiled.

Braxton wasn't impressed with General Banastre Tarleton, at least not at first. The British general looked indolent, even pudgy and soft, and not the bold fighter and sadistic killer he was reputed to be.

Braxton had never seen a Frenchman, but Tarleton looked spoiled and pouty and he suspected that was what Frenchmen looked like. But that was until Braxton looked into Tarleton's eyes and saw coldness and death, and realized that Tarleton was a poisonous viper. For the first time in a long while, Braxton knew the meaning of fear. He silently vowed that he would not make an enemy out of Tarleton.

"Burned Man Braxton," Tarleton said without emotion, "How incredibly fitting."

Braxton remained silent. Instead of the revulsion so many people felt when they saw him, Tarleton was not repulsed. Instead, he stared at Braxton almost approvingly. He was calculating.

"And you wish to kill rebels, do you not?"

"I do indeed, sir," Braxton said with what he hoped was proper humility.

It was for that reason and with Burgoyne's permission that Braxton and his band had traveled north and west to the British fort at Detroit. What had been a squalid little outpost had been augmented by the more than fifteen hundred British regulars Tarleton had brought from Pitt to reinforce the original garrison of only a couple of hundred soldiers. Rumor had it that Tarleton wanted to attack the rebels now, and not wait for Burgoyne to come with still more reinforcements. He felt that he had more than enough men to crush them this fall and there was no need to wait for reinforcements to arrive in the spring. If the British could get stronger, then so too could the rebels, he'd argued but to no avail.

He'd been overruled by both Cornwallis and Burgoyne. He would have to wait while more British soldiers arrived. Additional rumors said that several thousand more were coming overland and by boat from Montreal. Braxton wondered where they'd all eat, sleep, and shit, but that was not his problem.

"Other than killing people, what can you do for me?" Tarleton asked with a cold smile. "If I wanted people butchered in their beds, I can just turn loose the Indians."

Braxton nodded. "But will they report back on what they've found and will they do that in a language an educated man like you would understand? Hardly, General. What the redskins will do is kill, get drunk, fuck their squaws, and then exaggerate their enemies' numbers ten times over to make themselves seem like great warriors."

Tarleton smiled mirthlessly and looked out the window of his cabin and down to the muddy bank of the wide Detroit River. Across the river was Canada, under the control of General Frederic Haldimand, hundreds of miles away in Montreal. Tarleton was absolutely appalled at the thought of spending a winter in this miserable place. "The Indians are rather useless bastards, even when they are sober, aren't they?"

"Indeed, sir, and I have eighty men who can spread havoc among the rebel communities and kill them, which will mean fewer men for you and General Burgoyne to face."

From the look on Tarleton's face, Braxton was afraid he'd gone too far with his assessment of his own abilities. But then the

British commander looked intrigued and treated him to another icy smile. "Can you make your attacks look like Indian assaults?"

For a moment, Braxton was puzzled, but then it dawned on him. "So the rebels will attack the Indians in revenge and actually turn the red savages against them? I can do that, sir. Just turn me loose, sir, and I'll raise bloody fucking hell with the rebels."

This time Tarleton's smile was genuine. Death and destruction were going to be spread to his enemies. "Then go forth and smite the bastards, Captain, in full knowledge that whatever you do to them, however awfully it is done, will be forgiven by both me and a grateful king. And, oh yes, try not to get caught."

Major General Nathanael Greene lay in his bed. His once healthy and robust frame was but a distant memory. He was gaunt and pale, and his breath was shallow and each one a struggle. Nathanael Greene, the man who was once George Washington's trusted right hand, was dying at the age of forty-three. It was only a question of time.

Will Drake stood behind General Tallmadge at the foot of the bed. General Philip Schuyler stood beside Greene. Will had made his report on the trip up the Ohio to Tallmadge, who had thought Greene would like to hear it in person. He had. It meant that rumors of a British column approaching from the direction of the Ohio were unfounded. It also meant it was increasingly unlikely that any attack would occur this year.

"Burgoyne's in winter quarters or will be very shortly. It will be some time before he has the strength to mount an assault on us," Greene said weakly. "I only wish we had the strength to launch a surprise attack him like Washington did at Trenton." He took a deep breath. "However, that will not happen. We are more than two hundred miles away from Detroit, not the night's march from the enemy we were at Trenton."

"Still, perhaps we can do something?" inquired Tallmadge.

"What do you propose?" asked General Schuyler.

"Raids to keep them occupied and to possibly destroy their resources," Tallmadge answered. "Whatever we destroy this coming winter won't be available to use against us in the spring and summer."

Greene stared at Will. "I presume you'd send someone like Major Drake against them?"

Schuyler answered. "In some instances yes, General; however I was more thinking of George Rogers Clark and his men. I have it on good authority that he is in Kentucky and eager to help us. I've sent for him."

Greene managed a wan smile. "You mean there's somebody else the British didn't send to Jamaica?"

"Yes sir," said Tallmadge, "although there are rumors he's drinking heavily. Again."

Greene struggled to a sitting position. The effort seemed to exhaust him and he had to pause before continuing. "Actually, Clark is not in Kentucky and I have no idea whether he's drinking or not. Last summer we sent Clark out west to check on the feasibility of our retreating farther towards the Pacific if the need arose. He has not yet returned and I don't expect him until spring."

Tallmadge was surprised and puzzled, as well as a bit annoyed. He was the spymaster and supposed to know about things like Clark going west instead of getting drunk in Kentucky. "But who will lead the raids?"

"No raids," said General Schuyler and Greene nodded. "Not by him and not by Major Drake. We don't want to aggravate Tarleton into disobeying what may be Burgoyne's orders and coming after us. We might beat him, and we might not. Worse, we might provoke Burgoyne into bringing everything he has in a winter attack and we aren't ready for that."

Will wondered if they'd ever be ready enough to fight the British. Each day, the British got stronger. Were the rebels getting stronger than the enemy? He'd read the reports describing British numbers and knew better than to think that. He chaffed at the thought of doing nothing.

Will's frustration emboldened him to interrupt Schuyler. "By sending Clark westward, are you sending a message that we'll flee if the time comes?"

Greene chuckled. "We have no more intention of fleeing than you do of returning to that prison hulk, Major."

Will flushed. He had no idea that Nathanael Greene knew of his story. "I'm sorry, sir."

Greene waved off the apology. "Major, the problem is that people already see the British coming in one direction and a vast continent beckoning to the west. They rightly wonder whether we could or should pack up and move another thousand miles away, or even all the way west into lands held only lightly by the Russians or the Spanish, or by the widely scattered Indian tribes. If the land is fertile, there are those who feel we could exist out there for years, even decades, before the British even cared to come after us. With time on our side, we could truly become stronger, and who knows, the British might be more conciliatory after a generation or two. Lord North and King George can't live forever, can they? Perhaps their replacements would be more reasonable men."

Greene began to cough harshly. The speech had drained him of what little strength remained. When he gained control of himself, he looked sadly at those in the room. "Of course, some of us could easily be dead in the morning."

"If we are not going to raid, what would you have us do?" Tallmadge asked.

Schuyler answered for Greene. "We must have information, information and still more information. We must know their strengths and their weaknesses. More British troops are arriving almost daily and more are on the way. We want to know who they are, what they are thinking and what resources they have. General Tallmadge, I want you to send men like Drake and others to find out the answers to questions we haven't even thought of."

# Chapter 5 ★ ★ ★ ★ ★ ★ ★ ★ ★ ★ ★ ★ ★ ★ ★ ★ ★ ★

BENJAMIN FRANKLIN STOOD IN THE OPEN SECOND-FLOOR window and held his arms wide. He was stark naked and he enjoyed the gentle caress of the early morning the breeze on his pale, flabby body. It was likely one of the last days he'd be able to do this. In a brief while, it would be too bloody cold. In fact, it was chilly this morning, but he would not be deterred.

Franklin sighed at the thought. This would be his second winter at Fort Washington and he wondered how he'd survived this long without the comforts of civilization. He'd lived in London, Paris, and Philadelphia, but never a frontier outpost like Fort Washington or the surrounding villages collectively known as Liberty. He loved good food and wine and there was little of the former and less of the latter. He liked art and theater and there was none of either. Nor did many of the buildings have proper floors. Instead, the floors were dirt.

Franklin loved beautiful women, and some might be attractive, but there were damned few in Liberty who were up to his standards. That and so many of them bathed so rarely that they even smelled worse than the French women he'd flirted with at the court of Louis XVI. At least they'd had the decency to cover their personal stench with perfume, although that sometimes became suffocating.

Still, Franklin understood how fortunate he'd been. When the American Revolution collapsed, he'd been in Paris. A fearful King

Louis decided to placate a victorious and vengeful England by turning him over to them to be tried for treason. His execution, like Washington's, would be all but guaranteed. But Franklin's friends had smuggled him out of the country and, after a tortuous voyage, followed by hiding in numerous American houses, and several close brushes with the British, he'd found himself in Liberty.

"Mr. Franklin, will you please get dressed," demanded a female voice.

"Mistress Benton, will you deny an old man one of his few remaining pleasures? Or are you shocked by the sight of a magnificent naked man?"

Sarah grinned at him. "First, sir, I would never deny you your pleasures, but the people in the street below are getting a marvelous view of your distinguished presence, which might just terrify those who've never seen such a treasure. Second, I have indeed seen a naked man or two in my life, and, while you are truly magnificent, please note that I am not struck dumb or otherwise shocked."

Franklin laughed and reluctantly wrapped a robe around him without admitting that he was indeed cold. Sarah Benton had been his secretary for only a few days, and had quickly become his confidante. The fact that she was more than lovely further brightened his days and was making life in the frontier quite tolerable. She was a delectable exception to the general rule that women in the Fort Washington-Liberty area were plain at best. Just as important, she smelled clean.

"You've seen a naked man? I'm shocked," he said wickedly. "I was under the impression that you'd never been married, at least not by clergy."

"Since when are a marriage ceremony and a clergyman required for love and marriage? There are places in this vast land where the presence of clergy is nonexistent; therefore, young lovers do what young lovers must and consider themselves married in the eyes of man and God. And that is what my poor dead husband Tom and I did."

"What happened to him?"

"He went off and got himself killed at Brandywine. A friend told me he was hit by a cannonball and died instantly. Part of me says that's a polite fiction, but I am thankful for the information. So many families heard nothing after their men went off to war.

They spend their time waiting. Many will never find out whether their missing husband or son is dead or alive."

"I am saddened for you. Still, there is a place where people love freely and where there is no clergy? How absolutely wonderful; I think I shall go and live there when I grow older."

Sarah's responsibilities to Franklin were simple. She saw to it that he ate properly, dressed, and prepared himself to represent his beloved Pennsylvania in the Continental Congress that met in a large crude hall less than a hundred yards away.

"And what will Congress do today?" she asked.

Franklin snorted derisively. "Dither. You've seen them at what they call work. Instead, they dither."

Sarah had indeed seen Congress at what they called work. At first, she'd been fascinated to see men like John Hancock and others try to make a nation. Then she'd realized they had no idea what to do. With the British gathering themselves to come at them, talk of nation building seemed like an exercise in irrelevancy.

"We must make a constitution for this poor nation," Franklin said. "If we do that, then we are proclaiming to the world that we are a proper nation with a true entity. Right now, we are nothing more than a bunch of defeated revolutionaries who are on the verge of extinction."

"A constitution will change all that? Wasn't the Declaration of Independence enough?"

"No, not at all. The Declaration was magnificent, even though I didn't write it, but it was only a beginning. But a constitution will show that we have a purpose and laws along with a set of ideals. Thus, even if we should fail, history will recognize that we were far more than a pack of brigands who deserved to be destroyed by England. No, Sarah, even in our deaths we would then say to the world that men deserve to be free."

"And what about women?" Sarah asked.

Franklin winked, "Only the pretty ones."

Winifred Haskill jumped as she heard a sound from outside the cabin. Winifred was always jumping because she was always scared. She was thirteen and hated the fact that her parents had dragged her and the others in their deeply religious community out into a forest filled with wild creatures just so they could be nearer to a God who didn't seem to like them at all.

Why did she feel that God didn't like them? Was it because they lived in self-inflicted poverty in a land of wealth? Or was it because their neighbors in Philadelphia had mocked and laughed at them because of their extreme faith which required continuous bible reading, fasting, and hymn singing at all hours of the night and day—practices which had greatly annoyed their neighbors? Perhaps it was everything, she reluctantly concluded. Finally, even the tolerant Quakers had asked them to leave Philadelphia if they would not keep silent.

But why did her father have to locate them in the middle of a dense forest hundreds of miles away from home and who knew how far from other people?

Of course she was scared. The surrounding forest was filled with wild animals, and even wilder red savages who wanted to do unspeakable things to her, things she'd only heard about and didn't quite understand. Winifred did not try to fool herself. She was just thirteen and skinny as a twig and had stringy brown hair and a bad complexion. But, still, she was a female and was afraid.

In the year they'd been in the forest, they'd at least managed to build cabins and a barn as well as clearing out a field for planting. The cabin was made of rough logs chinked with mud, and did a miserable job of keeping out the weather. Wind, rain, heat, and cold air all took their turns entering through the cracks they didn't quite know how to fill properly. Even the shack they'd called home back in Philadelphia had been a better place.

And now they had to become farmers in order to survive since hunting could never provide enough food. It was backbreaking work, especially clearing out the stumps of chopped down trees, but she'd gotten used to that. Her mother often said it was God's Will that they work so hard and were all so thin. Winifred thought they were thin because there still wasn't much food and that God had very little to do with it. She kept those thoughts to herself lest she be whipped for them as she had in the past for being impertinent.

She heard a sound and jumped fearfully. She jumped again when she heard the sound of yelling. What was happening? Nobody yelled in their community except her father when he was angry. Muskets were fired and there was screaming. Then Winifred began to scream. And scream.

★　★　★

Burned Man Braxton's following had shrunk from a high of eighty to around thirty. A half dozen had been killed in raids, and another handful wounded, but they were not the main cause for the shrinkage of his band. A number had departed in disgust and shame at what they were being called on to do.

"I came to fight," said one as he led ten of his companions away from the camp, "not slaughter helpless women and children."

Braxton wanted to kill the man, but it would have started a brawl that, while he could win, would mean the deaths of some of those men devoted to him. The hell with what he considered deserters. However reduced, he had a company that was loyal to him and thought nothing of performing the most depraved acts to punish the rebel scum who deserved everything they got. He was more than pleased that Harris and Fenton, two of his deputies from Pendleton, had elected to stay with him. They'd always liked the way he operated.

The defections meant that pretending to be Indians was over with. That little secret was out. Tarleton professed not to care. Just keep killing, he'd instructed them.

Braxton and his men were about fifty miles south and west of Detroit, which, according to Tarleton, meant they were in rebel country. They should, therefore, assume the worst about anyone they met. That pleased Braxton. Anybody they met was going to get their worst.

Harris had been scouting and had reported finding a small settlement a couple of miles to their front. Three houses, a couple of barns, and a stable all indicated an extended group of probably a dozen people. He guessed that at least half would be male and able to fight. He also assumed that they were used to life in the wild and would be as ready as they could be for an attack. Well, Braxton thought, he would be even readier.

Braxton always chose midday for his attacks. At first that surprised his men, but then they understood his logic. Dawn was the traditional time for a surprise assault, which meant dawn was the time when people in hostile territory were watching most intently for danger. By midday, they should feel relatively secure and be going about their chores comforted by the fact that they could at least see clearly, which sometimes led to overconfidence.

Dead of night was out too. Braxton had learned from hard experience how difficult it was to coordinate a group of men and move them silently in the dark. At one settlement they'd made so much noise finding each other that the settlers had been prepared. It hadn't done the settlers much good, although they'd killed two of Braxton's men and wounded a third before they'd been overwhelmed. So much for his men being skilled woodsmen and able to move silently as a cat as some of them had bragged. Braxton couldn't either, but at least he understood his limitations.

Harris returned again and reported that the settlers had one man out in a field and a second man in the woods, probably hunting for squirrels and rabbits. Both were armed. The man in the field was out of sight of the main buildings.

Braxton smiled. With one man hunting, a distant musket shot would not alarm the rebel settlers.

Harris and three men were sent to deal with the farmer in the field, while Fenton and another three stalked the hunter. Fenton reported back within a couple of minutes. The hunter had been so engrossed in stalking a rabbit that they'd crept up behind him and stunned him with a thrown tomahawk and then Fenton hacked him to death with it.

Half an hour later, Harris and his men returned. A fresh and bloody scalp hung from Harris' belt. "At first we couldn't get close to him, but then he laid down his rifle and went and squatted in a hollow to take a shit," Harris laughed. "We rushed him so fast he never had a chance to even pull up his pants."

Even Braxton found that amusing. He had his men fan out in an arc and move towards the settlement. There was a point in the woods where they could get to about a hundred yards from a barn and one of the buildings. When they were settled and still in the shade of the trees, he paused and looked. Nothing. A child was playing in some dirt and a woman was hanging wash.

Braxton pulled a whistle from his pocket and blew one short burst. Immediately, his men began running towards the houses. They made very little sound and nobody had noticed the whistle which they might have taken for a bird call. Nobody saw them until they were halfway there, and they were in the compound before anybody could respond. The woman hanging wash went down from a rifle butt, and the child gained her voice and ran screaming.

Men and women tumbled from the houses and were cut down by Braxton's men. Perfect, he thought. He signaled and others of his band entered the barns and the houses. A couple of shots were fired, followed by screams and very soon all was silence.

"Bring me the survivors," Braxton ordered. Two men, four women, and a pair of small children were all that remained. His men knew what to do. The woman who'd been hit with the musket butt looked stunned and there was blood on her head. The men and the children were taken to a barn where they would be bound and gagged and then have their throats cut without the women knowing it.

He glared at the women. One he noticed was rather young, fourteen at the most. More likely twelve, he thought.

"You want to ever see your menfolk again? Then you do as you're told, you hear?"

One of the women, the oldest at maybe forty, nodded. "Why are you doing this to us?"

"Because you're rebels, that's why."

"Not true," she said. "We ain't nobody's people. We just want to worship our God in peace. That's why we came here. We don't want no part of no war. We are peaceable people of God."

"No peace here, woman," Braxton said, "and no God either. Now you're gonna do as you're told if you want your men to be alive when we leave here. Strip."

The women gasped and stared at each other. Braxton snarled. "Either you do it or my men will rip them rags off you right now."

"Obey him," the older woman said and made to comply. Within a few moments, the four were naked, including the injured one who had to be helped out of her clothing. The younger one was sobbing and trying to cover herself with her hands. She had small, bud-like breasts and just a wisp of hair between her thighs. Braxton thought she was maybe twelve, and not fourteen as he'd first guessed. It excited him. He liked them young.

Braxton took the young one by her wrist and dragged her into the house and into a bedroom. He heard his men starting to have their way with the older women who began to howl in terror and pain.

He threw the girl on the bed and she punched at him, hitting his still raw face. The sudden pain was intense and nearly stopped him, but he overcame it and struck her hard until she whimpered and lay still. She screamed the first time he took her, but not the second or third. She didn't scream again until he turned her over to his men. Not all of them took her. A few complained that she was too skinny or still a kid. He thought she was likely dead when she and the other women were piled on top of the bodies of the men and children in the barn, which was then burned. He didn't care.

As they took off with their plunder, Braxton was satisfied. He'd wiped out another nest of rebels at a cost of two men slightly wounded. He hoped Tarleton would be pleased. Tarleton frightened him.

Will and Sarah walked arm in arm through the muddy streets of Fort Washington. There was a chill in the air, and a light snow had fallen early that morning. Nothing had stuck, but it was an unsubtle reminder that winter was almost upon them. Sarah wondered if would be appropriate or just too shocking to wear men's trousers when the weather worsened. She had arrived with little in the way of feminine clothes and there wasn't much available in a town that was basically a military post. She would have to ask Abigail Adams. Franklin, she was certain, wouldn't care at all. She knew he would smile like a cherub and say she could work naked if she so liked.

"What are you going to do now," Sarah asked Will. She knew from his already familiar actions, that something was up.

"I guess you can keep a secret," he said with a grin. "Not that there's any British around you'd blab to, but I'm going east. We're going to keep people on watch at Detroit and Pitt and it's my turn to go to Detroit. I'll check things out for a while, be replaced, and return."

"What do you expect to find?"

"A British army that's growing bigger and stronger each day."

She shuddered and not from the cold. "Then they will come for us and finally destroy us, won't they?"

"Not if I can help it," he said and quickly realized how foolish it sounded. How could he, one man, stop a British army? Thankfully, Sarah seemed not to have noticed it.

Sarah changed the subject. "Mr. Franklin is a great man."

"So I've heard. However, isn't he getting just a wee bit old?"

She laughed. The great man was maddeningly and intentionally imprecise as to his age. It was presumed that he was at least in his middle seventies and possibly older.

"In some ways, he is old. He tires easily and it frustrates him because there's so much that he wants to do and feels needs to be done. In other ways, he's a child filled with wonder at the world around him, and, in still other ways, he is a genius. Have you heard his latest?"

"No."

"Well, after spending all his days trying to get the fools in Congress to institutionalize a form of government, he has devised a new way of making guns."

"He what?"

"Indeed," she said with some pride. She had become deeply fond of the old man. "It occurred to him that guns are made by gunsmiths, but that we have very few of them here at Fort Washington. Therefore, he said we had to make them without gunsmiths."

"Sounds logical," Will said. She was leaning against him and he could feel the pressure of her breast against his arm. Perhaps if he kept her talking they could walk forever.

"And logical it is, Will. He decided that we—I mean, the army—should only make simple weapons and that we should make them by making a large number of barrels, then make stocks and then triggers. If they were made simply enough, they should all fit together and we could make a large number of weapons very quickly."

Will found the concept intriguing and said so. "But what sort of weapons are they?"

"He's toyed with several types. But right now he's working on one that almost looks like an old blunderbuss. They have broad barrels into which powder is poured, and then followed by whatever is going to be fired—lead bullets, glass, stones. He thinks the effect will be devastating at short range. Franklin's going to have them demonstrated later."

"I would like to see that," Will said, and made a mental note to find out more from Tallmadge.

Major James Fitzroy was surprised and delighted when Hannah Doorn informed him that she and a woman servant were coming with him to Detroit, or at least with the army. He was unused to women making pronouncements concerning his life, but he accepted without hesitation. He was genuinely fond of her, and her presence would more than brighten up what promised to be a dismal winter in a miserable location—Fort Detroit. His planned trip to find Tarleton had been cancelled when information was received that Tarleton had gone to Detroit, instead of staying at Pitt.

Hannah also reminded him that she had business interests in Detroit, which would more than pay for any inconvenience he might feel about having to support a poor woman. She was, thank you, more than able to support herself. He'd long since concluded that Hannah Doorn was a very clever woman. She'd gotten around those laws that restricted ownership of property by women by using a cousin as a front for a small percentage. Or she simply ignored them. He'd concluded that much of the property she owned was still in her late husband's name and no one cared.

"Damned if it isn't strange," he'd told Danforth over brandies, "but the Dutchie women seem to be at least as smart about business as the men are. Must be the air here in the colonies."

Danforth pretended to shudder. "Thank God it's different in England where women know their place, which is either in bed with their legs spread or in the kitchen with their legs together."

Fitzroy was more than surprised to find that Hannah was in a partnership with a Jewish merchant who had a store in Detroit.

"After all," he'd told her, "don't they delight in cheating Christians?"

"I've known Abraham Goldman and his family since I was a little girl and he had a similar arrangement with both my father and my husband. I don't think he would cheat me. Each year, I receive an amount of money as my share of the venture we own jointly."

"I see," Major Fitzroy had said, not certain he saw anything at all.

"And they don't eat Christian babies either," she'd laughed, and he happily admitted he really didn't think they ever did.

They traveled by wagon from Albany north and then west to Oswego, a decrepit and nearly abandoned site on Lake Ontario that was being rejuvenated by the British for the coming campaign. Burgoyne commented, without apparent bitterness, that the direction they were taking took him away from the site of his defeats in 1777, at Saratoga. It was, he informed all, a part of his life that should remain closed except for the obvious lessons to be drawn from it.

Burgoyne also found Hannah Doorn quite attractive and made tentative efforts to influence her and take her from Fitzroy. When she would have none of it, Burgoyne simply shrugged, laughed it off, and went looking for another conquest. To his dismay, there weren't any other women in the caravan available to be seduced.

From Oswego, they traveled by ship as close as they could to the falls at Niagara, where they paused, rested, and gazed with amazement on the magnificent natural wonders. Burgoyne said that he'd heard of them from travelers, but assumed the descriptions were exaggerations resulting from too much to drink. "Not any longer," Burgoyne said. "There is nothing like them in all the world. I feel honored and privileged to be here and to have seen them."

It was a sentiment held by Fitzroy, Hannah, and almost everyone in their traveling party of several hundred. "You'd have to be insane to not see the hand of God in those falls," Hannah said, and Fitzroy could not contradict her. He was overwhelmed by the vision and the sound of the roaring water.

They continued by land to Lake Erie and then were jammed into a couple of small and filthy merchant ships to take them to Detroit. An eight-gun sloop, the *Viper,* escorted them. It was encouraging to realize that the Royal Navy had control of the lakes, and not the rebels. It was also incredible to Fitzroy and the others that lakes as immense as Ontario and Erie existed. Could it really be that other so-called great lakes were even greater? Even Burgoyne expressed astonishment.

On first sighting Detroit, Fitzroy was mightily depressed. A wooden stockade enclosed a number of muddy acres filled with ramshackle wooden buildings running inland from the equally muddy banks of the Detroit River. The military outpost was a little ways inland and attached to the town. It was called Fort Lernoult. Although small, the fort at least looked like someone with military experience had planned it. He'd been informed that it had eleven foot high earthen walls and contained several cannon.

A shipyard of sorts lined the riverbank where lumber was piled high and the barges that Burgoyne had ordered were under construction. News of the barges had been a surprise to Fitzroy and Danforth although, to Fitzroy's chagrin, Hannah had known all about them from her Jewish merchant friend who was selling them supplies. Regardless, the activity on the waterfront looked like chaos.

"One spark and the whole thing would go up like an obscene parody of Nero's Rome," Fitzroy muttered as he took in the piles of wood, the shavings, and the dust.

His low opinion of Detroit did not rise as their ship moved

against a crude dock that extended into the river and threatened to fall down as they were tied up to it. At least they would not have to wade the final few feet, or climb down into small boats, although he presumed that other, lesser mortals in the other ships would do exactly that. It was always good to be associated with the commanding officer since rank had its privileges.

Several score buildings had sprung up outside the stockade, and Hannah and her servant made for one of the larger ones while Fitzroy tried to figure out where Burgoyne was going to put his headquarters. He took in the hundreds of white tents that dotted the landscape and disrupted the lives of the farmers whose strip farms ran inland from the surprisingly wide Detroit River.

Danforth had pompously informed him that the river was technically a strait and not a river since it only ran thirty-odd miles and connected two lakes, St. Clair and Erie and, no, Lake St. Clair was named for a Papist saint, and not after the rebel general. Fitzroy told Danforth he was a bloody bore and that he'd rather have a drink than a lecture.

The tents housed the British contingent that now consisted of more than four thousand soldiers. Come spring, there would be many more. Pity the poor rebels, he thought.

Hannah entered the store owned by Abraham Goldman and looked at the items for sale. They included clothing, camping goods, pots, pans, stoves, and even some toys, although she wondered just how many children there were at the depressing outpost. Finally, she wandered over to a different section and looked at the neatly arranged stacks of cloth and blankets. She fingered several of them and nodded approval.

"Mistress Van Doorn?" inquired a small, wiry man of indeterminate age, although Hannah already knew he was in his sixties.

She smiled warmly. "Mr. Goldman, it is just plain Doorn and you know it quite well. There is no 'Van' in front of my name."

Goldman chuckled. "And why shouldn't you promote yourself? Everyone here is trying to better themselves, and what better place to begin than your name? Let them think you're even more important than you are."

To her surprise, Hannah thought it was a good idea. Beginning immediately, her name would be Hannah Van Doorn. She smiled sweetly. "Did you find quarters for me?"

"The army has taken everything that even resembled quality housing," he said sadly. "First Tarleton's officers and now Burgoyne's will require something warm and dry for the winter. The enlisted soldiers and officers of lower rank than generals are expected to live in tents or huts."

Hannah could not keep the dismay from her voice. "Then what will I do?" The idea of her sharing a tent with Major Fitzroy and Danforth appalled her.

"Don't worry," Goldman said with a laugh. "I've converted a portion of one of the warehouses into a bedroom with a kitchen and a study. There is even a fireplace and I will see that you are supplied with wood. I think you and your major will be quite satisfied."

Hannah blushed. How on earth had he found out about Major Fitzroy? She fingered a cloth and pretended to examine it. "I'm sure I will be satisfied. Tell me, do you think red and white will sell well this year?"

Goldman stiffened perceptibly and hesitated. "Perhaps not as well as blue and white," he said and asked softly, "You?"

Hannah Van Doorn smiled demurely, "And why not?"

The building assigned to Benjamin Franklin for the development of a new way of making guns was set up for display this afternoon, not work. He called it "Merlin's Cave" in a fit of whimsical honor to the legendary magician companion of the equally legendary King Arthur. On a series of tables were piles of the components needed to build a gun. Franklin beamed at everyone. He was in his glory.

"Kindly note, gentlemen, that what I have here are the parts of a gun that some people are beginning to call a 'Franklin' in my honor."

"It also bears your shape," said General Schuyler with a smile that brought chuckles from the others. A completed gun lay on the table. It was short and squat.

Franklin ignored the gibe from his good friend. He would take verbal vengeance over supper and relish it. "A group of people here are charged with making each component, while another group is responsible for assembling the, ah, marvelously and accurately named Franklin."

"What are the components, Mr. Franklin?" asked General Tallmadge. Will stood beside him.

"First, gentlemen, we have the wooden rifle stock, then the trigger and flint, and, finally, the barrel. The only really difficult part to make is the trigger. The wooden stock is made on a foot-powered lathe, and the barrel is made by a blacksmith, such as Mr. Benton here. Regardless of the degree of difficulty, groups of workers specialize in making only their own particular part of the gun. Then, others, and often women like the sublimely attractive and young Miss Faith, assemble the components."

"Why women?" inquired Schuyler.

"Many women are quite skillful at knitting and sewing. There-fore, it seemed logical that their nimble fingers would be able to fashion a weapon out of small and diverse parts. With women performing some tasks, it also frees up men to perform others. With your permission, General Schuyler, would you pick one part out of each pile and hand it to that young lady who, in deference to your advanced age, is pretending to gaze worshipfully at you?"

Schuyler flushed. Franklin had gotten him back. He grinned and took a part at random from each pile. Faith took them sol-emnly, laid them on a table in the order she wanted, and then proceeded to put them together. It took only a couple of minutes before the unique-looking weapon was completed.

"Impressive," said Schuyler, "but will it work?"

Franklin took the stubby gun from Faith and held it aloft. "I will test it and fire it."

"You will not!" exclaimed Schuyler. "If an accident happens, we cannot afford to lose you."

"You're right," said Tallmadge. "Someone less important should fire it. Will Drake, you do it."

Will grinned at Tallmadge and took the weapon, while the others laughed at his expense. He examined it carefully and saw no obvious flaws. Franklin suggested they go outdoors, where a wall of dirt-filled sacks had been constructed about fifty feet away. Someone had stuck some men's clothing to it as a target. Will loaded the weapon with a packet of powder and one large lead bullet, cocked the hammer and aimed. The thing was heavy and dragged down the barrel.

He fired and the recoil pushed him a step backwards. A huge flock of pigeons erupted in fright from Tallmadge's headquarters, flew around in circles and finally settled back down. Will noted that Tallmadge was a bit concerned about the birds. He hoped he'd hit something near the target and not one of the pigeons. Then he wondered just what all those pigeons were doing in the loft of Tallmadge's office?

They walked through the dissipating smoke. A sandbag just to the left of the target showed a huge hole. Franklin peered at it and winked at Will. "It would appear that the sandbag is dead, but the enemy soldier is just fine, thank you."

"With practice, sir, I am confident I can do much better."

"I'm sure you can," Schuyler agreed. "But I do wonder just what the primary purpose of your weapon will be? It doesn't have the range of a rifle, or even a musket, so how shall it be used?"

"I see it as a second weapon," Franklin said. "I visualize a soldier carrying it on his back and, when his musket is emptied, he takes it and fires at very close range at the advancing enemy who will think the soldier is helpless. I believe it would be quite shocking to an enemy, assuming he survives."

"That might work," said Tallmadge, "but I doubt it, sir. The heat of battle is confusing enough without having to change weapons."

"Can it take a bayonet, Mr. Franklin?" asked Schuyler.

"I don't think so," Franklin said, "although a short bayonet might be contrived for it."

"Then a second weapon it must be," Schuyler said, "Or something for cavalry to use if we ever get some horses. Tell me, how many of these can you make, and why not utilize your assembly method for some other type of weapon?"

If Franklin was disappointed at the less than enthusiastic reception his weapon had just received, he didn't show it. "When we get going, an initial goal will be ten of these a day. We can improve upwards as we continue to learn. Within a couple of months, I hope to be building a hundred a day. However, if you are not interested in that many of my Franklins, I am certain I can adapt my methods to other killing devices."

Schuyler nodded solemnly. "Such as muskets?"

"Indeed."

"And rifles?"

"The problem of cutting the grooves in the barrel is enormous."

Schuyler smiled. "Then work on it, will you?"

Owen Wells went looking for Faith Benton. He wanted to get her alone so he could talk to her, but that was proving unlikely as she was either working making Franklin's guns, or with her cousin Sarah, or with her father. He wanted to tell her that she was the loveliest thing he had ever seen. Owen had never been in love before, so he had no idea how to proceed. He alternated between periods of deep despondency and great elation. It was like he had been reborn. If only Faith might return his affections.

Sometimes he thought his position as her suitor was hopeless. She was beautiful, and he was nothing more than a stumpy caricature of a man with bulging shoulders and overlong and heavily muscled arms. Perhaps she would laugh at him. She had seemed friendly enough when they traveled from the battle on the Ohio to Fort Washington, but that was back then and he had helped save her life, and this was now and she was safe and secure. Worse, she was surrounded by young men who not only outranked him but looked normal. He didn't care. He had to know.

Finally, he was in luck. She came out of the women's quarters and just stood there, breathing deeply of a crisp afternoon, a shawl wrapped loosely around her shoulders. She was so beautiful.

"Good morning, Miss Faith," he said and walked slowly up to her. She turned and smiled at him in recognition.

"I believe it's afternoon, Mister Wells."

He flushed. What a wonderful way to start a conversation with the woman he dreamed about. He'd just shown her that he couldn't tell time. "I've been so busy it's easy to get confused."

"I know that feeling."

"I just wanted to speak to you, to let you know that I'll be leaving."

Was that dismay he saw on her face? "Where are you going?"

"I'll be leading a patrol out to the east, in search of Redcoats and their friends."

"You'll be leading it? But I thought you were only a corporal?"

"I was, but Major Drake suggested that I should be a lieutenant because of my experience in the Royal Marines and General Tallmadge agreed. So now I am an officer," although, he didn't add, one of the most junior ones in the entire American army.

She grinned. "And a gentleman?"

"Oh, I hope so," he said and spoke more boldly than he felt. "And I was wondering if you might like to go for a walk with a gentleman? Or perhaps just sit and talk?"

Faith was touched. The short, squat young man was only

slightly taller than she and only a couple of years older, but she knew his story and that he had been aged beyond those years by events far beyond his control.

For that matter, so had she. Her experiences at the hands of Sheriff Braxton's deputies were something she could not put out of her mind, even though she tried to make light of them when talking with Sarah. Wells had to be aware that something awful had occurred to her back east, but that didn't seem to bother him. Perhaps equally awful things had happened to him on board a British warship? And why not, she thought. He would have been a boy among older, stronger men. She'd heard terrible stories about what happened to boys surrounded by predatory older men.

Faith tightened her shawl around her shoulders. He looked so frightened at being with her and that she might say no thank you to a walk. Perhaps she should say "boo" and see if he'd fall over or just run. No, she decided. He was just too nice a young man.

"A walk would be nice, but not too long a one. I wouldn't want you catching a chill before your first patrol."

"Good idea."

She smiled warmly. "Perhaps after, we can sit by a fire and talk."

# Chapter 6 ★ ★ ★ ★ ★ ★ ★ ★ ★ ★ ★ ★ ★ ★ ★ ★ ★

MAJOR JAMES FITZROY ARRIVED BACK AT THE ROOMS HE shared with Hannah Doorn—no, make that Hannah Van Doorn. He was nearly shaking with anger and frustration.

"What is the matter, my dear lordship?" Hannah teased, trying to amuse him out of his anger.

"Anything and everything," he groaned. "I have just found out what a treacherous viper General Banastre Tarleton is, and to make matters worse, I am to blame for some of the evil he is doing. I do not understand how people in England can consider him to be a hero and a saint, while those in the colonies more accurately portray him as a criminal. I accept that war is a ruthless profession by its very nature, but he goes beyond the limits of decency, and I don't just mean killing prisoners or abusing civilians. I mean atrocities."

She smiled, asked him to be seated and calm himself, and poured him a cup of real coffee. Very few in Detroit had access to real coffee and the aroma was magnificent. It was one of the benefits of her association with the Jewish merchant. She waited until he took a couple of sips and felt more composed.

"That is so good," he said with a sigh.

"And now you may tell me what troubles you."

"Do you know what a loose cannon is, my dear? No? Well, it is a term that I believe comes from the navy. If a cannon on a ship breaks loose during a storm, it can career all over the ship, injuring and killing people, smashing things, and causing enormous damage to the ship until it is either gotten under control or hurled overboard. Some ships have been sunk by loose cannon, both literally and metaphorically."

"And Banastre Tarleton is such a loose cannon?"

"Indeed. He makes up his own rules and they are brutal. It has just come to Burgoyne's notice that Tarleton has been sending out raiders to pillage, torture, rape, and slaughter innocent civilians who happen to be in between the rebels at Fort Washington and here. He wished to convince the rebels that Indians are doing the attacking, which would cause the rebels to retaliate against the red savages, which would then cause the Indians to fight on our side. Even if the Americans won such a war, which is very likely, it would distract and weaken the bloody rebels."

"Awful," she said thoughtfully. "I suppose it makes some appalling sense from a military standpoint since it would necessarily weaken his enemies, but how absolutely terrible. But how do you know all this?"

Fitzroy sipped some more coffee. How marvelous it was and how wonderful it was to have someone like Hannah to confide in. He considered himself to be a truly fortunate man. Perhaps the colonies weren't as uncivilized as he first thought.

"It began with tavern rumors that we immediately pooh-poohed as coming from loudmouthed drunks either bragging or complaining. After all, who would even think of doing such horrible things? Then several men who had served with the monster in charge of these forays began to speak up. They'd left because they couldn't stomach being part of the atrocities. Burgoyne heard of them, talked to them, and then confronted Tarleton with what he'd learned."

"What happened then?"

"Tarleton laughed at Burgoyne; absolutely just laughed right in his face. In effect called him soft and an old woman for caring about the plight of civilians. He said the purpose of war was to kill the enemy and it didn't matter if the enemy was old or young, man or woman, they had to be destroyed. He said that anyone between here and the rebel enclave was presumed to be a rebel and should be hunted down and killed like dogs. Burgoyne was appalled. He asked if Tarleton had heard of a lady named Jane McCrea. Have you?"

"Of course," Hannah said solemnly. "She was the young lady

who was murdered by Burgoyne's Indians during his advance to Saratoga in '77."

"Yes, and it didn't matter at all to the Indians who murdered her that she was a Tory and not a rebel. She was an innocent, and it meant that people thought Burgoyne was hell bent on killing innocents. It inflamed the frontier and brought many hundreds, if not thousands, of undecided Colonials into the rebel camp, which was a major factor in Burgoyne's defeat at Saratoga."

Fitzroy managed a small laugh. "At least it was a major factor in Burgoyne's mind. He was able to blame the Indians on his defeat rather than his other shortcomings. Regardless, Burgoyne was determined not to let that happen again, and here he finds that Tarleton is doing exactly the same thing and laughing about it."

"What did Burgoyne do?"

"He ordered Tarleton to stop the attacks and call back his wolves. Tarleton said it was impossible. He said they operated on their own and without plans, and he had no idea where they were. He said he didn't expect to see them until spring. He's lying, of course. There must be a rendezvous point or some other means of getting messages to those animals."

She sprawled out on the bed and allowed the bottom of her robe to open, showing her shapely legs. "But why does that bother you so much, my noble little major?"

"Because I enlisted the monster who is preying on the innocents," he said angrily. "His name is Braxton, and back in Albany, I gave him a commission as a militia captain since, as I recall, he already led a group of about fifty armed men. His face was terribly burned and his hands were mutilated and he hated the rebels for maiming him. But I never thought his hatred would cause him to rape and murder when I sent him off to Detroit and Tarleton's sublime leadership."

Hannah walked over, sat on his lap and held his head in her hands, then buried his face in the warmth of her bosom. "Now how could you have predicted what this Braxton would have done, or that Tarleton would give him such odious directions? You couldn't, my dear major, so please quit blaming yourself for the actions of others." Curiously, she realized she meant what she'd said.

Fitzroy took a deep breath and exhaled slowly. She was right, of course. She was almost always right and he appreciated that. "You are good for me, Hannah Van Doorn."

"I know," she purred. She undid the strings of her bodice and let her breasts fall free. His lips quickly found her nipples and she felt herself becoming aroused. She would have to get this tantalizing information to Abraham Goldman so he could forward it to Fort Washington, but not right now. Fitzroy's hands had begun caressing the moistness of her inner thighs, and her body was responding as it always did to his gentle touch. The damned war could wait for an hour. Maybe a couple.

Sarah was surprised and pleased to see Will. "I thought you'd left?"

"And I thought you'd be glad I'm still here."

She tapped him on the arm and smiled warmly. "Of course I am. I had just reconciled myself to being without the pleasure of your company while you tramped around the wet and soggy forest looking for Redcoats."

"Apparently something's come up. General Tallmadge wants me to accompany him to one of the hospitals tonight. It seems there's a very unusual patient."

Sarah nodded grimly. "I know and I will be there too. Mr. Franklin has a similar appointment tonight at the hospital and it must be for the same reason. I am to accompany him and make sure he doesn't get into any difficulties. Sometimes he's forgetful."

That evening the small group assembled in the foyer of the small wooden building they grandly called a hospital. A short and youthful-looking man named Jonathan Young said he was a physician and guided them in. Franklin murmured to Sarah that his name was quite appropriate and she noted that the doctor seemed quite nervous.

"Not too many beds are occupied right now," Young said. "It'll be different when the fighting really starts. Right now all I've got are a couple of fevers and some broken bones brought about by brawling and accidents. Nothing that purging, bleeding, and leeching won't cure."

Sarah shuddered. She had no idea just how leeching or bleeding might help a sick or hurt person, but she'd always accepted it on face value because it was such a traditional way of caring for the sick and injured. But purging? Violently emptying her bowels had nearly killed her when she was in the stocks, so how could it possibly help, and particularly if a person was already weakened? She wondered if the same applied to leeching and bleeding. If so, did the medical profession know anything at all about how the human body worked?

Doctor Young guided them into a small room off the main ward. "We keep sick females in here. When there are no women patients, which is usually the case, we use it for storage."

One cot lay in the middle of the room. Boxes surrounded it, there was little light, and the air was stifling.

Will stepped in front of Sarah as she held back. She didn't know whether or not she wanted to see what was lying in the bed. Will leaned over and stared at the creature swathed in bandages and blankets.

"A girl," Will said, "A child."

"A little older," Tallmadge said grimly and Doctor Young nodded.

"What happened to her?" Will asked.

"We're not certain," Tallmadge said. "She was found in the woods by one of our patrols investigating rumors of an attack on a settlement. She was stumbling around the ruins, naked, burned and bleeding."

"Dear God," said Franklin, "The poor child."

Tallmadge continued. "The patrol located the settlement and found a stack of charred bodies in what might have been a barn. They had been butchered and burned, reduced to a pile of blackened bones and grease. The girl was able to say that her name was Winifred Haskill and that horrible looking white men had destroyed her home. Then she collapsed and hasn't spoken since then. The men in the patrol weren't certain she'd live long enough to make it here, but she surprised them."

Eyes turned to the doctor who added solemnly, "She turns and moans, but she hasn't said anything that makes sense. It may be that her brain has been affected. She did endure a savage blow to the head."

"And what do you plan to do about her?" Will asked.

"She is wrapped in bandages because of a multitude of scratches and bruises, including one large cut on her head where someone may have tried to scalp her. I have applied salves to her burns, which, while looking horrible, aren't serious. Otherwise, her body is that of a healthy young woman. I took a cup of blood from her this morning, and plan to purge her in a little while. A cleansing of the bowels often helps the mind think correctly."

Will took one of the girl's thin, pale arms and lifted it. "I don't think she has much left to purge or bleed."

Sarah looked at him and held back a smile. It was exactly what she was thinking.

"I believe I understand my medicine, Major," Doctor Young sniffed.

"But do you understand women's medicine?" Sarah injected and enjoyed the confusion on the doctor's face. "Not only are our bodies different, but the way women use them is different from those of men. Tell me, how many babies have you delivered? How many cases of serious menstrual bleeding have you treated? Or tumors of the breast? Oh yes, how many women have you examined when they were naked?"

Doctor Young was flustered, and seemed embarrassed that such would be discussed in mixed company. "None at all," he admitted.

"Then let me propose a solution to this dilemma," she said, suddenly aware that Abigail Adams had entered the room and was standing behind her, nodding grimly. "Remand her to my care and I will treat her, woman to woman."

"And I will assist," said Abigail.

The doctor bowed and Sarah sensed his relief. "I accept your collective wisdom."

"And where will you treat her?" asked Franklin. The look of dismay on his face said he already knew the answer.

"She will sleep in my room," said Sarah, "and I will sleep on a cot."

"And I will be there every day to help," Abigail said and patted Franklin on the cheek, "so you will not lose out on the skills of your precious and indispensable clerk. I am certain that other women in the camp, such as Mistress Greene and Mistress Morgan will be more than willing to aid us."

Daniel Morgan and his wife, along with several dozen riflemen, had recently arrived. Even though he too was ill, Morgan was a welcome addition to the list of general officers.

Doctor Young managed a smile. "I am thoroughly delighted as well as outranked."

They took a cot from the hospital and transported the unconscious Winifred the short distance to Franklin's quarters. Abigail Adams walked alongside the cot and gazed sadly on the injured young woman. Sarah walked behind, with Will.

"The doctor meant well," she said.

"Doctors are bloody useless unless they can stitch a cut or fix a broken bone," Will said. "When they start to think, they become dangerous because they feel they know so much and they truly don't."

Sarah slipped her arm in his. It seemed so natural and comfortable. "Now when are you leaving?"

"Tomorrow. I should be back in no more than six weeks."

"Will you be seeing young Lieutenant Wells?"

His mission was not public knowledge, but why not tell her? "I expect to meet with him somewhere near Detroit. Why?"

"Because my silly cousin Faith is fond of him and wants him safely back."

"Do you want me safely back?" Will asked.

Sarah smiled and kissed him gently on the cheek. "Very much so, Will Drake."

From Fort Washington to Detroit was about three hundred miles. A lean and strong woodsman could stride out at four miles per hour for ten hours a day, which meant that he could make the trip in less than two grueling weeks.

Unfortunately, Will was still not in as good a shape as he once had been, and the route taken was not a straight line conducive to quick journeys. It took him several days to even begin to be able to sustain the long, loping stride of a true woodsman. Then he forced himself and the others to make up lost time. Their goal was the farm of a man named Jean Leduc.

Leduc's farm stood directly across the river from Detroit. Like others, he owned a strip of the riverfront where he docked a small boat and a canoe. His actual farmland ran in a narrow band inland and well into the woods. From his cabin and barn, anyone could see much of what was going on across the river in Detroit, half a mile away.

Jean Leduc was a small, thin man about fifty. His hair was wild and scraggly and his eyes burned with hatred for the British. They had killed his brother on the Plains of Abraham in 1757 and wounded Jean in the same battle, which caused him to walk with a limp.

His left hand was mangled. He'd been briefly captured by Joseph Brant's Iroquois, and a squaw had happily chewed parts of it off while he screamed in agony. This had greatly amused the Iroquois braves.

Leduc had no great love for the upstart Americans, either, but decided that anyone who wanted to kill British soldiers was the lesser of evils. At least the Americans alleged to tolerate Catholics, while the British often persecuted them. He had to admit, however, that the British had left his coreligionists in Quebec pretty much alone.

When Will arrived at the farm, he made sure he did so after crossing the river at night and downstream from the British fort and town. There were few people around, but why advertise his presence until and if it became necessary.

Leduc greeted him without much warmth and made him get into a barn where he waited with a surprised Owen Wells.

"Is this our prison, Owen?"

"No sir," Wells grinned. "It's just Leduc's way of showing us this is his place and he's in charge. It also means he'll help us but he doesn't love us. Although he doesn't want too much attention drawn to us, he's not really worried."

And that was the beauty of the operation. As a semi-cripple, Leduc was always hiring men to help work his farm. Thus, the presence of one, two, or even three men was not unusual. Nor was it strange that they were generally transients who never stayed long. Leduc had a reputation as a bad-tempered Frenchman and a selfish bastard who frequently tried to cheat his help out of their wages.

They went to the barn's second floor loft and looked out across the river onto Detroit. A number of distant buildings had lamps or candles glowing faintly through the night. They were close enough to see people walking around, and the superb Royal Navy telescope given him by Tallmadge brought them into even more detail. Outside the fort, hundreds, perhaps thousands, of campfires twinkled and flickered and showed the dim shapes of a multitude of white tents. It was an impressive display of British might. More than a score of flatboats or barges were arrayed along the riverside and others were under construction.

Wells said. "It's even better in the day, Major. There will be thousands of Redcoats marching around."

"It's amazing we're safe here."

"Oh, I think they know someone's watching them, it's just that they don't think there's much we can do, regardless of what we see, and then there's the fact that his lordship, Bloody Tarleton, doesn't want to piss off General Haldimand in Quebec by coming over to this side and roughing up the farmers."

Prior to the colonist's revolution, frontier areas like Detroit had fallen under the jurisdiction of the British governor in Quebec. After the war, the boundaries had been redrawn so that anything south of the Great Lakes fell under Cornwallis in New York. Therefore, the land across the river from Detroit was considered part of Quebec-controlled Canadian territory. Haldimand, no admirer of either Tarleton or Burgoyne, had let it be known that no British soldiers other than his would be permitted to operate on the Canadian side of the river. So far, Tarleton had been cowed by Haldimand and it was presumed that Burgoyne would obey the rules as well.

"Tarleton and Haldimand," Owen said, "It sounds like a theatrical group."

"And a bad one at that," said Will. "By the way, my men are camped with yours."

Neither man had arrived alone in the area, but had shown up alone at the Leduc farm. Another ten men awaited their return a few miles into the woods. They were near a tavern owned by men Tallmadge said were sympathizers to the American cause.

"Sir, did you see Faith?"

Will couldn't stifle a grin. "I did, and she said to tell you she misses you and wants you to come back as soon as possible."

"Would it be all right if I left right now?"

Will laughed and punched him lightly on the arm. "It would not. Now tell me, what will farmer Leduc have us do tomorrow?"

"We will work in his fields and take frequent breaks just like the shiftless bastards he usually hires. This will enable us to observe the comings and goings as best we can from over here."

Will thought of Tallmadge's request for information and still more information. "Any chance of our actually getting into Detroit?"

Now it was Owen's turn to smile. "He and I have been talking about it. He does cross the river on occasion and likes the thought of insolently parading American soldiers inside a British fort."

Will yawned. The rigors of the journey were catching up to him. "I like the idea, too. However, I think we should get some sleep if we're going to have to pretend we're farmers."

★    ★    ★

"The girl takes nourishment, but doesn't speak," Sarah said and Franklin nodded thoughtfully. She ran her hand through the wispy hair on the Winifred's bandaged head. Sarah and Abigail had cut it extremely short to make it easier to treat her cuts and burns, and it made her look even more skeletal then she was.

Sarah continued. "She takes broth and even mushy solids and seems to be gaining strength. Her bruises are going away and the cut on her head is healing. Sometimes her eyes open and she seems to be looking at me, but then she closes them and goes back to sleep. I worry that we may be losing her."

Franklin reached down and took Winifred Haskill's small hand in his. He marveled at the fact that it was colder and frailer than his. "When you are sick, doesn't it feel better when you awaken after a good, long sleep?"

"Of course. Are you saying that this deep sleep is a natural way for the body to heal itself?"

"Not the body, Sarah. More likely it is the mind that is trying to heal itself, perhaps even the soul, if there is such a thing. We know so little about healing the body, as you've learned from Doctor Young, and we know so much less of the problems of the mind and the soul. We are total illiterates in those areas."

"I didn't know you believed in a soul, Doctor Franklin."

"Some days, my dear Sarah, I don't know what I believe. While I certainly believe in a supreme being, I have no idea what shape or form it takes, or what interest it might have in our activities. For instance, does a god really care if young Mistress Haskill lives or dies?"

Sarah nodded. "Perhaps he doesn't care if anyone lives or dies. Perhaps god just permits things to happen, which would explain such things as war and plague."

Franklin smiled. She was so very smart. "Perhaps someday you will have the honor of talking to Thomas Jefferson. He is a very complex man with equally complex beliefs."

He sighed and continued. "In the meantime we shall concern ourselves with Mistress Haskill. I've spoken to some of the men who found her and they say that the place where she lived was a place of absolute and bloody devastation."

"I know. I spoke to some of them as well."

"Our soldiers think she escaped from the bodies of her family while the fire was just beginning and crawled her way into a cellar before she either suffocated or burned to death. Perhaps the pain of the flames even awakened her. They found a tunnel leading from the cellar to the woods. It must have been put there to provide for just such a need to escape, either from fire, or storm, or the depraved animals that call themselves men, and that is how she made her way to the forest where she was found. It's no wonder to me that she stopped speaking after giving her name. Perhaps she gave it so that we would have something to put on her gravestone."

Sarah shuddered at the thought. "But will she get better?"

"Only she knows," Franklin replied softly. "And right now she isn't telling. Some people say I'm a great and intelligent man, but situations like this make me realize just how ignorant I am."

"Does she even know that we won't harm her?"

"Have you told her that, Sarah?"

Sarah nodded. "I hold her hand and whisper to her. I say her name and keep saying that she's safe. Sometimes she seems to moan. Mistress Adams does it as well, and sometimes Mistress Greene takes a turn even though it means leaving her ill husband. We try not to leave her alone too much in case she should awaken and be frightened at being in such a strange place, but we do have other things to do."

"Then keep doing it as much as you can. No possible harm can come to her. And if she should awaken and be frightened, then we shall have to deal with it."

Franklin left the room. Sarah sat on a stool beside Winifred, took her hand, and talked to her. She told her that she was safe and free. She told her how beautiful the outside world looked, even though the new-fallen snow had done little more than cover the mud. Sarah told her a little gossip, such as how Faith was moping for a soldier who had gone away. She thought it was good to include mentions of family and the gossip of Fort Washington as a dose of the new reality.

At length, Sarah tired. She went to leave Winifred and catch up on her neglected clerical duties. On impulse, she turned and saw Winifred Haskill's eyes wide open and watching her. Sarah moved to the stool and sat down. The two looked at each other. Sarah felt like she was being measured, assessed.

"Will you remain with us, Winifred Haskill? Or will you go back to the dark place where you've been?"

The corners of the girl's mouth flickered in what might have been the beginnings of a smile. "Yes," she whispered. "I think I'll stay for a bit."

Leduc was amenable to the idea of taking them across the river, even though there was ice drifting downstream. "Mostly mush," he said disparagingly. "Try not to fall in, though. The cold'll grab your nuts in an icy grip and you'll die in just a few minutes."

"We'll keep it in mind," Will said, unable to stop his hand from moving to his groin.

Still, Leduc wanted them to wait a couple of days before crossing. He said he wanted their presence to be noted as normal around the farm. Will also suspected that the old bastard wanted some work done before the two men gathered their information and departed.

When they finally did cross, they took a rowboat to push through the ice rather than a more fragile canoe, and Leduc, for once grinning happily, let Will and Owen do all the work. It was proper, he said, since they were supposed to be his hired hands.

"We are going into the belly of the beast," said Owen.

Will thought much the same thing, although the beast seemed almighty disinterested in their coming. No one glanced more than casually at them, and only a couple of men waved at Leduc, whose presence in and around Detroit was clearly considered normal.

Will tried to take in the area with a soldier's eye even though he knew it was extremely unlikely they'd ever attack the place. The ground was flat to gently rolling, and the area had been largely denuded of trees. These had gone to build small but sturdy Fort Lernoult. More wood had gone to make the flimsy stockade that surrounded the town, and the town itself, as well as for use as firewood. Farms had sprung up on the Detroit side and sent thin fingers of cultivated land inland, like Leduc's on the other side of the Detroit River. Will noted that a large number of buildings and homes had been built outside the fort. Apparently, there was no longer any threat from Indians, which was interesting since Pontiac's uprising and subsequent siege of Detroit had taken place only a couple of decades earlier. Of course, the presence of the British Army had a lot to do with that sense of security.

As they walked towards the town's wooden wall, Will found it a cause of wonderment that British soldiers walked by and past them without apparently noticing them.

"Arrogant bastards, aren't they," whispered Leduc. "I'd like to slice their fucking throats."

They entered the town of Detroit with only a nod to the guards. Leduc explained that the guards around Lernoult and the town proper belonged to the regular garrison of fewer than a hundred men and he knew most of them by sight. A transplanted Dutchman, Colonel Arent de Peyster, commanded them. The garrison troops hated the new arrivals since they clogged the taverns and chased what few women there were. The regular garrison couldn't wait for Burgoyne's army to depart so they could get back to their comfortable existence.

"What kind of man is this de Peyster?" Will asked.

"He's fairly decent. He won't hang you unless it's absolutely necessary." He laughed when he saw the look on Will's face. "No, he's quite genial and tolerant for an British officer. He took over from Richard Lernoult who built the citadel, and is a far, far better man than Henry Hamilton, the lieutenant governor who was known as the 'hairbuyer' because he delighted in buying the scalps of rebels. He didn't much care if the scalps came from women or children."

"Still, we will have to watch out for de Peyster's men," Will said. "They will likely be able to recognize most of the locals and might wonder where we came from."

"We will indeed," he said and pointed to a close by wooden building. "But now we will go to this store that has a barn. It's where we will buy feed and supplies that I don't need," Leduc said. "That will be my excuse for being here in case I should happen to need one. There is a loft above the barn where you can go and observe."

The barn was quite large, and they went into the back of it and up a ladder to the loft. The owner was a friend of Leduc's and a rebel sympathizer who said he was going out and discreetly left them alone. The loft overlooked a narrow road that led to a two-story log building that had been whitewashed. Sentries stood guard around it.

Leduc came and crouched beside them and sucked on his pipe. He'd lit it from a candle in the owner's office. Will thought it was dangerous to smoke a pipe in a barn filled with hay and straw, but declined to comment. Leduc was touchy enough without some stranger telling him how to live.

"Are you happy, Major Drake? You are now staring at the headquarters of Tarleton the butcher and Burgoyne the fool. Major De Peyster knows enough to stay in his little fort and leave them alone. Since there was no room for them in Fort Lernoult, the British command has had to make its headquarters in the town."

"I wonder if we could break in and find some information of use to us," Will mused.

Leduc laughed harshly. "First, Major, I don't think you could break in and, even if you did, what would you find that you don't already know? They are coming in the spring and, if there is any reason at all for the boats, at least some of the soldiers or their supplies will arrive by water." Leduc yawned. "Don't even think of trying to get in. I would have a devil of a time explaining why the men I hired as temporary labor had to be hanged."

"Then there's no real point in us being here, is there?" Owen asked.

"Not really, although please recall that this was your idea," Leduc said and added a Gallic shrug. "So I hope you are enjoying yourselves and will be satisfied soon so I can get home."

Will admitted that Leduc was right. It was nothing more than curiosity that brought them to the barn, although it was fascinating to see impeccably dressed and high-ranking British officers strutting about the headquarters only a literal stone's throw away.

He stiffened as another distinguished looking officer left the building. "Is that Benedict Arnold?"

Leduc chuckled. "That is the lord high traitor himself. No one likes him and I wonder if he can even stand himself. Burgoyne, Tarleton, and Grant are trying to figure a way to get him out of Detroit and away from the campaign."

Another man left the headquarters. He wore an officer's coat, but was decidedly unmilitary. "Joseph Brant," Leduc muttered angrily. "I didn't know he was here."

"This means he's brought Indian allies," Will said. Brant was half-Mohawk and half English, and had allied the Iroquois with the British in the revolution.

"Of course has brought his goddamned Iroquois," Leduc snarled, thinking of his mangled hand. "I hate those savages more than I hate the English."

"And why is it that you hate the English?" Will asked. "I know they killed your brother, but that was war. Haven't they treated you well since then?"

Leduc took another pull on his pipe. "They think they have treated me well, but I hate them because the English are liars and frauds. I am French and Catholic and they hate the French and Catholics. They tolerate us French men and women and they will tolerate our faith only for as long as they have to. When they have achieved full dominance here, which means after they have crushed you poor fools, they will turn on my people and treat them as poorly as they now treat Catholics in Ireland."

He blew smoke from his pipe towards Will. The tobacco was less than cheap and Will nearly gagged. "Personally, I don't care what happens to Englishmen who fight other Englishmen, especially since I don't trust your people at this Liberty place any more than I trust the English. Still, you seem to be the best possibility from a batch of very bad choices."

Will didn't comment. He did, however, think that sighting Brant made the foray into Detroit at least a little bit worthwhile. Still, it was time to go. Perhaps they could have a drink at a tavern and listen to post gossip. No, he decided, that would be too foolhardy. Time to get away safely. He nudged Owen and they stood up.

"Hey!" came a loud voice from the ladder. "What the hell are you sons of bitches doing up there?"

# Chapter 7 ★★★★★★★★★★★★★★★★★★

WILL FROZE AS TWO BURLY BRITISH SOLDIERS CLIMBED UP and joined them on the loft. One of them, a sergeant, pointed at Leduc. "I asked you what you were doing up here?"

Leduc smiled thinly, "Just trying to avoid work while minding the store for my friend, Sergeant. Is there something you wish to buy?"

The sergeant looked around and then out the window. He took in the view of his army's headquarters. He turned and glowered at them. "There was, but not anymore. I don't know what you were doing up here, but I think it's possible you're all spies."

"Sweet Jesus," exclaimed Leduc, "How can you say that? You must have seen me before. I live here. I have a farm just across the river. How can you dare call me a spy?"

"Maybe you are loyal and maybe I'm King George." The sergeant smiled wickedly and pulled a bayonet from its scabbard. They did not have their muskets, which was normal if they were simply running an errand. To counter the soldiers' bayonets, Will and the others had their hunting knives. Will noted that Owen had slid to the soldiers' side and a little to their rear. Will tried not to look at him. The two Redcoats had apparently dismissed the short and shabbily dressed Owen as a possible threat.

"What I think," said the sergeant, "is that we should have the provost talk to you."

Will's spirits sank. If they were taken, he had no idea how he would get out of this mess. Owen's accent was Welsh, and his own was from the east, while he had his branding scar. No one would believe they were farm help for Leduc. He saw another prison for himself and hanging for Owen, and God only knew what for Leduc.

"Non!" screamed Leduc as he hurled himself at the sergeant. At the same moment, Owen took the sergeant in the rear and wrapped his powerful arms around the man's throat. Will grabbed the second soldier, who was shocked by the suddenness of the assault. He kicked the soldier in the groin and he dropped like a sack, gasping and clutching his crotch. Leduc fell backwards and Owen tightened his grip on the sergeant's neck, which gave with a sickening crack. Will took out his knife and rammed it into the other soldier's chest. In seconds, he was as dead as the sergeant.

"Jesus, Major, what have we done?" Owen's eyes were wide with astonishment.

Will was gasping. He'd never killed a man so close up like that. "I think we've outlived our welcome. We've got to leave, right Leduc?"

Leduc's answer was a groan. He lay on his back with the sergeant's bayonet sticking out of his stomach. "My God," said Will. "We've got to get you out of here."

"Too late," gasped Leduc. "A knife in the gut kills. It may take a while, but it always kills."

Will sagged. Leduc was right. If the rising stench was any indication, the bayonet had ripped his stomach and bowels. The wound would be fatal and agonizingly painful. Nor could they move him out of the barn. There was no way they could hide such a seriously wounded man.

"I will die here," Leduc said with great difficulty. "Hide the two bodies."

Will and Owen buried the two dead British soldiers underneath a pile of straw.

"Now you will leave me," said Leduc. "You will take the boat and slowly row across the river like nothing is wrong. If anyone asks, and it is most likely that they won't, you will tell them that I am fornicating with a whore and you will come back for me in the morning. They will believe that because it is what I have done in the past. Now go."

The statement exhausted Leduc. Blood continued to seep from the wound. If they removed the bayonet, it would gush. Leduc was indeed dying.

They made Leduc as comfortable as they could. He asked for his pipe and some flints and they left them beside him. They walked out of the barn, down the street, and past the guards at the gate. The guards, of course, were not at all concerned about people leaving the fort, only those coming in, and made no notice of them.

They pushed the boat out into the water and rowed slowly across the river. It seemed ten times wider than before. Poor Leduc. Will hoped he was dead before anyone found him and could question him. Of course, someone was bound to recall that he'd come across with two companions and, sooner rather than later, someone would miss the two British soldiers. He and Owen would pack up and return to Fort Washington as quickly as they could.

They were pulling the boat onto the Canadian shore when they heard a strident clanging behind from the fort. Alarm bells? Had Leduc and the dead soldiers been discovered? No. A plume of black, greasy smoke was starting to billow upwards and it came from behind the stockade and just about where they'd left Leduc.

"God bless that man," Owen said softly, and Will agreed. There would be no alarm for them and no one would chase them, at least not right now. Jean Leduc had set fire to the barn and it was beginning to rage furiously. It was the funeral pyre of a hero.

Dispatches, reports, and orders that needed to be registered and copied were the bane of any staff officer, and Major James Fitzroy was heartily sick and tired of them all. He wished that neither the printing press nor paper had ever been invented. Damn Gutenberg and damn the Egyptians. Or was it the Phoenicians? He longed for the moment when his day would be over and he could leave the stifling atmosphere of Burgoyne's headquarters and return to the loving arms of Hannah Van Doorn. At least he thought that her arms were loving. Sometimes he had the nagging feeling that she was using him, but then, that was only fair since he was using her.

Love was unlikely, but he was fond of the little Dutch wench, and felt that she was fond of him. He would settle for life as it is, rather than as it could be.

He yawned. He was tired, bored, and the fire in the stove was overheating the room and making him drowsy. He shook himself awake. It would not be good to be found napping while at work.

Burgoyne might laugh, but Benedict Arnold was around and that arrogant turncoat shit would tear him apart.

Danforth entered the little room off Burgoyne's office and dropped another pile of papers on Fitzroy's desk. "It never ends," Danforth commented.

"I'd rather be in battle," Fitzroy muttered. "This is no fate for a soldier. In battle I might die honorably. Here I might die of boredom or worse, be suffocated under piles of paperwork."

"Then you shouldn't have told anyone how literate you are. Then you could be an infantry officer out there in the freezing muck with your men who, of course, would hate you and would, if the opportunity arose, run a bayonet up your ass and call it a regrettable accident."

Fitzroy laughed. "Thank you for your perceptive observation. You're right. At least we are both warm and dry. Now, is there anything of note in that pile of rubbish?"

"Nothing of importance, but one item that is mildly interesting. It seems we are to be honored by the presence of one Erich von Bamberg, a colonel in the army of the Kingdom of Hesse."

"I thought Hesse was a duchy. One of a hundred or so making up that chaotic mess called Germany."

"I don't know and I don't rightly care," said Danforth. "It can be a caliphate run by fucking Hindus for all that it matters to me."

Fitzroy told him the Moslems had caliphates, not the Hindus and received an insulting sound for his efforts. He checked the clock on the table. It was almost time for him to be able to stop working without getting anyone upset at his leaving early, especially since Burgoyne, Tarleton, and Grant, were elsewhere. "And why is the Caliph of Hesse descending on us?"

"He has been sent to capture soldiers from Hesse and the other German states who have deserted and who have been reported to be with the rebels at Fort Washington. Apparently their collective Germanic majesties are insulted by such treasons. They are further upset because they no longer have the soldiers to hire out to the highest bidder."

"I wish Herr Bamberg well," Fitzroy said insincerely. Like most Britons, he thought little of the innumerable petty German princelings. They were almost as bad as the countless minor royalty in India. He sniffed the air. A pungent smell assailed his nose. Burning wood and burning meat? "What the devil is that?"

At that instant, an alarm bell began to clang and the two men grabbed their coats and ran outdoors. A fire was burning on the second floor of a barn a little ways off. As they watched in horror, flames erupted and the wind began to whip burning ashes through the air.

"This is going to be bad," Danforth said grimly. A dozen small fires were already beginning on the tightly clustered wooden roofs. With fire suddenly everywhere, people were running around in a panic.

Fitzroy grabbed Danforth's arm. "Run back in, grab what you can of our sacred papers, and then run like the devil for the eastern gate. This whole bloody town is going to go up in smoke."

The two men ran in and in only a few moments were outside with important papers stuffed into bags and anything else that would hold them. Others in the offices were doing the same thing. The roof of the headquarters was smoldering and a half dozen other buildings were in flames. The barn where the fire apparently began was a raging inferno. Fitzroy thought he could smell burning flesh. It had to be a horse or cow, he thought. It couldn't be human, could it?

"Get out of the stockade immediately," Fitzroy ordered as loudly as he could, and the others ran to comply, joining a rapidly growing exodus from inside the walls of Detroit.

More and more flaming ashes were falling and Fitzroy needed no further urging to depart. A swirling downdraft covered him with embers. The smoke blinded him and made him cough. He staggered through the fort's gate and out into the open air. In front of him, a soldier was on fire. He hurled himself into a muddy puddle and rolled over to put it out, cursing, crying, and terrified, but not badly hurt.

Fitzroy checked himself over and saw that his uniform was singed, but not burning. The back of his left hand was red and blistering from a falling ember, but he was otherwise unharmed. More and more people thronged out and gathered in the fields outside Detroit. They stood in shock as the cramped wooden buildings of Detroit were devoured by flames.

By the river, Fitzroy saw Benedict Arnold leading soldiers as they frantically pushed the precious barges into the water. A couple of the raw wooden craft were on fire and workmen were frantically trying to put out the flames with buckets of water drawn from the river. All around, British soldiers were striking their tents so the ashes wouldn't land on the canvas and set them aflame as well. Winter was nearly on them and they would need the tents to survive. Fitzroy continued to move farther away from the fire. Finally, he was out of the smoke and falling ash. He took several deep breaths and his lungs began to clear.

A filthy and demoralized Danforth appeared beside him. "Bloody hell," Danforth said. "If this is sabotage, someone will hang for it."

Fitzroy watched as the flames consumed precious supplies and material. Barrels of gunpowder exploded while hundreds of soldiers continued to run or mill about in confusion and panic. The British Army had been routed by fire, an enemy far more fearsome than the rebels. "This is as bad as a defeat on the battlefield."

"Indeed," said General Burgoyne as he approached the two men who snapped to attention. The general's uniform was likewise filthy from soot. His face was set in anger. "Fitzroy, I want you to find out just what the devil happened."

"Yes sir."

"You will do that while the rest of us assess our losses and try to recoup them. It does look like General Arnold managed to save at least some of the barges, although at least several hundred of us will need a place to sleep tonight."

For a guilty moment, Fitzroy wondered just how Hannah Van Doorn had fared. He'd been too busy to think about her. Then he realized that the wind that had fed the fire had come from the west and that the rooms they shared were in a warehouse outside the stockade and to the west. With just a little luck, both she and their quarters were safe. It would be ironic if he had a bed tonight, while General Burgoyne did not. Then he realized that beds and cabins could be rebuilt. If anything had happened to Hannah, he'd be deeply saddened.

Across the river, Will and Owen continued to watch and to plan. Dozens of others had gathered on the Canadian riverfront and were watching the fire with morbid fascination. Despite the size of the blaze, they were safe, even though it appeared that the fire would rage for some time before running out of fuel.

"We should leave, Major," said Owen.

"Not yet," Will replied softly. "We'll wait until tonight. If we leave now, it'll look suspicious. Tonight we can take a couple of Leduc's horses, pick up our men, send the horses in a wrong direction, and be miles away before anyone realizes it. Besides, we should watch and assess the damage."

Owen nodded. "I wonder how the hell they're going to catch those barges?" Several were drifting downstream and didn't have anyone on board. "Maybe we could find one or two and set them on fire as well."

Will conceded that it wasn't a bad idea since they would have to go downriver to cross in the first place. Of course the odds of them finding even one of the barges were incredibly small, but it was a thought. More important, however, was the need to report to General Tallmadge at Fort Washington.

"Have you slept with Will Drake?" Faith asked her cousin as they sat in Benjamin Franklin's small office. Franklin was out on business of Congress, and Winifred Haskill was sleeping in another room.

"That's quite a question," Sarah Benton answered, "but the answer is no."

"Are you going to?"

"Perhaps, but not until he returns from his journey," she answered facetiously. "And why the questions? Are you sleeping with Owen? Or are you and he just having a little fun with each other?"

Faith grinned. Young women of her age and situation frequently did not have actual intercourse because of fear of premarital pregnancy. This would lead to being ostracized among a host of other problems, which included having to raise a bastard child. Still, many young women saw nothing wrong with mutually exploring each other's bodies and otherwise enjoying themselves with boys they liked. Just don't do anything that would cause a pregnancy, was the unwritten rule.

"No I haven't either, although I might when he comes back, too. You're right. It's a little difficult to manage right now." Faith sighed. "And why I asked the question is because I'm afraid he might not want me after all that happened to me."

"Does he know?"

"Yes. I told him."

Sarah did not think that was such a wonderful idea. After all, she had no intention of telling Will, or anyone else for that matter, about any previous young men with whom she'd had any sexual activity. He knew she'd been what she considered as married to Tom, but anything else was best buried in the past. But the damage to Faith, if any, was done. "And did he run away in fear?"

"Well, he did go to Detroit."

Sarah laughed. "I believe he was ordered to do so. Did he indicate that he would call on you when he came back?"

"Yes."

Sarah rolled her eyes. Her cousin was such a silly little twit at times. "Then wait for him and, when he does return, rush up to him and embrace him and suffocate him with affection and passion. That way he won't have a chance to think, especially with your ample breasts pressed against him."

Now it was Faith's turn to smile, and she did so wickedly. "Is that what you're going to do with Will?"

"I may," Sarah replied impishly, "I just may."

The door to the other room opened and Winifred entered, walking hesitantly. She was eating well and had gained some weight, but her face was still gaunt and many bruises remained, as did the terrible scar in her scalp. The fever was gone and she was more and more up and about, although walking with a serious limp.

"Are you feeling sorry for yourself, Faith?" Winifred asked.

"I suppose I am," Faith answered. "Aren't I entitled?"

Winifred looked at her coldly. "You consider that you were raped, don't you?"

"In a manner of speaking, yes."

"And so was I," Winifred said, "Raped by any number of men and then sodomized and then beaten and left for dead on a burning pyre made out of my own family. Yet I am trying to put that behind me to the extent that it's possible and get on with what I can salvage of my life, so please don't ask me to pity you."

"I'm sorry," Faith said softly. Winifred's horrors made hers seem irrelevant. It was also apparent that the very young Winifred was very intelligent and articulate.

"Are you sure you wish to talk about this?" Sarah said to Winifred.

There was anger and strength in the young girl's voice and a cold fire in her eyes. "Oh yes. I want to keep reminding myself so that I can feel good about killing the British when the time comes. And yes, I know it wasn't British soldiers who hurt me, but it was men whom the British hired and paid. Now, Faith, do you have any idea what a young boy like Owen might have endured in the Royal Navy?"

Faith shifted nervously. "He's hinted at some terrible things before he grew strong enough to defend himself."

"My father was a sailor and what others did to him at night in the bowels of the ship are part of the reason he too deserted and we settled so far away from the sea. The captains and admirals say it doesn't happen, but it does. They punish sailors when they are caught, but first they have to be caught, don't they? Such sodomy as occurs in Royal Navy ships is a crime against God and man, yet it happens and little is done to stop it."

"Your father told you?" Sarah said in astonishment that such a young girl could know so much.

"No, he told my mother and she told me so I could better understand his moods and his raging angers. We came out here to reject the world and find peace through God. Instead, I find that we cannot reject the world, and that there is no peace." She laughed harshly. "I often wonder if there even is a God."

"You said you would kill British, Winifred, just how do you intend to do this?" Sarah asked. "You will not be given a rifle, not even one of Mr. Franklin's new ones." She didn't need to add that someone as small as Winifred would not be able fire a musket, much less withstand its recoil.

Winifred glared at her. "I have no idea, but I will do it."

The other door opened and Benjamin Franklin walked in. "Well, how wonderful to see all my lovely and favorite young ladies happily conversing together. I trust you are all having a pleasant afternoon?"

"We are indeed," Sarah said, and the other two nodded, forced smiles on their faces.

Burgoyne now lived in a tent with sod walls and planking for a floor and with as much of his personal baggage as had been rescued. As an old campaigner, he'd lived in far worse, as had most of the other senior officers. Only Tarleton complained about his new living quarters. Arnold said nothing. This was trivial in comparison to what he'd endured commanding American rebels en route to Canada with an army in what some called an epic march. He often wondered where he'd be if his march had resulted in a rebel victory instead of disaster.

To Fitzroy's relief, there had been no attempt to evict either him or Hannah from their quarters which the fire had spared. As Fitzroy had suspected and hoped, the wind had spared virtually everything to the west of Detroit while destroying much of what lay to the east. Nor had Burgoyne made any attempt to move himself and his staff into the tiny fort, much to the relief of Colonel De Peyster and the garrison.

"I assume you have disturbed me here in my palace because you have something of substance to report?" Burgoyne said with an attempt at humor. He could have commandeered one of the several surviving buildings for his use, but hadn't. The hundreds who were still trying to find someplace warm and dry appreciated the gesture.

"You may begin, Major."

Fitzroy coughed and began. "First, sir, the confirmed death toll stands at only eleven, although several of the more seriously burned and injured may yet succumb. The fact that the fire had raged during daylight hours meant that few were asleep in their beds."

"A small blessing," said Burgoyne.

"One person drowned after jumping in the river, another had apparent heart failure, while the remainder were burned to death in the fire or died shortly afterwards. At least a hundred were injured, although most of the injuries were minor and many of the men have already returned to duty."

"And the missing?"

"Fourteen, and I think at least some of them have taken the opportunity to desert. I'm sure they hope we will think their bodies were destroyed in the fire, and, God only knows, they may be right. However, several of the so-called missing were considered malcontents and troublemakers by their commanding officers, which makes me doubt the likelihood of their heroic deaths."

Burgoyne chuckled wryly. "I'm surprised the number of missing is so low, but then, the disaster did strike before much planning could be done by any potential deserters. Now, you've had three days, have you isolated the cause?"

"Perhaps, although I'm not certain we'll ever know definitely."

Burgoyne gestured impatiently for him to continue. "Then tell me what you think you know."

"Sir, we've isolated the cause of the fire, or, more precisely, where it started. It began in a barn near the western gate and spread like wildfire throughout the buildings of the town, missing, however, Fort Lernoult. It was fanned by a west-blowing wind that, while it destroyed everything to the east of that barn, did not destroy anything to the west of it, nor did it destroy the barn in total.

"Inside the remains of the barn, we found three dead bodies." Fitzroy paused. The memory of the horribly charred corpses sickened him and he felt slightly nauseous.

"Get it over with, Major," Burgoyne said sympathetically.

Fitzroy took a deep breath. "Yes sir. The barn was owned by a man named Brownell who wasn't there at the time of the fire. He'd gone for a meal and left the barn in the care of a friend named Leduc who was accompanied by two laborers. This was not unusual as Leduc and Brownell had known each other for years. Leduc owns a farm across the river."

"So Leduc and his companions were the corpses. But that doesn't tell us how it started."

"Sir, they were not the three bodies, at least not all of them. Brownell identified Leduc's remains based on a missing finger on his left hand. The other two bodies were those of British soldiers."

Burgoyne sat erect. "What!"

"Through slightly melted brass buttons and belt buckles, I identified them as grenadiers, and two grenadiers, a sergeant and a corporal, are among the missing. They had been sent into town to buy forage for an officer's horse, and Brownell's was one place they were to try. Oh yes, there was a bayonet in the stomach of Leduc's body, which implies some kind of struggle."

Again Fitzroy fought the horrible memory of having to move the remains to try to ascertain their identity and cause of death. When I die, he thought, let it be quickly and not in a fire. He had no idea whether the men had been alive or dead when the fire consumed them and shuddered at the thought of burning alive. He recalled the horror of Braxton's face and shuddered again.

"I then took a boat across the river to Leduc's farm. I know I crossed into Haldimand's Canadian territory, but I decided that a casual and unauthorized visit wouldn't upset Haldimand, even if he were to find out about it."

"Which he won't, damn him," Burgoyne rose and began to pace in the confines of the tent. "You were prudent in not asking my permission, which I might have had to deny, and you did well to handle it informally. What did you find?"

"No sign of Leduc, which confirmed that his was the body we thought, and nothing of the two laborers seen with him in Detroit. However, a neighbor said he saw them coming back from Detroit just about the time the fire started. The neighbor said he'd heard horses sometime after midnight. No, he didn't go to inspect."

"Conclusions, Major."

"It's possible the fire was an accident, or even the result of some kind of brawl between the two grenadiers and Leduc and his companions, which would account for the bayonet. However, I believe that sabotage is the most likely cause. In my opinion, Leduc was either a rebel sympathizer or a spy and that the two men came from Fort Washington. Leduc's neighbors said he frequently mentioned how he detested us British. Whether they came to destroy Detroit, or whether it was an opportunity that arose, we'll never know. I regret that I cannot give you anything more definite, but that will have to wait until and if we have those two men in custody. However, I consider that prospect most unlikely as they are doubtless many miles away from here."

There was silence as Burgoyne digested what Fitzroy had said. "I concur," he said finally. "And you've done extremely well. This damn place may still be filled with spies and enemy sympathizers. For that reason, I want you to work with the provost in tightening security and ferreting out spies. I don't want any more surprises like Leduc."

Fitzroy was dismissed. He saluted and stepped outside. Leduc had been a native local with reputation that was beyond reproach. While in Detroit, he had never said or done anything against the Crown, which made his neighbors' comments all the more surprising. And, he had prospered under British rule. So what changed him or drove him, and who was the real Jean Leduc? Fitzroy stared at the hurried reconstruction of the outpost. Of most concern was the condition of the sailing barges. Six had been destroyed utterly and most of the others damaged to some degree, and one seemed to have simply disappeared downriver. Danforth thought it would wash over the falls at Niagara in a week or two if it didn't run aground somewhere, and Fitzroy agreed he was likely right.

Despite the fact that the fire had been out for a couple of days, fingers of smoke still wafted upwards as scores of soldiers attempted to move the still hot rubble out of the fort and dump it into the river. Only then could the rebuilding begin in earnest.

Fitzroy found himself staring at the civilians working around him. Who were they? Loyal or rebel? Friend or foe? How many were taking notes and making observations that would shortly find their way to Fort Washington. From Leduc's now very cooperative neighbors, he'd heard of a tavern a few miles up the road where rebels allegedly congregated. He hadn't gone there yet and wouldn't without Burgoyne's concurrence.

Who could be trusted? At least he could trust sweet, buxom little Hannah.

# Chapter 8 ★ ★ ★ ★ ★ ★ ★ ★ ★ ★ ★ ★ ★ ★ ★ ★ ★

TALLMADGE HELD HIS NOSE. "MY GOD, THE STENCH IS APPALL-ing. Are you waiting for the spring thaw to bathe?"

Will smiled. "You said you wanted to see me the moment I came in, didn't you? Well, here I am."

Even though few people bathed very frequently, and most even less so in the winter when it was common knowledge you could sicken and die from excess washing, Will knew he was a special case. Two weeks of trekking through thick mud and undergrowth had left him covered with filth. That he was also exhausted didn't seem to affect or impress Tallmadge.

"Well, you can clean up later, I suppose. In the meantime, stand downwind and give me all the details on the Detroit fire."

"You already know about the fire? Someone preceded me?"

"You might say that," Tallmadge said with a lazy smile.

"Damnation. I nearly killed myself getting you the information and here I'm second-best again."

"Will, all I got was a scant outline. Details, man, I need details."

Will complied and filled Tallmadge in on everything he knew, from Leduc's heroic death, to the curiously thrilling feeling of watching the British high command standing before him while he was in the barn just before the brawl and Leduc's setting the fire.

"The British looked so bloody normal. I found it hard to believe that they were the same people who imprisoned me in that hulk."

"If they catch you again, Will, you'll believe it. They'll flog you to shreds and hang what's left of you for the crows to eat."

They continued with an assessment of the damage done to the British effort and what impact it would have on an assault in the spring.

Will sipped on a cup of what was alleged to be coffee, but was more likely something made of crushed chestnuts. "The storm of fire swept away a number of buildings, but they can be rebuilt. I'd say that hundreds of tents were destroyed, but not the inhabitants. Casualties were likely relatively few and fatalities obviously less so."

"Too bloody bad," Tallmadge muttered. "When I heard of the fire, I'd hoped for the complete immolation of the British Army."

Drake continued. "I am most intrigued by the damage done to the barges they had under construction. In my opinion it was heavy. I don't know how important the barges were, or what specific plans the British had for them, except that they obviously planned on sailing them around Michigan. I don't know how long it will take to replace them; however, I am sure they are working hard as we speak. The fire hurt them, but the wounds are far from fatal."

"You don't know much at all, do you?" Tallmadge said grumpily.

"I know I need a bath. And then I need a meal and some sleep. I'm still disappointed that I'm not the first with the news of the fire. Tell me, was it someone at the tavern near where I quartered my men?"

"In a manner of speaking, yes."

Will's curiosity was piqued. "And just what do you mean by that, my dear General?"

Tallmadge winked. "Well, let's just say a little bird told me."

Braxton unsealed the message and read it carefully. The very young British officer who'd brought it looked distinctly uncomfortable and kept trying not to stare at Braxton's ruined face and hands. Braxton felt like killing him. Fucking officers always thought they were better than everyone else, especially the young British ones. If they weren't the only means to his ends, he'd have nothing to do with them.

"You'll stay the night. I'll give you a reply in the morning."

"Yes, Captain." The ensign's smooth little face sagged. He'd sooner be in hell than spend a night with Burned Man Braxton and his terrible men. The little bastard was probably afraid that someone would try to bugger him in the night. Braxton grinned. Maybe the little boy officer was afraid someone wouldn't.

At least the little turd had the decency to acknowledge his militia rank. Of course the young twit probably realized that he, Braxton, could have him killed and blame the murder on Indians, or rebels, or bears. He glared at the Brit and watched him shift nervously. Power was such a good feeling. He felt like growling to see if the British ensign would shit his pants.

Braxton took the message outside the log cabin he called home and gestured for his two lieutenants, Fenton and Harris, to come to him.

"You boys bored?"

"Hell yes," Fenton answered. While they were warm and comfortable in other cabins they'd taken over, they'd not been allowed to associate with others in Detroit or elsewhere. Burgoyne had decided that the stench from their raids was too much. Well, the hell with Burgoyne. Of course, now there wasn't a Detroit for them to visit even if they'd wanted to.

"The British want us to raid another village," Braxton said.

Fenton's eyes gleamed and Harris smiled, "Finally."

"Finally is right," said Braxton. "Just like the others, it's a compound of several buildings with maybe a dozen people and that includes some women. Word is they've been harboring rebel messengers and maybe even the traitors who burned Detroit. If we do this right, we'll show the British just how useful we can be."

Harris and Fenton nodded like puppets. The mention of women in the rebel compound had gotten their undivided attention. There'd been no sex from captured women in a couple of months, which made their inability to visit the whores in Detroit a particular hardship. They were only a couple of days away from the settlement that Braxton had described.

"How did we miss it?" asked Fenton.

"Probably because it's such a little bitty place out there in a great big forest," Braxton answered.

He was tolerant with Fenton because they went back a long ways, even though he thought his old deputy was more than a little bit stupid. Fenton wasn't totally useless, however. It had been Fenton's idea way back in Pendleton to extort sex from female prisoners, or the wives, daughters, and even the mothers of male prisoners. Hell, some of the older women had been great at what Braxton asked them to do in order to save their families from further harm.

Still, Braxton thought Fenton would fuck a goat if that was all that was available. "It's at a place where two streams meet. I know one of them. We follow it downstream and it'll lead us to the rebels. Maybe the fun we'll have will make some of the boys who left us regret it."

Braxton's band was now down to under twenty. Lack of action had caused some to leave while others were affected by the fact that they were pariahs and no one wanted anything to do with them. Bring back a few scalps and brag about new meat they'd screwed and the right kind of men would come running real fast.

Then Harris had a thought. "Hey, didn't Burgoyne say he didn't want us around? Did the fire change all that?"

Braxton spread his ruined mouth in a parody of a smile. "Maybe our new orders didn't come from Burgoyne."

"Who then?" asked Harris.

Braxton laughed. "Bloody fucking Tarleton."

Neither Sarah nor Faith had worked up enough courage to greet Will and Owen with open arms and passion as they'd discussed. Faith was still apprehensive about pushing Owen, and Sarah wasn't certain she wanted to go too far with Will, at least not just yet.

That and the almost total lack of privacy in Fort Washington conspired against them. Sarah was not going to copulate against a barrack wall or on a pile of hay in a cold barn. Others were always doing exactly that, but she would not.

Still, Sarah made sure Will knew she was delighted to see him even though he was as filthy as a pig dressed as he was in a mixture of dirty woolen cloth and ripe buckskin. She laughed and told him any pig would be insulted by the comparison. Will thought he was immaculate in comparison with what he'd been like when existing in the hold of the prison hulk. He shuddered at the memory and, with a twinge of guilt, wondered what happened to the Negro, Homer, the man who'd rescued him and given him a second chance at life and freedom. If a miracle occurred and the Americans won their war, maybe he would find out.

While Will went to his quarters and scrubbed his body with

ash soap and lukewarm water from a bowl, Sarah took his clothing to her barracks and cleaned them as best she could. They agreed to meet later in the evening. She strongly felt that people should be as clean as possible and bathed as frequently as it was safe, and was pleased that Will seemed to feel the same way.

Will still did not have a proper uniform and put on other civilian clothing. A badge showed his rank in the army. So accoutered, he went to Tallmadge for further information.

First, the news of the draconian laws to be enacted against the colonists, whether loyal or rebel, was beginning to get out and circulate throughout the colonies. Rebel households were horrified, while loyalists were either disbelieving or shocked, with disbelief being the prominent emotion. They wanted proof and they would doubt the news until they either saw the official documents, or when Governor General Cornwallis admitted it.

"I wonder if people will finally believe it when they are enslaved and have had all their property taken from them," Tallmadge said bitterly. "Of course, even if they do, we might not be here to laugh at them."

They wondered if confirmation of the report would result in mass emigration of Loyalists from the colonies to Canada and elsewhere. "South Africa would be my choice," Will said.

In other areas the news was mixed at best. On the negative side, Nathanael Greene's young wife had informed them that the already very ill general had taken a turn for the worse. He was now partially paralyzed and drifting in and out of a coma. Even the most optimistic admitted that he would never again command in the field. This was a particularly upsetting condition because Greene had been Washington's right-hand man and, in the opinion of many, a better tactician and fighter than Washington himself. It had been Greene who had taken command of the southern theater and maneuvered Cornwallis into a corner of Virginia called Yorktown that should have been the coffin of British hopes.

None of the remaining American generals had ever commanded an army or held a significant independent command. And, with few exceptions, the rank and file had little confidence in their abilities.

The closest to a war leader at Fort Washington was Daniel Morgan, the Old Wagoneer. He had led a wing at Saratoga and defeated the British under Tarleton at the Cowpens where he had utterly destroyed the British force. He had arrived along with Willy Washington, the dead General George Washington's nephew and a decent cavalry commander in his own right. Morgan, however, was often bedridden himself as a result of bouts of rheumatism and arthritis brought on by too much campaigning in the field. He was nearing fifty and old beyond his years. Willy Washington had been captured before the debacle at Yorktown and subsequently paroled. He'd been one of the lucky ones to have missed the later British sweep of rebel officers.

"It could be worse," Will had said, "we could still have Gates and Lee."

Neither Horatio Gates nor Charles Lee had distinguished themselves in command of an American army. Although Gates was widely considered to be the victor at Saratoga, the battle had been largely won by his subordinates—Morgan, John Stark and the subsequently traitorous Benedict Arnold. In a later battle and after being given command in the south, Gates had fled in disgrace from his defeat at Camden. He'd been captured by the British and now languished in a Jamaican prison. Lee had been sacked by Washington after his confused performance at Monmouth. He too had been captured by the British and, for reasons unknown, had been hanged. Few mourned him.

On the positive side, John Glover and his small regiment from Marblehead, Massachusetts, was rumored to be en route. Not only were they fine soldiers and well led, but they were boatmen whose skills had already proven useful. Their work during the retreat from Long Island and the crossing of the Delaware came to mind.

Still, Glover's presence would not solve the problem of an overall field commander. He was a fine regimental commander, but not a man to lead an army. Will had heard that at one skirmish on Manhattan, Glover had fought bravely but had openly longed for someone else to lead the effort.

Tallmadge fumed. "We have colonels and brigadiers, but no one with experience in independent command except for a sickly Morgan. And there's precious little time for anyone to learn. The only other experienced ranking officer we have is Schuyler and the men won't follow him."

"Don't you think he got unfair blame for losing Ticonderoga?"

Will asked. The defeat at Ticonderoga had resulted in Schuyler's removal and replacement by Gates.

"Will, it doesn't matter what I think. The army has no confidence in him. If Schuyler commands, they will fight with one eye on the Redcoats and one on an escape route out to the west because they think he can do nothing but lose for them."

"That reminds me," Will said, "Have you heard from Clark and his explorers?"

"Not a peep. Well, perhaps a little," Tallmadge said in the same smug way he'd said that Will wasn't the first with the news of the Detroit fire. What the devil was going on, Will wondered.

"Clark and his men made it well west to a fascinating discovery, a huge salt lake. But now they are hibernating for the winter. What they did find is that there is precious little likelihood of a large number of people finding sustenance in such a barren landscape."

"So we fight or die?" Will said.

"Wasn't it always that way, Will?"


"Benjamin Franklin is a brilliant man," Sarah declared. "Perhaps the most brilliant man who ever existed. He lets the others, like that pompous Hancock, think they are in charge, but then he comes up with ideas that they have to follow. He's like a very old and very skillful puppeteer and they are his puppets."

"Do tell," Will said with a lazy smile. They were seated on chairs across from each other in Franklin's study. The great man was puttering around someplace, so any sense of privacy was an illusion.

Sarah was unfazed by his apparent lack of interest in what she was saying. What did faze her was the way he kept staring at her. She continued, "Dr. Franklin has made a series of proposals. First, he thinks that we should come up with a constitution, a set of rules that our nation should abide by. He says it would be a counter to the dictatorial hand of the British."

"Sounds reasonable to me."

"Yes. It would show people that they have a choice. They can live freely as Americans, or as slaves under the British. He says there should be no restraints on religion, assembly, or the press, and that just about any man should be able to vote if he wishes."

"So what is stopping Congress from doing just that?"

She grimaced, "The curse of slavery. The representatives from the southern states want slavery reinstated so that when we win they can get their human property back. Dr. Franklin thinks the genie is out of the bottle and can never be returned. Another version of Pandora's Box, he said. He thinks that the British did the colonies a favor by freeing the slaves, since, in his words, they can never be re-enslaved without an uproar and even an incredible amount of violence. After all, it's been several years since they were freed. He is certain they are getting used to freedom and would fight to keep it. He feels the results would be a civil war with white against black, and with those whites who oppose slavery helping the blacks. He said the southerners would wind up killing many of the blacks so they can enslave the rest. He also thinks that many blacks would migrate west like we did. It sounds so logical when he says it."

"He's right. I can't imagine a slave going willingly any more than I can imagine myself going back into a prison hulk. I know this sounds overly dramatic, but I'd rather be killed fighting than surrender and be sent to that hell again."

"Will, I'd like to say I understand, but I doubt that I'll ever comprehend what you went through."

He reached out and took her hand. "Sometimes I don't think I comprehend it either. It's like a bad dream that happened to someone who looked like me."

"Do you still think about it?"

"Not as often as before. At first, a strange sound or a smell would remind me, and it would be like I had been sent back to that hell. Of course, I sometimes still dream about it at night and wake up shaking and sweating with my heart pounding like a drum."

She covered his hand with hers, anxious now to change the subject. "Franklin's second great idea was that we should admit new colonies. After all, the area in which we are living isn't a part of any of the thirteen even though we have thousands of people living here. He thought we could name the colonies after Indian tribes, like the Miami or the Saulk. Of course, there are problems with that as well."

Will smiled. "Let me guess. Virginia and other colonies are laying claim to the land based on ambiguous and irrelevant colonial boundaries drawn many years ago in England."

"Exactly. However, he thinks he can wear down the opposition with a combination of charm and logic."

"As he has done with you?"

"I am very fond of him," she admitted. "I can see how French women threw themselves at him. If he was younger, a lot younger, I can see where I might do it myself."

"And where would that leave me?"

She smiled impishly. "Well, in a liberated society, couldn't a woman have more than one lover?"

Will stood and pulled her to him. He tipped up her face and kissed her longingly. "I don't want to share you," he said huskily.

"And I don't want to be shared," she said. "Dr. Franklin will just have to find someone else."

"Do you always call him Dr. Franklin. Is it ever Benjamin??"

"Yes, when we're alone and he's tired."

They kissed again, and this time with deepening passion. "Does he ever leave you alone here?"

She felt his erection through her dress. "Why, so you can take me to bed?"

"Yes."

His hands strayed from her shoulders and cupped her breasts. She felt mild surprise and pleasure. Benjamin Franklin was talking to someone in the next room and could come in at any time. Did she care? It would take but an instant to unfasten Will's pants and straddle him while he was seated on a chair. It wouldn't be dignified or romantic, but it would solve, at least temporarily, the problem of her wanting him so badly.

She took a deep breath and pushed him away. "I want you, Will Drake, but not with the chance that Benjamin or anyone else will surprise us. Perhaps the next time he goes out for a sufficient amount of time, I will send for you and give you more pleasure than you could ever imagine or deserve."

"Just perhaps?" Will said with a strained smile.

She put her head on his shoulder. "Perhaps more than perhaps."

Will smiled wanly. "It cannot come soon enough."


Fitzroy did not always get invited to the generals' luncheon meetings. These were often times for Burgoyne, Tarleton, Grant, and Arnold to discuss matters freely and without anyone taking notes. This time, he was present because of his efforts to root out rebel spies.

"If I understand you correctly, you've found nothing," Tarleton said with his usual hint of a sneer.

"I have not done quite that poorly, General. I have found that Detroit is a sieve and that information flows out of here like the river outside. My problem is finding out just who is telling tales to impress tavern wenches in order to get under their skirts, and who is really traitorous, and sending information to Fort Washington and General Tallmadge, their spymaster."

Fitzroy winced inwardly when he mentioned about telling tales to impress women. He was as guilty as anyone since he talked more than freely to Hannah Van Doorn. But why not? She was a loyalist and a very dear friend along with being a lover. In fact, Fitzroy was spending a lot of time wondering about their relationship and any future they might possibly have together.

"I can see Fitzroy's point," Grant said. "There is a sense of invincibility here, or at least there was until the fire, and nobody seemed to care what was said and to whom. Talking and bragging, however, does not necessarily make anyone a traitor."

"So what do we do about it?" Tarleton asked.

"I've ordered the obvious," Fitzroy answered. "Invoking General Burgoyne's name, I've required people to be more aware of what they are doing and saying. It'll hardly solve everything, but it is a step. I've also set a handful of what I think of as mousetraps to catch people. I think, however, that I will catch harmless and talkative mice, and not traitors."

General Arnold nodded solemnly. "And then you will make examples of them."

"Yes sir."

Burgoyne stood and walked around the table. "I've gotten more information from General Cornwallis. He says that New York is in ferment and that other cities are almost in open rebellion. There are riots in Boston, which is nothing new. It seems that the report of the American Colonies' future has gotten out and even our tame Loyalists are outraged, and I don't blame them."

"Is Cornwallis denying it?" Tarleton asked. "God knows, I would."

"Apparently so," Burgoyne answered, "but the trouble is spreading. And there is interesting news from London. It appears that the French king and his idiot queen have reconciled with the Marquis de Lafayette. The marquis' moderate forces have won a few battles against the radicals who seem to have disaffected a lot of people by killing so many of them. It would seem that the boy general is becoming a force to be reckoned with."

"Dear God," exclaimed Grant.

"Dear God, indeed," Burgoyne continued. "Apparently their French majesties concluded that, if they did not cooperate with the marquis, the moderates in France would proclaim Lafayette as a new king and leave them to live out the remainder of their lives as exiles in England. As it is, there may well be a constitutional monarchy with Louis and Marie as little more than figureheads."

Tarleton laughed harshly, "Serves them right. They are utter dunces and probably incompetent to serve as anything but figureheads."

Burgoyne smiled. "That may be true, but it does not thrill our own beloved King George. He sees a constitutional monarachy as a potential threat to the House of Hanover and its control over England. King George would like the monarchy to have more power, not less."

"Is Cornwallis asking for his army back?" Tarleton asked.

"Not quite. He acknowledges that we need the time to do the job properly, but he does not wish us to dawdle. I have sent him a report on our condition and our intentions. However, he is well aware that so much of what we will be able to do is dependent on the weather. First, the ice must melt and the land must thaw and then it must dry up before we can move."

Tarleton nearly snorted. "Still, I want this ordeal to be over. Migawd, I first thought that New York was the most diseased crotch of the world, but this manure pile called Detroit is far worse. Now I actually find myself looking forward to New York or Charleston."

"Not Boston?" Grant asked in an attempt at humor.

"Never Boston," Tarleton responded angrily. "Puritans, rebels, merchants, and witch burners, along with pale, ugly women who think it's a sin to enjoy a good fuck. I think I'd rather be here than in Boston, thank you."

Grant turned to Fitzroy. "In the meantime we prepare and look for spies. Curiously, but I almost don't care if the rebels know everything we are doing. After all, what can they do about it? We outnumber them hugely, outgun them enormously, and have better trained soldiers."

"And superior generals," Tarleton said and drew laughter from the others, even from Burgoyne who normally didn't think Butcher Tarleton was funny at all. Or even that good a general.

★　　★　　★

"I still don't see how we missed this," Harris muttered. Beside him in the brush, Braxton was deep in thought.

"Only thing I can think of is that it's a new settlement," Braxton said. "I mean, look at the place. Just a couple of log cabins poorly thrown together. No crops yet and not much of a place for animals. These people just arrived, and that's why we missed it. It wasn't here for us to miss."

He didn't bother to add again that the forest was huge and the settlement small, and they might have continued to miss it if it hadn't been for the specific directions they'd been given. For all Braxton knew there were a score of similarly undetected settlements like this just waiting to be discovered and then wiped out by his men. He hoped so.

Following the directions received from Tarleton in Detroit, Braxton and nearly twenty men had labored through the winter snow and mud to find the settlement that was claimed to harbor rebels.

Braxton didn't much care if the claim was true or not. He and his men needed some action. The bad weather made their approach easier. There was no one out in the fields preparing the soil for crops and they'd detected no sign of any hunters. Of course there might be one or two, but it would appear that they'd successfully bypassed them. If they were discovered, it would be too late. It was already too late for the occupants of the settlement and he didn't give a damn if they were rebels or not.

The settlement consisted of a larger building that was likely a barn, and a slightly smaller one, which he assumed was the main house. The shutters were closed against the weather, which meant that the occupants couldn't see them very well if at all.

"Look," Harris hissed. Two women, their heads covered with shawls, came out of the main house and went into what Braxton had assumed was the barn. A moment later, they emerged with two men and returned to the main house. No one was carrying a weapon.

Braxton signaled the others with a soft whistle and they began to move forward at a crouch. At a hundred yards away, he ordered a pause. There was still nothing to indicate that they'd been discovered. He waved the men forward. One group of a half dozen headed toward the barn, while the rest raced toward the house.

At about twenty yards distance, the shutters opened and a dozen gun barrels poked out. Braxton screamed at his men to stop, but it was too late. Sheets of fire cut down his men. To his left, he heard a similar fate befalling the men attacking the barn. Harris, directly in front of him, took a bullet in the head. Blood and brain matter spewed onto Braxton.

"Ambush!" Braxton howled. "Run."

Armed men poured from the buildings, screaming and waving knives and tomahawks. A couple of his surviving men managed to fire their weapons, but didn't appear to hit much. Braxton felt a pain in his arm and realized he'd been shot. A wild looking rebel came up to him. Braxton screamed out his fury and shot the man in the chest with his pistol.

He turned and ran for the woods. He felt agony from his arm and nearly passed out. Almost all of his men were down and being hacked at by the rebels who had poured from the buildings. Maybe one or two had survived the slaughter and maybe not.

Somehow, he made it to the shelter of the forest. He was almost incredulous at his own good fortune. He managed to reload his pistol with his one good hand. If the rebels came close he would use it on himself. He had no urge to be imprisoned or hanged, which he knew would happen.

He had to make it back to Detroit. Someone had betrayed him to the rebels, and Tarleton would want to know that.

Nathanael Greene was dead. The brave and skillful general, a trusted subordinate and confidante of George Washington, went to sleep and never woke up. Many hoped that such a peaceful death would be theirs as well, but doubted they'd ever be that lucky. Large numbers would die fighting the British in the spring, and they might be the lucky ones. Hanging or slavery waited for the survivors. Perhaps a few could wander west and be assimilated into the Indian tribes. Either way, many thought that a miserable life awaited them.

Greene's passing hadn't been all that gentle. The illnesses that had racked his body would have felled a lesser man much sooner. He'd fought and fought, but the brave warrior was slowly overwhelmed.

The ground was frozen and a score of deeply saddened men hacked at it for the better part of a day before they'd dug a hole of appropriate depth and width. Greene's body lay in a plain wooden box. Everyone felt that such a hero deserved better but that was all they had. Reinterment at a better place and with an appropriate monument would wait for the future, if there was a future.

They buried him with all the honors they could summon up. A squad of soldiers fired their muskets over the grave while a pair of drummer boys manfully plied their trade, after which a preacher spoke. He was mercifully short. Tallmadge whispered to Will that the poor man was probably freezing. So too were the several hundred who had gathered for the ceremony. Greene's widow Catherine and Abigail Adams stood together. A handful of other women, including Sarah, Faith, and Winifred Haskill, stood behind them.

Officers and men felt the loss deeply. Greene was the man in whom they had confidence, but the now ranking officer was General Schuyler. Will noted that no one stood next to Schuyler. Was it out of deference to his rank or because they had no confidence in his ability to lead? He feared the latter. Even Schuyler looked unusually glum and depressed. The weight of the revolution was now on his shoulders.

"Poor man," Tallmadge again whispered. "Schuyler's an excellent organizer and probably the reason we're all alive right now instead of having starved to death, but no one wants him leading an army into battle."

"What about yourself? You're a general."

"Good God no! I'm a desk general, not a fighter." Tallmadge looked at the officers assembled across the grave site. "Look at who's here and then think of who isn't."

Will glanced over the solemn faces. There were a number of good men, but not enough. The British roundup had decapitated much of the American Army. George Washington was dead, and now so too was Greene, a man many felt was Washington's superior in battle. Von Steuben and Wayne were present, but where were Knox, Lincoln, St. Clair, Sullivan, and Stirling? In a Jamaican prison, that's where, along with scores of others.

Morgan was present in spirit, but it was too cold for his aching body to venture outdoors for the ceremony. He might have another battle in him, but not the stress of a campaign. The man who'd had such an impact on the battle of Saratoga was now a shell.

Anthony Wayne was a fighter but too impetuous. The men did not call him Mad Anthony for nothing.

Von Steuben, the genial imposter who had convinced Franklin he was a Prussian general, would be best at training an army, which was what he was doing now.

Willy Washington was on hand, but the other American cavalry leader, Harry Lee, apparently now shared a cell with Alexander Hamilton. Of course, what good was cavalry without horses, and there were precious few of those at Fort Washington.

Glover would arrive in a few days, and that would give them another excellent regimental commander, but still no one experienced enough for overall command. Regiments needed to be formed into brigades and brigades into divisions and only Wayne and Morgan were even marginally capable of that task. Thus, to promote one of them to overall command meant a lesser man would command a division. They needed another good general to assume overall command.

"Someone will have to be appointed and then learn on the job," Will said.

George Washington had endured years of disaster and defeat before learning how to command, and so too had Greene. There would be no time for such a bloody apprenticeship. There would be only one chance in the spring. One defeat and the revolution was over. They could not again retreat to the west. They'd done that already.

The services were over and the crowd had begun to drift away. Nathanael Greene lay under a mound of cold raw dirt. He deserved better, Will thought.

Tallmadge snorted. "We're fucked, Will. Properly bloody fucking fucked."

# Chapter 9 ★★★★★★★★★★★★★★★★★

"WELL, MAJOR FITZROY, WHAT HAVE YOU FOUND ABOUT SPIES and such?" asked General Burgoyne. He was in a good mood. An almost empty food plate was on his desk and a snifter of brandy was in his hand. He'd moved from that drafty tent to a hastily built cabin with a genuine wood floor, and a fire burned in a stove that some insisted had been designed by the rebel, Benjamin Franklin. If the old rebel had indeed designed it, Burgoyne silently saluted him as the device gave off plenty of heat, keeping him and anyone else in the one room cabin warm and dry.

Fitzroy took off his snow-soaked cape and hat and sat down. "Nothing firm, sir, but many suspicions."

"Such as?"

"Such as how did the rebels learn that Braxton was going to attack where he did? On top of the suspicious fire in Detroit, it is too much to be coincidental."

Burned Man Braxton had returned to Detroit the day before with a handful of men. He was wounded and hungry. Several of his toes were frostbitten, and possibly part of what remained of his nose. He would lose the toes and the joke around was that any loss of his nose wouldn't make him any uglier than he already was. He'd lost almost all of his men in what was obviously an ambush. He'd ranted almost incoherently about betrayal and Fitzroy had to agree with him. Someone had indeed betrayed him.

Burgoyne took a sip of brandy. "I can't imagine you're terribly distressed about Braxton's failure."

"I'm not, but if the rebels can find out about a matter so unimportant, what else can they learn about our major plans, our capabilities and, more important, our weaknesses?"

The general wiped some crumbs and grease off his chin with his sleeve. "Good point. What do you propose?"

"Sir, despite the wretched weather, there is still commerce between the Detroit community and the farmers across the river. I believe at least one of them might be playing a part in betrayal, and I continue to hear rumors that a tavern a mile or two up the road has been known to harbor strangers who might be rebels. With your permission, I propose to take some men across and raid that tavern."

Burgoyne nodded angrily. "Permission granted and the devil with Haldimand and his concern with provincial boundaries. I've already written him that such forays might be necessary. He won't respond, of course. Will you wait until spring?"

Fitzroy winced. The river was sometimes frozen solid and the rest of the time the ice flowed freely and with dangerous floating chunks. Even though the locals still crossed occasionally, it was not something he was looking forward to. Some enterprising souls had rigged a rope line between the two sides, and flat bottom sleds carrying people and supplies could be pulled across. If a ship did happen by, not likely at this time of year, the rope could be slackened so that the keel passed over it. If the sled being pulled went through the ice, it would float and could still be pulled along. At least that was the theory. Fitzroy shuddered at the thought of making such a trip, but had decided it couldn't wait several months for the river to be clear of ice.

"No sir, I plan on going over in the next few days."

"Then go and good hunting."

As Fitzroy left the office he nearly ran into General Banastre Tarleton. His face was flushed and his eyes were glassy. "Well, well, if it isn't little Major Spy-Chaser," Tarleton said with an undisguised sneer.

Fitzroy glared at him. "Sir, I believe you're drunk."

"I am and you ought to be," Tarleton answered. His breath nearly caused Fitzroy to stagger backwards. "It's the only way to exist in this miserable shithole of an outpost. At least I've accomplished something while you spend your days and nights fornicating with that Dutch whore who's just as likely a rebel spy as anyone in this primitive place."

Fitzroy seethed. How dare he call Hannah a whore, and how dare he imply that she was a spy. Still, one doesn't challenge generals to a duel, especially one like Tarleton who might accept and kill Fitzroy. No, he stifled his anger. He would have satisfaction some other time and place.

Fitzroy smiled insincerely. "And what wondrous deeds have you accomplished lately, General?"

If Tarleton was aware of the sarcasm, he didn't show it. "While you have been looking on and under mattresses for spies," he replied. "I have arrested a number of Hessian deserters who are doubtless sending information to the rebels."

"Hessians who are spies? Here? Why on earth would someone from Germany come here to spy? They would be so utterly obvious."

"Of course they would be, that's why we caught them. Twenty of the bastards are now in custody and they'll all hang."

Now it became clearer. Tarleton had captured his "spies" in advance of the arrival of the Hessian officer tasked with finding and punishing deserters. His name would go to London and be praised for his diligence.

"What proofs did you find them with?" Fitzroy asked softly.

Tarleton belched loudly and the effort pitched him off balance. He steadied himself with effort. "They're Hessians. Don't need proof."

"General, people from the Germanic states have been living in the colonies for generations. That doesn't make them spies, and they cannot be deserters if they were never in anybody's army. We need proof they deserted before they can be executed."

"They'll be what I make them to be, Major, and the bastards will all hang. That'll send the fear of God, or whatever Germanic totem they worship, into the Hessian deserters now at Fort Washington and preparing to fight us."

Fitzroy managed to extricate himself and went to the provost's office in the fort where he looked on the score of confused and bedraggled men crammed together in a small cell. They were in shackles and looked at him mutely. Some were bruised; it was obvious they had resisted being arrested.

How on earth could they be spies? Several were old enough to be his grandfather and others were still children. To hang these people would be an atrocity. But then, he reminded himself, Tarleton specialized in atrocities.

"Bloody Christ," he muttered to himself. "How do I stop this from happening?"

Benjamin Franklin loved to have little soirees where he could make the informal contacts that were his specialty and use his still considerable influence to affect the course of the young nation.

Sadly, his get-togethers were nothing like what he'd held in Paris, or even Philadelphia. The surroundings were plain at best, and the refreshments were Spartan. There was bread and butter, and some meats and jams, and a choice of raw whiskies or a kind of tea to drink. Nobody went hungry, but there was nothing impressive or tantalizing. Certainly, there were none of the French wines that had made dealing with the miserable French themselves so pleasant and tolerable. Most of those present were thankful for a surprisingly good beer that a former assistant of Samuel Adams had managed to brew. Even though these were the rebellion's leaders, their dress was shabby. Many men wore buckskins and otherwise plain woolen cloth. Again, none of the elegance of France or even Philadelphia was present. It was so depressing. It didn't help matters that the floor was dirt.

Every host needs a hostess, and Franklin had called on Sarah and a handful of others to fulfill those duties. The ladies had managed to find enough fair quality dresses to make them presentable. He made pains to ensure that everyone knew that Sarah was his hostess and not his mistress, although he also made pains to let anyone know that he would be delighted if she were. For her part, Sarah found it amusing, as did Will.

In return for her duties, she'd insisted that Franklin also invite Will, who stood against a wall, sipping a wretched tea and watching the great and the not so great mingle. Cyrus Radnor, a man who referred to himself as a congressman from South Carolina, stood by him and smiled affably.

"I understand you were rescued from prison by a Negro?"

"That is correct," Will answered, puzzled by the question. Radnor was one of many congressmen who represented absolutely nobody. An obscure militia colonel and an only moderately successful tobacco farmer, he'd owned property and slaves before being chased out of South Carolina by the British and their Tory allies. He had not signed the Declaration of Independence, nor had he been sent to Congress in Philadelphia. He'd been chosen by the others to be in the current Congress because of his South Carolina residence and the fact that the Congress needed someone from South Carolina to claim any degree of legitimacy. There were some who doubted that Radnor had ever been a congressman in the first place.

"Then you have opinions about slavery, do you not?" Radnor asked.

"The Negro who freed me was a free man himself. He was never a slave and I would not want him to ever be one. I owe him too much for that to happen."

Radnor nodded, causing loose skin from his face to shake. It looked like he'd lost weight, but then, so had many people in Fort Washington. Will thought he was one of the few who'd gained, since he'd still been suffering from his privations when he'd arrived.

Radnor persisted. "Doctor Franklin says we should abandon the slave issue, Major, do you agree? Do you think slavery is inherently evil?"

"Whether I think it is evil or not is irrelevant. The egg has been broken and cannot be mended. Slaves have been free for a while now and will not take lightly to being reenslaved. During the war, the British raised several regiments of Negro infantry and they acquitted themselves quite well against Indians, although, to my knowledge, they never fought against us. If we win and attempt to enslave them again, it will be another war resulting in a bloodbath that could destroy what we had won." Assuming we win anything, he thought.

Radnor sighed. "With extreme reluctance, I tend to agree, although not all of my southern friends are of like mind. At the worst, they feel that we can import fresh slave stock for our plantations; however, the British will not permit that. They suggested that planters use white prisoners as indentured servants, and that won't work for several reasons. First, there aren't enough of them to supply the needs of the planters, and, second, the two groups hate each other and there would be murders." He blinked owlishly and Will realized that Radnor was drunk. "There must be a third reason, but I can't think of it."

"And why can't the planters import fresh slaves?"

Radnor chuckled and took a beer from a passing serving girl. It was Sarah's cousin Faith and she winked at Will.

"Goodness, what great tits on her and I think she likes you, Major. Too bad her cousin does as well."

Will winced. Were there no secrets in this bloody town?

Radnor laughed at Will's discomfort and continued, "Southern planters cannot import a fresh crop of slaves because the British have used their navy to close down the slave trade from Africa and the Indies. The British government is beginning to come under tremendous pressure to abolish slavery altogether and it may come to pass. In which case, they will piously impose their decision everywhere they can."

Will thought that would be a good thing, but kept quiet.

"Franklin wants us to have a constitution," Radnor continued, "and he wants that document to include a statement of freedoms to all Americans so they can see what we're fighting for and why the British proposals are so odious. The British have, in the opinion of many people, seized the moral high ground by freeing the slaves, and Franklin feels that we can attract followers by declaring our freedoms within an official constitution."

"How do you feel, Mr. Radnor?"

"I heartily agree with the need for a constitution and reluctantly agree that the issue of slavery is over and must be put behind us."

Will added. "Then whatever document we agree on must be published throughout the colonies well before the British strike so it can be another weapon in our humble arsenal."

Radnor belched, nodded and walked away. A moment later, Abigail Adams took him by the elbow and steered him away from the wall.

"Are you having a pleasant time, Major Drake?"

"Indeed, and are you Mistress Adams?"

She laughed wickedly. "Surprisingly so. There are too many men and too few women. I do believe I've had my middle-aged bottom patted a good dozen times and not all of them by Dr. Franklin."

"Doctor Franklin is a most interesting man," Will said, grinning.

"And I think your poor Sarah is suffering the same fate. She is a quite remarkable woman, I hope you realize."

"I do."

"Then don't lose, her, Major. And how was your conversation with the distinguished gentleman from South Carolina?"

"We discussed slavery."

She arched an eyebrow. The arguments for and against slavery had been a divisive issue in Congress. "I've heard rumors that he was wavering?"

Will smiled. "They would appear to be correct."

Owen and Faith met in a dark and cluttered storeroom after Franklin's party. He was delighted that she was willing to be alone with him, particularly since they were in what could easily be considered a compromising situation. Even though he felt that she liked him, she had seemed withdrawn instead of drawing closer since his return from Detroit.

Now that they were together, he wasn't certain what to do. He arranged a pile of clothing as a makeshift couch. He wrapped a blanket around her shoulders and invited her to sit, but she shook her head and continued to stand as did he. There was no heat in the storeroom and the wind came through the plain wooden walls. He thought he heard scurrying in the piles of clothing and wondered how many small animals were making their homes there. He hoped they didn't bite or have fleas.

"I hope you like the smell of tobacco," she said. "So many of the men at Franklin's were smoking pipes and that I could almost cut the smoke with a knife."

"I think you smell wonderful," he said.

"I think you are very nice, but very foolish." She shifted and shuddered. "I'm still cold."

"Maybe we shouldn't have come here," he said sadly.

"No. It's all right. Make some more space in the pile and sit down."

Owen did as he was told and, to his astonishment, Faith sat on his lap with her legs curled up and the blanket wrapped around both of them. "I am shameless, aren't I?" she asked.

"Hardly."

"Well, you know I'm not an innocent little child, don't you?"

"And I am?" he said as he shifted her closer to him. She was referring to the horrors of the jail in Pendleton and the abuse by the deputies. His response was an opening to show that he understood, and that there would be no secrets, no taboos, between them.

"Do you know what terrible things happen to young boys in the hold of a ship when no one is around and someone has stuffed a rag into your mouth so you can't scream? And then, of course, everyone denies it, so everyone can claim it never happened? The Royal Navy has some nasty little secrets. I thank God I first made some true friends and then grew up strong enough to protect myself and others."

She shuddered at the picture that appeared in her mind. "But you had no choice. They forced you."

He squeezed her to him. "And did you have a choice? You told me enough so that I have a good idea what happened back in Pendleton and you didn't have much of a choice either based on what later happened to your cousin."

"So what do we do with ourselves?" she asked as she rested her head on his shoulder.

He kissed her forehead and she snuggled closer. "We start from the beginning, and without any baggage or remorse from a past over which we had no control. May I introduce myself, lovely young miss? My name is Owen and I am in love with you."

She giggled and kissed him on the cheek. "And my name is Faith and don't say love just yet, although you Welsh have a marvelous way with words."

"When can I say it?"

"When I tell you that you may," she said and they kissed deeply and passionately. "In the meantime, we enjoy each other's company."

They struggled within the confines of the clothing pile, embracing and kissing. "We are not consummating this tonight," she said, removing his hand from her breast. Despite everything, she still considered herself a virgin. "Do you understand?"

"Yes, but why?"

"Because I'm not ready, that's why. Because there'll be a battle in the summer and I don't want to be either a widow or a woman with a child on the way and her man dead on the battlefield, or worse, maimed. And I'm not alone in thinking like that. Many women are afraid of being abandoned. Lord, what if you were a prisoner like Will Drake had been, rotting away for years?"

"You're right. I do not wish to lose you so I will not push you. Do you want to go back to Franklin's party?"

She giggled again. He was so sweet. Other young boys in

Pendleton would not have been as understanding. A couple of them had tried to seduce her, but none had succeeded, at least not fully.

"No, silly. I only said we wouldn't consummate tonight. There's still plenty we can do to make this night a pleasant one."

He smiled and kissed her again and again and this time she let his hands roam where they wished. She slipped her dress down to her waist so he could kiss her glorious breasts while he ran his hands up her thighs to where she was already moist. A second or two later, she had his manhood in his hand and stroked him while he continued to caress her. Lord, he thought as his mind reeled, whoever said New England girls were frigid Puritans didn't know what they were talking about.

They scarcely noticed that it was no longer so cold in the storeroom.

Fitzroy was nearly frozen with terror as the sled he was on was dragged across the ice-choked river. Frozen with terror, he thought. That's a good one. He was frozen on the frozen river. He'd never seen an iceberg, but he thought some of the chunks of ice floating by qualified.

Beneath a veneer of ice that sometimes buckled and shifted, the wide and deep Detroit River flowed at its usual strong rate. Somebody said nearly four miles an hour, which was a goodly walking pace for a strong man. If he looked down he could see bubbles of air moving beneath the ice as the river continued to flow. He thought that he could see fish staring up at him and laughing at him. He decided not to look down anymore.

"Tell them to hurry," pleaded Danforth from behind him.

"If they pull too hard they might spill you into the river and everyone says your balls will turn blue and freeze solid before they can get you out of the water."

Danforth shuddered. "Right. Then tell them to slow down. I prefer my balls warm and dry." They were wearing heavy wool coats over their uniforms and were still shivering from the cold.

Fitzroy stared at the farther shore, willing it to be closer. Finally it was and he stepped shakily off the sled and onto firm frozen ground. Three of his men had preceded him and three more followed in a sled behind his. A corporal, five privates, and two officers would be enough to raid a small tavern, he hoped.

One of the soldiers led a string of eight horses acquired earlier from local farmers. To Fitzroy's eye, they looked old and decrepit and he was sure he'd overpaid for their rental. Whoever said the Canadians loved the British had never tried to deal with the financial aspects of that love. Damned Canadians, he thought, and especially damn the French ones, who loved money and loved even more taking it from the British.

But at least they had horses, which meant they wouldn't have to walk through the knee-deep snow and mush. His six troopers were all part of Tarleton's cavalry and could ride anything, they said proudly. Still, it would be hell if they had to launch a cavalry charge or even a short chase with these miserable beasts and in the awful weather.

They mounted up and proceeded down the trail at a sedate pace. There was no reason to even pretend to keep their existence a secret. He was certain that their presence had already been spread for quite some distance, and he wondered if their cover story, a food-buying expedition, fooled anyone.

A short while later they came upon their target. The sign said it was the King's Inn, but no self-respecting king would ever stay at such a decrepit place, although he wondered if the current refugee king of France might consider it. As they approached, a cloud of pigeons left the roof of the adjacent barn, circled, and flew away.

"Danforth, did you do that, scare those silly birds away?"

Danforth held on to his steed's mane. He was not a good rider. "Not that I'm aware of. I rather thought my boyish good looks would have charmed them, not frightened them."

They pulled up in front of the inn. Their weapons were in their arms and half-cocked, ready to be quickly fully cocked and fired. Fitzroy signaled for two of the soldiers to go around back and for two more to check out the barn. He dismounted and, along with Fitzroy and the other two soldiers, entered the tavern. Two local men were supposed to own the place and they might have hired hands to help them.

Of course the place was empty. Fitzroy cursed roundly. There was evidence that the owner's departure had been hasty as a small fire still burned in the fireplace and a pot of stew was simmering above it.

"Barn's empty, sir," the corporal reported. "And no one's come out the back. There are tracks. They left on horseback. Do you want us to follow them?"

Fitzroy considered it briefly and discarded the idea. His men were not woodsmen or trackers and didn't even know who they were looking for. Worse, even though they were cavalrymen they were riding horses that couldn't catch a dead man. It had begun to snow again, and the tracks they saw would disappear shortly, and they couldn't go arresting just anyone they might catch up with. Bloody Tarleton might do that, but Fitzroy felt he had to have at least have some suspicions before acting. Of course, the tavern's owners' flight was highly suspicious behavior, which meant their adventure had paid off at least a little bit by scaring off suspicious characters.

"Thank you, no, Corporal. Bring your men in and warm and feed yourselves. You've done a good day's work."

The soldiers grinned and began to help themselves to the abandoned food.

Danforth emerged from a back room. His expression was grim. "I think you should look at this."

Fitzroy followed him into what was obviously an office. There was a desk made out of planking and papers were scattered all about. It was as if the owner had been thinking of discarding them, but interrupted before he could do it.

Fitzroy sat down and began to rummage through them. Some were irrelevant, the usual mundane bills and notes of a tavern keeper. He'd bought beer from one local farmer and stronger stuff from another. He'd bought meat and bread from others, and chickens from still another.

"I see nothing remotely interesting," Fitzroy said. He was beginning to feel tired. Their day had been a long one.

"You're looking at the wrong pile," Danforth said, and handed another stack of papers to him.

Fitzroy sniffed, annoyed at his mistake, and began to read. Danforth was right. This was far more intriguing. First were lists of British regiments as they'd arrived, along with estimates of their strengths. Then there was information about supplies and equipment, and information about the army's commanders and the existence of the now damaged barges. It was a detailed compilation of the British Army's presence at Detroit.

While some of it could have been the result of simple observation, much required someone with an intimate knowledge of the British Army, and the sheer volume implied a nest of spies.

"Interesting reading, eh?" asked Danforth.

"The bloody bastards. I wonder how many spies there were and how they got the information to Fort Washington."

"Does it matter?" Danforth said happily. "We've stopped it at the source, although I'm certain they'll try to set up another spy center. At least finding this will keep Bloody Banastre Tarleton off our backs."

That thought cheered Fitzroy as he continued to look through the papers. Now he was finding observations on the Great Fire as those who had survived it were now calling it. Of course, some of the comments on the fire could have been made by simply looking across the river, but some of them contained detail about military losses that could only have been gotten first hand.

Fitzroy recognized a name and cursed. "Damned Jews."

"What?" asked Danforth as he looked up from some additional papers.

"It looks like Abraham Goldman, the Jewish merchant, is one of the spies. Damn. He's getting rich on us and betraying us at the same time."

Danforth yawned. "No surprise. The stinking Jews are capable of almost anything. We'll arrest the Shylock when we return."

Then a phrase on a sheet of paper caught his attention and he felt a chill go down his spine. "Dear God," he muttered, causing Danforth to start and stare at him.

Fitzroy put down that paper and picked up another. This one referenced Braxton and his orders from Tarleton to attack the newly found settlement. He had argued with both Tarleton and Burgoyne against turning Braxton loose, but Burgoyne had been distracted and Tarleton wanted the raid to go forward. Someone had betrayed Braxton, taken over the buildings, and baited what Fitzroy later realized was a trap. Worse, the phraseology of the document he was reading was familiar. It ought to be, he realized with a sickening feeling—the words were his.

He felt staggered and his head spun. He took a closer look at the handwriting and recognized it. He felt like weeping.

Danforth grabbed his arm. "James, are you all right?"

"Yes," he said and shook his head violently. "I mean no. I'm not all right at all. I've been betrayed. Damn it, I've been betrayed and played for a fool."

Danforth closed the office door so the enlisted men couldn't hear. They were busy feeding themselves, but could easily become curious.

"What is it, James?"

Fitzroy handed him a sheet of paper. "Recognize the words, the writing?"

"Can't say as I do," Danforth said, puzzled.

"The words are mine, they come from my journal."

"Somebody's been reading it?"

"Of course, and I've been sleeping with that somebody. The handwriting is Hannah's. She's been copying my notes and forwarding them to the rebels." He shook his head. "This could not get any worse."

There was a tap on the door and the corporal opened it tentatively. "Sir, there's a man here from the sled pulley. He says someone cut the rope on the Detroit side and we can't get back tonight, maybe tomorrow at the earliest. Could be even longer if the weather turns bad."

Will and Sarah were aware that they were watching history unfold. They only hoped that they would be around years from now to tell the tale to their grandchildren. The very small gallery that the general public could use to watch Congress in action was jammed. This in itself was unusual as popular opinion said that Congress never actually did anything except talk a topic to death.

But this time it was different. The Continental Congress was actually going to do something. The distinguished members were going to vote on and, if approved, sign a draft constitution, and it contained a fundamental bill of rights. Franklin had insisted on the bill of rights. He'd argued that it was all well and good to decide the mechanics of a republican form of government, which was based on the writings of a Frenchman named Montesquieu. But what, he'd insisted, would that government stand for? It had to go beyond mere words. The words had to inspire.

Franklin had enlisted Sarah as a counterpoint for his arguments as he rehearsed them, and she was flattered that he respected her mind and her judgment.

For instance, he'd drawn himself up and asked if she wished to be forced to provide financial support for the Anglican faith, the established church of England? No, she'd answered. Did she agree that only members of an established church could hold political office as was the case in Virginia as well as England? Of course not, she'd responded.

Did she wish the newspapers censored and restricted by the government? No. How could you trust what you were reading if the press was restricted? You couldn't, she replied.

What about quartering soldiers in her house without her permission? She'd shuddered at the thought of a squad of dirty, muddy Redcoats traipsing through her home and again answered with an emphatic no.

With these and other points that represented a counter to British tyranny, she'd found herself in complete agreement and had discussed them with Will who also agreed. "It defines what we have been fighting for," he'd said, and she'd laughingly asked what took him so long to figure it out.

John Hancock, in his role as President of the Continental Congress read the proposed document in its entirety while the participants and spectators sat, transfixed. If and when approved, copies of it would be sent to the British-occupied colonies so they could see the difference between a corrupt, distant, and unfeeling British monarchy and a truly American form of government.

According to the new constitution, there would be freedom of speech and freedom of assembly. There would be freedom of religion and minimal restrictions on a man's right to vote. The press could not be censored.

And slavery was forbidden.

That latter point was finally resolved as Franklin had foreseen. The genie was out of the bottle and could not be returned; nor could the broken egg be made whole no matter how hard one might try. Slaves were free and that was that. England had solved the problem of slavery within the colonies. Rumors had the British backtracking on their promises when faced with economic realities, but that was another matter.

Freedom of religion meant that Jews, Catholics, Quakers, and all other denominations and sects would be permitted to exist, and did not have to either belong to or support the Church of England in Virginia, or the Puritan faith of Massachusetts. Nor did anyone have to declare for any religion. It also meant that the near theocracies that had existed in New England were even less likely to occur again. Some congressmen were uncomfortable with the thought of coexisting alongside Papists, Quakers, Jews,

and even atheists, but the diversity of faiths already existing in
the colonies made defining these freedoms necessary. It was joked
that some Anglican ministers who had been supported by government funds would actually have to go out and work for a living.

The right to vote was another sore point. While most of the
congressmen favored some kind of a republic, there was concern
that too much democracy wasn't a good thing. There were strong
feelings that only those who owned property and who were educated should vote. It was feared that chaos might ensue if the
uneducated and the poor could vote and have their vote count
as much as their betters did. While there were still vestiges of
this in the new constitution, the result was that most men would
be allowed to vote. Education and property requirements would
be minimal although voters would, of course have to be able to
read the ballot and sign their name.

All of this had deeply upset the handful who had supported
the idea of a constitutional monarchy in the colonies. Benjamin
Franklin had snorted that perhaps they'd like to borrow some
of George III's unemployed relatives, or even find a home for
the luckless king of France here in America. When the laughter
subsided, it was determined that there would be no king in the
colonies. Had he still lived, George Washington might have worn
a crown, but King George's ax had ended those ideas.

Since one provision of the proposed constitution prohibited
slavery and another said that almost all men could vote, did that
mean that Negroes could vote? Probably, was the consensus, but
not just yet. Will found himself wondering whether his Negro
savior, Homer, would have the right to vote. He hoped so. Of
course he was biased, but Homer deserved it more than many
white men he knew.

The reading of the bill of rights was over and then the structure of government was outlined. There would be a two-house
legislature, with an upper house where each colony had one
delegate and one vote. There would be a lower house with a
limit of a hundred representatives and they would be divided by
colony according to each colony's population. A president would
be elected by the two houses and serve a single six-year term.

Hancock droned on, talking about judges and ambassadors
and such and, finally, mercifully, was finished. The document
was incomplete and everyone knew it. But it was a start. And

in the bill of rights, a dramatic statement was made that was so totally different from England's way of life and rule.

A roll-call vote was taken and the motion passed, and by a considerable margin. The delegates, under the prodding of Franklin and Hancock, realized that they had to do something significant.

One by one, the congressmen from the colonies stepped to a cloth-covered table and signed their names. Will wondered if Franklin and Hancock, the only signers of the Declaration of Independence present, were comparing this signing to that fateful summer in Philadelphia. There were serious doubts about the legitimacy of the Continental Congress back then and there were even more doubts about the current one.

When it was over, there was no applause. Participants and spectators strolled outside. Will shivered. It had been overheated in Congress Hall and the change was too abrupt.

"What did we just witness?" he asked. "And will it last?"

Sarah took his arm and squeezed it. "Ask again in a year."

# Chapter 10 ★ ★ ★ ★ ★ ★ ★ ★ ★ ★ ★ ★ ★ ★ ★ ★

"FITZROY, YOU ARE A BLOODY GODDAMNED FOOL AND YOU were totally diddled by that yellow-haired Dutch cunt!"

A drunken and outraged Banastre Tarleton was in rare form and scathingly holding forth on the hapless Fitzroy. It had taken a week before the tow line between Detroit and the Canadian side of the river could be fixed and he could return with the news that Hannah Van Doorn and Abraham Goldman were rebel spies. By that time, Hannah, Goldman, and Goldman's three associates were well away—along with much of their wealth and inventory. Obviously, they'd realized what Fitzroy would find at the tavern and had someone cut the rope. Still, either she or Goldman had managed to warn the tavern's owners and coconspirators in time for them to vanish.

"By this time," Tarleton went on, "the whole bunch of them is either in Fort Washington or back in Albany and gathering up more of their money. I've sent riders to arrest and hang them if they show up."

Fitzroy stood stiffly at attention. "If you wish my resignation, you shall have it."

"Don't be silly," Burgoyne said softly. "What's done is done, and I still need a good aide, although I'd prefer one that isn't so gullible. And look at the bright side, Major. You actually did uncover that nest of vipers and send them running. Your personal embarrassment will wear off. After all, I've had to endure

163

the slings and arrows of my enemies for years after surrendering at Saratoga and I've still survived."

Tarleton smiled tightly. "Actually, it could have been much worse. What if the silly slut had become my mistress instead of yours as I'd planned? Imagine my embarrassment if that had happened."

Fitzroy suddenly realized what Tarleton was saying and why he'd been so critical of him. Tarleton had attempted to seduce Hannah and she'd rebuffed him. But why? Bedding a general was a much better source of information than a mere major, even though Fitzroy was Burgoyne's aide and confidante. If her sole motivation was spying, why then had she stayed with him?

Dismissed, he walked slowly and sadly to the tent he now shared with Danforth. Fitzroy had been evicted from the quarters he'd shared with Hannah almost immediately after he'd reported her treason. Tarleton's provost had only grudgingly permitted him to take his clothing and other personal effects, including the damned journal that she'd copied.

Inside, he pulled up a stool and opened the journal. A folded up piece of paper fell out. He picked it up and opened it. It was from Hannah.

"*My dearest little lordship,*" she'd written. "*By now you have found that I have been reporting everything of import to my fellow Americans at Fort Washington. It was not an easy thing to do as I am deeply fond of you and fervently wish that our lives together could have been otherwise.*"

Fitzroy took a deep breath. She hadn't gone to Tarleton's bed because she was fond of him and not Tarleton. Or Burgoyne. Was that supposed to make him feel better? Strangely, it did—a little.

She continued. "*I am sure you are angry and outraged by what you consider my treason. However, I am not a traitor. If I were a traitor, then I would have betrayed America because that is my country, not England. I am an American. So too is Abraham Goldman. I know that English law will find my argument specious and call for my hanging, but I don't care. I can only do what is right and just, and that is to do everything in my power to drive the English, you English, from my land, my country.*

"*Please understand, my love, that I bear the English people, such as you, no ill. Indeed, it pains me deeply to write this and leave you. I only hate and despise your king and his vile and grasping ministers.*

*"I find it highly unlikely that we will ever meet again. Should it happen, it will most certainly be because you are a prisoner, as I have no intention of ever being taken alive. Nor does anyone else who call themselves Americans, so tell your beloved generals that they are in for a battle of no quarter, no retreat. It may well be that the winners will be as bloodied and devastated as the losers. It may well be that neither army will exist when the battle is over. If that is God's will, so be it.*

*"Good bye, my dear little major and I fervently hope you are protected from whatever terrible things may come. And finally, I had no intention of falling in love with you, but I did. I can only wish that the world had been different.*

*"Your dearest Hannah."*

Fitzroy folded the paper and put it back in his journal. He felt the tears rolling down his cheeks.

Will stood with Tallmadge and Schuyler as Glover's Marblehead Regiment marched slowly in. They were ragged and exhausted and made no attempt at a proper formation. Many were limping, and some men helped others with their muskets and packs, while still others were nearly carried by their comrades. Despite their exhaustion, however, they managed grins and waves which were returned. They had made it and were justifiably proud of themselves.

There were approximately two hundred of the Marblehead men, and they were trailed by about fifty other older men, and a handful of women and children. One of the older civilians was a man who was gaunt and even dirtier and more ragged than the others. He stared at Tallmadge and Will. He had a full nose, a thick white beard, bushy eyebrows, and his hair was long and disheveled.

That man knows us, Will thought, and I think I know him. But how? Had he too served in the army? The man looked out of place with the group of civilians. Despite his physical problems, he carried himself like a soldier. Will thought the old man should be leading the column, such was his presence. Will glanced at Schuyler and Tallmadge. They too stared at the man. Tallmadge seemed to nod slightly. The man turned abruptly and walked away.

It had been an epic journey for the Marblehead Regiment, all the way from the coast of Maine to this place near the shores of Lake Michigan. They had trekked through almost a thousand miles of British-held territory and lived to tell about it. To some of the more historical minded, it was like the journey of Xenophon's ten thousand Hellenes marching through Asia Minor to their homes. Even though North America wasn't Asia Minor, Glover's men had traveled from the seacoast of Maine, overland to the St. Lawrence River, crossed, and then hiked to a point just west of the great falls at Niagara. There they had built boats and sailed or paddled their way to a point south of Detroit, eluded Tarleton's patrols, and marched the rest of the way to Fort Washington.

To many, their success was no surprise. Though small in number, the Marbleheaders were a superb regiment and had a reputation for doing the impossible. It was they who had saved Washington's army from being trapped on Long Island. They had commandeered boats and ferried the troops across to Manhattan under the very noses of the British, and, months later they'd help ferry Washington's men across the Delaware to attack the Hessians at Trenton.

The Marbleheaders were led by their original commander, Brigadier General John Glover. He saluted Schuyler and led his men off to where they could be quartered, rested, warmed, and fed.

"We need more of them," Tallmadge mused.

"At least they have weapons," Will said.

Tallmadge laughed. "You've been away too long. Franklin's factories are now making muskets for us. We have far more muskets than we do soldiers to shoot them. Nor are we suffering for lack of powder. Our factories are also turning out pikes, cutlasses, and tomahawks in large numbers. No," he sighed, "what we need are soldiers."

"Just curious, General, but do the factories continue to make that weapon I tested, the Franklin?"

"Lord no. That abomination was discarded rather quickly after we couldn't figure out what to do with it. It was inaccurate at long range, and awkward at short. Thus, we decided to focus on more traditional guns and we are doing quite well. The 'Franklin,' however, was not totally consigned to the trash heap. Willy Washington has taken the inventory of a little more than a hundred of the things and further shortened their barrels. He plans to use them as close-up weapons by his cavalry, which will also be armed with sabers and pistols."

A soldier ran up to Tallmadge, saluted, and handed him a message. Tallmadge unfolded it, crumpled it, and swore.

"More bad news, damn it. The British have found one of my spy centers. Do you recall the King's Tavern across the river from Detroit? Did you know the name was a joke? The owners were two brothers named King and totally loyal to the American cause."

"Of course," Will answered. "I kept some of my men near there while I was at Leduc's place. I recall you said that the owners were sympathetic."

"Much more than that. The brothers King and their grubby tavern were the clearing house for many of the messages from Detroit and now they've been discovered. The brothers got away, but they've been closed down. I can only hope that the people supplying the King brothers with information got themselves away as well."

"Does that mean nothing more from Detroit?" Will asked.

"Of course not." He sniffed. "It simply means that the information will come in more slowly and in a less timely manner until I can effect repairs to the system."

"Which reminds me, General, just how the devil do you get timely information from so far away?"

Tallmadge grinned impishly and punched Will on the shoulder. "When you're old enough to understand such adult matters, I'll tell you."

Abigail Adams invited a number of women to have tea with her, although the tea was more hot colored water than a proper tea. It was an opportunity to talk about things that were of utmost importance to them. Like the slim possibility that they would even be alive the coming fall.

A good hostess, she waited until the score of women had finished at least a little idle chatter. When there was a lull, she tapped on a cup.

"Ladies, it is time to discuss some serious matters."

Silence fell. Abigail Adams was the most respected and admired woman at Fort Washington. If she said she had something important to say, then she would be listened to.

"We all know that the summer will bring a bloody end to our stay here. Either we will prevail and return to our homes, or we will be captured and enslaved, if not killed outright."

There was a mutter that she ignored. "I know that some of you have vowed never to be taken prisoner, never to be enslaved. Some have vowed to fight to the death, while others have decided to flee elsewhere, if there only was an elsewhere. Sadly, there is no elsewhere. We win or lose here. Even if we try to flee, it will be in small numbers and into areas filled with red savages who would like nothing more than to rape us and kill us, if they don't enslave us themselves. If we lose to the British this summer, our prospects are beneath dismal."

"Then what do you propose?" asked Sarah. Even though she'd been prepped by Mistress Adams and told when to ask questions, Abigail's spoken words had chilled her.

John Adams' wife smiled tightly. "With the blessings of the conniving Doctor Franklin, he has come up with some ideas to help the men in combat and extend their numbers beyond what we have."

"Would we have to fight?" someone exclaimed in shock.

"Are you afraid to?" Sarah snapped back, causing a momentary uproar.

Abigail Adams called for calm and, after a moment, got it. "I am not proposing that we women actually fight; however, I am suggesting that those of us who feel we can should be prepared to fight. After all, didn't a few of you say that you'd rather die than be captured, raped, and enslaved? Well, wouldn't you rather take a few Redcoats with you before death, or were you contemplating heroic suicide?"

The heavyset mistress of General von Steuben rose. "I want to kill the bastards. Any British soldier who thinks he can lie on top of me without my permission will be a dead one."

Abigail nodded and suppressed a smile. "Good. No matter what happens, we will be terribly close to the fighting, so I am proposing that we involve ourselves in it as much as possible without actually trying to join the ranks of soldiers."

"But aren't there women already masquerading as soldiers?" the wife of a colonel asked.

"Likely a few," Abigail admitted, "although their presence is not officially admitted and their numbers not actually known. However, there have been incidents of women joining the ranks and actually fighting and even becoming casualties, which is how their gender was discovered. And that brings us back to the point.

In order to help our men, and help ourselves, we must not just sit idly by while the battle that shapes our futures takes place a few hundred yards away from us."

Catherine Greene, the general's widow, spoke up. Grief was still etched in her still lovely face. "What do you want us to do? While there are women here in camp, the men far outnumber us, which means our impact would be small."

Again Abigail Adams nodded and smiled, this time knowingly. "Of course you are correct. Our actual numbers are fairly small, but, if we are clever, our impact could be enormous. As to what I want from you, perhaps it is what you want from yourselves. I wish you to discuss this with the others of our fairer and so-called weaker sex and find out how many will help. When I have a good number, I will present it to Doctor Franklin and he will confront the generals."

Daniel Morgan's wife, also named Abigail, rose and glared at Abigail Adams. "Just one thing, Mistress Adams."

"Yes?"

"Fairer and weaker sex my ass."

Lieutenant Owen Wells rested his rifle against a log and looked out across the stark and snow-covered meadow before him. He and his men were hidden just inside the tree line and had been so for almost a week.

It wasn't warm yet, but the sun was shining brightly and there was the hint of spring in the air. There might still be snow and rain and ice, but it would not last very long. Springtime was good, a time of renewal with colors that were bright and clean. Spring was also bad, since it meant that the day of reckoning with the British war machine was coming closer.

That was why Owen, Sergeant Barley, and the twenty-odd men in his command waited along the trail a few miles outside of Fort Washington. Someday the nicer weather would bring unwelcome visitors, thousands of them, but not this day. They had another reason for waiting.

"What're you thinking of, Lieutenant?" Barley asked.

Owen was jolted back to reality. "My duty, of course."

Barley laughed and looked around. None of the other soldiers was close enough to overhear them. "Bullshit. You were thinking of your girlfriend, weren't you?"

Actually, Owen had been thinking of Faith's bare breast and the taste of her nipple on his lips and the feel of her hand on his swollen manhood. But he'd be damned if he'd admit all that to Barley, even if the two of them were close friends, Owen decided it was time to change the subject.

"Do you see the irony in our being here? Wasn't this the place where you found Major Drake and me fumbling our way through the woods?"

"Yes, and clumsier than hell you were, by God. We heard you coming for miles."

"That's because we were hungry and tired, otherwise we'd have been as silent as a snake, damn you."

Owen shifted and scratched where a twig was digging into his leg, "Do you ever think that it's wrong for me to be in charge of you when it was the other way around for a while?"

Barley spat on the ground. "Naw. I figure it's God's will or something like that. Besides, you can read and write orders while I'd have a hell of a time with them."

Owen knew better but didn't argue. Barley could read and write quite as well as the next man. What he didn't want was responsibility. Almost everyone in the colonies could read and write, even though many rarely read books except for the Bible. Newspapers and pamphlets were other sources of information. This made it much better than England, where so many were illiterate. Owen wondered why the British considered the colonists their inferiors when the average colonist—at least the ones he'd seen—were much better educated, along with being bigger, stronger, and healthier.

"I still don't understand why we're out here," muttered Barley. "If we're supposed to protect these people, why don't we meet them farther out?"

Owen rolled his eyes. They'd been over this before. "Because this is where the trails converge. If we went out to meet them we could miss them by a few feet and never know it."

"I suppose," Barley grumbled. "But what if they get caught out there while we're waiting here?"

"Then they're totally and tragically out of luck. Don't forget, though, we're not the only patrol out looking for them."

"And one's a Jew? I've never seen a Jew."

Owen couldn't resist. "They're easy to spot. They're big and fat and have large horns on the side of their heads and their bodies are covered with long greasy fur. And those are the female Jews and all they want to do is screw your brains out, which, in your case, won't take all that long."

"Fuck you, Lieutenant. But seriously, didn't they kill Jesus?"

"Not lately, Sergeant, and I do mean that seriously."

"Seriously, I never met any Jews. Have you?"

"Some. Mainly traveling peddlers back in Wales. They were like everyone else, just people trying to make a living, although I admit they were a little strange. I did very briefly see a few wealthy ones in New York, but they dealt with officers and not men like me."

He didn't need to add that it was the only time the Royal Navy had let him off the ship.

"Haven't been many people coming in lately, and don't tell me it's because of the winter," Barley said.

The phenomenon had been noted by others. What had been a steady trickle of people seeking sanctuary in Fort Washington had just about dried up. The reason was obvious. Who wanted to go to a place that might be destroyed in a few months with everybody in and around it either killed or enslaved? In effect, everyone who really wanted to go to Fort Washington was already there. The people they were looking for were the exception.

"Movement in the woods," one of the sharper-eyed soldiers announced and they all strained their eyes to see. Owen had a small telescope and finally caught a patch of moving color.

"I see them." He paused as the picture became clearer. "I count five."

"So do I," said Barley. "The small one might be a woman."

And that would make the numbers just about right, Owen thought. Tallmadge had said there wouldn't be more than a handful and one of them might be a woman. Behind them, Owen could see a line of small horse-drawn carts laden with store goods.

The people stepped carefully into the meadow and looked around nervously. They were fully exposed and it made them uncomfortable. Owen saw a couple of muskets, but the little group was decidedly lacking in firepower. One man was older and overweight. Two of the younger men were helping him. The smaller one removed a cap and revealed blond hair that had been chopped short. Obviously, she was the woman Tallmadge had mentioned.

Barley again spat on the ground. "Does not look like an invad-
ing army."

Owen stood up and waited until they saw him. He walked
slowly toward them, his rifle in the crook of his arm. Barley
walked a few paces behind him and to his side. When they were
a few paces away, Owen stopped.

"Name yourselves," he ordered.

The older man stood as tall as he could. "My name is Abraham
Goldman. These two young men who think I am so weak I will
fall over are my beloved but idiot sons. The other two men used
to own a tavern across the river from Detroit. The little one is
named Hannah and she has been a great help to me."

"Are you really a Jew?" asked Barley, stepping up alongside
Owen. "The lieutenant tried to tell me that Jews were bigger and
all covered with fur."

As Owen rolled his eyes, Goldman smiled tolerantly. "As monsters
go, I'm a small one. And it's springtime, so my fur has molted."

Owen eased his grip on his weapon. "And what else are you
to tell me, Mr. Goldman?"

"Tell General Tallmadge that his 'doves' have arrived."

Owen nodded and smiled. "I will, but first let's get you some
food and water."


"Another epistle from Cornwallis," said Fitzroy. "And again full
of lamentations and complaints about us taking so long fiddling
in the forests while Rome, or perhaps New York or London, is
burning."

Danforth sat on the edge of his cot and sucked on his pipe.
If the stinking mess he was smoking was actually tobacco, then
dogs had just become cats. "Well, why don't you write the details
in your journal so they can be stolen again?"

"Unfair," Fitzroy said and hid a wince. It reminded him again
of Hannah and the wound was still fresh. He marveled that he
still held strong feelings for her despite her betrayal. And, he had
indeed been keeping his journal and the hell with what either
Burgoyne or Tarleton thought.

"So what does the great Lord Corn of Wallis worry about
this time?" Danforth asked. He had been spending less and less
time in headquarters. He was now tasked with working alongside
Benedict Arnold and overseeing the completion of the sailing

barges, despite the fact that he knew nothing about boats other than that they floated on water. Or were supposed to, he'd joked.

Fitzroy chuckled mirthlessly. "Despite denials and such from Cornwallis and their lordships in London, the American public is aghast at the information that they would become vassals or serfs at the end of the taking of Fort Washington."

"Can't imagine why?" Danforth said. "Who wouldn't jump with joy at the chance to become a serf on his own land? I would be absolutely enchanted at the thought of working endless days for starvation wages and having my wife and female children sent out as whores to supplement my income."

"Cornwallis reports that insurrections have broken out in many areas and that Boston may now be under rebel control. He further said that partisan activity in the southern colonies has increased to the point where Charleston is under virtual siege. As to New York, Cornwallis has strengthened the landward defenses of Manhattan and thinks that there would be an insurrection if not for the presence of a half a dozen Royal Navy warships and their assorted cannon."

Danforth scoffed. "And a British victory at Fort Washington would change all that? Methinks he pins his hopes on a slender reed."

"He hopes it would be so. At least it and the return of his army would only give him enough force to put down what he is confronting now."

Danforth put down his pipe. "Dear Lord, are you saying that this war could go on even longer? I thought this campaign was to end the war in the colonies once and for all."

Fitzroy sat on his cot and pulled out his journal. "It was, but that was before the king and his cronies fucked it up so royally."

Will and Tallmadge walked through yet another warehouse. As with the others, it was filled with weapons of all categories, although many were of the very simplest types. Along with muskets, these included pikes, bayonets, and tomahawks.

Still, there were enough muskets to supply far more than the army at Fort Washington. It was testimony to the organizational skills of Schuyler and the improvisational techniques of Franklin. Who would have thought that the iron ore to make them existed in quantity just a few hundred miles north of them? And who would have thought that it could be mined with relative ease, melted into ingots, and then brought down in the large canoes used by the Indians when making long trips with sizeable crews and cargoes? While there would never be enough quality iron or implements to cast cannon, there was enough to manufacture the smaller weapons that filled the warehouses.

"Who will use all these?" Will asked. "Are you expecting company or is this wishful thinking?"

"Perhaps a little of both. Surely, we'll have more soldiers coming in when the British begin to move on us, but I'm just as certain that a number of our heroic stalwarts will flee anywhere they can, rather than actually fight. Human nature, I'm afraid."

"Summer soldiers and sunshine patriots," Will mused. "Tom Paine was correct. And what of Mistress Adams' ideas?"

Abigail Adams and a deputation of women had proposed to General Schuyler that they function as messengers and couriers within the army. There was a hint that women should also be allowed to load weapons for the men during the fighting that was sure to come. All the suggestions had been met with shock and skepticism. However, they had not been rejected.

"Much will depend on the requirements of whoever actually leads the army," Tallmadge said, adding that it had been Schuyler's response.

"And who will that be, and who is that man I've seen you talking with? You know, the one who arrived with Glover. Or is he just another of your spies?"

"He's an old friend." Tallmadge said with a knowing smile. "Just like you are, which permits you to take such liberties as you do with a high-ranking general such as I am."

Tallmadge took Will by the arm and steered him out of the warehouse. "Don't pressure me about him and I'll share a secret with you."

"Which one?"

Tallmadge grinned wickedly, "As how I get my information so quickly."

Will allowed himself to be led back to Tallmadge's headquarters. As always, the wood-shingled roof was covered with scores of pigeons and stained white with their droppings. A dozen or so flew off and whirled around as the men approached, while others stayed and observed. Instead of going through the front of the building, Tallmadge led him through the back. Inside, Will's jaw dropped as he saw cage after cage filled with pigeons.

"What is this, dinner?" he asked.

Tallmadge laughed. "Hardly. Cook them forever and they'd still be too bloody tough to chew. Will, this is the secret. The pigeons in these cages are homing pigeons and have been trained to return here once released. A small, short message is tied to their legs and they can make it from a place like Detroit to here in an astonishingly short period of time. It is a trick that's been in use for perhaps thousands of years. Of course, I must wait for a more detailed explanation to arrive in the traditional manner, such as when you finally show up covered with filth after plodding through the woods."

"And this is what you lost when the British raided that tavern, isn't it?"

"In part. Of course it wasn't the only location sending messages by pigeon. It was, however, the best. I've been reconstituting other sites. When the British finally move, their location will be sent to us by a variety of means and we will be able to react rather quickly."

"Doesn't that presume we'll have an army to react with?"

"It does indeed," Tallmadge said sadly, "and that is the flaw in the plan. We have to have a bloody army and someone competent to lead it. And still that might not be enough."

# Chapter 11 ★★★★★★★★★★★★★★★★★★★

BRAXTON DIDN'T LIKE INDIANS. MOST WHITE MEN DIDN'T. They considered them drunken ignorant savages who would steal anything that wasn't nailed down and that included white women. In particular, Braxton didn't like Joseph Brant and his Iroquois. He thought Brant was arrogant, and as to his so-called Iroquois warriors, Braxton considered them to be nothing more than animals that happened to walk upright. He knew it was a strange distinction from someone who had committed so many murders and atrocities, and the few men of his who had survived the massacre at the so-called farm reminded him of it whenever the occasion arose. Sometimes he agreed and actually thought it was funny.

Thus, it was with a degree of pleasure that he fostered a friendship with Simon Girty, one of the few men whose reputation was more fearsome than his own. Girty had been accused of rape, the murder and torture of innocents, and cannibalism.

Braxton doubted that the rumor about cannibalism was true. It was something he'd never do, unless, of course, he were truly starving. Then nothing counted. Still, he made sure not to get Girty angry at him. The two men were approximately the same age with Girty being just a few years older. They shared many attitudes towards the war and how to survive in it.

Girty had lived in a cabin outside Detroit the last several years after changing sides from rebel scout to loyalist. The rebels wanted to hang him for a multitude of crimes, including treason, and that made Girty a good man for Braxton to follow.

Girty took a swallow of raw homemade whisky and smiled. The two of them and some of their men had just come back from a patrol, and had tried to intercept the group of rebel spies fleeing from Detroit. To no one's surprise, the spies had too much of a lead for Girty, Braxton, and the dozen men they'd taken to catch up to them. Still, they thought they'd only missed them by a couple of hours from the signs they'd read in the forest. The carts they'd taken with them had slowed them considerably. They called a halt when they decided they were too close to where patrols from Fort Washington were likely.

"Would've been fun," Girty said wistfully. "The Jews we would've skinned and then crucified. You ever hear someone squeal when they've been skinned?"

"Can't say as I have," said Braxton. He had, but he didn't want to annoy Girty by saying so.

"Almost as much fun as when the Indians take a long time burning someone alive. A real long time," Girty said and looked at him coldly. "Killing like that don't bother you, does it? Hell, all they are is rebels."

"Don't bother me at all," Braxton said sincerely as he took another swallow from his cup of whisky. He wanted to ask if Girty had ever eaten the people he'd cooked, but decided against it.

Girty took a swallow. "Then we would've fucked that blond bitch until it came out her ears. Gawd, that would've been funny. I saw her around the post a number of times with that tight-ass major she was fucking, and it would've served both of them right. When we were through, I would've cut off her head and tits and sent them to that fucking major as a present. I hear he's still moaning for her. I'd like to have heard him moan when she arrived all in pieces. Hell, maybe it'll still happen."

Girty laughed hugely and yawned as exhaustion and the liquor took control. "Joseph Brant is a fool and his Indians are worse. Brant thinks he's a white man because he can read and write, or he thinks he's as good as one. Either way, he's wrong. He's an Indian and not a damn thing more. Worse, his big, bad Iroquois will run like rabbits when the actual fighting starts."

"Why?" Braxton asked. The whisky was taking him over and

he felt like nothing more than sleeping. Still, Girty had a lot that was important on his mind and Braxton wanted to hear it.

"Because they've been here too long and they're too far away from whatever swamp they call home. And when they've deserted and all run back to upper New York, then Burgoyne will have need of people like us to scout and run the woods for him. How many men you got left, Braxton?"

"A dozen."

"Tell me the truth, damn it."

Braxton winced. "Maybe six."

"I got maybe twenty. We'll have to start recruiting hard if we're going to get our share of loot out of Burgoyne's victory. I want two hundred or more men in Girty's Legion."

"Girty's Legion?"

Girty laughed again. "How about Girty's Scouts, or Girty's Royal Americans, or Girty's Murdering Fuckers? I don't care what the hell we're called just so long as we get to kill a lot of rebels and, when the war is over, we get our share of the loot. How's that sound, Braxton?"

"Sounds pretty good to me."

"Good. Now let's have another drink and see if we can find some people who think like we do."

The return of George Rogers Clark and his small band of explorers was met with apprehension. What would be the results of his exploration of the lands to the west? Would they be able to transport Fort Washington and their concept of a new nation out into what people were openly referring to as a Great American Desert? And if they could, it might mean that a battle with the British could be deferred, perhaps permanently. If the rebels could only get far enough away from King George's claws, they might live a bit longer as free people. They knew they could never fully escape. Their only hope was to be far enough away for a long enough time to establish themselves and let England either forget about them or be willing to let them live in peace.

There would be no secrets. After Hancock and Schuyler met briefly with Clark, anybody who wished to was welcome to come to the room where Congress usually met and hear Clark's report.

During the war, George Rogers Clark had conquered much of the area around Fort Washington when he captured the British forts of Vincennes and Kaskaskia, and even threatened Detroit. They respected him and admired him; however, everyone at the meeting saw that he was ill at ease and that did not bode well for any who had hopes of a farther retreat.

Clark spoke softly at first, and then gained strength. He told them that the area to the west was a vast grassland, and not a desert, although there were long stretches without much water, and where crops would not grow. It was a paradox since he and his men had to cross a number of rivers, including a few that were extremely wide and deep.

These rivers, however, weren't all that far away and most people already knew about them. The British would be in striking distance if they moved along their banks. Thus, they would have to flee past the rivers.

Beyond the rivers was an endless plain. Clark said it could and did support life, just not much of it. The buffalo herds were immense and were chased by the Indians, many of whom were on horseback, although some were still on foot. According to Clark, some of the Indians were getting horses from the Spanish to their south and rapidly learning to use them to advantage.

"The savages are taking to horses just as fast as they can get their hands on them, and that generally means stealing them. If we go into their land, we'll have to be mounted and they'll try their best to take our horses. A lot of the Indians have guns as well, and they don't like us at all."

Clark added that only small communities would survive in such an environment, since there was no place where food was abundant. Small communities would, of course, be juicy targets for the Indians. "In order to move into the plains," he continued, "we'll have to fight the Indians and destroy them."

Farther to the west was what was referred to as a great salt lake. Clark hadn't seen it, but the Indians all agreed it was there. Since the lake was salt, it was obvious that any land around it must be barren. He had talked to Indians who had been to the lake and beyond, and added that he believed it was indeed a lake and not an arm of the Pacific Ocean which was much farther away.

Still farther beyond the salt lake were great mountains that, if crossed, would send travelers into the land bordering the Pacific Ocean. This land was rumored to be fertile enough, but, unfortunately, it was also occupied, or at least claimed.

"Indians are there, of course, but there are supposed to be Russians to the north and Spanish to the south. That reminds me," Clark added, "anybody who does go west will quickly find that they're in territory claimed by Spain and they don't take too kindly to strangers, especially non-Catholic strangers, coming into their land. We'd probably have to fight them as well as the British and the Indians."

Benjamin Franklin stood. "Let me ask you a few questions, General Clark." Clark nodded assent. "First, since grass grows on the prairie, why can't we plant wheat?"

Clark grinned. "Well, you could. But then you'd have to fence in the planted area to protect it from buffalo and other wild animals that would either eat it or trample it, and I don't know of any fence that could keep out a herd of ten thousand hungry buffalo."

"Are the herds really that large?" Franklin asked. Almost everyone had seen buffalo, but only in much smaller numbers.

"The herds are that large and larger. There may be millions of them roaming over the plains and they're all always looking for food. It's an incredible sight to see a herd on the move, especially when they're running, and they're terrifying when they stampede. The sound is almost deafening. In order to protect our crops, we'd have to kill off all the buffalo and that ain't gonna happen 'cause there's too many buffalo to kill off. Besides, if we did, there'd go our primary source of meat."

He was handed a mug and he took a swig. It was clearly not water. "Nah, if we went out there we'd have to become small groups of nomads just like the savages."

"But can't the buffalo be domesticated, tamed?" Franklin inquired genially.

Clark guffawed. "You'd stand a better chance of taming a bear."

"And the Indians are truly that dangerous?"

"Everything is dangerous out there, Doctor Franklin, the Indians, the animals, and the weather. Look, I went out with thirty men and came back with eighteen. The others are dead, and they were all well-armed and trained soldiers and woodsmen. Life is worse than hard out there. How the hell do you think a bunch of pilgrims would do?"

Clark smiled wickedly at Franklin. "I got one question of my own, Doctor Franklin. Were you cold this past winter?"

Franklin returned the smile. "I was miserable as you and everyone around here knows. My old bones nearly froze."

Clark nodded. "Then don't go west. The winds are ten times wickeder than they are here and the temperature's so cold it freezes piss before it hits the ground. We saw buffalo freeze to death and they got real thick skin and fur."

Franklin appeared to shudder. "Thank you General Clark."

There was polite applause. Clark had answered the question of continued flight; it wasn't feasible for the community of Fort Washington. Individuals could make it into exile, but not the several thousand people in the area. They would have to stand and fight.

Sarah held tight to Will's arm as they exited the barn. The press of bodies inside had caused the barn to be awfully warm. Will thought that some of his personal warmth might have been due to the fact that Sarah had stood directly in front of him and her back and bottom had been pressed against his body. He hadn't minded a bit.

"I'm cold," she said and wrapped a shawl around her shoulders, "And afraid."


Lieutenant General John Burgoyne was more than a little drunk, which wasn't unusual for those in the encampments that surrounded what was left of Detroit. It was presumed that the garrisons at Oswego, Albany, and Pitt were also drinking away the winter as they awaited the campaign that would begin in spring and commence fully in summer. There was no fear of a surprise attack from the rebels. Scouts were watching the trails and reported nothing.

"Gates, Arnold, Morgan, and Stark," Burgoyne muttered. "The four of them conspired to beat me at Saratoga. That cannot happen again. I will not permit it."

"It can't happen again," Fitzroy said. His voice was a little slurred. He'd been helping his commanding officer and distant cousin while away the evening. "I mean, at least not that way. Gates is disgraced and in prison, and Arnold is on our side."

Burgoyne snorted. "Gates was a fool. He commanded the rebel army but did nothing. Arnold, Morgan, and Stark won the battles and he got the credit. There was no justice."

Fitzroy settled back. It was going to be a long evening. "And

Morgan shouldn't be a factor, either," he said. "I understand the man's crippled and needed to be carried on a litter for his last battle."

"During which he annihilated a force led by Tarleton, who was on horseback and didn't need a litter," Burgoyne responded. "Yes, he's crippled, but he's still a viper with venom. He will command one of their wings and he will do so with skill, just like he did at Freeman's farm where he stopped my advance."

Burgoyne took another long swallow. "Anthony Wayne played a subordinate role at Saratoga, so that only leaves Stark among the ones who defeated me. He destroyed my Hessian wing at Bennington when I sent them out to forage for supplies. Where the devil is John Stark?"

Fitzroy shrugged. "Probably in prison. Either that or hiding out on some mountain in Vermont. Maybe he's even dead."

"I hope so," Burgoyne said. "I fervently hope so. The man's a demon."

Commanding only local, raw militia, Stark's skillfully led soldiers had wiped out the Hessian force at Bennington. The Hessians had gone for food and one result of their defeat was that Burgoyne's army went hungry.

Fitzroy tried to lighten the mood. "Perhaps Schuyler will lead them? You defeated him handily, didn't you?"

"For which he was court-martialed and acquitted with honor. Nobody could have won anything with the disgraceful force he had at his disposal at that time. However, the rebels won't let him lead them anyhow because of the taint of defeat that surrounds him."

"Are you that concerned we won't win, General?" Fitzroy asked.

Burgoyne unsuccessfully stifled a belch and glared at him. "Of course I'm concerned. I'd be a bloody fool if I wasn't. A battle never goes as planned." He finished his drink and lurched to his feet. "And now I'm off to bed."

Fitzroy left and walked on unsteady legs to his tent. The air was more bracing than cold and hinted at spring. Good, he thought, enough of this waiting. Were the rebels drinking themselves through the winter at Fort Washington? He hoped so.

And what was Hannah doing? How was she spending the cold winter days and nights? Had she found another lover? He hated the thought.

Danforth was sitting on his bunk and polishing his boots. This was another sign of their dismal state. No servants. And no reason to polish boots except that it killed time. Worse, they had to mend their own uniforms, and those were starting to look very ragged.

"How is his generalship?" Danforth asked.

"Having another bout of nightmares filled with monsters and goblins. He sees outstanding rebel generals everywhere and it doesn't help that some of those who were at Saratoga are at Fort Washington. He's afraid of failure, and why not. Another defeat and he'd be a laughingstock."

"So would you, James," Danforth said softly. "You're both his cousin and his aide and I know you have no money or position to fall back on. I would survive because I'm just an ordinary officer and because my family does have enough funds to buy me another commission, or even a seat in Parliament. That and I'm confident Cornwallis would welcome me back with open arms. But you? You'd be associated by default with Burgoyne's mess and become a military pariah. You'd be lucky to get a job in India sorting elephant dung into piles according to size and stench."

"Thank you for the kind thoughts," Fitzroy said and rubbed his forehead. He felt the onset of a massive headache. Still, Danforth's comments were nothing he hadn't thought of before. For better or worse, his star was hitched to John Burgoyne's. If Burgoyne soared, so would James Fitzroy. If Burgoyne plummeted to earth, so would he. Damn.

So, who would finally lead the rebels? Would Morgan regain his health or would Schuyler recover his men's respect? And where the hell was this John Stark?

The women were organized into ten groups of ten each. In front, directing each group was a sergeant or a lower-ranking officer. The women held pikes, and the spear-like weapons were longer than the women were tall.

Even though training women on pikes had been agreed upon and was strictly voluntary, there was concern on the part of Schuyler and others as to whether giving weapons to women was the right thing to do. First and foremost, training women on the use of the musket had been ruled out. The musket was a large and cumbersome weapon and it was doubted that many women would be able to handle it effectively in the heat of battle; thus, even though there was a surplus of muskets and even though there were women who already knew how to use them, they would not be issued to the women. It was tacitly understood, however, that whatever happened when the fighting began would be beyond anyone's control.

The instructors understood the fundamental problem. The pikes were far heavier and more awkward than anything the women were used to handling. Thus, after a few clumsy near-stabbings, the first part of each drill focused on developing strength and familiarity with the pikes. After a few weeks of training, it now showed. The women, thin Winifred Haskill included, wielded their pikes with a degree of alacrity, and some with unexpected and new found strength. Winifred enjoyed anything that might bring destruction to the British.

"Thrust," Sergeant Bahlmann yelled at a group that included Sarah Benton and Winifred. Faith was absent this day, because of female problems, but Hannah Van Doorn was enthusiastically present. Bahlmann was a Hessian deserter and an expert with both the bayonet and the pike. Sarah and the others yelled and jabbed at an imaginary target. They had done this a hundred times and were getting bored as their arms grew leaden. The sergeant knew it. "Shoulder your weapons and follow me."

Puzzled, the women did as they were told. They were among the first groups who were being trained. What they learned and how well they learned it would set the tone for future trainee groups. It was a technique brought to the American army by von Steuben.

Congress and General Schuyler had reluctantly come around to the idea that females who wished it should be taught to defend themselves. No one thought for a second that it would alleviate the Continental Army's shortage of numbers in comparison with the British, but it might help in some small matter.

Besides, it made the women feel that they were contributing to the cause and, as Benjamin Franklin told Sarah, that was more important than anything. Sarah had given serious thought to hitting the old man when he'd said it, but he'd laughed and she'd realized he'd been teasing her.

The ten women and their sergeant were marched over a hill and were quickly out of sight of the others. Bahlmann halted them, turned, and stood before them. Behind him, a dead sheep was tied to a stake. They stared at it, knowing what was to come.

"Can you kill them?" Bahlmann asked in his accented English. "Them" came out as "zem." "Or do you just hope that you can? Or maybe you are here to impress someone with your bravery? A lover, perhaps. That there thing on the post is a dead sheep, not a living Redcoat, so the wee dead lamb won't try to stab you or shoot you any more than a chicken would. But can you jab that pike into it? Because that's what I want you to do. I want you to know what it's like to stick a pike into meat, and feel it driving into flesh."

There was silence as some of the women were openly dismayed at the thought of actually stabbing something. That they'd killed chickens and sliced meat from a cow or a deer was somehow now irrelevant. This was supposed to represent a living human being.

"We can do it," Sarah muttered. Hannah nodded, while Winifred looked enthusiastic.

The sergeant grinned. "I thought it would be you, Mistress Benton. Take a position in front of the attacking sheep and imagine that it is about to kill you."

Sarah did as she was told. "Lunge," she was ordered and she complied, the pike stopping just short of the carcass.

"Into the damned thing, Mistress Benton! Tickle it like you're doing and he'll come at you and kill you and then go baa-baa over your body." Sarah lunged again and felt the tip go an inch or so into the sheep's torso before stopping.

"You just hit a rib, Mistress Benton. People have them and so do sheep, and they're supposed to protect people from things like pikes. If you're very lucky you won't hit one, but most likely you will because there are a lot of them, so you will have to hit with enough force to break your way in. Do it again."

Sarah tried once more and was again stopped by the cadaver's ribs. Bahlmann yelled that she was a weakling, a child, a fool. She was getting angry. She pulled back slightly, screamed, and pushed forward with all her might. The pike hit flesh, then bone, and then went through. She tried to pull it out, but it caught on something and she wanted to gag.

"Twist and pull back," the sergeant said, and she did. The pike released itself. The spear point was covered with congealed red matter. Behind her, she heard a couple of the women snuffling and crying. She turned on them angrily.

"And what did you think was going to happen when you stuck someone?" she said while Sergeant Bahlmann grinned. "Sergeant, what happens if I can't get the bloody thing out by twisting like you said?"

"Leave it and get another one if you have to, but first try hard to get it out. If the Redcoat's lying on the ground, just put your foot on his chest and jerk it out. It should come out if you do that. Don't worry about him looking up your dress and seeing your sweet furry cunny 'cause he's going to have other things on his mind if that spear's so far inside his gut. However you do it, you must get it out fast before another British soldier comes up on you."

Sarah glared at him. "I have no intentions of wearing a dress in battle, Sergeant."

Bahlmann laughed and chose another victim and put her through the same paces. One woman couldn't do it and was dismissed from the group. To no one's surprise, Winifred Haskill had no problems, attacking the carcass with a ferocity that surprised and impressed Bahlmann.

The sergeant was good. He'd made them do things they never really thought were possible. The drill instructors had been sent over by von Steuben from the Hessian camp and were considered the best. She could see why. Franklin might have teased her, but Steuben was serious about the women's efforts.

The group was dismissed after cleaning their pikes and Sarah walked over to the fence where Will lounged. He took the pike from her. They would put it in the armory on the way to their respective quarters.

"Feel like dinner?" he asked.

Sarah realized she'd worked up a tremendous appetite. "I would love dinner. What are you serving?"

Will grinned wickedly. "Mutton."

A few yards away from the building where congress met, and ignored by the Americans nearby, two Indians watched intently as important white people exited the hall. One Indian was a blind old man and the other a boy in his early teens. They were dirty and dressed in rags. They'd been in the camp on a number of occasions, selling game or just simply watching. They were considered harmless as were a number of other Indians who came and went. Some came simply to beg and scrounge and it was accepted that some were calculating the strength of the American forces.

The older man was named Owl and not only because he was wise. A birth defect had made him wheeze and hoot when he talked. He looked towards the boy he couldn't quite see. Age had made his vision cloudy.

"What are your thoughts?" Owl asked.

The boy was named Tecumseh and it was understood that he was going to be a chief someday. It was considered good that he would see people who might be his enemy. His uncle was Little Turtle, a Miami chief who had fought against the American rebels. Now, Little Turtle openly wondered which was the better side for the Indians to support? The British were more powerful, apparently, but the rebels simply would not go away.

"The rebel women will fight," the boy answered. "Not as hard as our women might, but they will fight. But that is not what is important, grandfather, is it?" Owl was not the boy's grandfather, but it was a mark of respect and affection. "The true question is whether or not they will win. Answer that question and we can decide who to back, can't we? If we back the right side, perhaps we will win their gratitude and peace within our own land."

It was still a sore point that the Americans had come and driven away the Indians, primarily the Potawatomi, who'd been living for many generations, in the area now called Liberty. Still, even the angriest among them fully understood that the Indians had no chance of driving away either the Americans or the British without the help of the other side.

The boy smiled. The old man couldn't see it, but he heard it in the boy's voice. "But which will it be, grandfather, and just when will we make our decision? Or perhaps we will not back either side?"

The older man smiled and affectionately put his hand on the boy's shoulder. Yes, he would someday be a good chief.

This afternoon General Burgoyne was the essence of confidence. Gone were the doubts of the previous night and present was the confidence of a man who believed he possessed overwhelming advantage against an enemy that was inferior in all ways. Today he was a man who felt that destiny had chosen him to succeed where he had failed before.

Perhaps some of his pleasure was derived from the fact that the lakes, while still bitterly cold, were finally clear of ice and that more sailing barges, fully loaded with supplies, had arrived from Oswego. Also, several thousand more men were marching along the Lake Erie coast and still more were coming in from Pitt. Soon the army would be all together and they could commence to move westward. For many—most—it could not come soon enough.

Burgoyne beamed at the half dozen men in the room. Grant, Arnold, and Tarleton were the senior generals present, while Fitzroy sat quietly behind Burgoyne, ready to do his master's bidding. Two secretaries were ready to scribble notes and compare them later for accuracy.

"This is not a true council of war, gentlemen, rather it is a meeting where we can begin to coordinate our thoughts and our efforts. First, the arrival of the boats from Oswego strengthens us and vindicates my plan for them. They are now proven seaworthy and will most certainly make it to their destination."

Eyes turned to Benedict Arnold who fidgeted slightly and then nodded. "They, their crews, and their precious cargo are all intact," the one-time rebel general said.

Burgoyne went on to announce that the boats built at Detroit would be sent in ballast to Oswego where they too would be loaded with supplies and shipped back to Detroit. The supplies largely consisted of heavier items, like cannon, shells, and ammunition that could only be transported with enormous difficulty through the dense forest and along the area's almost nonexistent roads. It was a bitter truth that Burgoyne had learned during his Saratoga campaign. Had he left his cannon behind, he might have arrived at his goal of Albany long before the rebels could gather and defeat him.

Burgoyne repeated the fact that Benedict Arnold would command the flotilla of sailing barges, which would be augmented by two armed schooners, the *Vixen* and the *Snake*. Burgoyne added that the trip from Detroit to Oswego and back would be an excellent shakedown cruise for those boats and their crews that hadn't been more than a few feet from where they'd been built.

Arnold had been chosen to command because of his experience commanding rebel boats at the battle of Valcour Island. He'd been defeated, but his aggressive efforts had forced a year's delay in the British attack that ultimately led to Burgoyne's disastrous defeat at Saratoga. He would also command the united flotilla when it ultimately sailed for Fort Washington. Fitzroy wondered if this was a form of revenge on Burgoyne's part but decided it wasn't. The decision made just too much sense. Arnold now had the independent command he so fervently desired, and the heartily detested turncoat would be out of the way of most of the rest of the British officers.

Arnold quickly informed them that the barges would have their decks covered over with planking to protect the cargo from the heavy seas that sometimes occurred on the lakes. The cannon and shot they were to take would be carried as ballast, although some barges would have cannon mounted as bow guns for defense. When Burgoyne commented that perhaps more of the guns should be mounted on the deck so they could fire broadsides, Arnold countered by saying that they could not make the decks strong enough to carry their weight and it might even make the barges unseaworthy. Fitzroy was impressed by Arnold's quick mind and grasp of the situation.

Burgoyne added that Captain Danforth would travel with Arnold as liaison from the army's headquarters and that they would sail on the *Vixen*. Arnold smiled tightly. Cornwallis' spy on Burgoyne was now Burgoyne's spy on Arnold. It also meant that Danforth couldn't report to Cornwallis on Burgoyne's advance to Fort Washington because he wouldn't be there to observe it.

"I will not make the same mistakes I did at Saratoga," Burgoyne added solemnly. "Except for the flotilla of barges, I will not divide my forces in any great manner, and I will not be held up for lack of supplies. Nor will I be dragging cannon through the forest. When Arnold's fleet finally departs from Detroit for Fort Washington, we will move out as one mighty army. We will move slowly and allow those supplies that aren't going by boat to catch up with us. We will build depots along the way so we won't have to depend on food and ammunition coming all the way from Detroit."

Tarleton yawned. "Won't that require garrisons and won't that result in the army being divided anyhow?"

"To a point, of course," Burgoyne said with a degree of exasperation. Garrisoning the depots was an obvious need. "But the numbers will be small in comparison with the army as a whole and represent no significant reduction."

General Grant nodded agreement. "You say we will move slowly. How slowly? For myself, I would prefer to get there as quickly as possible and smash them."

"I estimate that it will take two months for General Arnold's fleet and the attending sloops of war to reach a point close to where Fort Washington is supposed to be. Since we have no reliable maps, the exact location is still a bit of a mystery.

"We will target our arrival to be within just such a time frame. While we certainly cannot coordinate these things very tightly, we can at least be close.

"While on the march, General Tarleton's force will lead with those units led by Joseph Brant. Simon Girty's forces will provide scouting and distant flank support."

Fitzroy was mildly amused that Burgoyne could not bring himself to refer to those men under the control of Brant and Girty as soldiers.

"I hate having those white savages watching out for us, especially Girty," snarled Grant.

"Beggars cannot be choosers," Tarleton said with a smile. "Anyone willing to kill rebels is a friend of ours."

Burgoyne continued. "While on the march, it is possible, even likely, that our army will stretch upwards of twenty miles, We will be passing in a narrow column through thick forests where the danger of ambushes will be constant. Say what you will about Brant and Girty and their savage followers, but we will need them lest a raid cut our column in pieces."

"Understood," said Grant. "I just don't have to like the buggers. And I think both groups will run rather than fight against the rebels."

"They will fight as long as they think they are winning," said Burgoyne, "which means the promise of loot to them. My only wish is that they help get us to our destination in good order and then the devil can have them."

"The devil already has them," Tarleton laughed, "or don't you believe that creatures like Burned Man Braxton are already owned by Satan?"

"Would you be offended if I said this isn't much of a cavalry regiment?" Will asked as he observed both the small numbers of men in the "regiment" and the quality of their horses.

Colonel William Washington smiled bleakly. "I would like to say that it is an example of quality over quantity, but even that isn't true." William Washington was an experienced and resourceful cavalry commander. He had once fought Banastre Tarleton sword to sword while his cavalry defeated the British at Cowpens.

"I'm afraid these poor men and their even poorer mounts would not be able to stand against the British," Washington said. "However, General Tallmadge has informed me that the British won't be bringing much in the way of cavalry either."

Colonel Washington's regiment of cavalry consisted of a hundred and fifty men, and only half of them had horses. The remaining men were prepared to fight on foot.

Nor were the horses anything to brag about. They were small and thin and little more than ponies. Will thought he'd seen larger and healthier dogs. But it was correct that the British had little cavalry either. "You'll fight as dragoons, I presume?"

"Correct. And in order to make up the shortage in horses, I am prepared to send men into battle two on a horse, or even carried in wagons."

Will couldn't resist the jibe. "You presume that these horses can carry two. I find it hard to believe that some could even carry one rider."

Washington slapped will on the shoulder. "If it weren't true, Will, I'd have you court martialed for slandering my horses. I can only hope we get more mounts and that a period of eating good spring grasses will strengthen the ones we have; however, I will not hold my breath that either will occur. But then, all we have to do is be ready to fight one time."

Will noticed they were practicing with a familiar weapon. "Aren't those the guns Dr. Franklin designed?"

"Indeed. Those are Franklin's Franklins, if you'll permit the pun. We've shortened the barrel and plan to use them as a close-range fowling piece or a small blunderbuss. They will be loaded with several musket balls that'll be held in by wax or mud so the balls don't roll out. They won't be much on accuracy, but I dare say they will make life interesting for a formation of massed Redcoats when fired at close range."

"Assuming you can get your men there before the British fire."

He nodded sadly. "Then we will have to endure a volley and attack them after they've fired and before they can reload." Washington pulled out a watch and checked it. "Three o'clock and all is well. Do you think the meeting has started?"

Congress had finally acted. A commander for the army would be chosen and everyone had their own preferences and doubts. Will had some sympathy for General Schuyler who seemed a decent sort and who had possibly gotten a bad deal from an earlier congress over the loss of Ticonderoga in 1777. But then, Will thought, did he want his army led by a man who was a "decent sort," and who had lost his only major battle?

"I only hope they make the right decision," he said.

# Chapter 12 ★ ★ ★ ★ ★ ★ ★ ★ ★ ★ ★ ★ ★ ★ ★ ★ ★ ★

Benjamin Franklin took his seat at the head of the long table. He adjusted his glasses and peered at the men gathered in the small room. They were the cream of the crop of the small army's leaders. God help us, he thought, as he gazed at Schuyler, Wayne, Morgan, Glover, and Tallmadge. Only von Steuben wasn't present. He was away with his Hessians and had said that he would support any decision that was made, just as long as he wasn't given the command.

"The time for dreaming and hoping is over, gentlemen," Franklin began. "Nathanael Greene is well and truly dead. And now the army needs a leader, a man who can inspire confidence in our soldiers and a sense of dread in the enemy. All of you are candidates for the position, yet all of you have serious flaws. Like it or not, I shall enumerate them."

There was a small amount of shuffling that Franklin ignored. "You, General Schuyler, are a major general and, thus, the highest ranking officer at Fort Washington. By rights, you should have the command. Yet, the rank and file and many of the officers have no confidence in you because of what happened in the past."

"Unfair," said Schuyler, shaking his head sadly.

"Life is not fair," Franklin retorted. "I too believe you were shabbily treated when you were removed from command by Congress, but it was done and cannot be undone any more than Ticonderoga can be returned to you. I believe that, if you were

193

named to command now, many of our soldiers would simply melt away into the wilderness. Still, your obvious skills at organizing this settlement and creating the army we have cannot be denied. Indeed, they must be continued, which is a good reason for keeping you where you are. Without you, I am afraid that we would have starved to death a long time ago."

Schuyler accepted the compliment with a small smile. "My work has been made easier these past few weeks thanks to the Jew, Goldman, and the Dutch woman, Van Doorn."

Franklin understood the implication. Thanks to Goldman and Van Doorn, Schuyler would be free to lead the army in battle if named to command. He wanted it. He wanted to be vindicated. It wouldn't happen.

"Tallmadge," Franklin continued. "You have never led an army. Do you wish to start now?"

"Good God, no," Tallmadge said with enough emphasis to make the others laugh.

"Nor do I," said Brigadier General John Glover.

Franklin smiled. He appreciated their candor. "I didn't think so. So that leaves General Wayne and General Morgan, unless you wish me to promote von Steuben."

"That would be a disaster," said Schuyler. "He is a fraud, has no command experience, and barely speaks English."

"But he is such a genial fraud," Franklin said. Franklin had given the rank of general to that genial fraud because he'd been convinced that Steuben could be of great use to the army, and that confidence had been proven correct many times over.

Franklin turned to Anthony Wayne. "But you are right. Von Steuben the German could never command an army of Americans." He turned to Wayne. "Do you think you are ready for the honor, General Wayne?"

Wayne paled. He was ambitious and skilled, but inexperienced. He knew that his relative youth—he was under forty—was also against him. That and many considered his tendency to impetuousness to count against him.

"If offered, I would accept," he said softly. "And I would do my best."

"Thank you, and no man could ask for more than that," Franklin said. "And you, General Morgan?"

Morgan, the gruff Old Wagoneer and veteran of numerous

battles and campaigns, snorted, "I'd take it in a heartbeat if I were younger and in better health. And then I'd kick Burgoyne's ass all the way back to London."

He could have done it, too, thought Franklin. But Morgan's health was against him. Although only a decade older than Wayne, the harsh and rugged life he'd led now conspired to keep him largely immobile. He'd had to be carried in a litter on many occasions because of the crippling aches in his bones.

Morgan shook his head sadly. "I could fight a battle, Benjamin, but I could not fight a campaign."

Again Franklin smiled. Morgan understood exactly. There would likely be a campaign against the British, not just a climactic battle. He wondered if Schuyler and Wayne understood that.

Morgan leaned back in his chair and winced from the pain in his lower back. "It looks like all of us are soiled virgins, Benjamin. What will you do?"

Franklin smiled impishly. "John Hancock once offered to lead the army. Perhaps he can be talked into it again."

There were brays of laughter. "Johnny Hancock doesn't even know which end of a musket to use," Morgan said and then turned serious. "Benjamin, you didn't bring us here to ridicule us or to choose any one of us. You're too damned smart for that. You already have a man, don't you?"

"General Glover," Franklin smiled impishly and said, "Would you be so kind as to bring in your good friend and traveling companion?"

Glover stepped away and into another room. He returned in a moment with a thin man with long white hair and a full white beard. He wore a suit of dark blue cloth, which was vaguely military. Tallmadge recognized him as the man who had arrived at the tail of Glover's column. Then the light dawned.

"Jesus Christ," he said.

The white-bearded man smiled. "Don't blaspheme. I am not Jesus, Tallmadge. The beard has fooled better men than you."

"Enough," said Glover, grinning. "Since not everyone recognizes you, introduce yourself to the others, sir. Give them your name."

"John Stark."

Further discussions regarding leadership of the army were anticlimactic. Franklin asked Stark if he would command the

Continental forces at Fort Washington and he agreed that he
would. Franklin then asked the other assembled generals whether
they supported Stark's ascension to command. They did. For a
moment it appeared that Schuyler would protest, but he did not.
Some later thought he hesitated, but they may have been wrong.
But who could have begrudged Schuyler a moment's pause at
what might have been?

John Stark was in his mid-fifties and, thanks to the beard and
the hard life he'd recently led, looked older. Still, he was in far
better health than Morgan.

Stark explained that he had escaped the British sweep by
the simple accident of being out fishing when the British had
descended on his home.

"When I returned home I found my house burned to the
ground and my wife beaten to death. Why did they have to kill
Molly?" he said, the anger surging. "I can only surmise that they
thought she knew where I'd gone, but she didn't. All she knew
was that I'd gone fishing, but had no idea exactly where and
there were a score of places to choose from. So in their blind
anger, they killed her."

Stark blinked away the sudden moistness in his eyes. "I figured
they'd be back looking for me and, a few days later, they were,
but this time I was waiting. There were just a three of them so
I killed two of them right off. I shot one with my musket and
killed the second with my knife. The third one ran. I know who
he is and maybe someday I'll catch up to him as well. Then I
took some supplies and, after saying goodbye at my wife's grave,
headed into the woods."

"Which is where I found him," Glover said quietly. "Eating
berries and nuts and looking like shit. I thought, is this what the
man who saved our left flank at Bunker's Hill and destroyed the
British advance on Bennington deserved to become? I convinced
him to come with us."

"It was not my choice. He dragged me along," said Stark with
a trace of a smile.

Glover's meeting him was not quite accidental. Glover had
known of Stark's escape and had gone to find him en route to
Fort Washington with his regiment of Marblehead men.

"So what are your plans now that you command us?" asked
Franklin.

Stark glowered and there was a sudden fire in his eyes. "To destroy the British. When they move on us I want to make every step a living hell for them. I want them to pay in blood for Molly and everyone else they've killed or abused."

"That's not quite a civilized approach to war," said Franklin.

"War is always barbaric," Stark retorted. "And anyone who attempts to put rules to it is a fool, and anyone who thinks that any war can be civilized is worse than a fool. War is the killing of people by other people. It is mean, miserable, and destructive. It blows human flesh to pieces and leaves the survivors screaming for mercy, and their widows and children to starve."

"Is it safe to say you will fight such an uncivilized war?" asked a mildly surprised Schuyler.

"I will use any and all means at my disposal to kill them," Stark said. "We will poison their wells and their food, and knife them in their sleep." He turned to Franklin. "And for you, most revered doctor, I wish you to use your most inventive mind to conjure up diabolic devices to assist me."

Franklin looked shocked. He had never before been asked to do any such thing. Even his invention of the weapon that bore his name was more of a lark than a serious endeavor. And the production of muskets and pikes was nothing at all unique. He wanted to prove his concept of using interchangeable parts, not necessarily destroy people. "I will do it," he finally said.

"I have one question," said Glover in an attempt to lighten the mood. "John Stark, how the hell much longer are you going to keep that ugly damned beard?"

"Until the last Redcoat is gone."


Erich von Blumberg was a colonel in the army of Hesse. He arrived at Detroit accompanied by a hundred or so Hessian soldiers. They'd come by boat, jammed in one of the barges, which made their journey somewhat more comfortable than marching along the coast.

Von Blumberg was in his early forties, stout, and wore his gaudily colored uniform and numerous medals as if he'd been born to them, which he had. Military service to the rulers of Hesse ran deep in his family. His command of the English language was excellent and he was angry.

"What you are telling me, my dear General Burgoyne, is that you have managed to round up only four deserters?"

"If indeed they are deserters," Fitzroy answered for his general. "We began with twenty and, after careful investigation concluded that only these four could possibly have been in your army."

The Hessian stood and stared directly into Fitzroy's face. "Why? Who gave you such wisdom?"

Fitzroy decided he would like to slap the pompous twit. "Common sense, Colonel. Several of the twenty were very young boys and others were very old men. A few were crippled and at least one was a babbling idiot. How many such ancients, infants, cripples, and idiots do you have in the armies of Hesse and the other German states?"

"None," von Blumberg said grudgingly as he ignored the jibe.

"You've interviewed the four," Burgoyne said to von Blumberg. "What do you make of them?"

"I want them hanged."

"But what proof do you have that they were ever in the army of Hesse or any other principality?" asked Fitzroy.

"They are Germans and they are the right age."

"But Colonel," Fitzroy continued, "Germans have lived here for decades, generations. I interviewed them too, and they all claimed to be born here. How can you be certain they are your deserters? And wouldn't they be beyond stupid to live near a British army encampment if they were deserters?"

Von Blumberg glared at him. "And perhaps they are stupid, Major. I talked with them and I am convinced there is a strong likelihood that they are deserters."

"But likelihood is not proof," Fitzroy insisted. "Would you hang men who might just be innocent?"

Von Blumberg merely sniffed. "Innocence and guilt are totally irrelevant. They must hang as an example to others that the armies of the German states are not to be trifled with. We had a contract with Lord North to provide soldiers and there have been so many desertions that they have cost us money as well as credibility."

"But you're not positive of their guilt, are you?" Fitzroy repeated, thinking that the Hessians had been sent to the colonies as cannon fodder, little more than brutally drilled puppets. Who wouldn't desert under the circumstances? North America was a huge continent in which a man could disappear.

Von Blumberg pulled a piece of paper from his jacket. "This is from your king, who is, you will recall, of the Germanic House of Hanover, which he still rules along with reigning in England. He says that I and I alone will determine who is a deserter. You don't have to be convinced of their guilt, only I do."

He turned to Burgoyne. "According to my orders you are required to turn those men over to me and I demand it be done immediately. If any of the others your major so foolishly let loose are still around, I wish them taken and hanged as well."

"They have departed," Burgoyne said stiffly and glancing at Fitzroy who nodded. If the others hadn't yet departed, they would soon be far, far away. "As to these four, they are yours. I cannot prevent you from taking them, however much I too doubt their guilt."

Less than an hour later, the four men were dragged from their prison by von Blumberg's men. Chains shackled their hands and feet, which made them shuffle rather than walk. They were confused and stared around at the growing crowd. A rough scaffold had been hastily thrown up and they were dragged to it. Nooses were placed around their necks. One man began to scream while another prayed loudly in German when they realized what was going to happen to them. The men were hauled up on barrels and, without ceremony and only a moment later, the barrels were kicked away.

"You didn't even give them a moment to pray or to see a minister of their faith?" Fitzroy said.

"It wouldn't matter," von Blumberg huffed. "They are going to hell regardless."

The dying men twisted, kicked, and turned while hundreds of soldiers and civilians watched in silence. Their faces were contorted and their bowels and bladders began to release, the stench adding to the abomination.

"At least kill them quickly," Fitzroy pleaded. It was possible to hasten their end by pulling on their legs and breaking their necks.

"Let them suffer," von Blumberg said.

"This unnecessarily cruelty will only harden the resolve of those actual Hessian deserters at Fort Washington," Fitzroy pleaded.

"Do I care what a few dozen wretched deserters think? Let them fear the future."

"A few dozen?" Fitzroy said incredulously. "Is that all you think there are?"

Von Blumberg looked at him growing surprise. "How many are there? A few score, then?"

Fitzroy laughed harshly. "Hundreds, you fool, perhaps a thousand."
Von Blumberg paled. "Dear God."

"And although they said they were already willing to fight to the death to stay free, some must have harbored doubts about committing suicide. Thanks to you, those doubts are all swept away. They will fight like savages to keep from falling into your hands."

The "deserters" had finally stopped twitching and the spectators melted away. A number of the civilians ostentatiously spat in the general direction of von Blumberg, who ignored the insult.

If John Hancock was disappointed that no one had asked him to command the American army, he didn't show it. Instead, he seemed positively relieved that John Stark had taken the burden. Similarly, General Philip Schuyler had decided to swallow whatever thoughts he might have had regarding leading their small army to glory.

If Hancock was annoyed at anything, it was that Stark was being particularly closed-mouthed about his plans. "Will you at least tell me, General Stark, whether or not you intend to take the battle to Burgoyne or do you intend to wait here for the blow to fall on us here?"

"We will strike at him as soon as he leaves his devil's lair at Detroit," Stark finally responded. He noted Anthony Wayne leaning forward expectantly and shook his head. "But not with the entire army or even a large portion of it. Colonel Clark's men will nibble at the British and hurt them."

"You are certain that they will come from only one direction?" Hancock asked.

"I am. They will come directly from Detroit and take the shortest distance. They will not deviate significantly from the already established trails."

"Are you concerned that the British might come down the Ohio, march north, and strike at our rear?" Hancock asked.

"To do that," Stark answered, "they would have to march a couple of hundred miles from Detroit south to the Ohio River, set sail on boats that don't exist, and then, after the water portion of their travels was over, march several hundred miles north to where we await them. I rather wish they would do that. They would be exhausted and starving by the time they reached us.

"The force they had gathering on the Ohio River at Pitt has

made its way almost to Detroit. Thanks to General Tallmadge's spies, we are now aware that almost all of the scattered British units are at Detroit."

Will, sitting behind Tallmadge, sensed his pleasure at the compliment. "And when they leave for Fort Washington, we will know quite promptly," Tallmadge added.

"How?" asked Hancock, "Fires? Smoke signals? Witchcraft?"

Franklin smiled, "Witchcraft most certainly."

"Speaking of which," Stark said, ignoring the comment, "how are you coming with your infernal devices?"

Franklin sighed. "I had hoped to use electricity as a weapon that would at least terrify our enemies if not kill them, but I fear our knowledge of it is not advanced enough. Therefore, I am looking to the past to save the future."

It was Franklin's turn to be secretive. He had told no one of his plan to turn out breech-loading rifles modeled on the Ferguson rifle used by the British at Brandywine and by Ferguson's Loyalists at Kings Mountain. While it had many flaws, the rate of fire could be an incredible ten shots a minute and by a soldier lying prone, which meant he was a far more difficult target. He'd gotten one of the weapons from a man who'd fought Ferguson, and he was even now tinkering with it. He was going to strengthen the stock and simplify the complicated and fragile mechanism. The squat gun named after him would be but a limited success at best, but a weapon that could fire so many more times a minute would be a feather in his cap.

Franklin didn't think he could manufacture a thousand of them—a couple of hundred would be more like it, but he thought they would be a most unpleasant surprise for Burgoyne.

"Will you elaborate?" Hancock asked.

Franklin beamed. "No."

John Stark, newly appointed Major General Commanding the American Armies walked the low, sloping hill. A chill breeze from the lake a few miles away swept through his cloak and into his thin frame. He willed himself not to shiver. It would show weakness. Generals should never show weakness to their men.

His title, he sniffed, was more imposing than the reality of his command. There were no "armies." In fact it was difficult to say that the force he commanded was an army at all—just a handful of regiments that might be combined into a few brigades perhaps, but not an army.

By the latest count, he had three thousand men at Fort Washington, or Liberty, as some called it, and another thousand or so under von Steuben a few miles away. Tallmadge insisted that scattered communities like Liberty would also send men when the time arose, but Stark was not a fool. He would not count on people who weren't there.

For that matter, he wasn't so confident that those currently present would all stick around when the British arrived. He would not count on dramatically increasing his numbers.

Nor did he have much confidence in Benjamin Franklin's sometimes crackpot schemes to develop weapons that would turn the tide against an overwhelmingly larger enemy army. John Stark would fight the old-fashioned way. He would plan a killing ground like he had at Bennington and hope he could inflict enough casualties to defeat the British before they overwhelmed his small force. If Franklin and his cohorts actually did create a weapon that worked, then that would be wonderful. Until then, he would trust in the musket, the rifle, the sword, and the bayonet.

And courage.

He liked the hill on which he stood. Long and low and not even a hundred feet high, the British might not recognize it as an impediment until it was too late, and were committed to a slow and tiresome uphill climb. The hill was relatively barren and windswept, which meant the enemy couldn't hide as they approached. Grasses would grow before the end of summer, but there would be no trees and no heavy brush. If only it wasn't so damned long, he thought. There was, he admitted, more hill than he had army to defend it.

Stark turned to his entourage. The other generals looked serious, while some of the lower-ranking officers looked on curiously, wondering what their betters were thinking, and knowing that such thoughts could determine whether they lived or died.

"Here," Stark said, pointing to the ground. "We will make our defenses here. Our left flank will be on the marsh in that direction and our right flank will be anchored on that bloody bog. They cannot turn us."

"You're sure they'll come this way?" asked Wayne.

"They don't really have a choice," Stark answered firmly. "They will come directly from Detroit and will be funneled by the rivers and the location of Fort Washington. If they go to our south, they will have to cross the river under fire, and I cannot imagine that Johnny Burgoyne would ever want to do that. He had enough of river crossings at Saratoga. No, by coming this way, he can keep his feet dry and only have fairly innocent streams to cross as he gets closer."

Will was busy taking notes. The location chosen was near the portage where Indians and French hunters had been crossing from Lake Michigan. It led to the spot where they could put their canoes back in the water and commence a long journey that would ultimately take them to St. Louis and New Orleans. Stark was right, he thought. The geography and the wetlands would force the British to come this way. Still, he saw a problem.

"General," said Will. "It is several miles between the two bogs. How will we defend such a distance with the small force at our command?"

"We will fortify the entire length and defend where they choose to attack. I don't think they will spread their forces and force us to spread ours. With Grant as second in command, I see him attempting a single attack in overwhelming strength at what they perceive of as a vital point. We will watch them and be prepared to move along our line and confront them at a moment's notice."

"Fortifying that much hill will be a major effort," said Schuyler.

Stark nodded. "It will."

"And it will be virtually impossible to keep secret," Tallmadge added.

"Do the British still have spies here?" Stark asked.

"Doubtless, sir," Tallmadge answered. "We've caught some of them and hanged them, of course, but I do not think that we've found all. Besides, there is enough casual traffic between here and the surrounding communities that it will be virtually impossible to keep our efforts a secret."

Stark shrugged. "Then we shall presume no secrets. We shall presume that the British will know exactly where and what we are doing. You're right, of course, Tallmadge. Any man who counts on this being a secret is a fool. We will have to outfight them, not out-secret them."

Tallmadge smiled, "Your orders, then sir?"

Stark returned the smile. "Dig."

★     ★     ★

"Well, Admiral Danforth, are you ready to set sail?" Fitzroy said with a cheeky grin.

"Careful you ignorant landlubber, or I'll sail one of these ugly boats right up your ugly ass," Danforth answered with a mock snarl.

"Well, look at the bright side. You'll be away from here and on a North American version of the Grand Tour. Just think what wonders you'll see. There'll be unwashed savages galore, and many of the ugliest and filthiest females in the world will want to bed you while the deer and black bears watch. There'll be scenic marvels like unending forests and clouds of bugs just drooling at the thought of sucking your rich English blood right out of your veins. Just think, some poor fools have to make do with trips to Rome and Venice, or even Paris, while you get the forests of Michigan as your Grand Tour. Of all the lucky bastards in the world, you truly are the luckiest."

"I am too thrilled for words," Danforth said. "And don't forget that I also get to go with Benedict Arnold, a man who was a traitor once and might just do it again." Danforth's low opinion of Arnold was shared by most officers in the British force.

"I doubt it," said Fitzroy. "Good lord, where would he go? Think, how many turns can a turncoat turn?"

"Regardless, it isn't fair," Danforth said with almost a sigh.

"Fair has nothing to do with it, my brave young soldier turned sailor, and say, doesn't that make you a turncoat as well? Life is not fair and you should know that. I certainly do."

"True enough," Danforth grumbled.

"True, indeed. Consider the position of our leaders. The brave General Burgoyne, my mentor and distant relative, loses an entire army at Saratoga in '77, but is given another one to play with, while Cornwallis, a man who very nearly lost another one at Yorktown in '81, controls Burgoyne and very nearly the whole North American continent."

Danforth shuddered. The tale of Cornwallis' rescue at Yorktown by the last-minute arrival of the British fleet and the subsequent defeat of the French fleet was the stuff of legend. Cornwallis the lucky was more important than Cornwallis the very good general. In truth, he was both lucky and a very good general, and both he and Fitzroy would have been far more confident of success had Cornwallis been in charge of the expedition instead of Burgoyne.

And after Yorktown, the incompetent and stubborn Admiral

Graves was given credit for the overwhelming victory over the French when it actually was the result of Admiral Hood's initiative in not waiting for the French to come out and politely line up to do battle. Instead, Hood had taken his division and thrown them onto the disorganized French ships as they emerged from the bay and slaughtered them. With the French shattered, British reinforcements landed and the rebel force disintegrated. For all intents, the revolution ended that day.

As a result, Graves was made a duke, while Hood, the fighter with the initiative, now languished on the shore, commanding not ships but a number of warehouses in Portsmouth as reward for his brilliance. Fair? Fitzroy didn't think so. But Graves was a favorite of the corrupt Earl of Sandwich, who ruled the Admiralty.

"We should be in England, training the new regiments that are being developed for the real war against France, perhaps even commanding one," Fitzroy muttered. "I still can't believe that England has fallen so low that she now has to conscript men into her army as she has done for her navy."

The news of conscription had struck the army like a thunderbolt. The navy traditionally conscripted, or pressed, men into the service, while the army prided itself on taking only volunteers. Well, admittedly some of the volunteers were the dregs of society and others given the choice of join or hang, but technically they were volunteers, weren't they? But the manpower situation had grown so dire and the wars so unpopular that England was now forcing Englishmen into her army. Some other officers wondered quietly if it would result in a revolution like what France was enduring. It was all the more reason that the British army prevail both overwhelmingly and quickly.

"It's indeed a sad state of affairs," said Danforth as he looked around with a touch of pride. "At least this part of affairs afloat is going well."

Fifty barges laden with cannon, carriages, shot, shells, ammunition, food, and other supplies too bulky to take overland were just about ready to set sail. The two small warships that were to accompany the flotilla were in place and looked brave, albeit tiny. The *Fox* and the *Snake* were schooners carrying but a dozen small cannon in total. Still, they were considered to be more powerful than anything the rebels had. While the rebels might be able to build a good-sized warship, they did not have the ropes and cordage and sails; thus, any ships would have to be galleys which the armed schooners could outmaneuver with ease. Also, intelligence said that they did not have the ability to forge cannon.

For this voyage, the *Fox* would also carry Arnold and Danforth as the swift but diminutive warships could sail rings around the barges.

Each sailing barge would have a crew of a dozen, which meant they could row if becalmed by the wind and defend the crafts if necessary. It was planned that they would take about two months to reach their destination, where, it was hoped, Burgoyne's army would await them. Since it was equally possible that the barges would arrive first, the plans also required them to stay offshore until the army appeared. It was hoped that neither the army nor the fleet would have a long wait.

"We sail tomorrow," Danforth said. "Shall we celebrate tonight?"

"Do you want to be on a small boat with a hangover?"

"Either way, I'll be sick as a dog, so I might as well enjoy myself this evening."

Later, they were well into their second bottle of brandy and preparing for their third, when Danforth turned and looked grimly at Fitzroy. "James, have we been sent on a fool's errand? Are we being set up to fail? Are these damned barges the equivalent of the Spanish Armada?"

Fitzroy sighed. He had been thinking the very same thing. "You ask too damned many questions."

Lieutenant Owen Wells looked at the strange contraption in his hand. Had he been more educated and traveled, he might have recognized it. Still, he saw it as a weapon from the past and wondered about it. They were outdoors and in the same place where Will Drake had used an earlier invention to fire at a target. A straw-filled dummy of a man was at the end of the range. A half-rotten pumpkin was the skull.

"Doctor Franklin," he said, "I know you're a man of great wisdom, but surely this is a joke."

Franklin nodded tolerantly. "Lieutenant Wells, I assure you it is not. The crossbow was an effective weapon against knights in armor several hundred years ago. Indeed, it was so effective, that it almost destroyed the armored and mounted knight as a military class."

"But we fight Redcoats, not knights in armor."

"True," said Franklin.

"And the last I checked, Doctor, none of the red-coated turds were wearing armor, even though they weren't knights."

Franklin nodded. "But the bolt from a crossbow will just as easily penetrate cloth and flesh. It is accurate to well over a hundred yards, which is at least as good as a musket and can be reloaded at least as fast thanks to my clever innovations to an otherwise awkward device."

Owen grinned inwardly. The good doctor was getting exasperated with his questions. "But if you wanted a better weapon, why not give us longbows like my ancestors used to use against the English? From what I've heard, they raised holy hell with King Edward's men."

"Because, my incessantly questioning young friend, longbows take forever to make and take an eternity to learn how to use, or didn't you know that?"

"Oh, I did. I just wanted to see if you did."

"Lieutenant Wells, you are a devil."

"I've been called worse, good doctor. But since you compare me with Satan, let me tell you how I plan to use these crossbows that you are forcing me and my men to use."

Owen cocked the weapon. The motion was blessedly silent, barely a whisper, thanks to some padding and oiling the doctor had added. He placed it snugly into his shoulder and fired. The only sound was a soft thwack as the bolt released and a slight thud as it impacted into a dummy made of straw.

"Excellent shot," Franklin said.

Wells was also impressed. "I can do better and so can my men. What I want to do is fire these quietly at night and into their camps so they don't know what's hitting them and from where. If I have to lose sleep firing these things, then everyone does.

"Then I plan to have my men lie in wait along the trail and watch for stragglers or someone out of line having to piss or shit. There's nothing worse than getting an arrow up your ass while taking a shit."

"Indeed," said Franklin happily. Tallmadge had suggested Lieutenant Wells as someone who would respond favorably to the idea of using a medieval crossbow in this, the late eighteenth century. Wells was Welsh and the Welsh were romantics when it came to killing. It was ironic. In the very early days of the war, Franklin had actually proposed arming the American army besieging the British at Boston with bows and arrows, but had been laughed at. Now he would have a degree of vindication. He hoped.

Owen smiled and fondled the crossbow. "Then we shall simply wait for other targets of opportunity. I dare say we will have plenty of them. We won't win the war with these ancient weapons, Doctor Franklin, but we will make the damned Redcoats miserable and cost them plenty."

Wells armed his crossbow with another bolt, cocked, aimed, and fired. Benjamin Franklin couldn't hide a gasp as the bolt penetrated and shattered the pumpkin, the skull of the dummy.

Lord Charles Cornwallis climbed the observation tower at the base of Manhattan Island and looked across the harbor at the assembled ships of the Royal Navy. Three giant ships of the line, seven frigates and a gaggle of sloops and merchantmen lay at anchor and rocked gently. On the tower, Cornwallis was almost as high in the air as a lookout in the rigging and crow's nests of the fleet. As an army man he firmly believed that no sane man would ever go up to such a fragile place on a ship, especially when the world beneath you rolled and pitched. At least his newly constructed tower on the battlements of Fort George had the decency to stand still; except, of course, when it was windy and stormy.

He thought it was an almost peaceful and tranquil perch in the sky. The dark of night hid so many of the world's scars and this was no exception. He could have turned and looked landward at the ruined city of New York but chose not to. Jammed with more people then it could safely handle—some estimated more than fifty thousand—the city had become a diseased and running sore.

Cornwallis heard footsteps and nodded warmly as his brother. Commodore Billy Cornwallis climbed up and joined him. He was gratified that his young brother was huffing slightly; thereby proving that he hadn't been climbing any of his ship's rigging for quite some time.

"Excellent view," William Cornwallis said, also looking over the harbor and ignoring the city.

Governor General Charles Cornwallis agreed. "Your ships

look like predators that are poised to pounce on an unseen and unsuspecting enemy."

"If only that were true," his brother said ruefully. His ships were shorthanded and low on supplies. Their warlike visage was a facade. "How go things in the fair city of New York?"

Both men turned to take in the view of Manhattan Island. Neither was surprised to see a couple of fires burning as more dwellings fell to accidents caused by overcrowding. Of course, the loss of the buildings would make the overcrowding more acute with still more accidents occurring, and so on. Life in the city of New York was a spiral descending into hell. Bells began to clang as people gathered to put out the fires.

The wind shifted and the stench of the city swept over them. Each man looked at the other. Was it possible to catch the pox from the air as some scientists seemed to think?

"Does the situation improve?" the younger Cornwallis asked.

"As we speak, hundreds in the city are dying of smallpox," his brother answered. "So far I've kept the disease from the garrison but only by sealing off the military in the fort. I can't keep them there forever. I must begin to send out patrols and try to regain the countryside so these damned people will leave New York and go back to their homes. I would also like for Burgoyne to get off his arse and win his battles, and return my army to me."

William saw no need to comment. The dilemma was well known. With so much of the army with Burgoyne, the British had virtually conceded the lands outside the major cities to whoever could hold them. Tories and rebels were again fighting for control of the countryside and the rebels seemed to be winning. Many Tories were disheartened by what appeared to be a two-part abandonment of them by the British. The first was the disappearance of the army, their protection, and the second was the publication of Britain's shocking intentions for the colonies after the war was won. Offended, angered, with their livelihoods threatened, many Loyalists had gone over to the rebels, while many of the others waited in sullen silence, but without supporting the British.

At least, William thought, the smallpox that was devouring New York had so far spared his ships. When the plague erupted, he'd coldly ordered those ashore to remain ashore so they could not infect his crews. Of course, that also meant he couldn't take on supplies or press crewmen. The additional crew he could exist without, but his men had to eat, damn it. Something had to break and quickly.

"What can I do to assist?" William asked.

"Take me home," Charles Cornwallis said with a wry laugh. He wanted nothing more than to be away from this place and to be back in England with memories of his beloved but deceased Jemima. He was one of a small number in his social class who had married for love and her death had devastated him.

"Is there a second choice?" William asked sympathetically.

"Could you take me and my soldiers to Boston or Charleston should the crises worsen here?"

William stiffened. That would mean disobeying the orders of Lord North, who had commanded that the major cities, specifically including New York, be held while Burgoyne marched inland. Still, Lord North was thousands of miles away, while his brother was the commander on the ground.

"Do you think that will be necessary?"

"I don't know. If the disease threatens we may have to leave, at least temporarily. Perhaps we can construct a fort on Long Island or Staten Island and be far away from the sickness that is New York while still claiming we're here." He laughed harshly. "It would only be half a lie, a fact which our conniving Lord North would fully understand and appreciate."

William relaxed. That would enable Governor Cornwallis to claim he still controlled New York by dominating the harbor. Perhaps he could even offer the use of the several hundred marines on his ships as additions to the governor's depleted garrison. "My dear brother, we will do everything we can to assist should that prove necessary."

Off in the distance, a woman wailed in unspeakable anguish. Someone had just died, and perhaps violently, although it was more likely from the disease that ravaged the city. It was a sound heard very frequently now, and both men wondered what if anything would be left of the American Colonies when Burgoyne returned victorious.

# Chapter 13 ★ ★ ★ ★ ★ ★ ★ ★ ★ ★ ★ ★ ★ ★ ★ ★

"WHERE IS MY UNCLE?" SARAH DEMANDED, WAVING HER arms in frustration. "And where are all the people who used to work with him? Merlin's Cave has disappeared and no one knows where it's gone."

"And neither do I," Will said, "and neither does General Tallmadge, although," he admitted, "he could be lying. He so often is."

However, Will had known that the men and some of the women working in the laboratory and factory known informally as "Merlin's Cave" had been gradually moving out. Where they'd gone and why was a mystery. Apparently General Stark and Benjamin Franklin knew their whereabouts and purpose, but neither man was talking and Will was not about to ask.

"Sarah, you work with Franklin. You could ask him yourself, you know."

"He's refused to talk about it. Poor Faith is distraught. Her father and mother have disappeared somewhere and Owen has gone east to confront the Redcoats."

"Which is exactly where I'll be going very shortly. Will you miss me as much as Faith misses her young sailor?"

She slipped easily into his arms and kissed him. "Of course I will."

They were in Franklin's office, which afforded them a degree of privacy. She was beginning to think that privacy and restraint could go to hell. They were all in danger of being killed or enslaved in a very short while, so why not enjoy what remained of life?

"Sarah, I would tell you where they were if I knew. Many things are happening, and no one is going to tell me until I come back from observing the British again."

Sarah understood the grim reality. Will was going east with a very small detachment to see first-hand the pace and size of the British advance. If he was captured, then he had nothing to tell, even under torture. Sarah shuddered at the thought of Will being brutalized by someone like the man who assaulted poor Winifred, or chewed alive by the squaws who had accompanied Brant's Iroquois. There were indeed fates worse than death and ordeals that made what had happened to her seem trivial.

Their thoughts were interrupted by Franklin asking for Sarah's presence. Will kissed her again. "If you want to know what is going on, why not use your feminine wiles on the good Doctor Franklin?"

Why not indeed, Sarah thought.

The beginning of the march out of the camps around Detroit was bloody impressive, Fitzroy thought. Literally thousands of men began to march across the fields and into the woods like a long, powerful, red snake. He gazed at the sky and saw columns of smoke in the distance. These were doubtless rebel signaling devices and made it obvious that not all the rebel spies had been captured. Far from it, if the number of smoke columns were any indication.

More puzzling were the numbers of pigeons that had been released. They flew in circles for a couple of moments and then headed west. He had the nagging feeling that this must be a means by which the rebels communicated, but, for the life of him, he had no idea how. Danforth was well-educated and might know, but he had departed with Arnold's navy.

It was an immense and mighty undertaking, even though Burgoyne's army was moving agonizingly slowly. Problems were beginning to arise and no one was surprised. All the planning in the world could not anticipate what would happen when nearly fourteen thousand men, along with hundreds of wagons and horses, and accompanied by herds of cattle, began to move west. Burgoyne had done all he could to lighten the army, but it was still necessary to bring a large quantity of supplies. Fourteen thousand men ate a lot of food each day, more than several tons, and they had no choice but to bring it.

At least they weren't dragging bloody cannon through the forest, and, unlike the Saratoga campaign, Burgoyne had not brought his mistress and several wagons of personal supplies. Fitzroy grinned. To the best of his knowledge, Burgoyne had no mistress at Detroit and had been forced to remain celibate along with most of his army. At least he'd had the pleasures of Hannah for a little while.

Fitzroy urged his small, old horse towards the front of the column. He was one of the lucky few on horseback. The vast majority of the men, including some fairly high-ranking officers, would have to walk. His position as Burgoyne's aide afforded him some privileges and he saw nothing wrong with that.

He found General Grant watching the march as it slowed and then stopped altogether.

"Now what the devil is wrong?" Grant muttered angrily.

"Surely it'll get better as we go along and get used to this, sir."

Grant glared at Fitzroy. "It can hardly get any worse, Major. We've been at this for hours and most of the men haven't yet left the camp."

Fitzroy noted that the querulous general had lost still more weight. Bad food will do that to you, he thought. The previously portly general now looked more stout than actually fat.

"I'm still surprised at the number of wagons, sir. I thought we were traveling light."

"This is light," Grant snorted. "We still have to carry food and ammunition, don't we? Only the cannon, shells, and extra ammunition went by boat, along with additional food, uniforms, blankets, and, of course, the luxuries without which General Burgoyne cannot live and will require once we arrive." This last comment was said with contempt.

"Well, at least we get to ride," Fitzroy said in an attempt to make pleasant small talk with Burgoyne's second in command.

Grant sneered. "Are you that stupid, Major? When we really get into the woods, we'll all be walking. Any man on horseback will simply be calling out for the rebel sharpshooters to kill him. And yes, don't laugh. I too will be marching and I will hate every bloody damn moment of it."

Why hadn't he thought of that? Fitzroy wondered. He pulled away from the general and commenced to look around. Flanking patrols were out and the woods were sparse. No enemy could be hiding in them.

Or were they?

The British column snaked its way out of Detroit and began to move slowly westward. Even though Burgoyne had seen to it that many of the encumbrances that had delayed him on his march to Saratoga were either left behind or were going by boat, the march was moving exquisitely slowly.

"Bloody hell," Sergeant Barley said, "I've seen dead men move more quickly."

Barley, Owen, and two more men were hidden in the trees and bushes that lined the trail. The leaves and shadows made them virtually invisible if they didn't move. The British were less than a hundred yards away and struggling mightily against the forest that had only begun to envelop them. Flankers and Indian allies occasionally made their presence known, but they were looking outward and Owen and his men were already inside their loose perimeter. Owen wondered how the going would be for the British when the trees began to thicken.

They waited until dark and Owen ordered them to withdraw. When they'd reached the relative safety of woodlands outside the range of the patrols, Barley grabbed Owen's arm and grinned wickedly.

"We're not going to give them a good night's sleep, are we, Owen?"

The British column, with the tail of it scarcely out of their camp at Detroit, had bedded down for the night. Even the patrols had largely gone to ground to await the dawn and the continuation of the march. A patrol of about twenty men was only a few hundred yards away, protected by a pair of sentries.

"Why don't we see if Franklin's crossbows work?" Owen said with an evil grin.

They daubed their faces with dirt and moved slowly to the patrol's camp. Owen noted that the bloody fools had built a campfire and were cooking something, probably a stew with a local rabbit as the guest of honor. A sentry moved between them and the fire. He was less than fifty yards away.

"Mine," Owen said. "Officers always get first choice." Barley responded with an obscenity but didn't argue.

Owen silently cocked his crossbow and moved slowly closer. He didn't think the Brit would see him since the man kept looking towards the camp, the fire, and his dinner cooking; thus destroying his night vision.

Owen was only about ten yards away from the man when he fired. The sentry dropped immediately with a bolt through his skull. There had been little noise.

Owen sent Barley to watch for the other sentry while he and the other two men crept closer to the camp.

A scream tore through the night. Shit, Owen thought. Barley's kill hadn't been clean. The men around the fire stood in alarm. "Fire," Owen ordered and three more bolts flew silently to their targets. Two men dropped to the ground while the third howled and hopped around with a bolt in his leg. They loaded quickly and fired another volley, this time with Barley joining in. Two more men fell writhing.

The remaining British fired their muskets indiscriminately at their silent and invisible enemy, hitting nothing. Still, they were alert and angry. "Fall back," Owen ordered.

"One more shot," Barley pleaded.

"Christ no," Owen said. "They're aroused now and there will be others coming from all over the place. We run like the devil and come back tomorrow."

Barley's teeth shone white in the night. "Sounds like a wonderful idea to me, Lieutenant."

Sarah stood naked in the basin of water. She took a wet cloth from a basin on a table beside her and used it to rinse out her hair. She enjoyed the feel of the water running down her body. It was warm outside and the water felt cool and refreshing. She was in the storeroom where she now slept.

There was a knock on her door and she stiffened. "Who is it?"

"It is I," came the familiar voice of Benjamin Franklin. "May I come in? I understand you wished to speak with me. Or isn't this a good time?"

"I'm bathing," she said, thinking about the comment that she should use her feminine wiles to pry information from Franklin.

"Then it would be a marvelous time," Franklin said.

She reached over to the table, grabbed a thin shift and pulled it over her head. "Then do come in," she said sweetly.

The door opened and Franklin's head poked around it. He saw Sarah and his face lit up. The thin shift had plastered itself to her wet body. "There truly is a God and I am in heaven," he declared. "Thank you, God."

"You have to be dead to be in heaven, Benjamin. And for God's sake, close that door."

Franklin did as he was told and, grinning broadly, sat down in a chair a few feet away from Sarah. He made no move to come closer or to touch her.

"There is a painting of great renown," he said. "It's called 'Venus Rising From the Sea,' or some such and it's by an Italian with a name that's impossible to spell. Botticelli, I believe, although it doesn't matter. I believe you would have made a marvelous model for Venus. Or she for you."

Sarah stepped out of the basin. "I'm flattered."

"You are even lovelier than many of the French noblewomen I've had the pleasure of seeing undressed. They are such a pallid bunch, while you are so refreshingly healthy. Even your hair, though wet, is so lovely. Frenchwomen's hair is puffed and plastered and sculptured so that it weighs heavily. I also have it on good authority that Frenchwomen's hair is often rife with vermin of all sorts." He sighed. The wet shift was so thin that she might as well be naked. "Tell me, has Will ever seen you thusly?"

"No. At least not yet."

"Then I'm flattered. However, as much as I am thrilled beyond words to be in your presence, I cannot help but feel that you are using me, shamelessly taking advantage of an old man's now unfulfillable desires."

"As always you are correct. I wish to know something. Where is my uncle? What have you done with him and the others who worked in Merlin's Cave?"

"Nothing sinister, my exquisite young friend. I simply felt that they could concentrate on their efforts far better if they were away from the distractions of this town."

"Should I assume they are working on something secret? After all, I find it hard to believe that a man of your intellect could only come up with the crossbow and the pike as an answer to England's great army."

Franklin chuckled. "And believe me I have tried. At first I thought that my experiences with electricity would result in a weapon that would tip the scales in our favor, but it's proven beyond us. Electricity will someday make a good weapon, but it won't happen in this war."

"And nothing else?"

"Just small things that will annoy and inconvenience the English, but nothing that will stop them or offset their numerical strength."

"I'm genuinely sorry to hear that." Sarah stood in front of Franklin. His eyes again wandered down where the shift clung to her firm breasts and nipples and her flat belly and hinted at the pale hair between her thighs. She smiled and handed him a towel. "Would you please help dry my hair?"

"With consummate pleasure, dear Sarah," he said happily as he stood up. What a wonderful day. He'd seen a beautiful woman nearly naked and still managed to keep his secrets from her.

Is this going to happen every night? Fitzroy was nearly dead from lack of sleep. The attacks on the column had resulted in a half dozen deaths and several wounded. Worse, they had kept everyone in a state of alarm which prevented anyone from getting a good night's sleep.

"Bullets I can understand," said Burgoyne, "but this?"

Burgoyne held a length of metal in his hand. General Grant took it from him and laughed harshly. "Crossbow bolt. Jesus, are the rebels that destitute? We'll overrun them with ease when we reach their miserable town if this is all they have. It'll probably be like a mud and wattle village from some depressing part of Ireland and not a proper city after all."

"I don't doubt that the town will prove to be crudely made," Burgoyne said. "But I do wonder if this weapon is as crude as it appears."

Fitzroy wondered as well. Some of the previous day's and night's casualties had come from gunfire, but the crossbow attacks had come with the silence of a poisonous snake striking. The men were definitely disconcerted by something that could wound or kill before anyone was aware that anything had occurred.

"Do you suggest more patrols, General?" Fitzroy asked of Burgoyne.

"Indeed, and I want more men awake and prowling around during the night. Some may be tired during the next day's march, but at least they'll be alive and the others will have rested."

Fitzroy thought that the added patrols would further slow the column, which was already plodding and beginning to fall behind schedule.

As they spoke, a horse screamed and bucked. They ran to it and saw a length of metal protruding from its flank. The horse staggered and fell to the ground, clearly mortally wounded.

"Fucking bastards!" screamed Grant. "That was my best horse!"

For the women at Fort Washington, the training that some had taken on as a lark had taken on a high degree of intensity. The British were finally coming.

Will watched as Sarah, now a squad leader, led her charges through their drills. They had learned to carry extra muskets, load them for the men, and use their pikes with surprisingly deadly efficiency. They had also learned to carry wounded off the field and care for them. They had practiced on dummies and willing volunteers, but they all knew there was no way to duplicate the sounds, smell, and terror of the battlefield. They were as untested as so many of the male soldiers were. When the time came, some would collapse, and some would run in panic, while others would perform admirably and even heroically. And no one really knew who among them would do what.

Will was filled with admiration for Sarah as she grew as a leader. Always strong-willed, she had become much more. And she was not alone. Many women, young and old, had become forces in the community. Some men had openly wondered just what monsters they were creating. Would women ever again be subservient? Others had laughed and said that women had never been subservient, they had only pretended.

The drilling ended and the women put down their pikes. They picked up new weapons that had only recently been provided— maces. They were spike-pointed iron clubs straight out of the Middle Ages. Once again Franklin had gone to the past to help fight for the future. Everyone was getting one and Will had one tucked in his belt. They were crude, but, in close quarters, they might prove effective. At least they would surprise the hell out of the enemy, Will thought. One blow could easily crush a skull and if the enemy soldier tried to block the mace with his arm, the bones would be shattered. The maces were not light and someone commented just how easily the women now wielded them. What weaker sex, another chuckled, repeating the old joke.

The women practiced wielding the maces, first with one hand and then the other and, finally, with both hands, whirling and clubbing. Valkyries, Will thought, recalling what he'd read of Nordic legends. Or maybe they were Amazons brought back from ancient Greece.

Sarah tucked her mace in the belt that bound her dress and walked over to Will. Her face was slick and shiny with sweat. He thought she was beautiful.

Sarah took his arm and they walked away from the crowd. It was an open gesture of affection that would have been unthinkable a few months before. Affection was supposed to be private. So too were passion and lust.

"When are you leaving?" she asked.

"Tonight."

"I'll be miserable without you."

Will took a deep breath, "And I without you."

"I still don't understand what you hope to accomplish by going all that way just to see what the British are doing and what we are doing about it. Why not just wait? They'll be here soon enough."

Why not indeed? Will had argued exactly that point. But he had lost. Tallmadge wanted someone from his staff to actually see what was happening. How effective were the riflemen like Owen Wells in fighting the British in the forests? How did the British react? What about Brant's Indians and Girty's white savages? Oh, they got frequent reports, both by pigeon and by courier, but they were words on paper. Tallmadge, and Stark above him, wanted an eyewitness. Will could only hope he didn't get himself killed before the climactic battle began.

# Chapter 14 ★ ★ ★ ★ ★ ★ ★ ★ ★ ★ ★ ★ ★ ★ ★

T HE SIX BEDRAGGLED MEN HUDDLED TOGETHER, WET AND miserable and too exhausted to even strain at their bonds. Not that it would have helped. Their captors only waited for an excuse to kill them. All of them were wounded to some degree, which, in the eyes of their angry captors, entitled them to neither mercy nor pity.

Fitzroy glared at them. "What unit?"

"King's Royal Butt-fuckers," a man with a bandage on his forehead answered, drawing smiles from the others.

One of the British soldiers guarding them snarled and swung his musket butt, smashing it into the man's face. Blood and teeth flew and he flopped to the ground, his jaw broken. The lack of discipline dismayed Fitzroy, but he understood it. These rebels had been murdering British soldiers, ambushing them, shooting them in the back. Americans who'd been killing soldiers in the night were objects of a deep hatred.

"How many of them are branded?" Tarleton asked. Fitzroy was taken aback. He hadn't been aware that the young general was even present.

Guards checked and reported that five of them wore brands, identifying them as rebels who'd fought before against the king and his army. Tarleton grinned wickedly. "Well now, they doubt-less know their future, don't they?"

Fitzroy reached into a pile of their belongings and pulled out

221

a crossbow. He examined it for a moment and handed it to Tarleton who found it amusing at first, but quickly turned angry.

"A coward's weapon," he said and tossed it back. He grinned wolfishly at the number of British soldiers who'd gathered around them. "I've changed my mind. Hanging's too pleasant for them. Do whatever you wish," he said. He whirled and walked away.

As Fitzroy gaped in astonishment, the surrounding soldiers roared and set about the helpless prisoners, hitting them with musket butts and stomping them with their feet. Then they began to stick them with bayonets. The Americans screamed in fear and agony while Tarleton laughed uproariously. It was over in a minute. The six prisoners had been reduced to a bloody, broken pile of almost unrecognizable flesh.

Tarleton glared at Fitzroy. "And don't you dare tell me how this is going to affect any rebels surrendering. I don't want them to surrender, Fitzroy. I want them to die. Every Goddamned one of them."

Fitzroy returned his glare. "I wouldn't treat a hog like you treated those men."

"And I wouldn't either," Tarleton replied evenly. "Hogs are valuable."

The stream was wide, but not particularly deep. Will estimated it at waist level at its deepest point. Nor was it running very quickly. Men would not be swept off their feet. It would not stop the British, not even slow them very much. What was stopping them, however, was its openness. It was about fifty yards from bank to bank and each side was heavily wooded and bordered by thick, green bushes. The handful of Iroquois paused, doubtful of whether to continue. It smelled so much of an ambush. They said they could detect the scent of white men.

A British officer came up to them and yelled something that Will couldn't quite hear, but the intent was obvious. The Indians were to get their lazy asses across the creek and scout out possible American positions.

Will felt a twinge of sorrow for the Indians—their group now reinforced to about twenty—but his feelings passed. They were the enemy. Will had arrived the day before to observe the progress of the British army. He lay in the brush, his face smeared with grease and dirt to make him less visible. Owen Wells lay a few feet away. He commanded the small American detachment while Will was strictly there to observe, a fact that made Will just a little uncomfortable.

Owen made a slight gesture with his hand. Two Americans jumped up, shrieked, and fired their rifles at the astonished Indians. They hit one in the leg and he fell into the water, thrashing wildly. The remaining Indians recovered quickly and poured heavy but inaccurate musket fire into the woods around Will and Owen.

Another signal and two more men rose and fired at the Indians, hitting nothing. The Indians screamed their anger and surged forward through the smoke of battle. When they were in midstream, Owen hollered for the rest of his men to fire and a score of crossbow bolts struck the Indians, who for a moment were puzzled to see the deadly things sticking out of legs and chests.

The bowmen laid down their crossbows and picked up rifles which they fired into the now thoroughly rattled Iroquois. The Indians were courageous, but this type of fighting was something terrible and new, even for warriors who made the woods their home. They fell back to the British side of the stream, dragging their dead and wounded with them. At least a dozen Iroquois had fallen and the once clear stream was running red, while clouds of musket smoke obscured both sides.

Owen looked at Will and grinned. "That was well done, wasn't it?"

Will admitted that it was. "Now what do we do?"

Owen looked across the stream where he could see Redcoats forming for an assault. The Indians had disappeared. "Major, I believe it's time to run like hell."

General Tallmadge looked at the mess that was Will Drake and sneered in mock contempt. "Drake, every time I send you out east you come back even more disreputable and filthy than before. Is this a project of yours?"

Will managed a wan grin. He had been on horseback for several days and nights. He was exhausted, hungry, and, as Tallmadge pointed out, filthy.

"I wanted to get here before the British showed up," Will said.

"Who aren't hurrying at all," said General Stark.

"No sir," said Drake. "Not only are they not hurrying, but they've stopped and are setting up a fortified supply depot. They are building a palisade, and buildings inside sufficient to contain a great amount of stores."

"Which is what we suspected would happen," said Stark with a nod to Tallmadge who smiled at the compliment to his intelligence gathering techniques.

"And they'll do it at least once more," Tallmadge injected. "Burgoyne has no intention of repeating what he feels are his mistakes from his Saratoga campaign. He will ensure that he has enough ammunition and food before investing Fort Washington and Liberty."

Stark glared at Will. "Tell me, Major, are we hurting them? Killing them?"

Will took a deep breath. "To an extent, yes sir. But we are not stopping them. We have killed and wounded a number of British and Indians, but there are so many of them and so few men in Clark's brigade who are fighting them. Is there any thought of reinforcing Clark?"

Stark seemed surprised by the question and Will wondered if he'd been impertinent. Then he decided the hell with it. He'd been there on the trail and he'd seen the fighting and the damage that a small number of men could do. "I think more men could really hurt them."

Stark slowly shook his head. "No. We will not reinforce Clark. However tempting that might be, it would mean running the risk of fighting the major battle in the woods where we might be overwhelmed and not in the fortifications we are building. No, Major, we will stick with our original plan and fight them here, where we've been preparing the field for battle."

Will was dismayed. "Sir, Clark's men have been killing the enemy, but we've lost men as well."

Stark nodded grimly. "I understand, Major. And I know from your report that the British have taken to killing the prisoners they've taken. Our whole army now knows what befalls them if they should be so foolish as to surrender. Any doubts our people may have had should now be totally destroyed. They, we, will all fight to the death."

"The Indians," Tallmadge asked, "how are they reacting to our attacks?"

Will grinned. He was on surer ground. "Brant's Iroquois are a long ways from their homes and don't at all like fighting our men. They don't like the crossbows and they don't like being ambushed every time they reach a clearing or stream. If you want my opinion, the Indians will be through as a fighting force before long and will simply fade away and be replaced by Girty's people."

Tallmadge grimaced, "Which means we trade one band of bloodthirsty savages for another."

Stark rose and turned to leave. Will started to rise, but Stark waved him down. "You've done good work, Drake. Get yourself cleaned up and write down anything you can think of that might be important."

When Stark was gone, Tallmadge smiled like a cat. "Will, we do have some good news."

"Finally? Wonderful."

"First, additional men have been coming in and in numbers sufficient to offset those 'sunshine soldiers and summer patriots' who decamped because they suddenly realized that the British are indeed coming. The change in numbers is not all that great, but it is an improvement. Unfortunately, many of the new men are either poorly trained or not trained at all. However, we feel they will be adequate fighters when put behind barricades and earthworks."

Will yawned. He would kill for a cup of real coffee. Or maybe a long nap. "Good."

"Additionally, Daniel Boone and some other fighters will be coming from the south. Stark has called for their help."

"They're coming?" Daniel Boone was a legend for his fighting in Kentucky, while some of the other southern fighters like Sevier, Campbell, and Shelby had helped destroy a British force at King's Mountain.

"We are confident they will obey Stark's summons," Tallmadge said smugly. "Boone has about a hundred riflemen, and, while it's impossible to estimate what the others will bring to the table, any number will be helpful."

"Wonderful. When will they arrive?"

"And there's the rub, Will. Boone will be here in a week or so, but we have no idea when or where the others will come. There's the nagging feeling that they might not arrive until after the battle. Stark sent messengers to find them, but God only knows when or whether they will. I also don't know specifically what Stark is ordering them to do and whether they will obey his orders. 'Tis a sad state of affairs."

Will groaned. "I almost wish you hadn't built up my hopes and told me."

"It seemed like the decent thing to do, sharing my confusion and my misery, that is. Now, why don't you take a bath and go find your woman. And in that order, for God's sake."

Captain Peter Danforth cheered with the others as the last of the sailing barges made it to the relative safety of Mackinac Island and under the guns of the recently completed limestone fort that crowned the hill overlooking them. The crew of the tail end barge waved happily back. The journey had been an unqualified success and Danforth, who still heartily disliked Benedict Arnold, had been impressed by the turncoat's ability to coordinate the efforts of the little fleet. Arnold was unquestionably qualified as a leader. Too bad Danforth couldn't bring himself to like or trust the man.

Impressive, too, had been the sailing qualities of the barges. They had performed well as their untrained crews learned to sail them without sinking them. As a result, forty-eight of the fifty boats that comprised the hodge-podge fleet had arrived at the fort that controlled the Straits of Mackinac far more quickly than anyone had thought possible. One had sunk, the result of bad construction, and one had simply disappeared during a sudden squall. Still, forty-eight out of fifty was an impressive performance.

"Halfway there, eh Danforth?"

Danforth nodded. Captain Thomas Rudyard was the second in command of the garrison of Fort Mackinac. Like Danforth, he bemoaned the fact that they were both stuck in this military backwater while real glory was to be had in Europe. Rudyard reminded Danforth of his friend Fitzroy in that the man had no money to speak of and would need glory on the battlefield in order to rise above his current rank. Rudyard, however, was likely already too old for promotion. He was almost forty and took out his frustrations by getting drunk each evening after his duties were completed.

Still, Rudyard was a likeable sort of sot. "Halfway there, Thomas, although far less than halfway home."

"I can hardly wait," said Rudyard. "I hate this place."

Danforth was sympathetic. Only at Mackinac for a couple of days, he found it beyond boring. Other than staring at the trees, which never moved, or the vast lakes, which sometimes did, there was absolutely nothing to do. Even the Indians seemed relatively docile and unthreatening and unwilling to repeat their warfare against the British only a few decades past. That last Indian war, under the loose leadership of Pontiac, had resulted in the massacre of the British garrison of Fort Michilimackinac, whose ruins were barely visible across the straits. The old fort had been abandoned as indefensible and the new one built on the island.

The French had maintained a presence in the lakes for almost two centuries before surrendering control to the British. Danforth wondered how their soldiers had coped with being out of contact with civilization and Europe for years on end. He wondered if some of the French soldiers in the garrison had gone mad, and then wondered the same about the British garrison. He couldn't imagine anyone actually liking it in the wilderness.

But then, some people did live there. A village of sorts had grown up along the shore and beneath the fort. It included the usual shabby taverns and these featured local women working as prostitutes. Some of those of partial French ancestry looked attractive enough and Danforth commented on it.

"Stay here long enough and they'll look even better. If you do choose one of them, keep an eye on your purse and wear a condom."

"I wouldn't think of not wearing one," Danforth sniffed. "I brought a half dozen lambskin ones in case I run into an opportunity in this miserable place."

Rudyard laughed ruefully. "If you think it's miserable out here now, just wait until winter."

"I have no plans to be here this winter," he said and shuddered at the thought.

"Well, I hope your plans never change. The weather's not bad now, but just wait. There'll be snow three times taller than your arse and the wind will blow you right down. Then it'll get so cold that the lake will entirely freeze over and you can walk right across to that disgusting village of Mackinac on the mainland, or you could go north to that equally desolate city of St. Ignace. Of course, bears and wolves can walk across as well and pay us a visit, and sometimes they do which makes life interesting. Imagine opening your cabin door so you can go out and take a piss, and seeing a bear staring you in the face and trying to decide whether or not to eat you. Once the freeze happened, we'd get fresh meat by killing the deer that would come close because they were starving to death and willing to take chances for food."

"Good lord, Rudyard, how on earth did you survive your time here?"

Rudyard grunted. "I'm not too sure I did. Actually, we drank even more than we do in the summer. Officers, of course, can take one of those part French doxies in for company. Thank God I'm leaving here when you people depart."

Benedict Arnold had decided to take two companies of the garrison's British infantry with him. The fort's commandant had protested furiously but Arnold had prevailed. Actually it made sense. It was obvious that the flotilla had made such good time that it was going to arrive well ahead of the main army and would need soldiers to protect it from possible rebel attacks. Arnold had decided it would be imprudent to stay at anchor in the lake and had planned to seek shelter up the St. Joseph River; thus, the infantry was needed to provide security from the landward side.

Of course, Arnold could have decided that they wait a couple of weeks to ensure a more coordinated arrival, but the former rebel general was anxious to the point of being impetuous. He wanted to get moving. He wanted to be first to the rebel stronghold. Perhaps he could win a skirmish or even a small battle and gather some glory to himself.

"They know we're coming, don't they?" Rudyard asked.

Danforth answered by telling him of the spies in residence at Detroit. "They watched us build these craft and then they watched them depart. I rather think there are people across the straits looking at us and just waiting for us to set sail. Then they will sneak past us and be at the rebel lair well before we arrive."

Rudyard grunted, "I hate when there are no secrets."

After washing himself, Will succumbed to exhaustion and slept the sleep of the dead on a cot in Benjamin Franklin's office. When he finally awoke, it was the middle of the next day and he only vaguely recalled climbing into the cot before collapsing.

The office door opened and Sarah entered, smiling. "Awake at last, I see. You slept so long it reminded me of an old German or Dutch folk tale about a man who sleeps for twenty years and finally awakens to find the world a changed place."

"In which case, please tell me that we've won the war and I can go home with you and live in peace."

She shook her head sadly. "If only we could be so lucky. No, the

British are still coming, although slowly, and we are still working devilishly hard to prepare for them." She held out her hands. They were calloused and hard. There was dirt ingrained in them. She was barefoot like so many women and a number of men. Shoes, moccasins, boots, were in short supply and would be hoarded for bad weather or the coming battle when mobility would be essential.

"Once I was a delicate young maiden whose hands were soft as cream," she smiled and sighed mockingly. "Look at me now."

Will swung out of bed and wrapped the blanket around him while he looked for his clothes. He was wearing his shirt, which went almost to his knees, but felt awkward without his pants.

He tried not to laugh at Sarah's comments even though he knew she was teasing him. A delicate young maiden? Her? While slender and lithe, there was nothing delicate about her. She was not a fragile flower like the women of the eastern cities who seemed to imitate what they thought were how British and French ladies behaved. No, she was a new woman, an American.

As he was thinking, Faith burst into the room. "Where's Owen and how is he?" Then she realized that Will wasn't quite dressed. "Lord, you've got skinny legs. Not at all strong and powerful like my Owen's, and much too hairy."

Sarah professed mock shock. "And how would you know about Owen's legs and, I'll have you know, Will's legs are perfectly fine. I think they are slender and elegant, thank you."

Faith grinned. "I'll bet I know more about Owen than you know about Will."

"Let me break this up before it becomes bloody," Will said as he slipped on his pants while somehow still holding the blanket around him. "Owen is fine and sends his love. He will be back here when the British complete their march. Thus, in a perverse way, we are safer because he is not around. And why aren't you both working with Dr. Franklin?"

Sarah answered. "We are no longer needed. Whatever devilish devices he's making no longer require as many of our nimble fingers as before. We younger ones have been sent back to work on the fortifications. All we do now is dig moats and earthworks and weave tree limbs to impede the British when they do arrive."

Will made a mental note to see how the defenses have progressed. Once again he wondered if British women would work like Sarah and Faith and hundreds of others were. He doubted it.

"Have you heard anything about Braxton?" Faith asked. "May I hope he's dead and rotting in the ground?"

"Sadly, he is still alive and quite well. Our scouts say he commands a company under Simon Girty."

Faith nodded. "Just as well. I'll have Owen kill Braxton when he arrives. I know Winifred would approve as well."

"Do you recall a woman named Hannah Van Doorn?" Sarah inquired. "She wishes to know if a Major Fitzroy is still with the British. He's an aide to Burgoyne."

Will shrugged. "Insofar as I have not gotten close to General Burgoyne or his staff and insofar I have no idea who or what this Fitzroy is or looks like, tell Hannah I'm sorry but I don't know."

Will stuffed his shirt into his pants. "Do you have to go back to work, Sarah?"

"Not immediately."

"Then walk with me, Mistress Sarah. I need you beside me."

If Sarah were a cat, she would have purred. "I'm honored, dear Will."

Hundreds of miles south and away from either Cornwallis or Burgoyne, Jack Sevier spat into the log in the fireplace and grunted satisfactorily when it sizzled. They were sheltering in what had once been a tavern about twenty miles outside of Charleston, South Carolina. Now the tavern was a ruin. Its roof had collapsed and the walls were charred. It was as close to the British-held city as any of the rebels wished to go. From here their patrols could watch the British patrols and the British could watch them. A kind of truce had developed with neither side wishing to upset things. At least, not yet.

"So who the hell is John Stark and why should we do anything to help him and those people up north?" Sevier asked.

"To the point as usual," said Francis Marion, the rebel also known as the Swamp Fox. Marion coughed and covered his mouth with a rag that he quickly checked for traces of blood. Sevier and the third man, Isaac Shelby, turned away and pretended not to see. The legendary Swamp Fox was a very sick man.

Shelby answered. "According to the messenger, he is now the general commanding our forces up north. With Greene dead, they had to choose someone, and I guess Stark was the best they had."

"And he will never be half the man Greene was," Marion said

glumly. "And he isn't any Morgan either. Dan Morgan is even sicker than I am so that leaves him out as Greene's replacement."

Sevier chuckled. "So this Stark is the best of what they had left? Jesus wept. At least they didn't pick Schuyler. So what does this General Stark want?"

"He requests our presence at the coming battle up north," Marion said. "In case you've forgotten, Burgoyne is advancing on him with at least ten thousand men, maybe more."

"And what concern is that of ours?" Sevier said. "We took care of the British at King's Mountain when we destroyed that column under Patrick Ferguson. They come this way again and we'll do it again."

Marion hadn't been at that battle. Sevier and Shelby had. The British under Ferguson had chased Sevier, Shelby, and other rebels from their homes and then over the Blue Ridge Mountains where they were forced to stand and fight. The result had been a catastrophic British defeat at King's Mountain. Ironically, current British weaknesses meant that the rebels were now back on the eastern side of the mountains. All the fighting had accomplished exactly nothing for the British.

"Then you recall that Ferguson basically threatened us all with death and destruction unless we kneeled down to him and worshiped his king," Marion said. "And you also recall how that enraged all of us who lived out there. Well, it looks like Burgoyne is going to do the same thing up north. And, if he's successful, don't you think he'll be down here looking for us in a very short while?"

Marion paused and took a deep breath. "Or had you forgotten the report that the British planned to turn all of the colonies into little kingdoms ruled by nobles brought in from England and where we would be little more than slaves?"

It was a very long speech for the sickly Marion, who commenced coughing violently.

"We remember," Isaac Shelby admitted. "So, you want us to go north and help Stark, don't you?"

"Yes. Daniel Boone's already gone with his men."

"But won't that give the British in Charleston a chance to come out and take over down here?" asked Sevier.

Shelby shook his head. "Not if we leave a small force to keep an eye on them. The British stripped the garrison to reinforce Burgoyne, remember. And I don't think the Loyalists in the area are all that enthused about any more fighting. They're as confused as anyone about British intentions and, from what I hear, don't trust them at all anymore."

Shelby turned to Marion. "We had maybe a thousand men at King's Mountain, although I don't recall anyone actually counting. What say we send out a call for as many men as possible, with their guns and horses, and meet in two weeks? Say we raise even half of that, who will command?"

Sevier and Shelby looked at each other. The command structure at King's Mountain had been by committee and both men knew it wouldn't work this time around. They turned to Marion.

The Swamp Fox waved his hand in dismissal. "It won't be me. I'd be coughing blood all the way north. No, I'll stay here and keep an eye on Charleston for you."

Sevier took a deep breath. Both he and Shelby were men of property and education. They were also ambitious. Someone would have to give.

Finally, Sevier took a deep breath. "I'll serve under you, Isaac," Sevier finally said. He held out his hand and Shelby took it.

Lord Charles Cornwallis took the paper on which the latest message had been written, wadded it up, and threw it across the room. The aide who'd delivered it scampered out of the office and closed the door behind him. William Cornwallis could not contain his laughter and positively cackled with glee.

"Another urgent and unrealistic message from their lordships in London, I see," William chortled. "And here I thought I was the only one who got those ridiculous epistles."

Charles Cornwallis calmed himself and sat down. "Yes. Lord North and his minions wish me to tell Burgoyne to please hurry. Just how am I supposed to do that when I haven't heard from Johnny Burgoyne in weeks and have no idea where the devil he is? To the west of Detroit is likely, but precisely where and how would I reach him even if I did know? And how long would it take for a message from me to reach him? A couple of months, I dare say, and then, of course, another couple of months for the response to get here assuming that he writes me immediately in the first place. Lord North and the king have no idea of the size of this continent or the distances involved."

William yawned and concurred. "North America is like a vast ocean with trees."

"I also rather feel that Burgoyne is moving as fast as he can, or at least as fast as I can make him. Don't they realize that Burgoyne is not in the room across the hall? Damn it, he's halfway across a continent!"

Commodore Cornwallis smiled and sipped his brandy. "You will, of course, ignore their message."

"Actually, I will tell the king and Lord North by my own messenger, who will leave himself in a few weeks that I am attempting to do exactly as they wish."

William shook his head. "They really have no idea of the conditions in these colonies, do they?"

"Not for one second. Are you aware that I've just been informed that there is no longer any significant rebel activity outside Charleston in the Carolinas?"

"I was not and what does it mean?"

"I don't know. We are sending out patrols to locate the southern rebels, but it will be additional weeks before we find out anything certain. In the meantime, they could have flown elsewhere."

William Cornwallis looked grim, "Or they are planning to lure us into an ambush." He paused. "Do you mean elsewhere as in farther north? Are you afraid that they could be heading north to help confront Burgoyne?"

"Of course," Charles Cornwallis said. He began to pace nervously. "And which southern partisan leaders might be going? However, Burgoyne is well aware of that possibility. We discussed it at length and rather assumed it was likely, even desirable that the rebel forces all converge. If we can kill all the vipers at one sitting, so much the better."

"Have you sent messages to Burgoyne?"

"Just the same as I will tell Lord North, although with a few changes. In my message to London, I will state my opinion that Burgoyne is in grave danger from the southern rebels heading towards him. He isn't, of course, and I won't say a word of that to Burgoyne, but that will be my little revenge on London. Might as well let North have some sleepless nights wondering whether or not Burgoyne has once again been swallowed up by the forests of North America."

William laughed appreciatively. If they could tweak their unloved masters in London, it was a good day.

# Chapter 15 ★ ★ ★ ★ ★ ★ ★ ★ ★ ★ ★ ★ ★ ★ ★ ★

THE SCREAMS AND HOWLS OF RAGE AND FURY FROM BEHIND him were Owen's first and terrible indication that something was horribly wrong. He wheeled and found himself face to face with a horde of Iroquois who'd exploded from the woods to his rear.

He and the others fired the muskets and crossbows they'd just been aiming at a patrol of Redcoats. Indians fell but the press of numbers carried them into the small group of rebels before they could reload. For a moment that seemed an eternity, it was a brawl with musket butts, tomahawks, knives and, ultimately, fists and teeth. Men screamed and fell while others fought desperately.

An Indian grabbed Owen from behind and began to strangle him. With his strong arms, he pried the man's hands from his throat and smashed his fist into the Indian's face, blood gushed from the Iroquois' mouth. Something hard hit him in the back and knocked him to his knees. He couldn't breathe and the world spun. I'm going to die, he thought, but then his assailant fell beside him, a tomahawk in his skull.

Hands grabbed Owen and pulled him upright. "We'd better run, Lieutenant."

Owen nodded. The pain from his back was so intense that he could barely inhale. Talking was out of the question. The Indians had also pulled back, leaving several dead and dying on the ground. From the receding screams and pleas it looked like they'd taken prisoners from Owen's small force.

Despite wanting to rescue his men, Owen had to retreat. The British patrol they'd been stalking was approaching rapidly. His remaining men helped him into the darkening woods as yet another summer rain began to fall. In a matter of moments they were relatively safe, unless they ran into some more of Brant's Iroquois or Girty's white savages.

Owen was half carried, half dragged to the rendezvous point where Sergeant Barley waited with the other half of the platoon. He was laid on the ground and covered with a blanket. He was offered water and he gulped it greedily.

"Got yourself into a mess, didn't you, Owen?"

"Go screw yourself," Owen managed to rasp. The effort cost him dearly.

Barley laughed and checked Owen's wound. "Somebody hit you with a tomahawk, but with not enough force to go all the way through your thick skin. In fact, it just glanced off. We'll sew it and wrap you up since I think some ribs may be broken. Then you've got to go back to Fort Washington. You're useless as tits on a boar with that wound."

Owen groaned in dismay, but had to agree. In his wounded state he would be a handicap to a force that had to move quickly and lightly through the woods.

Then he saw the bright side. Even the slowest mule would move faster than the British column and he'd be back to spend at least some time with lovely little Faith while he healed.

To Fitzroy's disgust and dismay, Burgoyne agreed with Brant and Tarleton—the prisoners belonged to the Indians who had captured them. It was a gesture to keep the Indians more or less happy. They'd suffered heavy casualties and, along with those who had returned home in disgust, now numbered fewer than two hundred. It was apparent by their sullen looks that they were dispirited as well, and Fitzroy thought they were going to leave as soon as they could, no matter what Burgoyne did to placate them.

But first, the prisoners had to be disposed of, and in the traditional Iroquois manner. The two men were only slightly wounded and seemed fully aware of the horrible fate they were about to endure. Seeing the white faces in the crowd, they called out and pleaded for help, proclaiming that they were Christians and white men and didn't deserve to be slowly destroyed by red savages. Some of the spectators might have agreed, but was to no avail. The prisoners were stripped naked and each was tied to a pair of long poles that had been driven into the ground. With their arms and legs outstretched, every inch of their bodies was now vulnerable.

Girty sidled up beside Fitzroy. "This part they'd normally leave to the squaws, and they are really nasty bitches. The fucking female animals would eat the prisoners alive if the warriors let them. However, since there are no squaws around, the warriors will fill in for them. I hope you enjoy it, Fitzroy." Girty laughed.

The torture took time. While the Iroquois yelled and taunted their victims, wooden splinters were shoved under fingernails and toenails and then set afire. The prisoners screamed all the while, which further excited and encouraged the Iroquois. When they were done with this, they took burning twigs and poked them into the prisoner's genitals and under their arms and onto the soles of their feet while the screaming reached new and purely animal crescendos.

"The Indians despise them for howling like that," Girty said. "They think that only women and cowards scream, so they're going to make it worse for them. They admire someone who endures in silence and might even finish him off quickly."

"Could you endure in silence, Girty?" Fitzroy asked.

"Probably not, but if it meant dying sooner, I'd give it a hell of a try."

Fitzroy found it difficult to speak, and wanted to scream himself. There was vomit rising in his throat. He was disgusted and appalled that Burgoyne had permitted this atrocity. He turned and saw Burgoyne standing a few feet away, his face pale and drawn. Tarleton was behind him and he was grinning broadly. Of course he would enjoy this spectacle. General Grant was nowhere to be seen. Smart man.

Burgoyne stepped forward and whispered to Fitzroy. "I see your dismay, but understand this—if this is what I have to do to keep my army intact and defeat the rebels, then so be it. I will beg God for forgiveness later."

Fitzroy understood but did not agree. War was brutal and hellish, but this was pure savagery, not war. This might have been done by some barbarian Hun or Mongol, but should never be permitted or condoned by British generals in this, the eighteenth century. As a soldier, he had been trained to kill, not to murder and certainly not to torture for pleasure or to prove a point. He turned away from Burgoyne, not trusting himself to answer.

Girty laughed. "It'll be over soon, Major, and then you can go and puke all over your boots if you want." Girty laughed even harder when Fitzroy found himself unable to respond.

The Indians piled bushes underneath the feet of the victims and set them alight. The carefully controlled fires first seared their lower limbs and then their torsos. The prisoners writhed and twisted in vain attempts to escape the slowly rising flames. A few moments later, one of them slumped over. His heart had given out.

"Well that lucky bastard's dead already," Girty said as an Indian reached in and scalped the unmoving man with one quick motion.

The second man didn't stop screaming and writhing until the flames were almost up to his chin. An Iroquois warrior leaned in and ripped off his scalp, but got his arm badly burned for his efforts. This pleased Fitzroy and the other Indians thought it was hilarious.

As the bodies charred and the stinking fire died down, the Indians drifted off. "Now what?" asked Fitzroy. The stench of burned flesh was adding to his problem. He wondered what Hannah Van Doorn would have thought of this. Even though she was a child of the frontier, had she ever seen anything like this? He wanted to talk to her. She would know what to say to comfort him. He missed her. Damn it to hell.

"The brutes are satisfied," Girty said and spat on the ground, "At least for the moment."

Behind him a dull popping sound followed by laughter drew their attention. One of the prisoner's skulls had exploded from the heat. "Yeah, they're satisfied for now," Girty said. "Next they're gonna get good and drunk."

That, Fitzroy thought, was a magnificent idea.

Tallmadge looked at the small piece of paper in his hand. The pigeon who'd brought it stood proudly and heroically on the table and puffed out its chest. It promptly spoiled the scene by dropping a load on said table.

Tallmadge and the others chuckled. "How appropriate," Tallmadge said. "Would that we had a million pigeons that could do the same for Burgoyne and his army."

Will joined in the brief laughter. "But what's the message? Burgoyne's through building a depot and is on the move once again, isn't he?"

"And perhaps only two weeks away," Tallmadge said. "Time to prepare our wills, Will."

Drake winced at the bad pun. "I would if I had anything to leave. I am as poor as the day I escaped from that hulk in New York."

"Aren't we all," Tallmadge added. "But, think of all the wealth that was abandoned by so many of the people who are here. Yes, people like Franklin, Schuyler, and Hancock are considered traitors by the British and subject to be hanged. But don't you think that a goodly portion of their wealth could have been used to buy forgiveness, much in the way that the papist priests require a payment as penance from their parishioners before they're forgiven?"

Schuyler grinned. "The papists have the right idea. Say you're sorry and you're permitted to buy your way into heaven."

Tallmadge shook his head. "I think your understanding of Catholic theology is highly suspect at best, my dear General, but the principle is the same—forgiveness can be bought and sold. It is a commodity. It might be something that could be traded by those Dutch investors who congregate on Wall Street in New York if someone could figure out how to market forgiveness in the form of shares."

"In times like these, wealth doesn't much matter," Schuyler said quietly. "Whatever I have lost in the way of money and lands, I can make back if given the chance. However, I cannot earn back my life if I lose it."

Will thought back to his months—years?—as a prisoner of the British and how he'd been starved. His position then had been far more hopeless than the one he was in now. At least now he could fight back.

So too could people like Owen Wells. Owen had ridden back from the skirmish where he'd been wounded as quickly as any wounded man could. He'd ignored the pain from his body so he could heal and get back to the fighting.

Sarah was another example of the wealth that was now his although, he considered ruefully, he'd yet to possess her.

Tallmadge poured brandies into small cups. There wasn't much good liquor left, although, like the tea, they'd tried to distill some of their own. It had been only marginally successful at best, although a number of men and women had managed to get falling down drunk from testing the results.

Schuyler raised his cup. "Gentlemen, let me propose a toast to the one thing of value that we now possess that, if we are successful, we can bequeath to our heirs."

"Hear, hear," they chorused, "To Liberty."

Silent and menacing, they moved like Viking longships descending upon the hapless British coast where they would fight the soldiers of Alfred the Great or Ethelred the Unready. The cold mist and rain hid them from their unsuspecting prey. In moments they would be ashore, wielding swords and axes to chop down the inept guardians of the land. When that pleasant task was completed, they would begin pillaging the rude homes and ravaging the local women. Many women wouldn't resist much. Instead they would feel honored to be the concubine of mighty Viking warriors. Fires and destruction would show where they had been.

Danforth chuckled softly. At least it sounded good, he thought as Benedict Arnold's small armada moved slowly and soundlessly through the cold, wet Lake Michigan morning. The air was calm, so the crews used the sweeps to row through the flat lake.

As with the trip north to Fort Mackinac, they had begun by making better time than expected and, according to plan, Arnold's orders called for them to anchor in the St. Joseph River, which was about a day's sail from where Burgoyne was supposed to reach the lake and meet up with them.

Their schedule was somewhat disrupted by a couple of violent squalls that arose shortly after they had left Mackinac Island and cost them one barge sunk and two badly damaged after they collided with each other. Danforth had worked hard to help pull the injured from the water, along with a couple of the dead, and received the silent gratitude from the crews for his efforts. Even Arnold complimented him tersely. Arrogant shit, Danforth thought.

After that, they made it a point to sail closer to the Michigan shoreline, which would enable them to beach the barges should another storm arise. None did, but the route did give Danforth and Rudyard an opportunity to view the coastline. They were both astonished by a number of large sand dunes towering several hundred feet into the sky.

It truly was a land of wonders, Danforth thought. Not only

did North America seem to go on forever, but he had seen the marvel of the falls near Niagara and now dunes like those from the Sahara emerging from the lake.

There was significant evidence of Indian presence along the coast as well, and Rudyard informed Danforth that the lake was teaming with edible fish.

"Which is part of the reason the rebels haven't starved," Rudyard said. "You can even chop holes in the ice in the wintertime and fish. The silly creatures are just dying to take your bait and become your dinner."

As they continued to sail south, one new problem had arisen. The British fort on the St. Joseph River had been abandoned several years before, and there was no one with the flotilla who was certain where either it or the river was. Since it was incumbent that they not sail too far south and alert the rebels of their presence, they'd slowed to a crawl and sent the smaller warship, the *Snake,* to search the coast and find the bloody thing. So far the search had not been successful.

"You'd think we were searching for the Northwest Passage," Danforth muttered. The Northwest Passage was the legendary and likely mythical waterway that supposedly connected the Atlantic and Pacific Oceans via Canada. Its lure had drawn many explorers in earlier years, but few now thought it existed.

"Instead, we are looking for a piddling little river," Danforth muttered to his new friend. The *Snake* was in sight and approaching Arnold's Armada.

"Can't be too careful, now can we," Rudyard said. "Can't risk the rebels finding us."

Danforth thought that Rudyard had been drinking again. He was slurring his words, and one whiff of his breath confirmed it. Lord, and it was still early morning. How did the man do it and still function? Danforth liked to drink as much as the next man and then some, but Rudyard was something else, and he was afraid Rudyard's hobby would result in tragedy. At least his two companies of infantry weren't onboard to see their commander in his cups. They had been distributed among the barges.

A signal flag from the *Snake* indicated that they had found the mouth of the river and a chorus of sarcastic cheers came from the ships. Even the usually dour Arnold managed a laugh. How the devil does one lose a river?

A few hours later, the convoy entered the wide mouth of the St. Joseph River and anchored a little ways upstream and, hopefully, out of sight of the prying eyes of Americans who would be on canoes or small sailing boats. Rudyard's two companies of infantry disembarked and began patrolling the coast, while the *Snake* again sailed upstream with Rudyard on board. Danforth envied him. The urge to explore a strange land was strong. He was concerned that Rudyard was so drunk he might miss a herd of elephants, but was confident that his subordinate officers would be up to the task.

After several hours, the *Snake* returned and signaled that all was safe. As arranged, the sailing barges were anchored in the middle of the river, lined up three abreast and lashed to each other for security. In effect, they became a floating fort.

Rudyard's report to Arnold was simple—while there was obvious evidence that people, both red and white, had camped along the banks of the river, there was nothing to indicate any recent or current enemy activity.

"In my opinion, General, what little signs there were came from stray Indians or trappers, and not the rebels."

"And you saw this from the ship or by patrolling the land?" Arnold asked.

"Both, sir," Rudyard said confidently. "Where the forest permitted, we swept about a mile inland on both sides and found nothing to worry about."

Arnold accepted this and set about preparing defenses. The eight-gun *Viper* was sent to patrol along the coast, while the four-gun *Snake* waited in the mouth of the river. Rudyard's infantry dug earthworks facing the lake that both he and Danforth thought would be useless if someone attacked in force, but they had to do something. He made sure the works were covered with brush and tree limbs to disguise their presence.

Danforth was concerned that they were now vulnerable sitting in the river. He also had his doubts as to how far Rudyard had taken the schooner, and how far inland his men had actually patrolled. But then, how far was realistic? An old map showed that the river wound inland for a hundred miles or more. Certainly, they could not patrol all of it, and, besides, any rebel activity would be near the coast and not inland. The forest along the river seemed impenetrable and someone who went ten feet into the woods would be invisible.

Certainly, he repeated to himself, people had been there before and would be there again, but not until the rebellion was over.

In fact, all they had to do was exist in the river for a few days and Burgoyne would be joining them with the main army. So why was he at all concerned about the results of Rudyard's alcohol-soaked patrol?

Faith hurled herself on Owen's prone body, both waking him and sending a wave of pain through his body that caused him to cry out. He had left his hard and uncomfortable wooden slatted bed in the hospital and had gone into the woods where he found the sunlight and soft grasses far more comfortable and conducive to healing.

"Jesus, woman," he gasped. "You almost killed me. You want to finish what the bloody savages started?"

Faith was immediately contrite. "I was so afraid when I heard you'd been hurt," she cried. "I thought I was going to lose you and I couldn't stand the thought of it."

Owen grinned. "Does this mean you truly care for me?"

She smiled impishly. "It does."

"Love me?"

"Yes," she said softly, "but only if you love me too."

"I love you, Faith, and I will love you for the rest of my life." He laughed harshly and winced at the pain from his chest. "Of course, the way I'm feeling that might not be all that long."

She touched his mouth to silence him and then lay down beside him with her head on his shoulder. "For us, forever might only be a few weeks, dear Owen, I think we should make the most of it."

As she said this, her hands went to his waist and loosened the drawstrings of his pants. She reached in and found an old friend rising to meet her. She knelt and pulled his pants down. Then she straddled him. "It's time to finish what we've always started, dear Owen."

For his part, Owen loosened her bodice and pulled it down, exposing her exquisite breasts. "Are you certain, dear little Faith?"

"As certain as I am of anything," she said as his hands and lips caressed her nipples until she thought she'd go mad.

As always and like many women, she wore nothing underneath her skirts and he entered her easily. They both gasped. Faith was mildly surprised that there was none of the pain she'd heard about, but then realized that their several mutual explorations had doubtless resolved that little problem.

"I love you," Owen said as she rocked him gently, taking care not to touch his ribs. His hands grasped her bare buttocks and pressed her more tightly to him. He wanted to say something far more eloquent but couldn't. They both groaned and climaxed within seconds of each other.

"I thought you were afraid of the consequences of doing this," Owen finally managed to say as they again lay beside each other.

Faith kissed him on the cheek. "I was. Then I realized that, come the worst, I wanted to have this memory of you, of us."

"What now?" Owen asked.

Faith giggled. "Well, dear Owen, for the short while, let's just rest a wee bit and do it all over again."


Benedict Arnold's sailing barges remained anchored in the river and lashed together for safety. They resembled nothing more than a giant raft. The majority of their crews had joined Rudyard's infantry in preparing defenses facing outward from the mouth of the river and towards the lake. They'd been told that the rebels had nothing larger than canoes, but Arnold disagreed and Danforth concurred. If the British could make ships like the *Vixen* or even the sailing barges, then so could the rebels. They were also reminded that canoes came in a variety of sizes and some could hold more than a score of men.

Even though Danforth agreed, he wasn't totally comfortable with this decision to fortify the lake front. But General Arnold had been adamant—the danger would be from the lake if it came at all. Danforth didn't like putting all their defensive eggs in one basket and had gotten Arnold's grudging permission to send a handful of men up the river to warn against any surprise attacks. Rudyard had laughed at Danforth's cautious nature. However, he had agreed to keep half a dozen men on guard duty on the rafts at all time.

Still, Danforth was worried. Rudyard was drinking ever more heavily and his men had taken their cue from him and had become slovenly and lazy in their duties. Worse, Rudyard had confided that most of the men who appeared to be British regulars were nothing more than the scrapings from the various communities in the area, such as St. Ignace, Sault St. Marie, Detroit and Pitt, and had gotten little training as British soldiers. They were Redcoats in name only.

He'd thought about discussing Rudyard's drinking problems with Arnold, but decided against it. For all his flaws, Rudyard was the closest thing to a friend Danforth had. Arnold was also drinking heavily, apparently depressed by the fact that his attempts to find glory and wealth had so far failed.

The hell with Arnold, the hell with Rudyard, and the hell with the rebels, Danforth finally decided. He rolled into a blanket and quickly went to sleep.

Only a couple of miles upriver, Brigadier John Glover and the remnants of his Marblehead Regiment waited. At first they'd been shocked when the British began to sail up the river they'd chosen as a point from which to attack the rear of Arnold's Armada as it passed. They had arrived in canoes, which were not their craft of preference, but they were justifiably confident that they could handle anything that floated.

Still, they'd had to paddle furiously to stay ahead and out of sight of a very slow moving British patrol probing up the river that was clearly wary of an ambush. When they'd gotten far enough ahead, Glover had sent scouts downstream who had reported that the British had stopped and pulled back to a point closer to the mouth of the river.

When scouts confirmed that the British defenses faced west towards the lake and not up the river, Glover realized that he'd been handed a golden opportunity. He'd stroked his broad jaw and finally smiled. He had fewer than two hundred men and was outnumbered and outgunned, but then, the damned British didn't know he was here.

Glover waited until night was almost dawn, the time when everyone would be either asleep or groggy. Then silent as a mild breeze, his canoes moved down the dark river, hugging the north shore. A mist hovered over the water and provided more protection. A campfire's dim glow told him that the handful of British sentries on the shore were as stupid as he'd been told.

Glover signaled and several canoes peeled off and landed softly. Their men slipped into the water and moved through the woods while Glover waited and watched. The anchored sailing barges were dim shapes only about a hundred yards away. He could rush past the guards, but didn't want them in his rear.

A scream was followed by the sound of a musket. Glover

cursed. His men were magicians on the water but lumbered like elephants on land. Surprise was lost. "Go!" he yelled and his men paddled their canoes with desperation and fury.

At first Danforth was uncertain whether he'd actually heard the sound of gunfire or he'd dreamed it. He stood up and looked around. Like everyone else, his gaze was towards the lake which was empty.

"What the devil is that?" Rudyard screamed and pointed upriver where shapes could be discerned behind the barges.

Boats, Danforth realized with a sinking feeling. He grabbed his sword and pistol and raced to the shore. Not boats, he corrected himself, canoes. And they were alongside the barges and men were pouring onto the precious craft. Rudyard lurched to the water and drunkenly fired his pistol at nothing in particular. This was a signal for his alleged British infantry to start firing at their own barges.

"Fire at the canoes," Danforth screamed as Rudyard fell face first into the river. I hope the bastard drowns, Danforth thought. Rudyard had failed to patrol and protect their rear.

"No!" Danforth heard General Arnold sob as he saw the glow of flames on the barges that quickly became raging fires. A moment later, the powder on one exploded, raining burning embers on its neighbors.

The barges were made of poorly seasoned wood that caught fire quickly despite their being immersed in water. Worse, the wind was from the east, blowing flames from the rear of the column of barges towards its head. Now, however, many of the rebels were silhouetted against the growing flames and British fire increased in accuracy. The Americans returned fire and several men near Danforth fell to the ground. Rudyard had managed to pick himself out of the mud and was just about to say something when a musket ball struck his skull and blew his brains out, splattering Danforth with gore. This demoralized his men who stopped firing and backed away.

It didn't matter, Danforth realized sadly. The anchored barges had become an inferno and the remaining rebels were climbing back in their canoes. They were paddling furiously for their lives as yet another cache of ammunition cooked off, taking two canoes with it.

★　　★　　★

John Glover was one of the first men out of the canoes and onto the barges. He heard the sounds of men screaming and realized that his voice was one of them. An astonished-looking British sentry was suddenly in front of him. Before Glover could respond, one of his men shot the man in the face.

"Gotta be quicker, General," the soldier said.

"Indeed," Glover murmured as more men sped past him and jumped lightly onto the other barges. By this time, the British were awake and alarmed and bullets from wildly fired muskets splattered around the barges. One of his men howled in pain as a shot found home.

"Grenades," Glover hollered and pulled a pair of them from his coat. They were not the grenades used by the British soldiers which contained explosives. These were clay and glass containers filled with flammable liquid and with a cloth wick that had just been immersed in that same liquid. They were fire bombs.

Glover lighted the fuse from the flint on his pistol, held it until it was burning brightly and dropped it down the hatch of the barge. A few second later, the fire grenade exploded and the barge shuddered. The barge's hull was cracked and water began to pour in. He grinned with satisfaction and threw the second one down the same hatch. Others were also hurling their grenades and explosions began to rip the air.

Several barges in front of him, a store of gunpowder exploded, sending flaming debris over the ships around it and killing several of Glover's men. Glover had to duck as pieces of burning wood fell around him.

British musket fire had become more accurate and organized. Another of his Marbleheaders fell, and then another. Glover looked around. Every barge was burning and flames were racing through their heavily tarred rigging. It was time to go and he signaled the retreat. Whooping happily, his men ran back to their canoes and began to push off. Glover was happy. He had won a great victory.

It was his last thought as the second grenade he'd thrown down the hatch a moment before exploded next to several barrels of gunpowder, utterly destroying the barge and Brigadier John Glover.

# Chapter 16 ★ ★ ★ ★ ★ ★ ★ ★ ★ ★ ★ ★ ★ ★ ★ ★ ★

DANFORTH WALKED ALONG THE EDGE OF THE RIVER AS THE rising sun revealed the totality of the disaster. Not a single one of the barges remained intact. Most had sunk or disintegrated after burning down to their water lines, the weight of their cargo dragging the shattered boats to the bottom. Those with ammunition on board had exploded and the only things remaining on the surface were a handful of masts and a great deal of charred debris along with a number of burned and mangled bodies.

A handful of the barges had broken loose or had their lines cut and had beached themselves on the shore of the river. But these too were burned hulks.

They retrieved a number of bodies from the river and most of them were American, including one which Arnold identified as John Glover's. That should have made Danforth feel good, but didn't. The price the British had paid had been far too high. At least thirty-nine rebels had died in the attack, but it was scant comfort for the utter destruction of the barges and their precious cargo.

Benedict Arnold stood ashen-faced and stared at where his armada had once been. Danforth thought the term "armada" was singularly appropriate. Just as the Spanish Armada had been destroyed, so too had Arnold's. Along with it had gone any hope of glory for Benedict Arnold.

"How many men did we lose?" Arnold asked.

"Maybe a dozen, General," Danforth said, "Twenty at the most."

Included in that figure he counted the six men left to guard the rear and were now presumed dead. Of the half dozen sentries on the barges, three had survived by throwing themselves overboard before being immolated, and a handful of men on shore had been killed by American gunfire or by falling debris.

Arnold nodded. "And that damn fool Rudyard was one of the dead, wasn't he?"

"He was," Danforth said reluctantly. Rudyard had indeed been a fool, and a drunken one at that, but he'd also been Danforth's friend.

"Then he's fortunate he's dead, otherwise I'd be forced to court martial him and have him hanged for dereliction of duty. His incompetence has destroyed what remains of my dreams. Damn him," Arnold said, his voice nearly a sob.

He turned and looked again at the mangled corpses. Some of the fixed grins seemed to be mocking him. "Bury them. Then we'll finish our journey."

Danforth turned away. He didn't give a stinking shit about Benedict Arnold's dreams of money and glory. All he wanted to do was see a victorious end to this campaign and a return home to England where he could seduce and marry the wealthy daughter of a rural squire. He'd had more than enough of war.

Will helped the frail old man to the top of the hill. Benjamin Franklin was winded by the time he made it, and had to pause and gather himself before he could speak with General Stark. Will was worried about Franklin's well-being. The hill wasn't that tall or that steep. Will had barely noticed it.

Franklin regained his breath and looked about him. General Stark looked on quizzically. "What are you thinking, Doctor Franklin?"

"My dear General, I am thinking that I was expecting so much more. You've had a good deal of time to prepare for the second coming of Burgoyne and I'd rather expected defenses that were much more formidable and daunting."

"Impregnable?" Stark asked with a smile.

"Something like that, General, although I know full well that there is no such thing as an impregnable fortress. Something like irresistible forces meeting immovable objects, I believe. But still,

I had rather hoped to see so much more than some ditches and some earthworks protected by wooden spikes. While I admit that they run for several miles, they just aren't terribly impressive."

"If you had an army, do you think you could storm this hill?"

"I am many things, but a military man is not one of them. Still, General, I do think that Burgoyne's army could batter its way through if they were willing to pay the price."

Will moved a few steps away. He would let the two men discuss matters with a semblance of privacy. Of course, he would stay close enough to listen unless one of them told him to either join the discussion or move farther away.

Stark smiled tightly. "Let me guess, you expected something like the hundred foot tall triple walls of Byzantium that kept barbarians at bay for so many centuries in the days of Rome and the subsequent Byzantine Empire."

Franklin flushed with anger, "Hardly. But I did expect something more."

"And what would Burgoyne do if he saw what you wished us to build? Do you think he'd go away? Return to New York? No. His orders are to destroy us and anything less would be a disgrace to him and his ambitions."

Stark turned and waved at the work going on around them. "No, Doctor, what Burgoyne would do if he found us too strong to attack would be to try to find a way around us. He would probe to our left and he would find a stream in flood that presents a significant barrier and, beyond that, he would find miserable ground leading to the lake. Then he would turn to our right and he would find that the swamp to our right is an even greater deterrent. By the way, Doctor, we have spent a great deal of time and effort making sure that the stream and swamp are formidable barriers by diverting other streams into both."

Franklin shook his head. "In which case, he could still go farther around our flank and find the end to the swamp."

"Which would cost him valuable time, and that is a commodity he doesn't possess. Major Drake stands over there pretending he isn't listening to us, and he will confirm that, won't you, Major."

Will smiled. He was not at all embarrassed. "It's the truth, Doctor. We've intercepted a number of messages from Lord Cornwallis stating the need for Burgoyne to make haste and destroy us before New York and the rest of the colonies explode and take them all to hell. Add to that the reality that George III wants his army back to fight in France and you have the fact that Burgoyne is under great pressure to end this as quickly as is possible. Thus, he is unlikely to spend time maneuvering his army unless he absolutely has to."

"What a happy thought," Franklin mused. "But I still don't understand? Why not make the fortifications greater?"

Stark smiled. "Because, if they were indeed too strong, he would have a legitimate reason to defy Cornwallis and go beyond that damned swamp and devil take the extra time such a move would require. But now he will be faced with a conundrum. The defenses will be strong, but not all that strong. He will face the likelihood of both success and heavy losses if he attacks us here, but he will see no alternative given his orders to make haste.

"Everything I've heard says he is tormented by two incidents in his life. First, the tremendous casualties he saw the British army take when it launched frontal assaults on our positions at Bunker Hill and, second, the devastating impact of his surrender at Saratoga caused in part by his dividing his army and attempting to maneuver around us. We want him to come to us where we want him, not anyplace else."

The truth dawned on Franklin. "And this hill is the place where you want to fight him."

"Precisely, indeed," Stark said. "We stand little enough chance as it is, so I wish to be the one to choose the battlefield, not Burgoyne. I have no desire to see him turning our flank and us chasing him to God knows where and then possibly having to fight him in the open without the protection of any significant fixed defenses. No, Doctor, I wish to fight him here."

"And here we stand a chance of victory? This is reminiscent of Bunker Hill, is it not?"

"We stand very little chance of victory," Stark admitted. "But a little chance is better than no chance at all. And kindly recall that we lost at Bunker Hill, although I must admit we are now far better trained and equipped then the army we had back then."

He did not need to add that part of the reason for the British army's ultimate success at Bunker Hill was because the colonists simply ran out of ammunition. There would be more than enough ammunition for the coming fight, just not enough men.

Stark paced the hill's gentle crest. "Are you aware that the men are calling this Mount Washington? It's largely sarcasm of course, since it does not in anyway resemble a mountain, but they know that this is where we will make our stand. What Burgoyne will do differently than what he saw in Boston that day, is that he will prepare the field instead of charging straight into our defenses. He will try to clear the abattis we've weaved and fill in the ditches in front of the earthworks before he attacks, and that will tell us exactly where he must fall on us. There will be no room for subtlety."

"And this is to our advantage?" Franklin asked.

"To a very small extent, but yes."

"But won't we be in a better position when the men from the south arrive?" Franklin persisted.

Stark shook his head sadly. "They're not coming."

Burgoyne was livid. "Gone? All of them? Every one of the cannon on those barges? All the ammunition and supplies? This is not possible," he said as he paced the confines of his tent. "Not even Arnold could be that inept."

Danforth tried hard to stand at attention. He hadn't eaten in days and what remained of his uniform was caked with mud and hung in rags. Behind Burgoyne, Fitzroy looked at his friend with deep sympathy. Not only was Benedict Arnold's career ruined, but so too was Captain Peter Danforth's. But he quickly changed his mind. Danforth's family had more than enough wealth to buy forgiveness and even a promotion when the proverbial dust settled. Assuming Danforth wanted either forgiveness or promotion. He'd briefly told Fitzroy of his decision to leave the army.

It was Danforth's misfortune to be the first to arrive with news of the debacle on the river. With both schooners occupied in recovery operations, Danforth and a handful of men had set out on foot to find Burgoyne. They'd had to elude rebel patrols and could trust no one they found. Since they had no real idea where Burgoyne's army was, they'd had to backtrack to find its trail and then chase it westward. It had been an exhausting effort and Danforth had an overpowering urge to go to sleep. He wondered if he could possibly do it while standing at attention. Danforth had given Burgoyne both a written and an oral report.

"Is any attempt being made to raise some of the guns, the supplies?"

"Sir, General Arnold is using the schooners to try and do exactly that, but I don't think he'll succeed. They're just too small to lift something as heavy and inert as nine-pound cannon out of the deep mud of the river."

Burgoyne shook his head angrily, "Assuming, of course, that they can even find the damned things in the muck." He sighed and tried to calm himself. "Stand at ease and relax, Danforth, I hardly think this farce is your fault and nobody here will blame you for it when they have Arnold as a far more convenient target. After all, he was in command, not you. According to Arnold, the fault lies with the late and unlamented Captain Rudyard who was drunk on duty and allowed the rebels to sneak up on him. Is that correct?"

Burgoyne saw a flicker of hesitation on Danforth's. "Was this Rudyard creature drunk?"

"He was, sir," Danforth said miserably. The man was dead. Why heap scorn upon him? Still, Burgoyne was totally blaming Arnold and Rudyard for the debacle which boded well for Danforth's personal future. Perhaps he would come out of this with his reputation unblemished.

Burgoyne sighed. "And he was your friend, was he not? Of course he was. And don't worry about your reputation. You were an aide, a representative from me, and had no authority over the expedition. Arnold approved of Rudyard's plans for the defense of the fleet, did he not? Of course he did. That makes Arnold culpable because he was the man in charge. He can try to shift blame, but it won't work and Arnold knows it. Command and responsibility are often lonely, and the loss of the cannon is all Arnold's fault. Except, of course, for the unpleasant fact that I was responsible for putting Arnold in charge in the first place. Tell me, Danforth, despite the small size of our ships, is there any hope at all of recovering anything?"

"Sir, even if Arnold does locate and dredge up some of the cannon, the carriages have likely been destroyed and the gunpowder is soaked and gone. Carriages can be built in time, and I'm sure you have some powder, but where will we get sufficient cannonballs? They would have to be cast and that is simply not possible with the tools and metal we have at hand. Again, we may recover a few cannonballs, but not very many. Like the cannon, they've doubtless sunk deep into the muck."

Burgoyne rubbed his chin. "You are correct. Some powder is all we have. Our reserve supplies were on those damned boats. As for balls," he mused, "I suppose we might do without solid shot by using stones and such, but the range and accuracy of the weapons would be greatly diminished. And, yes, we could manufacture something out of local wood to function as sledges instead of proper carriages, but, lord, how far we have fallen."

There was silence while the general contemplated the disaster. He shook his head and smiled slightly. "Thank you for your report, Captain Danforth, and be thankful we don't behead messengers anymore. Your friend Fitzroy is standing outside the tent and trying to eavesdrop. Tell him to get you fed and bathed and rested."

Will Drake went looking for Sarah. He was told that she and a group of women were in the swamp and working on the system of dams and ditches that kept water funneling through to keep the area wet, boggy, and unattractive to people like Burgoyne who preferred to fight on solid ground.

As Will walked through the woods his feet sank to well above his ankles in what was little more than thick mud and he wondered just how much of the wetness was due to nature and how much was aided by the work of the men and women from Fort Washington. When he almost fell into a deeper pool, he used a long thin tree limb to probe the water and found that there were places where it would come up over his waist. He grinned. If the rest of the swamp was like this, Burgoyne would avoid it like the plague.

After a while he heard the sound of voices and moved cautiously in that direction. In a moment he came upon a group of women using wooden shovels to shore up the sides of a ditch through which water was flowing. He quickly realized that he shouldn't be where he was. The women were all wearing long skirts, but had hiked them up and tucked the hems in their belts; thus exposing their legs and thighs which gleamed whitely except where they were covered with black goo from the swamp. Obviously they thought they were working in private as they were unconcerned about their partial nudity that would have been unthinkable in other circumstances. One of them might have been Sarah, but he turned quickly and began to walk away before anyone could accuse him of staring.

He'd just about decided to wait for her to return to her quarters when he heard someone behind him.

"Ah, there you are, the rogue who was spying on us."

Will turned and grinned sheepishly. Sarah was filthy and sweaty and staring at him, her expression stern and set with anger. She'd let her skirt fall down to its normal length, although her feet were bare.

"I didn't mean to spy. I'd come looking for you to talk to you."

"And I'm supposed to believe that? You'd better be thankful that none of the others who saw you skulking in the woods knew who you were."

He was about to say he hadn't been skulking when he saw the twinkle growing in her eyes. "And you were the most beautiful of all the mud maidens," he said and she laughed.

"I'll bet you say that to all the women you find crawling around in a swamp."

He took her hand. "As a matter of fact, I do. Aren't your friends going to miss you?"

"No. We were just about finished our task and I pleaded that I had to get back to Doctor Franklin, which, by the way, is somewhat true. He needs his nap and I'm going to make sure he gets one. He gets involved in a project and sometimes refuses to quit, which results in his becoming exhausted. We need him alive and alert."

"I'm glad no one else recognized me," Will said and Sarah hooted.

"And you're the brave soldier who's fought the Indians and the Redcoats? Afraid of the sight of women's muddy legs, are you? Or did you think women don't have legs? And, if we don't, how in God's name do we walk?"

"You're right. Thank God for women's legs."

"Now, brave soldier, why had you come looking for me?"

"To give you the good news," he said, thankful for the change of topic. "Arnold's fleet's been destroyed and this has caused Burgoyne to make another halt so the supplies he'd expected to get from the ships can be replaced from the depots he's so carefully built up behind him."

She clapped her hands in delight. "Wonderful, but it's obviously not a mortal blow to him. However, we'll all take any kind of victory, even small ones, won't we?"

As they walked back to her room at Franklin's office he told her of the grievous price Glover's regiment had paid for the victory and the loss of Glover himself. It sobered both of them.

Still, by the time he and Sarah had checked on Dr. Franklin and confirmed that he was sound asleep, and then gotten to her room, they realized that the good news far outweighed the bad. "Get a bucket of water," she ordered and he complied.

When he returned, her door was open and she had discarded her dress and stood in her shift, which was tattered and came scarcely to her knees. "Don't stare. You've already seen my legs and, if you'll notice, they are still covered with dirt." She took a cloth and first wiped herself down her face and arms with the water, and then her legs and feet. She rinsed the dirty water into another bucket. She was reminded of bathing in front of Doctor Franklin. Having Will see her was much more pleasant.

"Now I feel better," she said and then looked at him quizzically. "It's been time enough, hasn't it?"

He was uncertain of her meaning, so just nodded. She sighed and removed the shift. Will could only stare at her nakedness and she smiled wistfully at him. "Undress," she commanded softly and he complied.

"You're still much too thin." She said as she put her hands on his chest. "I can still feel your ribs."

She sighed and took him by the hand and led him to the bed. They lay down facing each other. He was almost afraid to reach over the scant inches to her. She smiled. "You will not rush things, Major Drake. You will take all the time in the world and you will do exactly as I tell you. Understand?"

Will laughed softly. The bed was narrow, but they'd make it more than adequate. "Fully, Mistress Benton, but may I ask why you have changed your mind about waiting?"

She sighed as his hands caressed her. "Because Faith and I had a long talk about living for today because tomorrow may never come." His lips were on her breast and his hand had begun to caress the moist softness between her thighs. She groaned with long-denied pleasure. "And because we love each other, dear Will, and, regardless of what happens, I want to have as many moments with you as I possibly can."

In the room next to theirs, Benjamin Franklin lay on his bed with his eyes open and smiled as he listened to the sounds of their lovemaking. About damned time, he thought.

★    ★    ★

Burgoyne was not in a good mood. "Fitzroy, please remind me why I should not have you executed?"

"Because, dear General, it's taken you so long to get used to me and because we are related, albeit distantly, which means my mother would be angry with you."

"Good points both," Burgoyne growled in mock anger. "Then upon whom might I take out my righteous wrath?"

"Might I suggest General Arnold?"

"He would be a marvelous target but for the fact that he is so self-centered and dense that he would not understand my displeasure with him. Which, by the way, is why I feel the urge to punish you instead. At least you would feel pain, whereas Arnold never would. Do you realize he considers it my fault that he lost his ships? In a way, he's right. I should never have put the bloody fool in charge."

Arnold had not yet arrived although, instead, he had sent a series of messages trying to explain away the disaster and blame someone else. He was now on board the *Vixen* and would arrive as soon as it was safe for him to land. The remainder of his men, the crew's barges and the late and unlamented Rudyard's infantry, were marching overland following much the same route as that taken by Danforth.

"Sir, may I ask if he's managed to salvage any of the cannon?"

"All of two of them, Fitzroy. Two out of all he had. Of course he has no powder, no carriages and very little shot for them. We can improvise some sort of carriage, but, as discussed, I'm afraid they will be reduced to firing rocks."

Burgoyne looked out his tent. It was raining heavily, which further made him gloomy. "After all the damage he has caused, can you believe that Arnold has the effrontery to remind me that I had promised him command of one of our wings in the coming battle and he expects me to keep his promise. It would be ludicrous if it wasn't so pathetic."

Fitzroy shook his head in disbelief. "And what will you do with the man, sir?"

Burgoyne glared at him and Fitzroy wondered if he'd gone too far with the implied slur of a general officer. No matter that general in question was so heartily despised by one and all, there were lines junior officers didn't cross.

Suddenly, Burgoyne laughed. "Oh he'll get command of a wing, all right, but like a chicken's wing, he won't be able to fly very well with it."

# Chapter 17 ★ ★ ★ ★ ★ ★ ★ ★ ★ ★ ★ ★ ★ ★ ★ ★ ★

THE RAIN HAD CEASED FOR THE MOMENT, ALTHOUGH THE low gray sky promised more. Sarah was delighted since it meant that nature would fill the swamp and the creek and the efforts of the women would not be needed for a while.

She and Faith were casually wandering the area between Fort Washington and the low hill that had been fortified against the British when they saw men running towards it and clambering up its rain-slickened slope. The two women looked at each other and began running as well. By the time they slipped through the mud and reached the crest, the trenches were beginning to fill with soldiers and a number of civilians. There didn't seem to be much of a plan or sense of urgency.

To her delight, she found Will standing by General Tallmadge, and both men were peering through telescopes at the distant tree line. He was so intent he didn't notice her at first, so she tugged gently on his sleeve.

"What's out there, Will?"

He handed her the telescope. "Look towards the edge of the woods at the line where we've cut the trees and made the meadow that much larger."

She squinted and looked through the lens. The area in question was a good two miles distant and, at first she saw nothing except a wall of trees. Then her eyes began to pick up flashes, almost drops, of unnatural color. Red. She gasped. They were here.

All the blood seemed to rush from her and she almost felt faint. Like virtually everyone, she'd hoped and prayed that this day would never arrive. "Those are the British, aren't they?"

"Yes, dearest, those are the British. Just scouts and patrols, and not even the advance guard, but the British have finally arrived."

She looked again, hoping she was wrong. She wasn't. A couple of Redcoats had moved out of the tree line and stood in plain but distant sight. They were merely specks, but they moved and had arms and legs. Will commented that the British were probably officers accompanying Indian scouts, and that they likely were watching through their own telescopes. She wondered if they should all wave.

"What are you going to do?" Faith asked.

Tallmadge answered. "I rather doubt that General Stark will have us do much of anything except continue to observe them. We'll watch them draw closer and they'll watch us watching them. I also rather doubt that the British will do anything until they are in place, rested, fed, and organized."

Three red-coated horsemen emerged from the distant woods. They paused and appeared to be examining the American position, doubtless again with their own telescopes.

"Is that Burgoyne?" Sarah asked.

"More likely it's Tarleton, as he commands the van," Tallmadge answered. "I would think that Burgoyne's farther back."

"Will you shoot at him?" Faith persisted. "Your cannon can reach that far, can't they?"

Will was about to answer that the cannon taken from the stockade were small and their shells would need wings to carry that far when the horsemen obliged them by turning and moving back into the forest.

"What will they do now?" Sarah asked. "And what will we do?"

Will took her arm and led her away. Faith followed, caught up and then took his other arm. "First, it will take some time for the entire British Army to arrive and, when they do, they will doubtless encamp so they can rest and get organized for a battle. Given the length of the column and the supplies that Burgoyne requires, that could take at least a couple of days. What we will do is continue to prepare our defenses while our patrols keep an eye on them and make sure they do not try to move away and flank us. We don't think they will do anything of the sort, but we must be prepared in case they do."

Sarah nodded. "I'm not very religious, but I will pray for a great storm to come and sweep them away."

Will thought of the terrible funnel-shaped storms the Spanish called tornadoes and considered that this was a wonderful idea.

General John Burgoyne tried to hide his frustration with the three generals who stood before him. Each was supposed to be subordinate to him, but each was angry with him, although with varying degrees and for different reasons.

In Grant's case, it was simple frustration with the maddening delays that accompanied the march, while Tarleton and Arnold's anger grew from a lack of any opportunity for glory and advancement, and their anger bordered on insubordination. Burgoyne could only hope that the rebel generals were as insolent with Stark as his commanders were with him.

Behind the four men, Fitzroy prepared to take notes. He was present as more of a witness than a clerk. The three subordinate generals reminded him of the three witches in *Macbeth*—or was it *Hamlet?*—because they were stirring up trouble.

"I say we attack as soon as possible and that means tomorrow," Tarleton said. "None of this damned fool waiting. One attack in overwhelming force and the rebellion will collapse and we can all go home."

"Here, here," said Grant. "I've campaigned long enough in this forsaken wilderness. I would like a bed to sleep in, a decent meal to eat, and a white woman to pleasure me. Let's finish this and get back to New York, which, although it's a stinkpot of a city, is a thousand times better than continuing in this miserable existence."

They continued to argue. Tarleton wanted freedom of action, but Burgoyne would not permit it. With ill grace, he had to settle for the right to patrol and probe the American lines. He could even demonstrate his forces, but not launch an attack against the rebel positions which consisted of a dry moat and earthworks behind the moat. An abattis of felled trees and stakes had been built both before the moat and along the earthworks. Tarleton said he wasn't impressed with rebel efforts and continued to press for the chance to make an immediate attack. He crudely reminded Burgoyne of the need to respond to the most recently received messages from Cornwallis and Lord North in which their lordships from faraway London and New York urged a quick victory and the prompt return of Burgoyne's army.

Burgoyne fixed him with a glare and reminded Tarleton that Cornwallis wanted the whole army returned and not half of it, which would be the case if they attacked without proper preparations. Tarleton stormed out of the tent and Fitzroy didn't like the almost feral look in his eyes.

Arnold continued to be indignant. His command would be the British left which butted up against the swampy wetlands. It would consist of Girty's men, the handful of remaining Indians, and the men he'd brought from Detroit in the sailing barges. It would be fewer than five hundred strong and Arnold was insulted by the paltry number.

Burgoyne, however, was not impressed. "You've lost your ships and my guns and you wish a reward? Do you realize the plans I had for those guns? I was going to line them up, wheel to wheel, and pound the rebel position to pieces. And what about the ships that were sunk on your watch? Not only did they contain guns and ammunition, but supplies of food that we will soon need. Moreover, I had given serious thought to loading them up with men and landing them in the American rear while we launched a frontal attack on their defenses. At the very least, they were going to demonstrate that possibility and force the Americans to split their forces to face that contingency.

"Now we have to prepare for the assault in an entirely different way. We have to risk the lives of our soldiers to enemy fire while they fill in the moat and are pulling away the barriers that confront us. Don't tell me your feelings are hurt, because I won't hear of it. Or would you prefer to be sent back to Detroit under arrest and awaiting court martial for your monumental stupidity in losing those ships and all they carried? If we lose here, I promise you that your failures will be published and you will be disgraced and become even more of a pariah than you already are."

Arnold gasped and almost ran from the tent. General Grant shook his head. "I may be the closest you have to a sane subordinate, which means, my dear General, you are in terrible trouble." He laughed harshly and also departed. Fitzroy looked questioningly at Burgoyne who waved him away.

As he walked away, an angry Colonel von Bamberg of Hesse

marched up towards the tent. Fitzroy gently but firmly took his arm. "This might not be the best time to disturb the general."

"More arguments? Dear God, what is it with you British that you can't get along? Or better yet, why can't you simply obey the orders of your commander instead of spending so much valuable time squabbling like washerwomen?"

"Just our nature, Colonel. What was it you wished to see the general about? Perhaps I can schedule you later."

Bamberg calmed visibly. When he wasn't yelling at his troops or hanging innocent civilians, the little Hessian was really rather decent. Now he even regretted hanging the suspected deserters, although he wouldn't quite admit that he'd made a mistake.

"The usual problems for me as well, Major. At least four more of my men have deserted and likely gone over to the rebels. I cannot comprehend this. Are they fools? In a few days they'll all be recaptured and hanged. Only now they will be flogged mercilessly before they are hanged."

Indeed, thought Fitzroy. What madness compelled the Hessians to desert and the American rebels to wish to die? He shuddered. And these are the people we are going to do battle against? Was everyone mad?

The next morning brought to the Americans the unpleasant fact that the British had worked through much of the night erecting their own breastworks to prevent the rebels from making surprise attacks on the British camps that sprawled across the front of the American lines.

A little before noon, the sound of drumming was heard. A drummer boy and a British officer carrying a white flag moved cautiously forward.

"Don't tell me they're surrendering," someone said and even General Stark laughed at that one.

"They wish to parley," General Schuyler announced with a rare smile on his face. "I do believe they think they can talk us into surrendering. Why in God's name should we surrender when we've all been promised a date with the noose? Shall we negotiate with them for new ropes?"

Stark lowered his telescope. "Still, it is a surprising gesture and one which courtesy says we are required to reciprocate. I do not think they are sending anyone of great rank, so we will not either." His eyes fell on Major Will Drake, who flushed. "Once again, Major, I do believe you can be of service. Take a white flag and meet their representative, but do make certain that he doesn't come too close to our lines. What he doesn't see can't hurt us."

Will grinned and grabbed a cloth that could have passed for white in a previous life. He tied it to a stick and walked across planks that were quickly laid across the moat, and wound his way through the abattis. He noted that the British officer had halted less than halfway and wondered if the man feared being fired upon. Drake shared his concerns and wondered how many British muskets were aimed at him.

As they approached, Will noted that they were of equal rank. Good, he thought, none of that nonsense about saluting an enemy. He stopped and bowed slightly. "I am Major Will Drake of General Stark's staff," he announced, promoting himself to a staff position he didn't quite have.

"And I am Major James Fitzroy of General Burgoyne's staff."

They nodded slightly and each professed to be honored to meet the other, although Will had the nagging feeling that Fitzroy's name was familiar.

"Tell me," said Fitzroy, "are you the same Drake who was with the French farmer at Detroit? We found your name in his journal after the fire."

Now Will remembered. Fitzroy had been the inadvertent source of so much information about the British Army thanks to Hannah Van Doorn and the Goldmans. "I am."

"Not that it matters, but I'm curious. Did you set the fire, or was it Leduc?"

"I wish I could claim credit, but I can't. I was back across the river when it started and it was as big a surprise to us as it was to you," he said and explained that Leduc had been mortally wounded in the brawl and had chosen a fiery death. Fitzroy admitted that Leduc's death had been heroic and honorable as well as inevitable.

"Had he survived his wounds, he would have been hanged of course," said Fitzroy.

Will continued, "And I recall a lovely lady asking about you, one Hannah Van Doorn."

Fitzroy smiled wanly. "She is well, I trust."

"She is."

"Then tell her I miss her, even though she betrayed me so thoroughly."

"I will."

"Now, Major Drake, we must attend to the formalities. Will you surrender and prevent the bloodshed and carnage that must otherwise occur?"

"Major Fitzroy, all carnage and bloodshed could be avoided if you and your army would simply march back the way you came. North America is a huge land. Right now you English share it with the Spanish and even the Russians. There must be room for our little nation. Why must you chase us and hound us? Why not simply leave us to our own devices? Why not let us live in peace these hundreds of miles away from the reach of king and Parliament? I cannot see how we can be any threat to the mighty British Empire."

Why not indeed? Inwardly, Fitzroy thought they were good questions. "If I told you it was because certain people in London think you are all traitors and bandits and threats to established order, would that satisfy you?"

"No."

"Would you be satisfied if I told you it was because the entire world has gone mad?"

"Yes," Will said with a grin. "And why on earth would we even think of surrendering? Haven't you promised to hang our leaders, brand and flog the rest of the men, and sell everyone into slavery, including the women and children? Surrender to what? A long and lingering death? Of course, we know that Burgoyne is under great pressure to win quickly and return to England with an intact army. Do you really think that either can occur if we do battle?"

Will gestured behind him, where, a few hundred yards away, the American earthworks were heavily manned with additional regiments of reinforcements waiting in the rear. Only Will knew that the large numbers were an illusion. The "regiments" in reserve consisted of every woman and child in the camp, now dressed in men's clothing and holding a pike. Nor were the heads and shoulders of all of the men behind the earthworks real. Many of them were scarecrows.

Still, at this distance, Will could see that Fitzroy was impressed. "Major Drake, are you aware that we have repudiated the draconian policies towards the colonies that originally came from London?" Fitzroy asked. "They were ill-advised at best and will not be implemented."

Will was unimpressed. "They may have been rescinded, but they could be reinstated at any time. We all remember your betrayal and capture of our leaders after the collapse of the rebellion. It was scandalous and scurrilous. Thank you, Major, but I think we will take our chances on freedom and independence. Nothing other than fighting you English will give us the rights other Englishmen have. Surely you must find that ironic."

"Indeed." Fitzroy nodded and bowed slightly. "Then our meeting is over. Perhaps we shall meet again under more pleasant circumstances."

"Perhaps," Will said and turned to return to the American lines.

"But will you please give my regards to Mistress Van Doorn?" Fitzroy added.

Will smiled. The major was a love-sick puppy. "I will."

"Mistress Van Doorn," Tallmadge said with a wide smile. The lady, if she was a lady, had lost some weight during her stay at Fort Washington, but remained a ripe and most delicious-looking woman. "It is so good of you to come and see me."

She smiled and seated herself and he felt charmed. "I always obey the orders of a general, especially one who commanded me in the past."

"I trust you have been informed of the British major's concern about you?"

Her eyes misted for a moment. "I have. Major Drake is the soul of courtesy in forwarding Major Fitzroy's thoughts."

"He is. And we have not forgotten your great aid in supplying us with information regarding the British at Detroit. May I ask if you would be willing to help us again?"

She shrugged and smiled. "As long as I don't get hanged, or at least not hanged right away."

"I have been told that you have some skills as an artist. Is that true?"

"I paint and sketch. I likely think I have more talent than I actually do, but I enjoy it and others have complimented me."

"Can you draw accurately?"

She looked puzzled. "Of course."

Tallmadge opened a drawer and pulled out several papers. "Could you draw these?"

Hannah Van Doorn looked at the sheets before her in puzzlement. Then the realization of what he wanted dawned on her. She smiled wickedly. She had done such drawings before, but not for such an important personage as Tallmadge was requesting.

"Of course I can, and they will be so accurate that not even his mother could tell the difference."

Fitzroy reported his failure to Burgoyne and Tarleton, neither of whom had expected anything else. "I never thought for a moment that they would surrender, but honor dictated that we make the effort," Burgoyne said. "There was always the off chance that they would see the hopelessness of their situation and save us the blood price we will all have to pay."

Burgoyne shuddered as he remembered the blood-soaked fields at Bunker Hill and Saratoga. Along with the piles of dead there was the stench of war and the screams and moans of the wounded and dying. Not for the first time did he wonder if he was too old for this type of endeavor. Win this one battle, he told himself, and there would be no more war for him. Win this battle in the wilderness and he could go back to London and luxury and, oh yes, the theater.

"The rebels seem to feel they will pay that terrible price regardless of what they do," Fitzroy said. "It would appear that they have decided to perish honorably rather than die later and more slowly as prisoners or slaves. It appears to be brave on their part, although it may just be desperation."

"Scum," snapped Tarleton. "They are all nothing but scum. Let me have one good attack and they'll scatter and we can gather them up at our leisure."

"We will attack when we are ready and not a moment sooner," Burgoyne bristled. "And your role in that attack will be sharply defined. You will be secondary to Grant and that will not change."

"Did you see the men they had behind their earthworks?" asked Fitzroy. "It seems their army is larger than we thought."

Both generals laughed and Fitzroy flushed. What had he missed? Burgoyne responded. "While you were arguing with this Major Drake, we had men creeping as close as possible and checking out their army with our telescopes. Many of those 'soldiers' were either women or cleverly contrived dummies. Their army is no larger than we thought it was."

Fitzroy felt just a little foolish. "And what about their cavalry? I saw maybe a hundred riders, which is a hundred more than we have."

Fitzroy decided to sting Tarleton, who loved commanding swift-striking cavalry more than anything. "I believe they are commanded by William Washington. You crossed swords with him at the Cowpens before you retreated after losing your entire command, did you not?"

Burgoyne hid a smile as Tarleton's face grew red at the memory of the destruction of his force at Cowpens. Morgan had commanded the Americans, and Tarleton had indeed briefly and literally crossed swords with Colonel Washington.

"The bastard had an unfair advantage of me. This time I will catch him and kill him." He wheeled on Burgoyne. "Give me half a chance and I will kill them all."

With that, Tarleton stormed away.

"Your attempt to get them to surrender, Fitzroy, was well done. Futile, and the results unsurprising, but well done," Burgoyne said. "A shame they didn't take it, but I don't blame them and I know you don't either. On the other hand, you really shouldn't be so unkind to dear Banastre Tarleton, now should you?"

Burgoyne laughed and walked away, leaving Fitzroy to his own thoughts. They were of the probability of battle in the next few days in which he could be killed or wounded, or worse, maimed.

And, to his surprise and dismay, his thoughts were also of Hannah Van Doorn.


Braxton's feelings of disgust increased with each step his feet took into the muck of the swamp. At one time he'd been a commander to contend with, a man whose name and ruined visage inspired fear. Now he was reduced to leading a dozen malcontents through a stinking swamp.

"How much farther?" a very young and junior British officer asked. Ensign Spencer was miserable. His bright red uniform was getting filthy. According to British army regulations, Spencer was in charge of the patrol, but he was terrified of both Braxton and the idea of taking a patrol away from the safety of the camp. Braxton wondered how the pale little boy had made it this far without wetting himself. Perhaps he had. They'd all stumbled and were wet enough to hide that little problem from the others.

"I'll let you know," snarled Braxton. Spencer was beginning to realize that signing up to fight for the king might actually mean fighting for the king and possibly even dying. And in a swamp at that.

"And spread out," Braxton ordered. Like all inexperienced troops, they had a tendency to bunch up in the mistaken perception of mutual security. Of course, this made them marvelous targets. At least they'd gotten rid of all the Indians. Only Brant and a couple others remained out of the hundreds of Iroquois who had begun the march. Screw 'em, he thought.

And screw Benedict Arnold. Nobody wanted to serve under a turncoat, but that's what Braxton's world had become. At least checking to see if the swamp was passable by an army made a little bit of sense, even if it was the turncoat Arnold who'd come up with the idea. If the British could swing through it and get in the rebel rear, there would be no need to storm those fortifications. Not that Braxton would have any part of storming the rebel earthworks. That's what the regular forces were for. The thought of marching straight into enemy guns sickened him. How the devil did the regulars do it?

Of course, they had to make sure that the rebels couldn't get through into Arnold's rear either. He laughed to himself. Somebody ought to do something to Arnold's rear. Or maybe to Ensign Spencer's plump little rear.

Spencer stumbled and swore petulantly. The water was now up to his knees and the heavy rains were making it worse. Each step was now a major effort. It had rained all day and that was turning everything into mud.

Spencer lurched to his feet. He looked like a drowned little dog. "They tell me the rebels are diverting streams to make this swamp even worse than it is."

Braxton didn't answer. He'd heard the same rumors but didn't think much of them. How could anyone divert streams?

At least the water wasn't particularly cold. In a perverse way, it was almost refreshing, assuming, that is, that there weren't any snakes lurking around. He shuddered. He hated snakes.

He stopped and Spencer halted beside him. They were almost a mile into the swamp and the water was now up to his waist.

He took a few steps more and the water got deeper. He made a decision. No way in hell that an army was going to come this way, especially not the British army. Not the way they liked to march in neat formations and keep their uniforms bright and red. Nor did he think the rebels would try it either. They just didn't have the manpower, or so he'd been told.

Braxton froze. Was that motion in a pile of branches and other debris? Logic said the rebels would have their own scouts checking on the swamp. Now it really was time to return.

"Now what?" Spencer asked, his voice trembling. He had picked up on Braxton's fears.

"It's time for us to go back and tell Benedict Fucking Arnold that there's no way an army can get through this shit. Maybe a handful could and they'd be too exhausted to move, but not an army. You agree, don't you?"

Spencer nodded solemnly, obviously relieved at the thought of returning to camp. "I concur."

Braxton didn't care whether Ensign Spencer concurred or not. He just wanted to get back to the camp. All they needed to do was keep a few men a little ways into the swamp to check on possible spies since determined individuals could always make it through. Again Spencer concurred, and this time Braxton laughed in his face.

Owen and Barley lifted themselves out of the muck of the swamp. The leaves and twigs they'd been hiding under fell away from them. "Think they saw us?" Barley asked.

"I think they did, or at least they suspected something. That's why they stopped."

"And that hideous-looking mess was Burned Man Braxton, wasn't it?"

"Nobody else could be that ugly," Owen said. "Excepting maybe yourself."

Owen said it in jest. In truth, he'd been stunned to see Braxton standing just a few feet away. He was the man who had abused both Faith and Sarah and raped poor Winifred Haskill. He could have killed the monster, but that would have alerted the British to the fact that the Americans had crossed the swamp, if only a few. Braxton would wait. Owen would not tell Faith or the others that he'd seen their tormentor.

Barley plucked a twig from his hair. "They're gone, Owen, and what tales will they take back to tell Arnold?"

"That the swamp is wet and the water is deep and the rain is making it worse."

Barley chuckled. "Did you see the little ass in the red uniform? Is that really an officer of the crown? He's just a damned little baby. I wonder if he wears diapers under that uniform. Christ, I thought you were bad enough."

Owen punched his companion lightly in the arm. "The boy's probably the youngest son of Lord Fumble-Dumble or maybe his lordship's illegitimate child born out of a barnyard coupling with a slow-witted milk maid who bent over at just the wrong time. But you're right, if that's an officer, I should be a general at least."

The two men laughed and began to crawl back to their lines. They now knew how deep the swamp was, and they also knew how deep the British thought it was.

# Chapter 18 ★★★★★★★★★★★★★★★★★

"To arms!" the lookouts hollered and the cry was echoed down the line. Men scrambled to take their positions behind the earthworks as drums added to the din.

A stunned Benjamin Franklin stared at an equally confused John Hancock. Both turned to General Stark. "General," Franklin said, "what the devil is going on?"

Stark had pulled out a telescope and was watching down the line to his left. "British skirmishers," he said. "Likely nothing more than a probe."

"That's Tarleton's wing," Tallmadge added. "He probably wants to see if we're awake."

Franklin took a proffered telescope and squinted. A scattered line of Redcoats had emerged from behind the British works and was advancing on the portion of the American lines commanded by General Anthony Wayne.

"Why aren't we firing?" Franklin asked, his voice quavering. He had never been this close to an actual battle.

Stark's face twitched in what was almost a smile. "They're just a little too far away, my dear Doctor." The distance was about a mile and well beyond rifle or musket range.

Moments later, the main body of the British right wing emerged behind the skirmishers and began to advance purposefully towards their American counterparts.

"Dear God," said Franklin, "they're going to attack, aren't they?"

Now Stark was truly smiling. Perhaps the short but maddening waiting was over. "One can only hope so."

The silence was broken by the sound of the drums and spoken commands coming from the American lines. In a short while, British officers could be heard ordering their men to keep order. The British force moved forward with a precision that was enviable, admirable, and chilling. The British were the consummate professionals, while the Americans, although good, simply were not up to those standards when it came to marching and maneuvering.

"Are you going to reinforce Wayne?" Tallmadge asked.

Von Steuben's Hessians were the reserve force and were behind the hill and hidden from British sight. Stark nodded and turned to Will Drake. "Tell my good Prussian friend to move his men over behind Wayne's but not to deploy or show themselves unless I deem it necessary. Impress on von Steuben that he is to move closer on my orders only, not Wayne's."

American marksmen started firing and the British skirmishers began to fall. The rest melted back into the main body which continued to advance at a deliberate but steadily ground-eating pace.

"Tarleton's mad," said Tallmadge.

"That is not a surprise," Stark said. "This is either a feint to pull us away from the center in order to leave us weakened for an attack by their main force, or Tarleton is trying to grab the glory of victory for himself." He turned to Franklin. "Nor is it quite time for any of your strange devices, Doctor Franklin. Insofar as the remainder of the British force hasn't begun to move, I rather think that this is Tarleton acting on his own initiative."

The British were now within range of the Americans and an American volley ripped through their ranks. Men fell, some jerking and some still. Suddenly, the British stopped and the whole mass appeared to stumble. They were enmeshed in the webbing of tree branches and shrubs that came to their knees and was very difficult to walk through. The British advanced slowed to almost nothing. Another American volley and more British fell.

Commands were screamed and Redcoats began to pull at the entanglement while others returned fire at the Americans who were fairly safe behind their earthen walls. Smoke billowed over both sides and a bitter cloud wafted its way over Franklin and Stark, causing the older man to cough violently. A third American volley and then a fourth and the British began to pull back. A ragged cheer came from the American lines. In a moment, the firing ended, as suddenly as it began.

"We've stopped them," Franklin said, incredulous.

"We stopped nothing," Stark replied. "That was not their main force. God only knows what Tarleton planned, although I'm rather certain it was as much a surprise to Burgoyne as it was to us."

Franklin checked his pocket watch. The fighting had lasted less than fifteen minutes. Scores of Redcoats lay on the ground. He felt his stomach churning. The sights and sounds of battle had sickened him. He could hear the wounded moaning and screaming. Standing beside him, John Hancock was pale but in control of himself.

"Your first battle, Doctor?" Stark asked, not unkindly.

"It is." Franklin answered. "And I would prefer it be my last."

Stark glared at Franklin and Hancock. "Then think upon this, Doctor Franklin and Mr. Hancock. The men who are lying still are dead. A few moments ago, they were laughing, cursing, and sweating, and doubtless thought themselves immortal. Now they are dead. And the ones who are moving and who you hear calling for help are the wounded. Some will lose limbs, eyes, faces, and many will die before the night is over. This is the price of the folly of war and we have not even begun to pay the full amount."

"Damn the British," snarled Hancock. "Why can't they just leave us alone?"

A white flag of truce showed from the British lines. A handful of unarmed men moved out to pick up the dead and the wounded. They were unmolested. Franklin could hear the cries of the American wounded, which told him that the fight had not been totally one-sided.

Franklin walked alone back down the hill. Hancock had already departed to go and give such solace as he could to the wounded. Franklin's stomach was still churning. He wanted to vomit. He was too old for this. He was too old for anything. And what had he gotten himself into?

He gazed into the face of Will Drake. "I confess that I had no idea," he said.

"And it will be worse, far worse, when the main battle begins," Will said softly.

Franklin nodded and allowed himself to be aided to a cart

that would take him back to his quarters. Perhaps Sarah would be there. She was a good listener and he needed someone to hear his rantings at this moment.

Tarleton stood at attention. He barely concealed a smirk. Burgoyne was again livid with anger, which seemed to amuse the younger general.

"Your folly has cost us more than a hundred casualties, and all for nothing. What in God's name were you thinking? Or were you thinking about anything at all?"

Tarleton was unconcerned. "Actually, my dear General, I was thinking and quite profoundly. I decided that it was time that we actually did something instead of sitting around on our asses. And so what if I lost a few men? They were soldiers and they died for a purpose."

"And what purpose might that be?" asked Burgoyne, his anger barely under control. He had a paternal attitude towards his men and hated to lose them. More pragmatically, he especially hated to lose highly trained professional soldiers for no apparent reason. It took a long time to turn raw material into a British soldier and wasting their lives was to be avoided.

"Simple," Tarleton answered, his tone implying that Burgoyne was the one who was simple. "If we had succeeded and penetrated their lines, then they would have been forced to use their reserves, which would have permitted General Grant to advance with his main body and crush them. Either way, the battle would have been over, and we could shortly find ourselves on our way to home and glory."

Burgoyne shook his head in disbelief. "Did it occur to you that General Grant was uninformed of your intention and was totally unready to assist you?"

Tarleton shrugged. "Then he should have been ready. And I rather think he was ready a few moments after my men began to advance. Victory, General, belongs to the bold."

"But you accomplished nothing, did you?"

Tarleton laughed, "Hardly. The almost invisible presence of that low and man-made thicket that stopped my men was an unpleasant surprise of the highest order. Think how catastrophic it would have been if the main attack had become entangled in it. The rebels would have had a wonderful time shooting and slaughtering our men while we could do nothing about it, except ultimately withdraw. It would have been a massacre most awful. Now we can take steps to eliminate that obstacle."

Burgoyne had to admit that the insolent and arrogant Tarleton had a point, albeit a small one. Twenty-eight British regulars were dead and seventy-four wounded and, as in any battle, many of the wounded were lost for this campaign if not forever. It had been far too high a price to pay to find out about the obstacle. A simple nighttime patrol would have been more than sufficient. Of course, no such patrol had occurred nor had one been planned. Damn Tarleton, he thought.

A thicket of twigs and branches? And it had stopped Tarleton in his tracks? Who would have thought it possible? And what other devilish tricks did the Americans have up their sleeves? Or, he grinned wryly, were they up Benjamin Franklin's sleeves?

Someone hailed him. A horseman was approaching. Burgoyne began to seethe. It would doubtless be another epistle from Cornwallis filled with unwanted advice and asking for the return of the army. He felt like throwing a clump of mud or horse dung at the rider.


Will Drake watched sternly as the delegation of four men came forth and stood before him. Their spokesman was a large, dour, and bearded man about forty. His name was Ephram. "Have you considered our request?" he asked without preamble, although he did glance nervously at the detachment of fully armed soldiers behind Will.

"We have, and we don't quite understand it." Will said. "Why in God's name do you want to go back to the British now?"

"It's simple, Major Drake, we all have families and we wish them to live out their lives rather than have them snuffed out in the next few days. We made a mistake in coming here. We honestly thought that the British wouldn't come this far to chase us and that we would be allowed to live out our lives in peace. We sincerely felt that the great distance between us and what the British call civilization would be our salvation. That and our faith in the Lord."

"And there are about fifty of you?" Will asked, although he already knew their numbers. "And you no longer wish to fight for your freedom?"

Ephram shrugged. "Yes to the numbers of us who wish to

leave, and yes we would be willing to fight for our freedom if the fight would be a fair one, and where we would have a chance of winning. But you can see the vast array before us. We would have no chance at all and it would result in a massacre followed by the enslavement of the survivors."

Will shook his head in disbelief. "Yet you think you stand a better chance by just walking up to the Redcoats and announcing that you're so very sorry you rebelled, and that you would be good and loyal subjects of King George if you would only forgive us for our trespasses."

Ephram flushed angrily. "Please do not blaspheme by misusing the Lord's Prayer, Major. We are protecting our families."

"You are what Tom Paine wrote about, aren't you. You are the 'summer soldiers and sunshine patriots,' aren't you? You stay with us when the times are easy, but run like rabbits when difficulties arise."

"I would not refer to being slaughtered as simple difficulties, Major, nor do I think of us as rabbits. We are honest godly people who have made what is to us a highly moral decision. Yet, if that's what you think of us, then yes. Now, may we leave?"

Will pretended to ponder. In truth, the matter had already been decided by General Stark and communicated through General Tallmadge.

"No."

Ephram looked flustered and the other three men showed obvious dismay. "Will you please tell us why not?"

"How many reasons do you want? First, you know details of our defenses and would doubtless tell everything to curry favor with your new masters."

To Will's surprise, Ephram actually smiled before he replied. "Of course, and, second, we might also unleash a trickle that would soon become a flood of people like us if the British did indeed welcome us back to their bosom, now wouldn't we? It might eliminate the necessity of a war or a battle in the first place."

Will matched his smile. "There is that. I won't lie to you. But the answer remains the same. And, in order to ensure your cooperation, you and your people will be kept under guard until the fighting starts. At that time you can make a final decision as the guards will probably then be needed elsewhere. When you are no longer under guard, you can run straight to hell for all I'll care."

"You will be damned for the innocent lives your rejection of mercy will cost," Ephram said with a sigh of resignation.

"Just as you will be damned for being a fool, a turncoat, and a traitor. You will be compared to Benedict Arnold."

Will signaled for the detachment of soldiers to take up positions around the men and take control of them and the others. He turned and walked away. A few paces on, Sarah stepped from behind the corner of a building. She took his arm and they walked away.

"Will, are you afraid that there are others like them?"

He squeezed her hand. "No one knows, and that's the problem. Deep down, many must be wondering if there is an alternative to fighting the battle that is coming. Tell me, dear Sarah, would you have us flee if there was a place we could go?"

She rested her head on his arm. "I have indeed thought of it and, you're right, doubtless every person here has pondered it. But no, sweet Will, I would not flee, at least not without you."

John Hancock poured a cup of what passed for coffee and handed it to General Stark. "I confess that I was at first dismayed when you sent a low-ranking officer to deal with the British envoy, but I somewhat understand it."

Stark nodded. "It was a formality and a preliminary one, at that. They sent a junior officer, so we responded in kind."

"But you say it was a preliminary meeting?"

"Indeed. I do not think that Burgoyne actually wishes to fight this battle. He is under orders to return his army for other purposes after crushing us, and now he is realizing that we may be more difficult to destroy then he and London envisioned. Indeed, he now must confront the possibility of a Pyrrhic victory in which his victorious army would wind up being in no shape to help Cornwallis or Lord North or anyone."

"So there will be other meetings. But for what purpose?"

Stark yawned. He hadn't had more than a few hours of sleep in the last several days. He really didn't want to waste time talking to Hancock, but the man was the president of the Congress and had to be humored.

"He wants his army rested and ready, and he wants us intimidated. Those people who wished to leave us and others like them are his goal. If he can convince people to flee, then his task becomes all that much easier. In effect, he inflicts casualties without blood and fighting."

"Especially if they reveal our secrets," Hancock said.

Stark laughed. "With all the spying and counterspying that's going on, I rather doubt that either side has many secrets." Except, he thought to himself, the devices that Doctor Franklin was conjuring up. Even Hancock was not privy to all of these.

"No, Mr. Hancock, I rather think Burgoyne will realize that he has two choices. Attack us here where we are the strongest, or try to turn our flank by marching around that bloody swamp that your people are keeping so well filled with water. And based on what we have learned, I do not think that he will be granted the time to do that."

"How do you know this, General? More spying and counter-spying?"

Stark finished his tea. "Something like that, Mr. Hancock, something like that."

Colonel Arent De Peyster was disgusted, tired, and drunk as a lord. The backwater fort at Detroit that he'd commanded for so long was even worse and more decrepit then it had ever been. The arrival of Burgoyne's army and its subsequent and unlamented departure, along with the fire, had utterly ruined what had been an uninspiring posting in the first place. The wooden stockade that surrounded most of the town had been destroyed by the fire, as had a majority of the buildings, and very little in the way of rebuilding had begun.

Thus, the Swiss-born and middle-aged major was forced to drink either in a miserable and filthy tent that passed as a tavern, or alone in another tent that was his quarters. This night, he'd chosen to be alone in his quarters.

De Peyster had helped defend Fort Pitt during the uprising led by Pontiac nearly two decades earlier. He was now an over-the-hill major and would never be promoted again. He also felt abandoned by Burgoyne and the rest of England. Once, during the American Revolution, the garrison numbered nearly four hundred men. Now it was fewer than a hundred and De Peyster was of the opinion that maybe only half could find their boots without help.

The fort itself, the citadel, had been built a few years earlier by a Captain Lernoult, who promptly named it after himself. De Peyster chuckled drunkenly and thought he would rename it Fort De Peyster just to see what, if anything, London would do. Nothing, he concluded, and had another drink.

Lernoult's fort would have been a strong one, with thick, high walls, but for the fact that it had been neglected and now was so seriously undermanned. While the great fire had destroyed much of the town, another fire a few weeks ago had destroyed or damaged the barracks and commandant's quarters inside the fort, which was why De Peyster was sleeping in a tent. This time there was no question as to who started the fire. It had been a drunken soldier and not a spy. The soldier was rotting in jail and would doubtless be either hanged or flogged so severely that he would die of his injuries.

Bored, De Peyster got up, left his tent, and walked towards the riverfront. A handful of good-sized bateaux had arrived with a large number of men who said they were Loyalists and on their way to reinforce Burgoyne. De Peyster thought it more likely that they were thieves and bandits who would prey on innocent people, so he ordered them kept on their boats and had a guard posted.

The bateaux were lined up on the riverbank, much like Burgoyne's sailing barges had been. De Peyster blinked. The bateaux appeared empty. Where were the crews? "Damn it," he muttered angrily. Obviously, they'd gotten away and were off in the town drinking. He turned and strode towards the fort. He would roust the handful of men on guard duty and send them and anyone else he could find to locate the missing Loyalists, if indeed that's what they were.

"Major?"

He turned towards the sound. A group of men quickly surrounded him and took his small sword and pistol before he could even blink.

"What the devil is this?" De Peyster snarled as he regained his poise.

He gasped as he felt the cold metal touch of a knife against his throat.

"Now please be a good little British officer and nothing will happen to you or your men. If you understand, please nod." De Peyster nodded emphatically and the pressure was lessened. He also thought that the man spoke with a southern drawl.

He became aware of scores of men moving quickly and silently past him and into Fort Lernoult. "Who are you and what do you want?"

"Major, my name is Colonel Isaac Shelby and I've come a hell of a long ways to help out the people in Liberty and bring ruin to your General Burgoyne. In case you haven't noticed, we've just seized Detroit in the name of the independent colonies, and another force from the south has likely done just the same thing to Fort Pitt."

De Peyster sighed. He was a realist. The fort, the city, and what remained of his career were all gone. The fort and the city might be regained, but his career? Never.

"Colonel Shelby, I hereby give you my word that my men and I will not attempt to escape. Will you treat my men kindly and allow my officers their parole?"

Shelby smiled in relief. He'd been terrified that he and his men would have to storm the fort. Even undermanned, the defenders would have exacted a terrible price. "Agreed," he said.

De Peyster smiled wanly. It was time to make the best of an atrocious situation. "Excellent. Now kindly let me buy you a drink."

# Chapter 19 ★ ★ ★ ★ ★ ★ ★ ★ ★ ★ ★ ★ ★ ★ ★

B URGOYNE GATHERED HIS SENIOR OFFICERS IN HIS TENT. TAR-leton, Grant, and Arnold were in attendance, along with several other brigadiers. Girty and Brant were there as well, and Fitzroy thought it amusing that the regular British officers didn't want to get too close to the disreputable pair. As usual, he stood behind his cousin and commanding general and waited for events to transpire.

Burgoyne cleared his throat and began. "Gentlemen, after reviewing the situation and after watching the defeat of Tarleton's attack, I had come to the reluctant conclusion that a frontal assault on the rebel works would require that we pay a dreadful cost."

When Tarleton started to protest, he was waved to silence. "I felt that such a frontal assault would ultimately prevail, but that our effectiveness to aid Cornwallis in New York, or Amherst's efforts in Europe, would be significantly diminished. It would be a battle not unlike Bunker Hill and after it our army might not exist as an effective force.

"Therefore, I had determined to march to our left and find a way around that bloody swamp and away from their fortifications; thus forcing the rebels to meet us on an open field, however long that might have taken. Sadly, that will not occur. We no longer have the luxury of time, if, indeed, we ever had that luxury in the first instance."

Burgoyne took up a few sheets of paper. "Last evening, I received this from Cornwallis."

"Another epistle?" Tarleton jibed. "Or would Papal Bull be the more proper term?"

Burgoyne joined in the wry laughter before continuing. "Indeed, bull is quite the appropriate term. And this is the twenty-third letter to the heathen, who are us, and I am ungodly sick of them. However, this is by far the worst of them and will greatly impact on what we do here."

That silenced the laughter and he continued. "This first sheet is a letter from Cornwallis with fresh orders for us, and the other is a summary from Lord North as to what is transpiring in France. According to North, the situation in France has gone from mildly hopeful to catastrophically bad. Thinking that the situation had calmed down enough for them to return, their foolish majesties, Louis XVI and Marie Antoinette, departed for France where their welcome was lukewarm at best. However, they forgot that their new role called for them to become limited monarchs, and, with monumental stupidity, had some local leaders summarily hanged for their part in the rebellion. The result was that the mobs arose again. Louis and Marie were captured trying to flee back to the coast. He was literally torn to pieces while she was thrown down a well where she drowned or suffocated under large quantities of excrement that were dumped on top of her as she struggled."

"The animals! Barbarians!" exclaimed Grant, and the others joined in shouts of anger. "Regicide," Tarleton added, somehow forgetting that Englishmen had killed Charles I a century and a half before. Only Arnold was silent.

Burgoyne continued. "As a result of the brutal murders and fresh uprisings, the situation is even more dire than it was before. Hundreds of moderates like Lafayette have again fled to England leaving the mob in control of France, where it is busy butchering what remains of the aristocracy along with anyone who ever even helped the nobles. The revolutionaries have raised an army of several hundred thousand peasants and, while untrained and poorly equipped, are so great in numbers that they could overwhelm a smaller army of British regulars should they meet in the field."

Burgoyne handed the letters to Grant who began to read them for himself as Burgoyne went on. "Simply put, Lord North and Cornwallis want their army back, and as immediately as possible. I was required to sign a receipt upon receiving the message from Cornwallis, which also informed me that I had but a week after signing said document to finish things here. If the rebels have not been subdued by that time, we are to return to New York as quickly as possible. Even though that could take some months, and would leave the damned rebels in charge of this land and their own destiny, it would have to be done."

Voices rose in protest and Burgoyne silenced them with a wave. "And yes, gentlemen, I understand fully that the information received by Cornwallis and now by us is many months old, and any request for urgency could have been overtaken by new facts we are not privy to, but our orders stand. We will move much more quickly on the rebel works than I had wished even though it will result in higher casualties than I had desired. I can only hope that we will not destroy the army Lord North wants returned to his bosom.

"Therefore, we will not march around their flanks in search of a weak point to force them out of their works. We will indeed attack frontally, but only after we have prepared the field to limit their advantages. I have spoken of this to General Grant whose force will lead the assault, which will consist of the bulk of our army attacking as a great phalanx across a narrow front. The phalanx will consist of a number of columns, each column ten men across, approximately as we did at Bunker Hill. They will use only the bayonet since the men behind can't fire without hitting those in front. We will rush them and overwhelm them with cold steel, the most frightening weapon we have. Then the columns will spread out and destroy the remnants of the rebel army. We will have three days to remove those thickets and fill in such ditches as we can. Then we will attack and smash our way through them, and we will prevail come what may."

Tarleton stood up. "I beg for the honor of leading the attack."

Burgoyne smiled inwardly. Getting the arrogant ass killed might be a good and pleasing thing, but with Tarleton's luck, he might pull it off and be proclaimed a hero.

"Your courageous offer is duly noted," Burgoyne said, "but that command will still fall to General Grant. It is a decision based on his seniority, his rank, and his experience. You, however, will use what will remain of your force to protect our flank and harass theirs, as well as being available to support Grant when his phalanx smashes through the rebel lines. Fear not, Banastre, there will be plenty of honor to go around."

Tarleton appeared to sulk for a moment, but Fitzroy thought he actually looked relieved that his request for glory had been denied. "Has the messenger departed?" Tarleton inquired. "I have some correspondence to send if he hasn't."

"No, he has gone. He had orders to leave as soon as I had signed the receipt. He didn't even have time to wait for a response. Curious though, that he couldn't even wait for a little while."

Fitzroy thought briefly about the short but powerfully young Welsh ensign who'd brought the message and departed so quickly. He'd wanted to quiz the messenger about a multitude of things, but the man had pleaded the necessity of duty, jumped back on his horse and ridden away. He'd been in such a devil of a hurry that he hadn't even waited to be fed. Curious indeed.

Ephram and four of his cronies quickly overpowered the two men detailed to guard the would-be changelings during the night. They were bound and gagged, but, other than a few bruises, not harmed. Ephram had no urge to kill them. He considered himself a man of peace. He gathered the rest of his men along with the women and children and headed towards the rear of the American defenses.

As hoped, the American sentries were watching the British and not very much caring what was going on behind them. If they heard anything from the fifty-odd people, the soldiers probably thought that a detachment of fellow soldiers was moving around behind them.

Just before they reached the earthworks, they paused. In the night they could hear the sounds of the British pulling and hacking at the thicket that had destroyed the earlier British attack. The British soldiers were lying prone as much as much as they could and hurling grappling hooks into the thicket. Once snagged, the British pulled on them and dragged the abattis apart. He thought it was curious that the rebels weren't firing on the British workers, but concluded that there were no good targets in the night.

Ephram was pleased. The British efforts meant that they would have that much less distance to run to safety. He had all his people bunch together. The women and boys would hold the youngest children as they dashed towards the British. As a sign of good faith, they were unarmed. Their faith was in British mercy and their god.

"Now!" he ordered and they all rushed over the parapet and out into the no man's land between the two lines, and headed through the narrow gaps in the abattis he knew existed.

"Save us!" he hollered to the British and ran towards them with his hands in the air. The others picked up the chant and "save us" was chorused by more than two score throats.

Ephram was conscious that the British diggers had abandoned their shovels and were also running towards their lines and it confused him. Why would they do that? Gasping and stumbling, he and his followers continued on.

Then, only a few yards away, they perceived a line of soldiers. They were indeed safe, Ephram thought smugly. A few more strides and they would be behind British lines and with much to tell. Damn the rebels for not releasing them and forcing them to go through with this charade.

A ripple of fire shattered the night as a hundred muskets fired into them. Ephram died immediately, a bullet in his skull. Most of his followers fell to the ground, wounded and screaming, or, like Ephram, dead. Deprived of their leader, the survivors simply milled around in confusion and dismay, howling at the loss of their love ones.

A second volley scythed through them and most of the survivors were killed or wounded. The literal handful who still lived, turned and ran towards the American lines, screaming that the British were murderers. There was no third volley.

Behind the embankment, General Tallmadge watched with General John Stark. "Did you expect that to happen?" Stark inquired angrily.

"No," Tallmadge said. "I had no idea they would try such a thing." The slaughter sickened him. "But I cannot say I am disappointed. Such butchery will drive home the fact that the Redcoats are murderers, and that neither they nor their promises can be trusted."

"What will you do with the survivors?"

"Those who made it back will be allowed to do whatever they wish. They can even leave if they so desire, although I doubt that they will want to go to the British after what has happened to their friends and families. They will stand as living proof of British perfidy. In the morning, we will attempt to see if any remain alive out there and ask for a truce to recover bodies if the British don't do so first. I would think parading dead children throughout the camp would again be a reminder to our people that the British will show no mercy."

"You, General Tallmadge, are a devious, conniving bastard," Stark said with a small smile. "I admire that in a man."

Tallmadge nodded solemnly. "Which is exactly what you need to stand a chance of winning; thus, I will accept your compliment."

Dawn brought another flag of truce and another meeting between Will Drake and James Fitzroy. For his part, the British officer looked shaken, while Will was righteously grim, although sickened by the carnage.

"Major Drake, I want you to know that we had no idea that those people were unarmed civilians. Had we but known, we would never have fired on them. The officers and men who fired on them are stunned by what has happened."

Will responded solemnly. "If it's any consolation, we understand fully how it must have looked to your men. In the middle of the night, what looked like a large number of people came out of our lines, yelling and running up to the men who are trying to destroy our defenses. I cannot see how your men could have behaved otherwise. It is a tragedy, Major, and the only ones truly to blame are those foolish, foolish people who ran at you like that."

"The officer in charge of the guard detail is very distraught," Fitzroy added. "Several small children were killed and he blames himself for the atrocity."

"Tell him that neither General Stark, nor, for that matter, the survivors who made it back, hold him responsible. They were under the spell of a messianic leader named Ephram and to the extent that any individual is to blame for that piece of horror, it is Ephram."

"I will tell Captain Blaylock that, although one wonders how much solace he will get hearing it from his enemy."

Will considered it ironic that the British were so concerned about the inadvertent killing of people they'd come to destroy in the first place.

"Do you have any survivors on your side?" Will asked.

"Three, and they are badly wounded, although," Fitzroy added wryly, "don't worry about them betraying your secrets. I rather doubt that they know anything that we haven't already learned.

On the other hand, I am certain you have figured out that the massacre, however unintended, can be used to your advantage. I rather think that your people consider us vile killers of women and children, and that you will do nothing to change their minds."

Will shrugged. "I cannot help what people think, although I rather doubt that they were favorably disposed towards you in the first place, since you've marched all this way to either kill us or enslave us."

"You're right, of course, Major Drake. At any rate, thank you for accepting our sincere apologies, however useless they are."

"As I said, we understand fully. And, by the way, Mistress Van Doorn sends her regards, and, for your information, she is a lady who is most highly regarded and respected in our camp." He held out a piece of paper. "She asked me to deliver a small note if I thought you'd be favorably disposed to receive it."

Fitzroy almost grabbed it and Drake laughed, "Just a little anxious, Major?"

"So how do you like consorting with the enemy?" Sarah teased. "You and that major must be good friends by now."

Will lay back on the grass and looked up at the clouds that scudded across the sky. They were about a half mile from any houses and in a world of their own. They had made love, bathed in a small pond, and made love again. For his part, Will was sated, but he had the feeling that Sarah was not. He could only hope he would be up to the occasion. It was almost sunset and he didn't have to be back until morning, so maybe he could manage it.

"He actually seems like a decent sort, as, frankly, so many of them do. The people I dealt with on the battlefield were professional soldiers and our enemy, but human beings nonetheless. The animals were the sort who ran the prisons and the hulks. They were looked down on contemptuously by the regular line officers."

"Tarleton's one of those professionals that you admire, isn't he?" she teased.

Will chuckled. "Tarleton's an exception to any rule. He's a monster. And people like Girty and Braxton are animals, and not professionals. In any other time and place they would be nothing more than criminals. I still cannot fathom why Tarleton is considered a hero in England."

"Will, has it occurred to you that they haven't really sent their best generals to conquer us?"

He raised himself on his elbow and thought it unusual that they would be talking military matters while lying naked on the grass. "We've talked about it. Tarleton's not experienced enough, and Arnold isn't trusted by anyone. However, Grant is as solid as they come, and Burgoyne is an experienced professional who seems to have learned from many of his past mistakes. We all hope that he hasn't learned too much."

Will sat up, pulled up a long grass and began to chew on it. "Still, you raise a good point. The British are stretched as a result of the deteriorating situation in France, and many of their best leaders want no part of tramping through the forest to take us, any more than they did when the revolution first broke out so many years ago. No glory or honor doing that. No, they all want to be in France when Paris is liberated from the mob."

Sarah moved beside him and put her head on his shoulder. He flicked the grass away. "So now they spend every day whittling at our defenses and filling in the traps we dug for them."

"Surely they can't fill in all of them?" She said.

"No," he said. "Not all of them."

She pushed him on his back and rolled on top of him. "Enough of that ugly world. All I want is the here and now." She reached behind and took his manhood in her hand. To Will's pleased surprised, he was indeed rising to the occasion. She guided him inside her and began to rock on top of him. "This is all I want today, Will Drake. Tomorrow will take care of itself."

Fitzroy was the presenter. He stood in front of the crudely drawn map of the area. "The rebel order of battle is really quite simple. Morgan commands an American division in the center, while Wayne is to our right and Clark to our left. The divisions are not equal in strength. Morgan's is the largest at close to two thousand men, and Wayne has another thousand. Clark has five hundred at most, although a high percentage of them are woodsmen and considered deadly shots."

"And the Hessians?" Grant asked. "The bloody deserters? How many are there, and where the devil are they?"

"We estimate their strength at perhaps another thousand, and they are under von Steuben," Fitzroy said. "We believe they will be behind the center of the line, or wherever they feel we will launch our major attack."

"They will be extremely dangerous," Grant said softly. "They know that their best option is a fast death."

Or victory, Fitzroy thought but was tactful enough not to say it out loud. "We estimate the total rebel numbers at well less than five thousand, which they will attempt to defend against our thirteen thousand."

Grant nodded. They had started with over fourteen thousand men, but the constant skirmishing and the need to garrison depots along their route had reduced the number to actually less than thirteen thousand. The crews of Arnold's Armada had been used to form an additional regiment, which Arnold had as part of his command.

Fitzroy continued. "As to artillery, we have the two nine-pounders recovered from Arnold's ships, and have them on sledges. Sadly, there are no shells for them, so they will fire langrage only. They will not be effective at long range. We will also have the small guns and ammunition which we've removed from the two schooners, a total of ten four pounders, and they do have their shells. What they don't have, however, is proper carriages for being moved about on land or being secured from damage caused by recoil. The carriages they are on are meant to be tied down to the hull of a ship."

"We will make do with what we have," Burgoyne said softly.

"And what of their peasant army?" Tarleton inquired with a sneer.

Fitzroy eyed him coldly. He was referring to the group of women, old men, and young boys that would likely include Hannah Van Doorn. "We estimate another thousand ill-armed and poorly trained people of both sexes and all ages who will be used against us. As you are aware, they will be primarily armed with pikes, axes, and anything else they can find or that the evil mind of Dr. Franklin can devise. We believe they will be led in battle by General Schuyler."

That surprised them. Schuyler was a major general and to lead such a host would be demeaning. Or was it? Like the Hessians, those in what Tarleton contemptuously referred to as a peasant's army would fight with incredible desperation when the time came.

Burgoyne stood. "As we've discussed, General Grant will command a phalanx of ten thousand men. It will be a hundred men across and a hundred men deep, with the first several ranks consisting of grenadiers. Without pretension or subtlety, the phalanx will crash into the center of the American lines and push its way through. It will succeed for the simple reason that the rebels do not have the manpower to stop it. And, if they try to reinforce their center from their flanks, we will attack their weakened flanks and overwhelm them. Casualties will initially be heavy, but the attack will quickly force the rebels to fight us on our terms and we cannot lose such a battle. At the end of a bloody but decisive day, the rebels will cease to exist as an army."

As might we, Fitzroy thought.

Burgoyne looked away. "There will doubtless be rebel survivors, particularly among the women and children, who will run and, quite frankly, I am inclined to let them run as far away as they wish. Let them flee to the mercies of the Indians, or try to get back to their homes in the east. Let them be messengers of doom. Those people can be picked up at our leisure or simply left to rot in the backwoods."

There was a round of cheers. Grant seemed confident, and even Tarleton looked pleased at the prospect of such a slaughter. Only Arnold seemed less than enthusiastic. Fitzroy wondered if he was having second, or even third, thoughts about his treason. He almost felt sorry for Arnold. He was a man without a home.

The shifting of thousands of men did not go unnoticed. Will and Sergeant Barley lay in the grass and watched as large numbers of Redcoats moved hither and yon. They were behind the British, having had little difficulty sneaking through the enemy pickets. Either they were incompetent or they were indifferent as to what the rebels might find out. Will depressingly thought it was the latter.

"What the devil are they up to?" Barley muttered. Will smiled. Finding the answer to that question was why they were there.

"I rather think it has something to do with the coming attack, don't you?"

Barley grunted and spat on the ground. "Not that I don't like you, Major, but I'd much rather they'd sent Owen instead of you. He's a much better tracker."

Will had wondered the why of that as well. Tallmadge had explained it simply. Will was more of a professional soldier than Owen and would be better able to interpret what the movements all meant. And, for some unexplained reason, Owen was not to be used. Tallmadge kept his intelligence efforts compartmentalized, which meant that Owen was involved in something important and the possibility of his capture could not be allowed to jeopardize it.

Unfortunately, this meant that Will's capture could indeed be risked. He was out of what little he had that passed for a uniform and he'd be hanged if caught. Fortunately, the only Englishman who might recognize him was his counterpart, Fitzroy, and they'd only met twice. While he was fairly certain he'd recognize the Brit, he wondered if the reverse were true. Probably, he admitted sadly, even though he was unshaven, dirty, dressed in a frontiersman's buckskins and carrying a long rifle. The rifle was a difficult weapon, but he was confident in his abilities. He also hoped it would help his disguise as a member of an irregular unit.

"Enough," Will said and stood up. With forced casualness, he stepped boldly out onto a trail and walked to where a number of British officers were examining stakes that had been driven into the ground. They barely noticed him as he watched their deliberations. To them he was just another colonial bumpkin with a long rifle in the crook of his arm and doubtless one of the handful of loyalist militia that had been arriving in very small numbers.

However, a small, trim Hessian officer in an impeccably clean powder blue uniform with gold facing stood apart and Will nodded politely to him. The officer turned and walked toward him. Will gave the Hessian the casual salute that a colonial might give and it was returned.

"And who might you be?" the Hessian enquired.

"Captain John Smith of the newly formed Loyal Connecticut Rangers, sir," he answered, hoping that the German didn't recognize such an obvious alias. Foolishly, he hadn't thought anyone would ask him his name. "And who might you be?"

The German was momentarily surprised that anyone might question him in return. "I am Colonel Erich von Bamberg of Hesse."

Will immediately recognized the name of the man who had hanged innocent people on the suspicion of their being deserters. If von Bamberg was annoyed at Will's posing a question to him, he didn't seem overly concerned. Obviously he'd grown somewhat used to the ways of the colonies.

"Are you with Girty's people, then?" von Bamberg asked.

Will allowed his distaste to show. "Hardly, sir. I am a soldier. They are animals."

Von Bamberg chuckled. "Good for you. And when did you arrive?"

"Just yesterday along with some more messages for General Burgoyne. I'll be going back to Detroit shortly."

"Well, that explains why I never saw you before or ever heard of your Loyal Connecticut Rangers."

Will decided it was time for a change in the conversation. "Colonel, may I ask what all this activity means?"

Von Bamberg smiled happily. "Why, captain, we are trying to prepare for the grand assault which will take place either tomorrow or the next day. Surely you've heard that the good and wise General Burgoyne has ordered a massive frontal assault on the rebel works and that the attack is designed to destroy them?"

"I have, sir."

"Indeed. Approximately ten thousand men will line up in ranks about a hundred across and a hundred deep. They will charge the rebels and be an irresistible force. The wooden stakes are here so the men will know exactly where to line up. It is quite a project and may require a rehearsal, which, since Burgoyne loves theater, he might appreciate. Of course, Burgoyne is telling the rebels exactly where the attack will fall because he certainly cannot shift this mass of soldiers around like chess pieces. There will be no surprise at all, I fear."

Will nodded. "I sense you do not feel total approval, Colonel."

"I'm just a guest here, Captain, but perhaps you could tell me what problems such an attack might cause?"

Will pondered. He wasn't certain if he was being condescended to or if the Hessian genuinely wanted his opinion. "I can think of a couple. To begin with, only the very first rank or two would be able to fire on the enemy. The rest would be useless, although they could certainly use the strength of their push, plus their bayonets, when they closed on the rebels."

The Hessian was visibly impressed. "Very good. Now what else?"

"By concentrating his forces on such a narrow front, General Burgoyne is forfeiting much of his numerical advantage. We outnumber them, so he might have launched a strong attack at several places and stretched the rebels too thin to withstand all the attacks. If only just one of several attacks succeeded, the rebels would have to retreat. Also, such a narrow front attack means the rebels can concentrate their numbers as well."

"Excellent. What did you do before joining the Rangers?"

"I was a farmer, but I read a lot."

"Then you might have heard of the ancient battle of Thermopylae, where a Spartan named Leonidas and three hundred men held off a large Persian host because the Spartans held a narrow front."

"Indeed, and I also know that the Spartans were ultimately overwhelmed and destroyed. Do you fear that this attack might be another Thermopylae?"

"Not quite," said von Bamberg. "I do fear that a great loss of life will occur, however, and, by the way, the Spartans were not overwhelmed. They were betrayed."

Will smiled. "I'd forgotten."

Von Bamberg nodded and smiled grimly. "Enjoy your observations, Captain, and have a safe trip back to Detroit. Or are you going to stay for the fight?"

"I plan on leaving as soon as possible."

Von Bamberg turned and walked towards where a pair of his Hessian soldiers were resting. They were about a hundred yards away and snapped to attention as they saw von Bamberg. When he reached them, Von Bamberg turned and began to yell and point to Will.

"Spy! Spy! Grab him, he's a spy?"

Will ran as hard and fast as he could. The cluster of trees that had hidden him and Barley was almost a quarter mile away. He looked over his shoulder. Von Bamberg and the two soldiers were pursuing, but all his yells had attracted little other attention, although a couple of unarmed Redcoats were looking at them, slack-jawed with confusion.

What the hell had gone wrong, Will wondered as he ran. Did the damned German know there was no such unit as the Loyal Connecticut Rangers? Perhaps Will had just been too inquisitive for an ignorant colonial. It didn't matter. If he didn't reach the trees and Barley, he'd be caught and hanged.

To his astonishment, von Bamberg seemed to be gaining. Of course the Hessian wasn't trying to run while holding a long rifle. Will thought about turning and firing, but, if he missed, the Hessians would be almost on him. No, he would try for the woods before defending himself.

Less than a hundred yards to go and Will could hear von Bamberg's heavy breathing.

"Stop, you rebel bastard," von Bamberg yelled and gasped. The man was clearly out of shape and might not be able to run much farther. However, he might not have to.

A shot rang out and Bamberg screamed. Will turned to see the Hessian falling backwards. A red stain was spreading across his chest.

"Get your ass in here," Barley shouted as he rose up from the ground.

Will ran into the trees, ducked behind a thick trunk and prepared to fire at the two remaining Hessians who had stopped and were bending over their fallen leader.

"Don't," said Barley. "I haven't reloaded yet."

Will agreed. One of them should always be ready to shoot. The two Hessians were picking up their colonel who hung limply between them. There was little doubt that he was dead. They showed no interest at all in continuing the chase. Barley had finished loading and the two men looked at each other. There was no reason for more killing.

"Thank you, Barley."

The sergeant grinned. "If my memory serves me, this isn't the first time I've saved your worthless ass."

Will punched him on the shoulder. "Try 'worthless ass, sir,' and let's figure out a way to get back to our lines before the unfortunate death of von Bamberg, the murdering Hessian swine, brings more attention than we can handle."

# Chapter 20 ★ ★ ★ ★ ★ ★ ★ ★ ★ ★ ★ ★ ★ ★ ★ ★ ★

Fitzroy stood over the lifeless body of Colonel Erich von Bamberg. The dead German had been laid out on the ground beside an open grave and he tried to generate some sympathy for the man. That he couldn't was not a surprise. After all was said and done and despite his belated efforts at civility, the Hessian had been a coldblooded and callous murderer of both his own men and those who were innocent. He wondered which part of hell was reserved for men like von Bamberg and monsters like Tarleton and Girty. Perhaps they'd share a cell for all eternity.

That there were rebel spies watching the army maneuver into position came as no surprise, although the audacity of this particular spy was worthy of note. It took courage to simply wander around as if he belonged there and ask questions. In a way, such openness was better than skulking behind trees and peering through telescopes.

The two Hessian soldiers who had been chasing the spy were dumber than oxen and had not seen the face of the spy. All they knew is that he was very tall, very fast, heavily armed, and was accompanied by a large number of rebels, which is why they had given up the chase when Bamberg had been shot. They'd added that it had also been necessary to try to give aid to their beloved colonel whose death the entire Hessian detachment would deeply mourn.

"Bull," Fitzroy muttered and then concluded that the two Hessians weren't as dumb as he'd first thought. They'd avoided a possible ambush by pretending to help a hated officer who was dead before he hit the ground. And mourn my ass, he thought. The Hessians who remained out of von Bamberg's original detachment would celebrate their loathsome commander's death, and Fitzroy wouldn't blame them for one minute. Von Bamberg's second in command was a very young lieutenant who looked overwhelmed by the responsibility thrust upon him.

Fitzroy caught Burgoyne's eye. The general winked. Von Bamberg would not be missed.

Fitzroy wondered just who the spy had been. Perhaps the next time, if there was a next time, that he saw the rebel Major Drake, he would ask him. Then he chuckled. Did he really expect Drake to give him the name of a spy?

"I must be getting old," he mentioned to Danforth who had just joined the group.

"I dare say we all are," said Danforth, "just remember that growing old is far better than dying young. You will join me in a drink or several in honor of the dead German to speed him on his way to Valhalla, will you not?"

Fitzroy smiled. Why not indeed?


Tallmadge looked over the crude map that Will had drawn. The position of the gathering place for the British attack showed that they would attack at very near the center of the American lines. Stark, Schuyler, and Von Steuben watched.

Von Steuben's English had improved over the years from impossible to understand to fairly good. He turned to Will. "Why did your man find it necessary to shoot von Bamberg? I was so looking forward to hanging him by his testicles. Don't let it happen again."

"Sorry, sir," Will said with a smile.

"Their attack will not be very subtle at all," Tallmadge continued. Stark and the others silently agreed. "You've done a good job, Will. This proves that the British are locked into a specific plan of action with little flexibility at all."

Von Steuben growled. "That is the good news. Additional good news is that they will be so massed that virtually anything we fire at them will hit someone and most of them will not be able to fire back at us. The bad is that we will be hard pressed to repel such an overwhelmingly strong attack. We will fight hard, especially my Hessians who have no choice and no hope of a life if we do not win, but I do not think we can stop them."

There was silence as this sunk in. "But we can slow them," Stark said.

"Of course," said Schuyler, "but slow them for what purpose? Or do you propose that we pray for miracles?"

"That would not be a bad idea," Stark added. "However, think of the battle as a vast and bloody test of wills. Yes, they out-number us badly, but they are not fighting for their lives as we will be. Even if they are defeated, the worst that could happen to the survivors is that they would be captured and someday be exchanged and returned home. As for us, any who survived would be hanged or enslaved and, frankly, I'd rather be hanged than live the life that Hamilton, Jefferson, Adams, and so many others are living in Jamaica and elsewhere."

Stark glared at Will. "What about returning to a prison hulk, Major, and starving to death after being flogged and branded anew? If you were lucky and not hanged outright, that is. What do you think about that?"

Will stiffened. "I'll be dead before that happens, sir. I will not be taken prisoner."

Von Steuben chuckled. "Live free or die again, General Stark?"

Stark smiled. "If the statement worked at Bennington, it cannot hurt to use it again."

"Mark this date," Benjamin Franklin said. "It is September 15, 1784, and it is the day on which the fate of our nation will be decided. If it wasn't so frightening, it would be glorious."

Sarah smiled fondly. The old man was dressed and ready even though it wasn't yet dawn. He'd put on old clothes and let it known that he would be present at the battle whether anybody wanted him there or not. Incongruously, he had a pair of duel-ing pistols in his waistband along with a thick knife taken from someone's kitchen. He noticed Sarah staring at them.

"Like so many people, dear Sarah, I too will not be taken alive. I don't fear hanging. Or death, for that matter. After all, I've avoided it for quite a long time and I fear it's ready to catch up to me. No, what I dread is being taken prisoner and carried back to London and put on exhibit like some caged but senile animal. I am far too proud to handle living in my own filth and hearing the ridicule of the British nobility."

Sarah started to speak, but found she couldn't. She began to sob and reached out for him and embraced him. "Except for Will, there is no man on earth that I love more than you, Doctor Franklin."

Franklin returned the embrace and she felt his tears. "Would that you were forty years older, Sarah, or that I were forty years younger."

Owen was awakened from dreams of Faith well before dawn. He grumbled for a moment, then became fully alert. One of General George Rogers Clark's aides was going around and shaking the officers who dutifully followed to where Clark waited.

"Today's the day," Clark said grimly. "Word has it that the British are through rehearsing and will attack before noon. We have orders. We will be dividing into two groups. The first will stay here and shoot as many Redcoats as they can from the flanks of their major attack. You will also try to disrupt the flankers they will have out to protect their so-called phalanx. If you can get any of them to flee, then more the better.

"The second group, the smaller one, will have the pleasure of mucking through the swamp and making sure that the British don't attempt an attack through that miserable body of water that extends to our rear."

Clark glanced at Owen. "Since you've been through the swamp a number of times, Wells, you will lead that group. If they start to come through in force you are to retreat and make sure that we are informed, although I have to admit I have no idea where we'll find reinforcements for you. You are not to stand and fight and be overwhelmed without us knowing that the devils are coming."

Owen was aware of the number of eyes staring at him. He would not make a mistake if he could possibly avoid it. But something bothered him and Clark picked up on it.

"You have a problem, Wells?"

"Not really, General. I understand fully that we are to withdraw and not fight a superior force, but what about an inferior force? What if we see that we can defeat a small force and get into their rear and raise holy hell with them?"

There were chuckles and Clark smiled. "If you think you can destroy the British army by attacking like that, then go ahead. However, I don't think the Redcoats will be so cooperative, even if it is Benedict Arnold commanding that flank. However, don't hesitate if the British offer up themselves as a sacrifice."

The meeting broke up and Owen returned to where Barley and the rest of his men awaited. Along with the twenty men in his command, another sixty would be attached to him and he'd be given the temporary rank of captain. Not bad for an enlisted deserter from the Royal Navy.

"So what do we do?" Barley asked.

"Very simple," Owen said. "We get wet and dirty while watching and waiting, and, if the gods and the British cooperate, we get to raise holy hell with them."

Barley nodded. "Sounds good to me. Just one thing, Acting Captain Wells, there's only one God so don't say gods. Don't tempt the Lord by blaspheming. Like a lot of us, Owen, I've been thinking about death and God and we're in enough trouble without getting Him mad at us too."

Drums rattled and thundered, with fifes piercing the din, as thousands of men marched to their places and their destiny.

Fitzroy thought it was an impressive, even awesome, sight even though the numbers were far less than some of the great and epic battles the British Army had fought. When victory came, and the histories written, this battle would be its own epic.

The men had been fed and almost all looked rested. Some looked confident, while others showed fear and concern on their faces. At least they felt that all their efforts, for good and ill, would come to fruition this day. And, as they looked around, they openly wondered just what if anything could stand before the mighty host of which they were a part.

Frequently, a unit would break into spontaneous cheers if they saw a particular general, like Grant or Burgoyne, or sometimes just for the sheer devil of it.

Burgoyne grinned. "With men like this, just how can we lose?"

Fitzroy agreed.

Banastre Tarleton watched the display of bravado with contempt. In his opinion, Grant was an obese pig and should not be in command of the main attack force, although Tarleton had to admit that Grant had once been a very good and brave general. He also had to admit that Grant had lost a considerable amount of weight on the march, although he still had a ways to go before anyone would consider him trim.

Tarleton's anger, however, was directed more at Burgoyne than Grant, who was simply following orders. That Burgoyne had more confidence in the sixty-four-year-old Grant than in the younger Tarleton was simply beyond his comprehension. An attack like this would require bravery and strength and, while Tarleton acknowledged Grant's fundamental bravery, he doubted that the old man had the strength to follow through. No, he fumed; command of the main assault should have been his.

Nor was Tarleton pleased that Arnold held the left flank which abutted the stinking swamp. At least there was the remote possibility that some of the rebels would come sneaking through, but nothing like that was even remotely possible where he commanded the two regiments that were all that Burgoyne had left him.

Skirmish with the rebels, he'd been told, but don't hazard an attack of your own. Burgoyne had left Tarleton with no doubts as to what would happen if he disobeyed and again went off on his own.

Still, one could hope. In his fantasy, he had terrible things befalling Grant and the attack, and Burgoyne calling on him in desperation to save the day. Were that to occur, he wondered if he would even honor Burgoyne's request. Let Grant and Burgoyne be defeated. Then, the next day, he would assume command and a new attack would succeed.

Or perhaps he should wait until the last bloody damn minute before sending his troops to help pull Grant's chestnuts out of the fire?

Tarleton sighed. He knew his fate. Grant's attack would succeed for the simple reason that he was too strong to fail. Tarleton's men would be permitted to follow and help clean up the debris of what had been an American army.

Still, his first version of the future was the one he liked best.

On the other British flank, Benedict Arnold was equally glum as he contemplated his lost reputation and fortune. His beautiful wife Peggy would be so disappointed in him. She had such expensive tastes.

There would be no glory in holding a flanking position that would protect Grant's enormous and illustrious phalanx and, at the same time, keep an eye on anything that might happen in the swamp.

Like Tarleton, he too had only a pair of regiments and only one consisted of British regulars. The other was made up of the remnants of Joseph Brant's command mingled with Simon Girty's

animals. What a comedown for a man who had commanded armies
to victory! Not that he envied Grant in his position. Arnold was
convinced that the attack was going to be bloodier and far more
difficult than anyone envisaged. Still, it would succeed and all the
glory would be Grant's. Damn it to hell, he thought.

He paced angrily. He was a man of nervous action and standing by doing nothing was not something he did well He turned
to where the swamp would be if he could see it. A low mound
obscured his view and he knew that Burgoyne could not see it
either. He didn't like that, although earlier patrols had proven
that a large detachment could not get through the swamp to
his rear. However, what about a small one? A handful of rebel
irregulars could play holy hell with the British rear.

Arnold smiled. He could actually do something while getting
rid of Girty's swine who would be of no use at all in the coming
fight. He called over an aide.

"Ensign Spencer, go to Mr. Girty and direct him to send Braxton's men into the swamp where they are to watch out for any
rebels attempting to get into our rear. You will command them
as you did previously. This time, however, please let them know
that you are truly in charge and please act like it."

Spencer paled. Going back into the swamp was the last thing
he wanted to do, especially with Braxton the monster. Arnold
smiled inwardly. Spencer was the type of person he both hated
and admired. Spencer was skinny, spoiled, whiny, and totally
unworthy of being an officer in any army. However, he was
also rich, titled and descended from Normans who had landed
in England seven hundred or so years earlier. This made him
privileged, while Arnold was not. So damn him. Arnold also
thought that Spencer's Norman ancestors had likely been made
up of stronger and sterner stuff.

Arnold did smile. "And again, don't forget that, as a British
officer, you will be in command. Don't let those filthy wretches
tell you what do to; no, you tell them what for. Do you understand me, Spencer?"

Arnold saw a flicker of hatred replace the fear in the boy's
eyes. "I understand, sir."

Should the women wear dresses to the battle or not? Sarah
thought the question ridiculous at a time like this. Who cared

what one wore? The British drums were growing louder and it looked like they were ready to march.

Still, the debate had been interesting. One group said that the women would be better off wearing men's clothing because pants were so much more functional. They also said that the British might momentarily think that the Americans had more men than they supposed and react accordingly.

The other side had agreed, but thought that the impact of seeing they were opposed by women in skirts would bring home the fact that putting down the rebellion was so much more than fighting an army of men. The British had to know they were fighting a people.

Abigail Adams had settled the issue. Each woman could do whatever the devil she wished.

Sarah decided to wear a skirt, but she hedged her bet by having pants underneath them. If the skirt proved cumbersome, she would yank it off.

"Or a Redcoat will rip it off for you," Hannah Van Doorn said with an impish grin. "And won't he be shocked to see pants instead of something more intimate."

Beside her, Faith tried to laugh, but she was too nervous, too pale, too scared. So too was Hannah and everyone else. She couldn't imagine how soldiers steeled themselves to go into battle time after time. Sarah looked around and saw her aunt and uncle and then, to her utter astonishment, there was Benjamin Franklin and he was holding a pike. Behind him was John Hancock cradling a light fowling piece, and with them stood virtually all of the members of Congress.

She caught Franklin's eye and he walked over. "I believe I may have said something about hanging separately or hanging together, and this is another one of those moments. If we prevail it will be because of all of us. If we fail, the results will be too dismal to be contemplated."

She was about to say something when a host of men rushed by. They were part of Morgan's contingent and they were heading to their posts behind the earthworks. It was beginning. God help us, she prayed.

In his quarters in New York, Lord Charles Cornwallis had awakened that morning in a cold sweat. He'd had a terrible dream. The only problem was, like most dreams, there was bloody little he could remember of it. He seemed to recall a great battle involving the British Army and a vast mob that obviously represented the American rebels. Or perhaps it was the damned French peasants who still swarmed about the French countryside and threatened to overwhelm the smaller British army that was trying to reinstate the remnants of the monarchy.

Or perhaps it was both of them.

The dreams had been frequent of late. Most had resulted in him awakening overwhelmed with concern about what might be happening to Burgoyne's army.

It was maddening. Time and distance were doing unto him what time and distance did to His Majesty's government in faraway London. For a moment, he felt a twinge of sympathy for Lord North, Stormont, and the others who, like him, were so out of touch with events they desperately needed to control. But only for a moment. The devil take them all.

He would not, of course, mention his dreams to his friend and brother who, with a pair of ships of the line and six frigates, had returned from Boston with the news that the rebels in Massachusetts were largely inactive. It was much the same in New York. It wasn't safe for small British patrols to go too far out of the town, and he didn't have enough men to risk in a larger patrol, but both sides seemed to have adopted a live and let live attitude.

So be it.

He welcomed William to his crudely furnished quarters in the massively reinforced fort at the tip of Manhattan Island. Cornwallis had given up the idea of governing New York from Staten Island, and besides, the plague and fires had almost entirely vanished. So too, unfortunately, had most of the population and almost all of the buildings outside the military encampment. The city of New York was very nearly a ghost town.

William Cornwallis took a seat and glanced at the leather case on a shelf. "Please don't tell me you still have that ghastly thing?"

Cornwallis chuckled. Like himself, William had seen more than enough death, but the idea of a skull in a box along with other bones managed to appall him. "I have my orders," the general said, "or rather, the orders I was originally given have been reiterated. I am to keep Mr. Washington's skull until the appropriate moment, which, I presume would be notice of Burgoyne's victory. At which time I am to make it the centerpiece of a monument to our victory."

"And if we lose?"

"Then I throw the abominable thing in the river and we all sail away."

"And how likely is the likelihood of such a defeat, my dear General."

"The thought of it is the stuff of nightmares, but it is not bloody likely at all, my dear brother."

William laughed genially. Usually the army and the navy did not get along well, but the relationship between Cornwallis and his younger brother was the exception.

"And what do you think of the latest news from England?" William asked.

Lord Cornwallis merely smirked. "More of the same, I'm afraid. There is chaos in France, although the bloodletting does appear to be winding down and it may just be time for some member of the surviving French nobility—Lafayette, perhaps—to take the crown, even though it is likely that any kingship will be under tight controls. Such controls are anathema to our own beloved king, but apparently he will acquiesce if such a limited monarchy can end the killing in France and end any threat to the house of Hanover in England."

William Cornwallis nodded thoughtfully. "And what news from Burgoyne?"

"Nothing," Cornwallis said, "and I am frankly a little worried. There is rebel activity between here and Fort Pitt, which is raising hell with our limited ability to communicate with Burgoyne in the first place."

William poured the two of them a brandy. He raised his glass in a slightly sardonic toast. "Then here's to the next messenger bringing word of a stupendous victory."

At first glance, the three-masted sailing ship looked like a large but disreputable merchantman, the type that was always putting in at Kingston, Jamaica, and delivering cargoes that varied from clothing, to foodstuffs, to slaves.

The name painted on her filthy stern said she was the *Flower*, and, given her appearance and the ripe smell coming from her, the name was utterly incongruous. Once ships like the *Flower* sailed in fear of American privateers and the occasional rebel naval vessel and either sailed in convoys protected by Royal Navy ships, or were heavily armed. Now, they sailed alone, which was just fine with their captains who were a touchy and independent lot, always jockeying for additional profit even if it meant taking on additional risk. Convoys, however safer, stifled creativity, which meant reducing opportunities to make money, often through discreet smuggling. But now there was relative peace since the rebellion had been quashed. The French navy was in disarray, and there was no reason to hide in a convoy.

The *Flower*, however, was not an ordinary merchantman. She was a floating lie. Her captain was a small hard man named John Paul Jones, and she carried no cargo. Along with her crew was a detachment of eighty Marines, men who had sailed on other, regular American Navy ships. Nor was the ship as disreputable as she seemed. Her original clean lines had been purposely and skillfully obscured to make her look totally unthreatening. Rough, even sloppy, painting covered the twelve gun ports that lined each side and totally hid the nine and twelve pound cannon behind them. Additional hastily applied planking altered her true shape.

Nor was the ship's real name something as vapid as the *Flower*. Instead, her true papers showed her to be an American naval warship, the *Liberator*, and she'd been chosen and named for this singular mission. That she was a regular navy ship and not a privateer or a pirate was a distinction that meant a lot only to the officers and men of the *Liberator*, all of whom couldn't wait to paint over the ridiculous name of *Flower*. So far as they knew, she was the only regular navy ship the Colonies now had. John Hancock had signed the commission a few months earlier and it was clearly of dubious legality. The officers and men of the *Liberator* didn't care. She and they had a job to do.

The frigate did not put in at the major port of Kingston. Instead, she anchored in a cove a dozen miles away from the city. This did not attract undue attention. Many planters had their cargoes unloaded at places more convenient to them than the town. As long as duties were paid, no one cared. And if duties weren't paid, then sometimes nobody cared either, especially when a bribe to an underpaid local official was cheaper than paying duty.

When darkness fell, there was no one to see the ship's boats lowered. They were filled with heavily armed Marines who were dressed as ordinary seamen, a fact that they accepted as necessary but resented nonetheless. They were proud of their uniforms, particularly the leather collars that kept their heads proudly upright.

Captain Samuel Nicholas commanded the Marines. Nearly

forty, he'd served with Jones when, in 1775, the pugnacious little Scotsman had command of the *Alfred* and attacked the British in the Bahamas. Thus, neither he nor Jones were strangers to each other or to the Caribbean waters.

Nicholas marched his men quickly overland to their target, a sprawling farm compound a couple of miles inland. However, it was no longer a farm. It was a prison.

It was a little after midnight and all was quiet when they approached. A handful of the stealthier Marines reconnoitered ahead and returned with the information that only a few British soldiers guarded the compound and seemed to be uninterested at best. After all, where would the occupants go even if they did manage to set themselves free?

The Marines waited until a squad was in position to block anyone from escaping down the road to Kingston.

A scream and a musket fired. Nicholas cursed—surprise was lost. "At them," he hollered and his men swarmed into the compound. British guards tumbled out of their barracks and were quickly and brutally cut down by Marine muskets and then by cutlasses and bayonets. It was over in a couple of minutes, and a score of dead and wounded British soldiers were sprawled on the ground, while a handful of others stood with their hands in the air.

"Any of them get away?" Nicholas asked and no one was certain. Nor could the British commander tell them. He had fallen with a musket ball in his neck. The Marines would assume the worst and make all haste back to the ship. Nicholas was suddenly aware of many pairs of eyes watching him and his men from behind the barred windows of the prison buildings.

Nicholas gave the order and the prison buildings were broken into. Scores of confused and bleary-eyed men poured out and stared at the Marines who stared back in dismay at the wretches. The men the Marines had come to liberate were thin to the point of being little more than sticks. Many of them were half naked and their backs bore signs of floggings. Some couldn't stand up and Nicholas suddenly despaired of getting them back to the ship anywhere near as quickly as planned.

Nicholas swore and sent a runner back to Jones with the bad news. It would take longer then planned, and he would need additional manpower from the *Liberator* to help with the men they'd freed while the Marines maintained a rear guard.

Damn, he thought. But that was the way with plans. They never worked out as they were supposed to.

Thus, it was mid-day before the last of the wretched men had been aided across country, and then been helped aboard the *Liberator*, and put below decks. Some of the freed prisoners had to be carried, which meant that litters and stretchers had to be improvised, and all of them needed to be aided during the slow, tortuous journey back to the waiting ship. Many of the Marines and crew of the *Liberator* wept openly at the misery they were witnessing, while all of them treated the freed prisoners with a degree of tenderness and compassion that would have surprised those who'd seen them in battle.

Fortunately, no attack from the city materialized. While the crew of the *Liberator* made ready to sail, the freed men were given soup and fruit and some seemed to improve dramatically. Food and the prospect of freedom will do that to a man, Jones remarked to Nicholas, even though more than a few of them had vomited their meals.

As they raised anchor and put to sea, a small cutter showing the British flag rounded the point of land that had shielded them. Jones ordered the guns run out and a dozen cannon made ready to blow the tiny vessel out of the water. The cutter mounted only swivel guns.

"Chain shot and aim for their rigging," Jones commanded as the cutter came within range.

Twelve cannon fired as one. The two masts on the cutter disintegrated and the little ship began to wallow helplessly.

"Are we going to sink her?" Nicholas asked.

"Nay," said Jones in his thick Scottish accent. "They're now no threat to us and, besides, let them describe us to their British masters. It won't matter. In a matter of hours, this ship won't resemble the one that they saw."

A small, thin man with a scraggly beard and dressed in rags stood before Jones. "On behalf of all of us, dear sir, thank you. A few more months and we might all be dead."

Jones bowed. "You are more than welcome, sir. Now, may I ask who you might be?"

"John Adams," he replied.

Jones smiled. He knew they'd struck gold in Jamaica. Adams was one of the surviving American leaders they'd wanted most to free. "Welcome aboard."

Adams smiled and Jones winced. Several of Adams' teeth were missing and others were rotten. They had paid a terrible price in their Jamaican prison. They had survived, sort of, but the health of many of them was doubtless ruined. Jones wondered why the bastard British hadn't killed their prisoners outright instead of letting them live on in agony. Because the British truly were bastards, he decided.

"Captain Jones, may I inquire as to our destination?" Adams asked.

Jones wished he had a simple answer for Adams and the others. So much was out of his control. Almost everything would depend on the actions of others many hundreds of miles away. His plans called for him to call at a French port for food and news of the war and, if all was well, he would choose between Boston and New Orleans as a destination. And if all was not well? Well, he thought he could find a place, but the current political situation was complicating matters. During the revolution, the world was against Britain, but now, the world was on her side and against the madmen in revolutionary France. A handful of islands remained under French control and these were being ignored by the British, but they represented nothing in the way of long-term safety. The only good thing about the fighting in Europe was that it had pulled away many of the Royal Navy warships that ordinarily prowled the Caribbean.

In truth, the only nation he could think of that might be sympathetic to the American cause was Russia, where Catherine the Great ruled. He had no idea just how he might make it to St. Petersburg if he had to, although he did have a Russian flag in his quarters and a letter from Catherine inviting him to come and join her navy. He wondered what either would get him if a British seventy-four gun ship of the line stopped him.

Still, he'd gotten his orders and fulfilled them. What the devil to do next was the problem.

"Hopefully, sir, we'll have a home in a free country. If not, we may have to sail the seas forever. Perhaps we might be fortunate and find a tropical paradise in the South Pacific."

# Chapter 21 ★ ★ ★ ★ ★ ★ ★ ★ ★ ★ ★ ★ ★ ★ ★ ★ ★

THE SOUND OF THE DRUMS CHILLED THEM, AND MEN ON BOTH sides shivered despite the summer's warmth. The red-coated beast was beginning to stir. What had been almost casual lines of British soldiers changed into straight lines that were intimidating in their precision.

To either side of the British phalanx, cannon boomed. Fitzroy watched as the two rescued nine-pounders belched out the rocks that were all that could be fired from them. Predictably, they did little more that stir up dirt on the hill, resulting in derisive taunts from the defenders. Their intended use was to frighten the rebels and Fitzroy was afraid that they'd become laughably ineffective.

The same happened with the guns taken from the two schooners. Since the ships were now defenseless, they had been sent back to Mackinac. These small guns also sent their projectiles into the earthworks with no apparent effect.

Not a most auspicious start, Fitzroy thought. As he approached Burgoyne, he saw Tarleton ride off, whipping his horse in petulant anger.

Burgoyne smiled calmly. "You saw Tarleton depart, I trust?"

"Indeed, sir, and he looked very angry."

"He was. Once again he asked for the honor of leading the army and once again I declined his offer. I did think, however, that the timing of his request was most unusual."

"Sir?"

"Yes, because he waited until he knew it would be impossible for me to honor it under any circumstances. If anyone hasn't noticed, the attack is commencing and there would be no reason on earth to remove Grant at this late moment, and replace him with Banastre Tarleton even if I desired it, which I don't. This proves only one thing, in my opinion. Do you know what that is, dear cousin?"

"I have thoughts, General."

"Share them."

Fitzroy laughed sharply. "Deep down, Banastre Tarleton is a coward. He's fantastically good at raiding small units when he outnumbers them, and butchering prisoners and civilians. But put him up against a good fighter, as happened when he took on Morgan at the Cowpens, and he fails and runs."

Burgoyne nodded and smiled, "My sentiments exactly. Where General Arnold is both brave and foolhardy, Tarleton is merely foolhardy and not brave at all. No, General Grant is the professional whose services I trust. Ergo, he commands the attack."

Burgoyne took a deep breath. "Regardless, to what do I owe the honor of your presence? Do tell me that you wish something other than you too commanding the assault."

Fitzroy flushed. It wasn't that far from the mark. "No, but I do wish to be released so I can join General Grant in the center of the phalanx."

Given the size of the British formation and the potential difficulty in controlling it, Grant had placed himself and his small staff almost exactly in its middle. It was a unique solution to a unique situation.

"Sorry James, but you may not. I need you here in case something unexpected happens, which is usually the case when two armies collide. I understand and commend your desire to be at the center of the fighting, but my and the army's needs must come first. I must have someone I trust nearby."

Fitzroy was disappointed, but understood. But he also felt relieved. Even if the rebel defenses collapsed, they would not do so until they had taken more than the proverbial pound of flesh from the British attackers. The thought of the carnage to take place chilled him. Perhaps Tarleton wasn't the only coward on the field of battle.

★   ★   ★

Burned Man Braxton stared in disbelief. Behind him a battle was beginning and this arrogant young jackass was giving *him* orders. Worse, the snot had the power of General Arnold and the British hierarchy behind him. It was all due to a rule that said a British officer of any rank was superior to a militia officer of any rank. Thus, the very young Ensign Spencer, whose nose actually was draining snot onto his chin, had announced that he would command the detachment going into the swamp.

For a moment Braxton understood why the colonists had rebelled. He put the heretical thought out of his mind. He would obey orders no matter what he thought of them. English victory would put him that much closer to wreaking vengeance on the people who had maimed him.

He also thought that he would put a musket ball into Ensign Spencer's head if the little boy's actions threatened Braxton's existence. Glancing at the men around him, he thought he wasn't the only one who would finish Ensign Spencer if the need arose.

"I want the men closer together than the last time," Spencer said. "There's too much danger of us getting separated and losing contact if we spread out."

Braxton nodded and passed on the order. He had his doubts, but he also understood that the boy was at least a little bit correct. If his men got separated and if any of them ran into the rebels, there was the real danger that they could be destroyed by an inferior force. They might also get lost.

"Then let's go," Spencer said and wiped his nose on his sleeve.

The approaching horde of British soldiers was slightly obscured by the dust that thousands of marching feet were kicking up. Will could not begin to fathom what was going on in the minds of the British soldiers as they marched forward. A pennant was raised in the middle of the block of men and he presumed it showed where whatever senior officer who commanded the army was located. Intelligence said it was General Grant, and Will had no reason to doubt it. Grant was a logical choice. Still, the pennant made a splendid target, or it would when it and the British army came closer.

He mounted his scrawny horse and took his position alongside Brigadier General William Washington, who nodded. Behind them were the hundred and fifty men who constituted the entire mounted force that the Americans could field. Not even Washington could call them cavalry and keep a straight face. They were mounted infantry on bedraggled ponies that were so small that several men's feet almost dragged on the ground.

Still, they remained better than Burgoyne's cavalry, which was nonexistent. The British had brought fewer than fifty horses and most of those that hadn't been killed by crossbow bolts were being utilized by the British for use by couriers and ranking officers.

If opportunities presented themselves, however, William Washington's men could cause damage. With knowledge of exactly where the British were going to attack, Stark had ordered that lanes be opened through the thickets in hopes that spoiling attacks on the British could take place. The lanes were not visible to the British as the brush entanglements had not been removed, merely loosened so they could be pulled aside quickly.

The small American cannon boomed. If they hit anything, no dust was raised up so Will couldn't tell. "I hope they are aiming at that damned pennant," he said.

"Why bother," said Washington. "At a point, whoever is commanding won't control anything and, besides, how do you know that the pennant isn't a ruse to get us to waste our ammunition shooting at it?"

Will agreed. A small commotion behind the American lines caught his attention. "You won't need me for a few moments, will you?"

William Washington laughed good-naturedly. "Didn't think I needed you at all, Drake."

Will found Sarah's uncle Wilford sweating heavily as he pushed a wooden contraption into position. It and a number of others had been hauled up the hill and manhandled into place by groups of older men and women. Some of the men, however, had the look of artisans and seemed pleased with themselves. For his part, Will could only gape. He had only seen things like this in history books.

Wilford wiped sweat from his brow and smiled at Will. "Damn it, son, I am too old for this."

"Wilford, have you and Dr. Franklin gone out of your minds? You have brought us catapults with which to fight the British."

"Catapults, Will, were used to batter down the walls of many

enemy castles and cities in the Middle Ages. These little devices
are designed to kill soldiers."

"How?"

"Originally, it was thought they could hurl pointed and weighted
projectiles at the enemy. The balance of the projectiles would cause
them to fall point down and find British flesh. Sadly, we found
we didn't have the ability to make enough of the projectiles to be
worthwhile, so we determined that they could be used to throw
rocks at them, large, man-killing rocks and large numbers of them."

Drake shook his head. "Clever and good, but they won't stop
that army."

"No, but they will cause casualties and annoy the hell out of
it. Anyone who is hit by a good-sized rock will be either killed
or seriously injured with badly broken bones."

Wilford was correct, of course. But the ultimate truth was
that only another army could stop the British. Still, the idea of
distracting and bleeding the British had considerable merit.

"Any other ideas from yours and Franklin's fertile minds,
Wilford?"

"See those jugs half buried in the ground?"

"I do."

"And see the ropes leading from them?"

Will grinned, his curiosity piqued. "Of course."

"When the time is right, I and others will pull on those ropes
and when that happens, do yourself a favor, Will. Don't be anywhere near those jugs."

Owen Wells led his men behind the Loyalists commanded by
Braxton and the little British officer. With the British bunched
up, it had been a simple matter to wait for the men led by Braxton and the little ensign to go past. Nor was there any problem
staying unnoticed. Individually, a man traveling through the
woods could hear other sounds, but a group of them, however
hard they would try to, just couldn't remain silent. Nor could
their ears easily pick up other sounds as they sloshed through
the water and the muck.

Owen ordered his men to move out in a manner that basically mirrored Braxton's force. To his delight, Braxton and his
men were totally focused on their front and not their rear. The
two groups were approximately the same number as they slogged

through the dank water that came well over their knees. Owen signaled his crossbowmen to go to the front. When they got to within twenty or thirty yards of the enemy he waved his arm and a score of crossbow bolts flew to their targets.

A dozen enemy soldiers screamed or fell silently into the water, their bodies pierced by the bolts. The remainder turned and milled, searching for their attackers. Owen heard a high-pitched and youthful voice calling for the Loyalists to open fire. Muskets barked, but at what? Owen's men had dropped to the water or taken position behind trees.

The crossbowmen quickly reloaded and fired again, striking several more targets. Owen urged his men up and toward the enemy soldiers who were frantically reloading the muskets they'd so foolishly emptied at the trees. At nearly point-blank range, Owen's men fired their own muskets with devastating effect and hurled themselves at the confused survivors of Braxton's force.

The two groups became a howling, splashing, bloody tangle as men clubbed each other with rifle butts, stabbed with knives or hacked with tomahawks. Men wrestled and bit and fell beneath the water, some to remain there. Braxton's Loyalists fought desperately. The Americans now outnumbered them and were between them and refuge back in the British lines.

Owen saw Braxton with a pistol in one hand and a tomahawk in the other. He was bleeding from a crossbow wound in his leg and was having difficulty standing. The little British officer lay face down in the muck, his arms and legs twitching. One of Owen's men ran up to Braxton, who shot him in the face. Another of Owen's men took a tomahawk swipe in the arm and reeled away, screaming. Braxton was a wounded and dangerous animal and several Americans were keeping their distance.

"Mine!" yelled Owen. His own rifle was empty and his remaining weapon was a broad-bladed knife. As he approached Braxton, the scarred man seemed puzzled. "I want to kill you, Braxton."

"Who the fuck are you?" he snarled.

Owen decided he didn't want to inform the gathering circle of men in any detail about what had happened to Faith and her family. Or for that matter, Winifred Haskill, who was slowly recovering from her even greater ordeal at the hand of Braxton.

Owen swung his knife in a lazy arc, confident that Braxton couldn't escape. "Let's say I am a friend of some people you hurt."

Braxton laughed. "That'd be a large number, short boy." he said. To Owen's surprise, he threw the tomahawk, causing Owen to duck, and charged awkwardly at Owen. The two men collided, and Owen lost his knife. They grappled with their hands and Owen was astonished at how strong Braxton was. But being shorter gave him greater leverage than Braxton. The two rolled around in the muck, seeking advantage. Finally, Owen managed to get his arms around Braxton's waist and buried his head in the other man's back before the other man could find his throat or eyes.

Owen began to squeeze with his heavily muscled arms.

Braxton grunted and tried to break Owen's grip. He couldn't. Nor could he reach behind and find Owen's eyes to gouge out as Owen's head was in his back, and Owen's testicles were also out of reach. Braxton's grunts turned to groans and his body began to thrash and arch as Owen squeezed the life out of his chest.

The groans became cries of agony and Owen used all his strength and energy to increase pressure. Finally, there was the terrible sound of bones breaking. Owen continued to squeeze even though he thought his own lungs would explode from the effort. Braxton tried to scream, but he couldn't gather his breath to do it.

There was a nauseating crack as Braxton's spine snapped. Braxton sagged and was still. His eyes were open, but he couldn't move. In a moment, Braxton's eyes glazed over and he was dead.

Owen allowed Barley to pull him off and help him to his feet, shaking and exhausted. "He's dead and that's good," Barley said. "Now maybe you can get over your personal feud and let us get back to fighting the British."

Owen inhaled deeply and realized his mistake. All his remaining men, maybe thirty of them, were gathered around them, wide-eyed. They'd been watching the brawl. Any survivors from Braxton's group had fled and probably gotten back to the British lines. Worse, the little officer had managed to get up and run away as well.

"How many escaped?" he asked.

"Maybe six of them. Not more than ten," Barley answered. "One of them was that officer. I saw him waddling away like he'd crapped his pants and he probably did."

Owen wished Barley had thought to stop them as he counted his own survivors. Thirty-two effectives. Ten of his men were dead and another handful too wounded to continue. He ordered a couple of men to help the wounded back to the American lines. He turned and addressed the rest.

"The swamp ends in a little ways and there's a hill just beyond it. I want to see what's on the other side, don't you?"

Barley laughed. "What if it's the whole British Army?"

"Then we'll run like our pants are on fire back into the swamp and hide. But before we do that, maybe we can cause some more harm to the Redcoats. Are you with me?"

His men gave him a ragged cheer. They had already begun picking up their rifles and other discarded weapons and were loading and cleaning. He told them to load any weapon they could find. He gave them a few moments to get organized and ordered them forward.

The old man's open eyes stared vacantly in the direction of the two men who sat before him—one a young man and the other a boy barely into adolescence. Owl couldn't see them, but he knew them well. He had sent them and others out to watch the white men and their armies. And to learn.

The young man was a skilled and brave warrior who had fought the Americans. He was named Little Turtle and the boy was his nephew, Tecumseh. The old man knew he was going to die soon, which was the reason he'd been chosen to make the important and terrible decision regarding their destiny. The fate of the tribes in the area depended upon his judgment. If he chose correctly, then his name would be remembered in song as a hero. If he was wrong, well, he'd still be dead. His bones ached and his leathery skin was cracked. He would not see another spring. Some days he thought death would be a welcome friend and in the cold and lonely dark of night he was certain of it.

The old man spoke. "And what is happening to our future enemies?"

"They are killing each other, grandfather," Little Turtle said. "And they are doing so with ferocity and skill I never thought the white man possessed."

The old man nodded. The loose alliance of tribes had first been shocked when the Americans came to their area, and their shock had turned to horror when they saw how many Americans there were and how well armed and disciplined they were. When they'd heard that another force of white men was gathering to drive the Americans away, they'd rejoiced at the thought that they would be rid of the white invaders. As they waited for this miraculous event to occur, they'd decided to remain peaceful with the Americans, trading with them and observing them until the British arrived. Then they would pounce and earn the gratitude of the British.

The British had come in astonishing numbers, but had brought the hated Iroquois as their allies. All the tribes in the area felt betrayed. If the English were allied with their enemy, then they too were the enemy.

"You are my eyes, Little Turtle, did you see the armies prepare?"

In the distance they could hear rumble of war. "I did, grandfather, and I watched them begin to fight. They are not like real warriors the way they march and move. In some ways it is almost funny, but in others it is frightening. They have discipline and guns, while we have neither. They also have numbers far larger than we can gather even if all the tribes united as one. And, despite the foolish way they fight, they are very brave. They would be formidable enemies." He shook his head sadly. "Others of our people remain to observe them while I speak with you."

Although Little Turtle had fought the Americans, it had been in the form of raids, not battles like the one beginning to take place.

The old man was concerned. "You and Tecumseh have not been detected have you?"

Tecumseh answered. "No, grandfather, we have not. But I wonder if it would matter if we were? Both sides know we are out here because these are our lands. Indeed, grandfather, I would be surprised if they did not expect us to be out here, watching and waiting. I'm sure they wonder what we are going to do as do we."

The old man smiled inwardly. The boy was so smart. Little Turtle was a war leader, but Tecumseh possessed the wisdom of a far older man. Tecumseh, if he lived, was the future. If there was a future for the red man, he thought sadly.

The old man smiled. "Tecumseh, tell me what you did when you heard the first cannon?"

Tecumseh grinned. "I nearly jumped out of my skin."

Owl grinned and Little Turtle laughed, "And the second time?"

"Then I merely flinched, grandfather, as I realized they weren't aiming their flying stones at me. Then they became like the thunder in a rainstorm."

The old man nodded. "Little Turtle, could we fight them?"

Little Turtle shrugged then remembered with mild chagrin that the old man couldn't see the gesture. "Of course we could fight them, but we wouldn't win, not even against their smallest army. They all have muskets or rifles, which we do not, and, as has been said, they have many more warriors then we have. You are right, father, we must not have the white men as enemies."

"Yet at least one of the two groups must be," the old man said softly.

But which one, he wondered? The Americans who said they only wished to return to their homes in the east, or the British who wished to drag the Americans away? Both groups had said they wished to depart, which would be good for the tribes. But who could believe either of them? The white men always came, but they never left and it didn't matter who they fought for. The British, if they won, would doubtless leave a fort, like Mackinac, and traders would come who would corrupt the tribes with liquor and cheap goods in return for furs. The Americans would return to their homes in the east if they won, but would all of them depart? Certainly not. Where the white men went, they always stayed. They had contempt for the red man who they thought of as ignorant, drunken savages. Sadly, the white men were often correct. Alcohol and smallpox had ruined so many tribes.

So which of the two armies would be the enemy? Or would it be both? The several hundred warriors gathered in the woods behind him wondered the same thing.

Danforth was in the middle of the British Army with Grant, and it was rapidly becoming a mob. Even General Grant grudgingly admitted that he was losing control. Grant professed to be unconcerned. "Everything breaks down when the fighting begins. Just keep marching towards the enemy and all will be well."

Danforth agreed except for one thing—the fighting hadn't really begun. American and British cannon had been firing at each other for some minutes and to little effect. American riflemen were firing slowly and carefully at the ponderously moving British horde, but were of no concern to any but the men in the first few ranks. Those men in front would be terribly bloodied before this day was over, but that was their fate. The ones who fell would be replaced by those behind and the inexorable advance would continue.

Danforth was concerned that the structure of the British force was proving even more unwieldy than thought. Even Grant had been a little surprised by that fact. Still, the British Army moved forward. The Americans would be crushed.

A soldier near them screamed and fell to his knees. "What the devil?" Danforth exclaimed. The man had been wounded by a falling rock.

Benedict Arnold looked at Ensign Spencer with some sympathy. The boy's left arm dangled uselessly and there was a large and growing welt on the boy's forehead. He was in intense pain and was having difficulty standing.

"General, we went into the swamp as you ordered and we were ambushed. There must have been hundreds of them and they had us surrounded. Only a handful of men managed to get away."

"Where's Braxton?" Girty snapped.

"I don't know," Spencer said and began to blubber.

Arnold was sympathetic to the boy. "Go have your wounds tended to. Your first battle is over. And for God's sake wipe your nose."

Arnold thought quickly. He doubted that "hundreds" of rebels had infiltrated through the swamp, but there had obviously been more than enough to overwhelm Braxton's and Spencer's command. Whatever numbers out there could play hell in the British rear unless he did something to stop it.

As if to punctuate his thoughts, puffs of smoke appeared on the hill blocking his view of the swamp. Arnold stood and swore. The insolent bastards were firing on them. He made up his mind.

"Girty, I will take your command and all but two companies of regulars and attack those rebels coming at us from the swamp. That should be more than enough to send any American force packing."

That and it would show him acting decisively in the face of an unexpected enemy. Perhaps the day would turn out well for him after all.

★　　★　　★

Burgoyne also saw the firing from the hill and was dismayed by the obvious fact that an unknown number of rebels had worked their way behind him. The impassible swamp was obviously not as impassible as he'd been led to believe. Had a large force gotten in his rear, or was it just a minor thing?

Damn Arnold, he seethed, could the man do nothing right? Quite obviously reinforcements were needed to plug the rebel entry point from the swamp.

"Fitzroy, get over there and tell Arnold to send more men to reinforce the swamp area. Damn it," Burgoyne raged, "must I do everything myself? Why the devil didn't I get generals who could think?"

Fitzroy was about to ask for a clarification of the orders, but the look of fury on Burgoyne's face told him it was not a good idea. If the general wanted more men sent to their left, then more men would be sent.

Fitzroy mounted his bedraggled excuse for a horse and urged it where Arnold was supposed to be. If Arnold wasn't there, he would issue orders on General Burgoyne's behalf. He would do it and return as quickly as possible as the furious sounds to his right and front said that the battle was rapidly approaching its climax.

# Chapter 22 ★★★★★★★★★★★★★★★★★

A T JUST UNDER THREE HUNDRED YARDS, AMERICAN RIFLEMEN opened fire, carefully aiming at the officers. These were easily recognized by the metal gorgets, reminders of medieval armor, that hung from their necks. The shiny devices also made excellent aiming points, and, even at extreme range, the riflemen quickly made kills.

At two hundred and fifty yards, both Morgan and von Steuben realized that there was no reason to hold back the musket-firing regulars. Even though their weapons weren't at all accurate at that range, the mass of enemy meant that shots didn't have to be aimed or accurate to hit someone.

The American Hessians in von Steuben's brigade grinned openly as they began to blaze away with their new weapons.

In the British mass, General Grant listened to the volume of fire to his front and realized something was wrong. "What the devil is happening?" he said to Danforth. "They can't possibly reload a musket as quickly as they are. Could people be passing extras to them?"

Danforth thought it was a logical conclusion and one that didn't bode well for the men in the British front ranks. It now looked like they would suffer even heavier casualties than expected. Worse, the absurd but potentially fatal steady rain of rocks continued.

Danforth hopped onto a fallen tree and got a view of the field in front of him. He watched as some of the Americans received loaded weapons passed on to them while others continued to load and fire at an astonishing rate. The truth dawned on him.

He jumped down and grabbed the general by the arm. "Some of them appear to have Ferguson rifles," Danforth said breathlessly.

Grant paled. The breech-loading Ferguson rifle that could be loaded and fired many times faster than a musket was thought to have disappeared after the defeat and death of their inventor, Colonel Patrick Ferguson, at the Battle of King's Mountain. The British army had earlier rejected them as too expensive and the totality of Ferguson's defeat had put an end to any further debate on the value of the weapon.

But now, somehow, Ferguson rifles, or something very much like them, were being used against them. What in God's name were the rebels up to, Grant wondered? First they threw rocks at them like uncivilized barbarians and then they followed up with a gun that might be superior to anything the British had.

This was indeed going to be a long and bloody day.

As the first British ranks neared the American lines, their dead and wounded were pushed aside, even trampled, some to a bloody pulp, but the mass of Redcoats continued on. At fifty yards, they were at the lip of the shallow dirt moat that protected the Americans.

Behind the earthworks, General Stark looked to where a number of Schuyler's men were waiting to pull the lanyards that were connected to the jugs that were half buried in the ground. He took a deep breath, nodded, and turned away.

One of the men pulling a lanyard was Sarah's uncle, Wilford. He looked at the approaching mass of screaming faces and pulled.

The entire front of the British line was shattered by the explosions that blew up clouds of dirt, flames, bodies, and parts of bodies. Behind them, others were shredded by the rocks and pieces of metal that had been buried in the jugs along with quantities of gunpowder, or burned by the oil that had been in the jugs. There was silence and then the screams began. The entire mass of British soldiers seemed to groan and then stop.

In the middle, but now much closer to the front as the result of heavy British casualties, General Grant quickly recovered from the shock of the explosions. He had to get the army moving again or everything was doomed. Beside him, Danforth was almost too stunned to speak.

Grant lay about him with the flat of his sword. He screamed and cajoled and, within moments, so too did his officers and sergeants and they began to reassert control. Slowly, painfully, the British mass began again to inch its way forward, covering the remaining few yards to the American earthworks. American bayonets protruded and rifles fired, but the British pressed on until, finally, the two forces collided with screams and primal howls.

Only half aware of what was happening to the bulk of the army, Fitzroy galloped up to the captain commanding the remainder of Arnold's command. Arnold wasn't there, which puzzled him, but no matter. He quickly gave the order as he understood it to a captain of regulars—reinforcements were to be sent to stop an attack from the swamp to their rear. The captain saluted and began to bark out orders. Satisfied that his orders would be obeyed, Fitzroy turned and rode back to Burgoyne.

The British captain was puzzled. How many men were needed to plug the exit from the swamp? The silly boy, Spencer, had gone and failed, and he had been followed by reinforcements led by Girty and Arnold, and yet, apparently, it wasn't enough.

He had fewer than two hundred men with which to hold a flanking position that now seemed irrelevant. The two armies had made horrible contact and were locked in mortal combat.

He came to a conclusion. Nothing was going to be decided where he was and his latest orders were specific—reinforce the flank. At least he would be away from the horror of the two armies clawing each other to pieces and the possibility that he would be ordered into the charnel house. He ordered his remaining men to follow him and move rapidly towards the hill where they'd seen shooting.

From the top of Mount Washington, William Washington watched incredulously as the last of the British skirmishers trotted, almost ran, towards whatever fighting was going on in the swamp. What the devil was happening there, he wondered. It didn't matter. He decided that what he saw was an opportunity.

At his command, men ran forward and cleared away enough of the thicket to permit horsemen to ride through them in a column of twos. He signaled and his men rode their horses forward at the trot. They could not gallop. In his opinion, half of the nags would collapse and die if they tried it. They were less than a hundred yards away from the side of the British phalanx; most of whom didn't even see his men, so preoccupied were they with advancing forward over their dead and dying comrades. Those who did turn and see just looked on incredulously. Not a shot was fired in the direction of the small force of American cavalry, and it occurred to Washington that the British weapons were empty to prevent accidentally shooting their own side.

Will was with Washington's force and soon found himself in the position of being behind both the main British army and out of sight of the British force that had just disappeared over the hill.

"Now what?" he asked of Washington.

Washington winked. "Damned if I know. Never thought we'd get this far and still be alive. See those cannon to our right front?" Will did. "Why don't we ride over there and take them?"

With yells and whoops, Washington's hundred-odd cavalry trotted towards the two pair of guns that had been firing ineffectively at the American works.

Some of the gunners ran, but most tried to defend their weapons with pistols and cutlasses. Washington's men responded with the blunderbuss-like Franklins and sabers.

Will slashed at a British sailor and saw him fall. Another tried to pull him from his horse, but Will hit him on the head with the handle of his sword, while, a moment later, another American ran the man down with his horse.

It was over in a couple of minutes. A dozen dead British and half as many Americans littered the field. The remainder of the British contingent was running in all directions. It was a sweet little victory, Will thought. It felt good, damned good, to finally come to grips with the enemy, and even better to win a fight, however small.

Will Washington was flushed but happy. He'd come to the same conclusion. He looked at the four cannon and grinned. "Anybody here know how to work these damned things?"

"I do, at least a little bit," Will heard himself say.

Washington grinned engagingly. "Damned if you aren't a man of parts, Drake."

Astonished by the surprisingly overwhelming British response to their foray, Owen led his men back into the swamp where they continued to snipe at the British who were lined up at its edge, apparently unwilling to get their feet wet. Girty's men, never the bravest, were holding back, content with occasionally firing their rifles at some target visible only to themselves.

Owen had received a few dozen reinforcements and was using them to good effect. The British force now numbered several hundred men and, if they chose to advance into the swamp, could easily push him back and leave the way open to the American rear. He could not allow that to happen, although it seemed that, at least for the moment, the British had little intention of trying it. He saw a man he presumed to be some general running around and waving a sword. Just out of range, he decided, and Barley concurred. Too bad, they both concluded. It would be great to take down a British general.

The American army was dying.

Nearly half of von Steuben's Hessians were dead or badly wounded or crawling back to find help that didn't exist. The same was true with Morgan's men. There were just too many British and, no matter how hard or how desperately the Americans fought, additional Redcoats clambered over the growing pile of bodies to hack and slash at the dwindling number of rebels.

Musket fire had ceased to be effective and the battlefield was strangely void of the sound of gunfire, with only howls and screams being heard. Slowly, the Americans were forced back from the earthworks. As the rebels fell back, the British instinctively stretched their lines to the left and right in an attempt to overlap the Americans. In desperation, Stark called for Wayne to attack from his flank even though it meant virtually abandoning the works confronting a strangely quiet Tarleton. It was a chance that had to be taken. Every chance had to be taken.

General John Stark stood a few feet behind the churning, howling mass of humanity that was the battle. His orders to Wayne meant he had no more men left. It was over. He had no other troops to add. Now the real dying would begin.

He turned to Daniel Morgan who had painfully struggled out of his litter. Stark drew his sword and shrugged. "Live free or die," he said softly. "Time to make good on that statement, isn't it, Daniel?"

Morgan grinned and drew a pistol and a tomahawk from his

belt, while Stark pulled out one of Franklin's maces. "As good a time as any, I'd say."

Both men bulled their way into the savage fighting.

Tarleton read the order and dismissed it. Burgoyne wanted him to use the regiments at his disposal to attack the American lines directly in front of him, the very same defenses that had cost him so dearly just a few days earlier. Didn't the man realize that nothing had been done to reduce them?

Apparently Burgoyne thought that the rebels had abandoned their works and sent all their men to support those trying to stop the advance of the British phalanx.

But why, Tarleton wondered. The phalanx seemed to be making progress and Redcoat soldiers were beginning to lap over the rebel works like an irresistible wave. And yes, he could hear guns firing to his left and beyond the main British thrust, but surely Arnold had things well in hand. The man might be a turncoat and a traitor, but he was a damned good fighting general for all that.

No, Tarleton thought. He would not advance, at least not yet. His original orders called for him to attack when the main attack broke through and that must be what Burgoyne was reminding him of. With just a little more than a thousand men at his disposal, even a small number of rebels behind their defenses could stymie him and cause enough casualties to result in another sardonic tongue-lashing from his beloved commanding general. Another debacle as perceived by Burgoyne might be injurious to Tarleton's career.

Tarleton smiled. He would not attack. At least not just yet, he repeated. If Burgoyne had gotten himself into trouble, he had more than enough men to solve his own problem. He, Banastre Tarleton, would wait for the right moment and then strike. That, he decide, would be the way to win glory for himself and erase any memories of the disaster at Cowpens.

The naval gun carriages had been built for use on a ship and were designed to be stabilized and controlled by ropes and pulleys. On land they were awkward and cumbersome and prone to topple over. However, some clever minds in the British Army had figured out how to stabilize them through the use of strong tree limbs that projected in various directions.

The British were not able to develop wheels for the cannon, which meant that the American soldiers who had captured them had to use muscle power and their horses to drag them into a better position to damage the British advance.

After what seemed like forever, the American cavalrymen wrestled the four guns—two four pounders and two nine pounders—into position. Under Drake's cautious direction, they charged them with powder and poured a combination of rocks and trash down their muzzles. Drake wasn't certain just how much powder the guns took, so he intentionally underloaded them. At least he hoped he had. An exploding cannon could kill a lot of men.

Curiously, the British rear ranks seemed oblivious to what they were doing; the British were totally fixated on the bloody action to their front. They probably thought the men working the guns were British, he concluded.

Drake grabbed Washington's arm, startling the more senior officer. "William, I think we'll have a chance to get off two rounds, maybe three, before they realize what's happening. Then we'll have to leave the guns and run like the devil."

Washington nodded, then grinned wolfishly. "Then let's get started."

Will was uncertain as to the safety of the guns and decided that only he would fire them. He told the men to step back about fifty yards and lie down. He took a deep breath and touched a burning match to the firing hole. When the powder began to sputter he ran to the second gun and repeated the process.

By the time he'd reached the third, the first and second had fired. He grinned at the fact that he was still alive, and fired the third and fourth. When the dust and smoke cleared, he saw that the rear ranks of the British Army had been shredded. Men were piled up in bloody heaps.

"Don't gawk," Washington yelled. "Reload, damn it, reload!"

Many people said that little Winifred Haskill was still more than a little mad from the abuse she'd received, and they were right. As the day of battle approached, she rarely spoke and rarely ate. She existed and nothing more.

The only persons with whom she did speak were Sarah and the Hessian sergeant, Horst Bahlmann. Bahlmann was the one who had given her a pike and taught her to use it, which pleased her.

She longed for the day when she could use it to take revenge on the people who had raped her, murdered her family, and then tried to burn her alive. That the British regulars were not the same as the scum that Girty and Braxton commanded didn't matter. She had correctly concluded that the British were the paymasters and leaders of people like Braxton. She had also learned that it had been Tarleton who had ordered Braxton out to destroy her people; thus, the British were at the heart of the disaster that had befallen her. Now they would pay.

She held her pike in her small hands and stared at the carnage that was taking place just a few yards in front of her. Behind her, Sarah, Faith, and hundreds of other women also watched. They were shocked and horrified by the sights and sounds and smells before them. The training they'd received now made them think they had been children playing at war. Many had seen death and fighting, but nothing on a scale like this.

The women had held back. They were on the American right flank and could see where the larger British force was pushing the Americans back and lapping over their flank. They were losing and it would be over soon. General Schuyler was with the few hundred older men who were not part of a regular unit. He had dismissed the women's role as irrelevant.

The women wanted to do something, but were stunned into immobility. At first, Winifred Haskill had been standing with them, but she had gradually moved forward. It was as if she was possessed by a mad desire to get closer to the killing. Sarah had grabbed her arm, but Winifred angrily shook her off. She mumbled something about Bahlmann being in danger and lurched toward the battle.

Winifred recoiled as a wounded American soldier staggered by her and stumbled to the rear. He was screaming soundlessly and trying to hold his intestines inside his ripped stomach. Then, to her utter horror, a Hessian walked out and fell to his knees. The top of his head and much of his face was gone.

Winifred shook like a small tree in a wind. In her mind she saw Bahlmann, her guardian, lying dead before her. She screamed like an animal and ran towards the British. She pointed her pike at a British soldier and rammed it into his chest with all the force her little body could generate. He collapsed in a heap. She tried to pull it out, but couldn't. Another Redcoat ran his bayonet through her chest and lifted her body into the air, shaking it like a dog before it came free.

At that moment, cannon fire erupted in the British rear. The crowd of American women snapped. Madness of their own overtook them. Primal howls came from hundreds of female throats and they surged at the British.

Now the British flank was being overlapped by the horde of screaming women, who jabbed and hacked at the stunned Redcoats with pikes and axes, or smashed at them with their maces while the British only slowly began to fight back at them. In their insane fury, the women never heard the cannon fire again.

In the middle of the American ranks, Wilford Benton placed the last load of rocks on his catapult. He had no idea whether he'd hit anything or not, although it seemed more than probable that he had. It was obvious, though, that his efforts had been for naught. The British advance had been staggered but not stopped. Like the tide, or maybe a lava flow, it continued inexorably.

Wilford heard the cries and screams to his right and knew that the women had attacked. "God bless them," he mumbled, "and God help them." He pulled the rope that launched the rocks skyward.

"We're done," he said to the two men who were helping him. They nodded and grabbed their own pikes and axes. A British soldier had bulled his way through and stood before him. Wilford took his ax and hacked downward onto the surprised Redcoat's head, splitting it nearly in two.

Someone brushed beside him. It was John Hancock. There was blood on his waistcoat and a loaded pistol in his hand. "Well done," Hancock said with a smile.

Major General James Grant whirled about, "What the devil is happening, Danforth?"

Danforth didn't know either. In their front and to their left came the sound of screaming banshees, while cannon boomed to their rear. All around them, soldiers looked about in confusion. The attack was stalling. Again. Grant grabbed soldiers and hollered for them to press forward. His efforts began to work as the advance resumed.

Then General Grant stopped moving. He stood as if at attention, but his sword slipped from his hand and fell to the ground. Danforth was at his side and turned to see why his general was silent. He gasped and gagged. He had seen horrors this day but nothing like this. A large rock protruded from the middle of Grant's skull, just above the bridge of his nose. Danforth dropped to his knees and vomited, while Grant simply stood. His eyes were blank and his jaw moved sporadically, but with no sound coming forth. Other soldiers saw the unnatural creature that Grant had become and recoiled.

Tommy Baker was twenty-two and had been a British soldier for seven years. He knew that sometime in the dark and best forgotten past he'd had an ancestor who'd been a baker. Lucky man, he'd often thought. At least the bastard had likely been able to eat what he made and stayed warm by his ovens.

But not so for Tommy Baker. He'd spent his early years always hungry, growing up in a poor and dying village a few miles north of London. He had been only thirteen when his father pushed him out of the house and informed him that he was on his own. Dear old dad had too many other mouths to feed. His mother had looked on him sadly and turned away.

He'd tried odd jobs but wasn't much good at anything. He was too small and thin for farm labor and he soon wandered into the bustling city of London where he'd tried his hand at the infernal places called factories that were sprouting up all over the city. They were either stinking smoky horrors or places where white-faced women worked at giant looms while he lugged their materials back and forth. The lucky ones gave sex to the owners in return for food and better conditions. A couple of foremen had squeezed his arm and suggested how he could earn money and favor. He hated them all.

He'd quickly lost a series of jobs and tried begging. When that didn't work, he tried stealing and was caught and sent to prison where a recruiter for the army found him. Tommy was given a choice: enlist or be hanged for the capital crime of stealing a loaf of bread. Tommy thought it over for about two seconds and made his mark on the enlistment papers. He didn't even get the enlistment bonus called the King's Shilling. The recruiting sergeant said he needed that to bribe the guards. Tommy thought the bastard sergeant had kept it, but what the hell.

Tommy quickly found that he loved the army. It fed him, and his body filled out so that he no longer looked like a starved dog. It clothed him, trained and disciplined him, and gave him a musket he could use to shoot at people. Best of all, they paid him. It wasn't much but it was more money then he'd ever had in his life. He soon found himself trusted and respected and after a few years was promoted to corporal.

Tommy served in the colonies and had been in combat during the last days of the insurrection, which made him a battle-hardened veteran. He didn't much like being shot at but it was part of his duty.

The trek from New York to Detroit had been pleasant enough, and even educational. He was impressed with the vastness of the Americas. But the journey from Detroit to what the rebels called Fort Washington had been an ordeal. He'd been shot at by unknown assassins who had waited like snakes in the grass. He'd lost a good friend who'd taken a crossbow bolt in the throat. He'd raged for days. Who killed with a crossbow? Savages, that's who.

He hated the rebels for the way they fought and he hated them for rebelling against his king who had given him so much. Thus, Tommy Baker and the thousands of others like him couldn't wait to get their hands on those rebels and destroy them.

Tommy had exulted when he'd first seen the defensive earthworks and the enemy soldiers behind them. They weren't much at all and the bastards couldn't run and hide anymore.

And when the army was formed up for the grand assault, he'd cheered when General Grant took a place of honor with them. Grant was a fat old bastard, but he was a tough one and he cared for his men. Grant told them the rebels would collapse under the weight of the British assault and run like they always did. They all thought that Grant was clearly the best of the British generals. Tarleton was a lunatic who might just be a coward to boot, and Arnold was a turncoat, which said it all. Burgoyne had already lost one army and that too said more than anybody wanted to think about. No, Grant would lead them to victory and glory.

But it wasn't happening that way. Instead of running, the rebels continued to fight with a maniacal desperation that neither Tommy nor the other Redcoats had ever seen. Tommy and his comrades managed to bull their way over the embankment but they'd paid a heavy price. He found himself stepping over and on to piles of bodies. Some wore the homespun clothing of the rebels, but so many wore the king's red that it was dismaying.

Tommy had started about a third of the way back in the phalanx, whatever that word meant, and didn't regret at all not being nearer the front. Many of his comrades were dying up there and they'd all been horrified when the series of explosions had rocked them on their heels with debris and pieces of flesh landing on them.

They'd been shocked by the amazing rate of fire that the rebels had sustained and the accuracy with which they'd shot. Then came the showers of rocks that threatened to break bones and bash in skulls. Still, the attack continued and Tommy and his mates were slowly winning. They were tired, angry, and frustrated, but they were winning. The American bastards would pay in their own damned blood for this day.

Finally, he'd reached the front and it was his turn to fight. He didn't even give a thought to the fact that it was because everyone who'd started out in front of him was dead or wounded. He felt release and lunged with his bayonet only to have it parried by what he quickly realized was a well-trained Hessian wearing the remnants of his old uniform.

No matter. Tommy was British and that meant he was better than anyone. He was also fresh and the Hessian was tired. He skewered the Hessian who screamed and collapsed, and looked for another. He was distracted by the sounds of screaming to his left. Out of the corner of his eye, he saw that hundreds of women had descended on the British lines and were hacking and stabbing with axes and pikes. Bloody fucking hell! Was he supposed to fight women? Damned if he wouldn't if one of the bitchy American whores came at him with a pike.

Behind him, he heard cannon fire followed by screams from within the phalanx. More bloody hell, he thought. Had the rebels gotten behind them? This was not right. He began to look around nervously. He laughed harshly. No problem, he decided. General Grant would fix it all in a minute. In the meantime, he had to keep his thoughts to the front.

"Grant's dead," a voice hollered and it was picked up by others. "Grant's dead," echoed throughout the phalanx.

"Fuck me," Tommy said and a soldier beside him nodded agreement.

Throughout the attack there had been physical pressure from behind him, pushing Tommy and the others forward, just as he had pushed others ahead of him through the defenses and up over the American works.

Now there was no pressure. He stepped back, astonished that he could do so. Others were doing the same thing. A gap of a few yards appeared between the ragged, exhausted American remnants and the British. It grew larger. A woman appeared in front of him, but just out of the reach of his bayonet. She'd been cut on her shoulder and was covered with blood. She was screaming at him like an animal and she held a pike like she knew what she was doing. What the bloody goddamn fucking hell was going on? Other rebels, men and women, were kneeling, either wounded or just plain exhausted.

He backed up a couple of more steps and turned around. British soldiers were falling back. All around him they were turning and retreating. Some were beginning to run. Grant was dead. It was over.

Tommy Baker felt naked. His musket was unloaded as some fool had decided that only the first couple of ranks would carry loaded weapons lest they shoot their comrades in the back.

He took a few more steps backward, signaled to the men beside him, turned, and began to trot to the rear. He fumbled to load his damn musket.

"Grandfather, the red-coated soldiers are retreating. What is your wish?"

The old man jerked awake at the words from his beloved Tecumseh. The British were retreating? Impossible! That was the last thing he had imagined. He had decided to support the British when their victory became evident. He felt that their presence would be less onerous than the Americans who were always grasping at the land.

"Where is Little Turtle?" he asked.

"I am here, grandfather."

"This is the worst of all options," Owl said. "If we support the British, then we will have supported the losing side. If we support the Americans at this time, it will mean nothing to them. They will hate us no matter what we do."

The old man was dismayed. Why hadn't he urged them to

support the British in the first place when it might have affected the fighting? Why hadn't he told them to attack the American rear? The answers didn't matter. It was too late.

Little Turtle spoke. "Then what shall we do? We can still attack the Americans and perhaps turn the tide."

Owl man took a deep breath. It hurt his lungs and he coughed. There was blood on his hand where he tried to cover his mouth. "We will do nothing."

Little Turtle was stunned. "Nothing? We have hundreds of warriors with more arriving each day, and they cry out for blood. We cannot go away like skulking animals. We must fight one side or the other."

The old man shook his head. "If, as Tecumseh says, the British have been defeated, then supporting them will be of no consequence. If we now attack the British, the Americans are likely to attack us because we would be attacking other white men. No, we must not do anything. This is no longer our fight, if it ever was. I was wrong," he said sadly. "We should now be miles away from this fighting. The white man now controls this land and there is nothing we can do."

Little Turtle was furious. "We must fight. We are not cowards."

With that, he stormed away. The old man was saddened. "He will do something terrible."

Tecumseh did not answer.

# Chapter 23 ★ ★ ★ ★ ★ ★ ★ ★ ★ ★ ★ ★ ★ ★ ★ ★ ★ ★

DRAKE AND WASHINGTON SAW THE BRITISH FORCE START TO turn and pull back and quickly recognized their peril. If they stayed put, they would be overrun by a mass of angry humanity. They quickly determined that pulling the guns to the American lines was not practical. "Destroy them," Washington ordered.

Will Drake signaled and a number of men ran forward. They loaded as much powder as they could find down the barrels of the four cannon and then jammed in cannonballs and rocks.

Will set a long fuse, lit it, and ran like the devil was after him. As before, he had no idea what was a safe distance. Nor did any of the others. They all just ran. He found a depression in the earth and threw himself in it. He had just covered his head with his hands when the first of a rapid series of explosions rocked him, sending shock waves over him. He closed his eyes tightly as debris rained down on him.

"I think we're still alive," William Washington said after a moment. Drake looked up. He and the others were covered with dirt.

Drake stood and looked at the four craters that marked the location of the guns. Their barrels had been ripped apart and were lying well away from where they had been. Their carriages were nowhere to be seen. "Well," he said happily, "I guess that was enough powder."

They ran to their horses and mounted quickly. The retreating British had been slowed by the explosions, but had recommenced their movement to the rear. The small American cavalry force again skirted the British and moved back through the gap in the defenses. Once through, they rode to the rear of the American lines where hundreds of American and British wounded and dying were being tended. They found General Stark. His uniform was torn and he looked exhausted. Still, there was a ferocious glint in his eye.

"Well done," Stark said to Washington. "Now I have another assignment for you."

"Name it, sir," Washington said.

"Look around you. Our army was mauled and is in disarray. It is exhausted, wounded, and out of ammunition. Right now we are trying to care for the wounded, bury the dead, and provide food and water for the living. While we do this, much of our defenses have been destroyed by the British. Since your men appear reasonably healthy, I want you to repair the earthworks and the wood thicket. Will you do that?"

Washington and Drake looked at the milling hundreds. Drake wanted desperately to find Sarah. Was she alive? Hurt? Was she as worried about him as he was about her?

Still, they had their duty. If the British attacked again, the American lines were wide open and would collapse.

Washington shrugged and grinned amiably. "Where are the shovels, General?"

Burgoyne's head sagged and his chin nearly touched his chest. "How long has it been?"

How long since what, Fitzroy wondered. He pulled out his pocket watch. "It's been a little more than two hours since the fighting began, sir."

Both men looked at each other. It had taken just two hours for the rebels to defeat, at least temporarily, the greatest army in North America. Thousands of soldiers streamed disconsolately by them. Few bothered to look at their commander. The men were looking out for their own well-being and cared nothing for what generals thought. Despite the chaos, Fitzroy saw a number of officers trying to impose order and control and, to a large part, succeeding. The regiments had been stopped and mauled but not destroyed. Even so, it would be a while before they fought again.

Burgoyne walked away, heading to the privacy of his tent. He didn't wish to see or speak with anyone until he had come to grips with the situation. Reports would be taken later. Everything could wait, along with the inevitable excuses and recriminations.

Fortunately, the Americans were in no shape to counterattack. From where Fitzroy could see, they were working on repairing their defenses. Thank heaven for small favors, Fitzroy thought.

"Have you noticed it's raining?"

It was Danforth. His uniform was in shreds and a large scab had formed on his forehead. "Perhaps it will clean you up," Fitzroy said and put his arm around the other man's shoulders. "Good to see you."

"Good to see you, too, James," Danforth said and plunked himself down on a folding chair that Burgoyne had been using. "And don't ask me how bad it was, damn it; it was bloody awful. I've never seen such a slaughter and I've never seen British soldiers take such punishment. They only gave up after enduring more than any men should be called upon to endure. I hope history will be kind to them."

"Agincourt," Fitzroy said, "only we played the role of the French on this date," he said referring to the climactic battle of 1415 in which a smaller British army had slaughtered a much larger French army that had attacked them on a narrow front.

"We attacked in a narrow front mass that invited flanking attacks and eliminated our strength in numbers. Had we won, of course, Burgoyne would be proclaimed a genius. Now what will happen to him, to us?"

Fitzroy thought that history would be kinder to the soldiers than it would be to the generals. "And General Grant is truly dead?"

Danforth found a bottle with some brandy in it and took a long swallow. "Well and truly dead and with a rock stuck squarely in the middle of his skull like some great and unblinking third eye." Danforth shuddered. "Absolutely hideous. No man should die like that and he took forever to collapse and finally stop breathing. I swear he was trying to talk, to say something." He laughed bitterly. "Perhaps he was saying something like take this fucking rock out of my head."

"You stayed with him, I take it?"

"Of course. Now you're going to ask me how I got away. Well, it was quite easy. When our own soldiers fell back, some of them knocked me over and likely trampled me for good measure. I do believe I was stunned for a few minutes. When I came to, I simply crawled away until I thought it was safe enough to stand up. At that point, I got up and walked back to our lines with as much dignity as I could muster. I wasn't the only one. A lot of lightly wounded men or some unwounded soldiers simply trying to save their own skins were doing the same thing. Thank God the Americans were not in the slightest bit interested in stopping us from departing. They had a handful of men working to repair their defenses and, by the way, I think I saw the man you were negotiating with. Drake, I believe."

Fitzroy took it in. For some strange reason he was pleased that the rebel had also lived to fight another day. It had begun to rain again, a fitting end to a miserable day and it was still early afternoon. Damn.

"What's going to happen now?" Danforth asked.

"Well, we won't be attacking again, at least not for a while. Burgoyne's called for a council of war, which will now only include Tarleton and Arnold, since Grant is dead."

Danforth shook his head. "Why in God's name couldn't either Arnold or Tarleton have been killed instead of Grant? Better yet, why not both of them?"

Why indeed? Fitzroy could not think of an answer.

Drake was working with men who were repairing the defenses and was soaking wet from the sudden rain and up to his knees in the mud it had created.

Along with repairing the earthworks and replacing the thicket, they'd been dragging dead British soldiers out to where other Redcoats could retrieve them and carry them back for a proper burial. The British wounded were allowed to either return to their own lines if they were able, or were cared for as best they could by the Americans. These activities caused the British and American soldiers into close proximity with each other. Either out of respect or exhaustion, there was little or no conversation and no hostility. Simple nods and grunts sufficed. There had not been a formal truce. The men simply decided to solve their problem without any help from higher-ups.

A mud-splattered British officer appeared and politely requested permission to search for the remains of General Grant and Will gave it. Within a few minutes the dead general was found and his body taken away. The officer thanked Will profusely. They both agreed it was a strange way to run a war.

Thus, Will had no time to search for Sarah. Instead, she found him. She rushed to him and they embraced, with both of them weeping from relief. No one noticed. Similar reunions were taking place around them as the fortunate ones found each other. There were also howls of pain and grief as a loved one was found dead. There was a cut on Sarah's cheek and another on her arm. Both would leave scars. He didn't care. Her clothing was bloody and torn. But she was alive.

Finally they pulled apart. "What about the others?" Will asked, half fearing the answer.

"Too many are dead," she said sadly. "Faith is alive and unhurt, as is Owen who is still out in the swamp. But my uncle Wilford is dead with a bayonet in the chest, and my aunt is badly wounded and may not make it. Little Winifred Haskill is dead. She thought her friend Sergeant Bahlmann had been killed and went crazy. Ironically, Bahlmann did survive, but most of his fellow Hessians didn't."

The loss of so many civilians saddened him deeply. Soldiers were supposed to die, but the civilians? "Thank God Stark lives."

Sarah nodded. "Unhurt, as you are aware, but Wayne and von Steuben are dead and Morgan is wounded. The army is in grievous shape. Dear God, Will, if there's another battle there'll be no one left to fight it."

Hannah van Doorn approached and interrupted. "Then let's see that there isn't another battle," she said grimly. Like the others, she was filthy and exhausted and the once plump woman had lost a considerable amount of weight.

"How do you propose to stop it?" Will asked.

She handed him a folded piece of paper. "When you next see Major Fitzroy, will you give him this? Since his place was with his general, I am presuming that he too lives."

Will was puzzled. "Just why do you think I am going to see the British again?"

"Because General Tallmadge asked me to find you and bring you to him and General Stark. I can think of no other reason than that you are going to speak again with the British and that likely means Major Fitzroy."

Despite his exhaustion, Will almost laughed. What kind of world was it coming to when women were part of the military?

"I have decided to assume direct command of our center as well as the army as a whole," Burgoyne announced. Night had fallen and only one small and flickering candle lighted the interior of the general's tent. Arnold and Tarleton simply nodded. Each knew that neither was acceptable in Burgoyne's eyes as eligible for promotion to Grant's position. Nor did they think for one second that Burgoyne would divide the army into two divisions instead of three.

"What are our casualties?" Burgoyne asked and winced. He didn't really want to know the answer to that question.

Fitzroy took a deep breath. He'd been all over the field for as long as daylight lasted, inquiring and compiling the awful numbers.

"I can only give estimates, sir, but we have suffered at least twelve hundred dead and likely twice that many wounded, with many grievously."

He shuddered, thinking of the long rows of moaning and crying soldiers, some of whom were being cared for by their comrades while others simply lay and waited for someone to help them, or for death to end their pain. The worst ones were those whose wounds were the most terrible and who said nothing, simply awaiting their fate. Even if they lived, many, perhaps most of the wounded would never fight again. So many had lost limbs or eyes, or even both, that a host of smashed and broken men would have to be carted back to Detroit to begin their long arduous trek to England. If they lived, of course. It was understood that many would die en route to New York, and so many others would pass on before ships made it back to England.

There had to be a better way to care for the wounded, he thought ruefully, but could think of nothing. Doctors were not an answer. Few in their right mind would trust anyone's health to a barber-surgeon who thought it wise to bleed people who had already bled copiously because of their wounds.

Fitzroy continued. "And there are at least two thousand missing, although most of them will doubtless turn up sooner or later when they get tired of running and regain their senses. When all is said and done, I estimate our total casualties will be in excess of four thousand."

There were gasps. Even the normally unfeeling Tarleton was shocked. Four thousand was about a third of the force they'd committed this day and four thousand was approximately the number of men in the whole American army. This did not include the women and old men among the rebels. Those old men and women had inflicted terrible casualties while sustaining many of their own.

"It is worse than the numbers," Fitzroy added. "Many of the survivors are the remnants of the regiments that were in the fore of the attack and those units no longer exist as anything more than disorganized clusters of men. I would estimate that our true fighting strength is about half of what it was this time yesterday."

"Any thoughts on American casualties?" Tarleton asked.

"None whatsoever, except for the obvious. They too must have suffered heavily. I would not be surprised if they lost half their army as well."

"Then what do we do?" Arnold asked.

"Attack," Tarleton snapped. "We do what we should have done in the first place. We attack all along the line and overwhelm them. They are too few and cannot be everywhere in strength."

"With respect, General," Fitzroy said, "Based on what I've seen, it'll be some time before the army is able to attack. Even so, I doubt there'll be any enthusiasm for another frontal attack, however overwhelming our numbers might appear. Our men might just refuse to go. It wouldn't be the first time an army has refused to attack. Besides, we have other problems, ammunition and food, for instance."

Burgoyne smiled tightly. "You are simply full of good news, Major."

Fitzroy flushed. "Sorry, sir, but I assumed you wanted the truth."

"I do, however little I might like it. Continue."

"Our food supplies might last us a week, sir, but that's all. We must either withdraw to our closest depot or arrange for supplies to be shipped to us. Either way, our men might be hungry for a day or so before we got there."

No matter how he'd tried to phrase it, the statement was an implied criticism of Burgoyne. The army had continued to use supplies when it had been expected that they would be on their way back down the trail to the depots with large numbers of prisoners.

Fitzroy continued. "Ammunition is a more severe crisis." He turned to Arnold. "I hope I don't have to remind you that our reserve supply is now on the bottom of the St. Joseph River. What ammunition we now have is what our men carried less what was expended today. We were perversely fortunate that General Grant insisted that only his front ranks actually fire their weapons so that the bulk of the army still has what ammunition it started with. However, there is little more. One more battle and we will be using bayonets simply because we are out of powder and lead."

Burgoyne looked stunned. He stood and the others did as well out of courtesy to his rank. In the dim and flickering light, Burgoyne looked like a confused and wounded animal.

"What now, my dear General? What will you do to save the situation and our hopes?" Tarleton asked sarcastically. Fitzroy wanted to punch the smug bastard in the mouth.

Burgoyne had too much dignity to respond in kind. "We will rest this night. All of us, and that includes every general and private in the army, will rest so we can think clearly and dispassionately. Tomorrow we will have hard decisions to make."

Hannah Van Doorn deposited Will with General Stark and departed with a sad smile on her face. The note she'd given him was in his pocket. Stark was in conference with Schuyler and Tallmadge. Both of them were bloodied and worn, but they had survived. Stark, by far the older, looked exhausted. Tallmadge looked up and nodded. Will stepped forward and stood at attention.

"Relax, Drake," Stark said. "We've got more important things to do than stand on useless formality."

"Yes, sir."

"Are you well? You're not wounded, are you?"

"Only in spirit, sir. This has been a dreadful day."

Stark continued. "Indeed it has, which is why I wish you to once again be an intermediary for me. We must do whatever we can to end this, once and for all, at least once and for all for this time. I wish you to get a good night's rest, either alone or with your lovely Sarah. Then I wish you to be dressed in a fine and clean uniform and then to go out and discuss a serious proposition I wish to make to General Burgoyne. As a sign of my good faith, you will also take with you the sword that once belonged to their General Grant and return it. One of our men had liberated it," he said wryly. The once lucky soldier had doubtless thought it was worth a fortune.

"I'm sure the gesture will be appreciated, sir." Will was astonished that General Stark even knew about Sarah.

Stark clasped his hands behind his back. "I hope more than that. I hope it will be an opening as well as a reminder. Go get some rest. I need you alert when you meet with the British."

Later that evening, Will thought he'd be too tired to even think of making love. However, Sarah had other ideas. She wanted to purge herself of the savagery of the day and her way of doing it was to draw him into her, crying and sobbing, and hold him so tightly that there was nothing else in their world. Then they slept.

Will and Sarah were awakened a little past dawn by a wild-eyed and haggard Tallmadge, who wasn't in the least embarrassed to see the two of them in bed and scrambling to cover themselves. "I hope you're not planning to sleep all day, Drake, we have a task for you. I'll be outside. Don't dither. And Sarah, you look absolutely lovely."

"You can go to hell, too, General Tallmadge," Sarah snapped, but then smiled.

Will washed and dressed in a clean blue uniform, the same one he'd used the last times he'd met with the British officer. He then ate a couple of biscuits with butter and washed them down with something that was called coffee but was not. After that, he reported to duty.

A visibly shaken Tallmadge was again with Stark and, to Will's mild surprise, so too was Benjamin Franklin. The old man looked haunted by what he had seen, although he managed to smile warmly at Will, while Tallmadge looked away. Will thought he saw a hint of madness in his eyes. He wondered if stresses were finally getting to his friend.

They sat Will down and discussed with him what they wished him to say and do. What they told him more than surprised him and he shook his head, puzzled.

"Why are you having me do this? This isn't like the first meeting where we were all fencing around. Shouldn't someone of higher rank be involved in something this important? Why not yourself?" he inquired of Stark.

"Perhaps later," Stark answered. "In fact, hopefully later. For this preliminary meeting, I still think it best that you meet with someone of equivalent rank and that you are simply a messenger, although a messenger who is free to discuss and even negotiate."

"Dear God," Will said.

"Doubtless so, if you believe in God," Franklin said with a twinkle in his eye.

Stark put his hand on Will's shoulder. "Just do your best and if you fail, we shall try again. Perhaps what you say will be rejected out of hand, which would not surprise me. Burgoyne may require more time to come to grips with reality. Thus, while a rebuff to you would be annoying, a rebuff to me or Schuyler or Tallmadge would be far more serious."

"I will do my best," Will answered in a soft voice. He wondered if he would be up to the task at hand. Then he thought of the tremendous opportunity he'd been given and the easy out if he failed.

A few moments later, he stood on the earthworks with Grant's blanket-wrapped sword under his arm while a boy drummer beside him banged away on his drum. On the earthwork behind him, a corporal frantically waved a white flag. Nobody was shooting this day, but nobody wanted a mistake to happen.

All of the dead had been dragged away and much of the earthworks had been repaired. The thicket of tree limbs had been replaced, with only a narrow path for Will to walk through. The rain of the previous day had washed away much of the blood, although there were dark stains here and there as ghastly reminders. One could almost imagine that thousands of men had not been killed or wounded on this field. Even the craters caused by Franklin's exploding bombs had been filled in, perhaps to give the impression that there were more exploding bombs. The ground was still muddy and slippery, which would further impede any British attacks.

Will had a dire thought. What if there actually were more bombs, or what if all the bombs hadn't gone off? What if one exploded when he walked over it? He smiled and supposed that Stark would find another volunteer.

A white flag waved from the other side. Will signaled the silly little boy to stop his drumming and began the lonely walk to meet the future.

Will and Fitzroy greeted each other reservedly. Whatever good will they might have felt for each other after the first meeting had been dispelled by the flowing of so much blood. Still, each was pleased that the other had survived the carnage. For his part, Fitzroy was slightly embarrassed that he had personally seen no combat as he'd been beside Burgoyne throughout the fighting.

"Let me extend our thanks for the return of General Grant's sword," Fitzroy said as he received the peace offering. "It will be sent back to England along with his remains which you so graciously permitted our men to retrieve." Fitzroy smiled wanly. "Grant's remains will be pickled, of course, which is a devil of a demotion for one so brave."

Will nodded and reached into his pocket. He withdrew the note from Hannah. "This is for you. A very nice lady who apparently thinks highly of you requested that I give it to you."

Fitzroy blinked and took it. He looked over Will's shoulder and grinned. "Is that her on the earthworks?"

Will turned. Hannah was a couple of hundred yards away but her blond hair stood out like a beacon. "I believe so," he laughed.

Amenities done, Will turned serious. "I have a message from General Stark. The slaughter of yesterday was a lesson for both of our sides. It cannot be allowed to repeat itself. He has a very simple proposal to end it. Are you interested?"

"Of course, assuming that you realize we are both pawns."

"Indeed we are. If our conversation turns to nothing, then we will be removed from the board."

Fitzroy chuckled. "Understood. Now let me hear your proposal."

"General Stark implores General Burgoyne to surrender."

Fitzroy nearly staggered. "You must be joking."

"I am not."

"We are within an instant of destroying you Americans. One more attack and what's left of your army will crumple and disappear."

"Quite possibly, but you know as well as I do that there will be no second attack. Your army is spent both physically and emotionally. It needs time to recover and refit, and you will not have that time. Neither General Stark, nor Cornwallis, who wants his army back, by the way, nor the weather, which will begin to turn cold in a few weeks, will permit you that luxury. And let's not forget the fact that you must replace your brave General Grant and many others who fell yesterday.

"And even if you did manage to muster an attack, it is highly unlikely that your army would be willing to destroy itself again against our defenses. They would simply go to ground rather than repeat yesterday's horrors. And even if everything I've said is wrong and you do indeed manage to push us off this bloody hill, you will have accomplished nothing. We have changed our strategy. If you take Fort Washington and Liberty, you will have taken nothing. We will burn everything and retreat west with all the food and supplies that we can carry and leave you here to starve and freeze. At least until Burgoyne is again reminded that he has to return what would then remain of his army to Cornwallis."

This last statement was a lie. Will knew that nothing had changed and that his fellow Americans were not in a position to migrate anywhere at this time.

Fitzroy found himself both amused and frightened. The Americans fully understood Burgoyne's dilemma. "We would hardly starve. We would get supplies from our depots or by water from Detroit. I think Burgoyne would decide that Cornwallis can bloody well wait."

Will smiled. "You will get no supplies."

He gestured and a man appeared on the earthworks. He was guarded by two American soldiers. Will gestured again and the man began to stumble forward. A few minutes later, he stood before them, his hands bound behind his back. Fitzroy was astonished.

"Girty?"

Simon Girty, bloody and bruised, his clothes in rags, snarled his answer. "Of course it is. Now untie me so I can kill this rebel bastard."

"Time enough for that," Fitzroy said quietly but firmly. Girty's eyes glowed with hate. "There is a truce here, and I don't want it broken."

Will nodded agreement and Fitzroy continued. "What happened, Girty? You and your men deserted, didn't you?"

Girty spat on the ground. "You can call it deserting if you want, but I call it retreating to save our skins. But it didn't work out that way. First we were attacked by the fucking red savages on our way east. Then, when we'd fought our way through them we were attacked by rebels coming east from the bloody damned depot. They captured me and killed the rest of my men. The rebels have taken your depot and all the supplies, and yes, Fitzroy, and don't look so damned shocked. The Indians have declared for the rebels and there's another rebel army coming down the road and ready to jump all over your ass."

Will smiled. "Why not send him on to tell his tale to Burgoyne?"

Fitzroy recovered from his shock and agreed, sending Girty stumbling toward the British lines. "I rather wish you'd kept the pig," he muttered.

"I like the idea as well, but there would have been a riot. Too many of our people wanted to skin him alive. Now, let me elaborate on what Girty said. There are two American armies in your rear. One consists of a force commanded by Isaac Shelby and has come from the south. They have taken Detroit and are rolling up your precious depots. Detroit fell quite easily, by the way. The defenses were in ruins, the garrison stripped by Burgoyne, and a very discouraged Major De Peyster was found drunk in his bed.

"The second force came from Boston and is commanded by General Edward Hand and, while he isn't the best and brightest of the litter, he is smart enough to have taken a defenseless Fort Pitt and is moving on your base at Oswego.

"In sum, Cornwallis holds only New York and Boston and may be evacuating Charleston. Further in sum, you and General Burgoyne hold the ground on which you stand and nothing more. Girty will confirm what he has seen and heard and Burgoyne will, of course, send scouts out to confirm it. You have not won anything, although you might yet take some useless ground and cause more deaths. You are surrounded and cut off with any possible reinforcements half a continent and many months away. That is, if Cornwallis sends them at all on something which he might think is a fool's errand. General Burgoyne is in even worse shape than he was at Saratoga. In effect, the frontier of our new nation has been pushed westward by a good five hundred miles and I cannot imagine Parliament at all enthused by the thought of sending another army to take it all back."

"I'm sure General Burgoyne will be glad to hear that," Fitzroy said drily. He dreaded the possibility that Drake's claims were true. His worst fears would have been realized—his own career would be just as ruined as Burgoyne's. He would have to leave the army and find another way of supporting himself, which would be more than difficult. He had no family money like Danforth to fall back on. If what Drake said was true, he faced a dismal future.

"Will you convey General Stark's message?" Will asked.

"Of course. And will you convey my regards to the lovely Hannah?"

Will grinned wickedly. "Surrender and I'll see to it that you convey them yourself."

Burgoyne awoke with a splitting headache. He groaned and swung his legs off his cot and tried to blink away the pain that throbbed behind his eyes. He, Tarleton, and Arnold had waged a long and furious argument while drinking brandies the night before. Tarleton wanted to withdraw and regroup, while Arnold, true to his belligerent nature, wanted to attack and damn the results. This had confirmed Burgoyne's notion that Tarleton was basically a coward, and that Arnold was an opportunist who was most concerned about his own advancement, no matter how many people were killed in the process.

He groaned again. Where the devil was Grant? Why the devil had the man gotten himself killed? What the hell was he supposed to do now without his right-hand man?

Surrender had not been discussed, other than to be ridiculed. Still, the word and the concept had hung over their heads like the sword of Damocles. Girty had been interviewed and the disgusting man had repeated his original story: a large rebel force under Isaac Shelby was in their rear. Whether they had actually taken Detroit or not wasn't relevant, although they did believe it was likely. Burgoyne had left Detroit with only a virtual corporal's guard under De Peyster and taking it would have been no great achievement. So too with Pitt. If the rebel General Hand had conquered Fort Pitt, that too would have been easy.

He sighed. Obviously, he should have left a stronger force behind him. Why had he believed Cornwallis' vague assurances that the rebel's strength was concentrated at Liberty and Fort Washington and that any other rebel forces in the colonies could be discounted?

Or had Cornwallis actually said that? He seemed to recall something about rebel activity simmering and the need for the rebel forces to be destroyed, but had there been any mention of other rebel armies? Not that he could recall. He had a terrible thought. Perhaps he was supposed to believe that there were no other rebel forces that could threaten him. Neither the war nor his position as commanding general was popular in England. Had he truly been set up to fail? The thought made him even more ill.

Burgoyne dressed and opened the flap of his tent. As usual, Fitzroy was there, like a faithful dog.

"Some coffee, General?"

"Splendid thought." Why, he wondered, did Fitzroy look so concerned? "I have made a decision, Major, we shall attack and damn the mud. Arnold shall lead and we shall press them at several points. Please send messengers and call them for a council of war."

Fitzroy looked stricken. "I can't, sir."

"Why not?" Burgoyne asked, confused.

"Sir, I thought you might wish such a council so I set out a while ago to inform the two generals to be prepared."

"And?"

"They're gone."

Burgoyne staggered as if shot. "Gone? Where? How in God's name can that be?"

"No one seems quite sure, but they departed during the night along with a number of men and several other ranking officers. Apparently they felt that surrender was all too likely and neither man felt they would survive capture and imprisonment because of the crimes they've committed against the rebels. Tarleton is a murderer and Arnold is a traitor to the rebels. Joseph Brant and his handful of surviving Iroquois have also fled, as has Girty."

Burgoyne sat heavily on his camp stool. He began to shake and an unbidden tear fell down his cheek. It couldn't be happening again, could it? He had spent so much time and political capital recovering from his surrender at Saratoga and now was history going to repeat itself? The gods could not be that cruel, could they?

Of course they could, he thought bitterly. His army was effectively leaderless, low on food and ammunition, and surrounded by an enemy that would only grow stronger as word of his weakness grew. He could march his mauled army to a strong point and fortify, but to what avail? What relief column would be coming to help him? No, they would starve. The rebels ate the fish from the lakes, but he doubted there were enough fish to sustain his mauled army.

Even if Cornwallis were so inclined, he had been left with

only a small, defensive force with which to hold New York and a handful of other cities.

Burgoyne pulled himself to his feet. He loved theater and it was time for him to put on a bravura performance. He forced a smile.

"James, my dear cousin, kindly find a drummer and inform General Stark that I would talk with him."

# Epilogue ★★★★★★★★★★★★★★★★★★

A FEW DOZEN MOUNTED SCOUTS UNDER WILLIAM WASHINGTON rode well ahead of the main body as it entered the city of New York. Behind them came a company of mounted rangers led by Owen Wells.

The British appeared to have left the devastated city, but no one trusted them. The last of their ships, a pair of frigates, were still in sight but well out of cannon range and headed towards the Narrows. The ship of the line carrying Lord Charles Cornwallis was but a distant speck on the horizon. But who knew if they'd left bombs or assassins in the ruins of what had once been the proud and prosperous city of New York?

The scouts signaled that all was well and the main body, some fifty senior officers on horseback, plus a thousand or so infantry marching behind, moved cautiously forward. After a while, they reached the tip of Manhattan Island and halted.

"What a dismal sight," General John Stark said. There was no argument. They were surrounded by ruins. Before leaving, the British had torched what remained of the city and blown up the fortifications in what appeared to be nothing but an act of mindless spite.

"No matter," the general said laconically. "New York didn't exist at one time and it can be built again."

This was important as a rebuilt New York was high on the list of possible locations for the capital of the new country. The congress currently resided at Philadelphia, and there was agitation for a decision to be made regarding its permanent location. Was it to remain in Philadelphia or elsewhere, such as New York, or even a new city that would be built in the south? Some were campaigning for such a new city along the Potomac River. For the time being, it would be in Philadelphia.

Even if New York didn't become the capital, the magnificent harbor and the wide Hudson River leading to the country's interior meant that a new and prosperous city would soon be rebuilt on the site.

It had been a year since Burgoyne's surrender at what Americans were referring to as the Battle of Fort Washington, despite the fact that Fort Washington had been a couple of miles away from the fighting. But then, thought Will, the battle of Bunker Hill had taken place on Breed's Hill and nobody seemed to care.

Burgoyne had been paroled and allowed to go home in disgrace, while his army had been held in captivity until a treaty was signed. When that occurred, the British found to their dismay that about half the men taken prisoner had no intention of returning to Great Britain. The addition of several thousand trained soldiers was welcomed by Stark, although many in Congress argued that, with victory, there was no need for such a large standing army.

Numerous people had escaped death on both sides. Tarleton and Arnold had emerged in Canada after a long trek through the woods, and Simon Girty was now active down the Mississippi, stealing and killing near Spanish-held New Orleans.

On the American side, John Adams, Alexander Hamilton, and Henry Knox had escaped from captivity on Jamaica, thanks to the exploits of John Paul Jones. Diplomat John Laurens had been released from the Tower of London. He and John Jay had negotiated a treaty between Great Britain and the colonies. After the defeat at Fort Washington, the British decided they wanted nothing more to do with fighting the thirteen colonies who were now calling themselves the United States of America. The defeat had struck George III particularly hard and there were rumors that he was mentally unhinged by the event.

Thomas Jefferson, author of the Declaration of Independence, was dead of a fever that had gripped him while in prison. Dead, too, was Benjamin Franklin. His aging body had finally given out, but not his mind, which had remained sharp and clear to the end.

Franklin's death had struck Sarah particularly hard. She had come to love the old man as a father or grandfather. Will had become fond of him as well, and his well-attended funeral had served as a memorial for all who had died in the war and the final battle at Fort Washington.

Will was maybe fifty yards behind the more senior officers and generals, which gave him time to think and muse. He realized that he had ridden past the spot where the prison hulk *Suffolk* had gone down. There was nothing, not even a piece of rotten wood sticking out of the water to remind him of that horrible part of his past.

To his astonished pleasure, Homer had simply showed up the night before. He'd been living in Halifax, Canada, and had returned to see just what the new nation would be like. Since he considered himself to be a rebel, he was uncomfortable with the fact that thousands of Tories were migrating to the Halifax area. He also wanted to see what remained of the city where he had spent almost all of his life.

"It's my home and the home of my ancestors," he'd said. "Of course I'm interested in what's going to happen. If I like what I see, I'll return here, find a good woman and set up shop doing odd jobs. It's also too damn cold up in Canada. Of course, I'll probably have to stop stealing stuff and killing people."

"Probably a good idea," Will had said with mock solemnity.

"Unless, of course, they try to cheat me or steal from me. Then they might deserve it."

"Understood. Now, do you still call yourself Homer or something else?"

Homer had laughed. "My real name *is* Homer. Homer Brentwood, and I come from a long line of Brentwoods and, no, I have no idea where the name Brentwood is from. I was having you on when I said that Homer might not be my real name."

They'd spent the rest of the evening talking and catching up. Homer declined to march in the victory parade. Instead, he was back with Sarah, waiting for the reoccupation of the city to take place.

Benjamin Tallmadge had suffered an emotional collapse and simply disappeared. It was said that he felt responsible for the carnage of the battle. After all, it was Tallmadge who had Hannah forge Cornwallis' signature to a "message" from Cornwallis ordering the army's return to begin within a week of receipt.

Owen, dressed in a British uniform, had delivered it. Even though the battle had resulted in an American victory, it had been too much bloodshed for Tallmadge to deal with.

But that was the past, Will reminded himself. Now the future beckoned. He spotted the waterfront land that Hannah Van Doorn and the Goldmans had recently purchased from Tories who were more than willing to sell at almost any price. Will wondered just how he was going to like working for a woman in the import-export business. He was a shareholder in their venture, but only a junior one. He would stay with the army for the time being, and then become a merchant.

He expected he would do no worse than James Fitzroy, who was now married to the very clever Hannah. Fitzroy had tendered his resignation from the British Army after seeing Burgoyne safely on his way back to England and whatever the fates had in store for him. The British Army had said, in effect, that they didn't much care what he did.

Before dying, Franklin had made it clear to anyone who would listen that the only way to ensure and preserve peace was to prepare for war. He was certain that the British would be back, and that the Spanish and French would be looking for American weaknesses to exploit. Stark emphatically agreed.

Marriage. He thought of Sarah, who was now very pregnant. If they had a boy, they would name him Benjamin Franklin Drake. If a girl, they hadn't made up their minds, although Sarah had laughingly ruled out Will's tongue-in-cheek suggestion of Benjamina.

Will wondered if other marriages wouldn't soon occur. Catherine Greene was more and more seen in the company of John Stark. Widow and widower, Will thought. Why not? Neither seemed concerned about the age discrepancy, and Cathy Greene had been much younger than her late general husband.

And did Stark have political ambitions? John Hancock was currently president of the new nation, but the constitution called for free elections. What would happen the first time they occurred and an incumbent was defeated? Would there be a peaceful transition of power or a civil war?

Already, also, the southern states were arguing that the prohibition on slavery was causing them economic ruin. Will thought it was good that there was no crop that required large numbers of laborers, or slaves, like the growing of sugar in the Caribbean did. Until such a crop came along, if one ever did, perhaps slavery would remain a dead issue.

When the ceremonial retaking of New York was over, Owen and Faith would return to her old home in Pendleton, Massachusetts, while Sergeant Barley had agreed to farm Will's place in Connecticut now that Will's thieving relatives had departed to Canada.

It was all so neat, or it seemed to be. Things had a habit of unraveling, however well-laid plans might be.

Stark dismounted. "We will build a fort here." No surprise. He was at the spot at the tip of Manhattan where earlier forts had been constructed. "It will defend the island and serve as a testimonial to our existence as a free nation."

"George Washington would have loved it," Will said to Owen who had ridden up beside him.

"You ever meet George Washington?" Owen asked.

"A handful of times, but nothing of significance. He had more important things on his mind."

Washington's mortal remains—his skull and a handful of bleached bones in a leather container—had been turned over to Stark by Cornwallis as a goodwill gesture. He could just as easily have dumped them in the river, but he hadn't. Now they were interred at Washington's estate at Mount Vernon at the request of his widow, Martha, who had been living quietly with relatives. There had been thought of building an enormous cathedral for his remains, but the forceful widow had put her small foot down and the thought was forgotten. For some reason, the British hadn't destroyed the Washingtons' elegant Mount Vernon home. Perhaps they had envisioned a plantation on the Potomac as a residence for some new British lord once the war was over.

The British frigates had disappeared from view. The last of their sails vanished beneath the curve of the earth. "They're well and truly gone, Will," Owen said.

"Truly gone indeed, Owen, but now we have a nation to build."